A DEAD MAN'S SECRET

A DEAD MAN'S SECRET

Simon Beaufort

This first world edition published 2010
in Great Britain and in 2011 in the USA by
SEVERN HOUSE PUBLISHERS LTD of
9–15 High Street, Sutton, Surrey, England, SM1 1DF.
Trade paperback edition first published
in Great Britain and the USA 2011 by
SEVERN HOUSE PUBLISHERS LTD.

British Library Cataloguing in Publication Data

Beaufort, Simon.
  A dead man's secret. – (A Sir Geoffrey Mappestone mystery)
  1. Mappestone, Geoffrey, Sir (Fictitious character) –
  Fiction. 2. Great Britain – History – Norman period,
  1066–1154 – Fiction. 3. Detective and mystery stories.
  I. Title II. Series
  823.9′ 14-dc22

ISBN-13: 978-0-7278-6972-2 (cased)
ISBN-13: 978-1-84751-303-8 (trade paper)

All Severn House titles are printed on acid-free paper.

Severn House Publishers support The Forest Stewardship Council [FSC],
the leading international forest certification organisation. All our titles that
are printed on Greenpeace-approved FSC-certified paper carry the FSC logo.

Typeset by Palimpsest Book Production Ltd.,
Falkirk, Stirlingshire, Scotland.
Printed and bound in Great Britain by the
MPG Books Group, Bodmin, Cornwall.

For Chuck Garrity Sr,
dear friend for many years

Prologue

William fitz Baldwin was pleased with the little castle he had built. It guarded a ford in the River Tywi, and he felt it was as secure a fortress as any he had seen. It comprised a sturdy motte topped by a wooden tower, and there was a palisade of sharpened stakes that protected a sizeable bailey. He intended to begin work on a proper bailey later in the year, reinforcing the fence with earthen ditches and a moat. And perhaps, in time, he would add a stone curtain wall. That should please the King, who, some three years earlier, had ordered him to establish a military base in this restless part of his domain.

He climbed to the top of the tower and stood on the battlements, resting his elbows on the rough wood and inhaling deeply of the fresh, salt-tinged air. Behind him were the densely forested hills of the Tywi Valley, and in front were the marshes, a lonely, peaceful swath of mud and grass, dappled with sheep. He had called his castle Rhydygors, after the Welsh words for 'marsh' and 'ford'. To his right, just visible on a slight promontory, was the little town of Kermerdyn.

William liked Kermerdyn. Less than a mile distant, it was a prosperous place with several busy wharves. The River Tywi was navigable to the sea, and, as Kermerdyn served a vast hinterland, the town contained wealthy merchants and traders – Welsh, Saxon and Norman. And they were not the only reason the area was rich: its fields had been silted by meandering rivers and were fertile and easy to till. The air was full of the scent of ripening crops, and the bleat of sheep and the contented lowing of cattle could be heard from all directions.

Of course, the region had its problems. The Welsh were no keener on the Normans than the Saxons had been, and resistance to William the Conqueror's invasion had been fierce. King William Rufus had continued the advance, but although the

Normans had managed to secure a strip along the southern coast that extended as far as Pembroc, there were huge tracts to the north that were still held by Welsh princes. Many made life difficult for the Normans.

One of the most powerful was Hywel ap Gronw, an astute politician as well as a mighty warrior. He had reached an agreement with the Normans that worked to the benefit of both sides. It brought a degree of stability to Kermerdyn, and William was happy to work with a man whose word he trusted. He had entertained Hywel just the previous evening, in fact, a pleasant, amiable occasion full of music, stories and good wine. William was less fond of Hywel's chief counsellor, Gwgan, who was sardonic and clever, and never revealed what he was really thinking.

In his defence, Gwgan had made an excellent marriage to Isabella, a daughter of Lord Baderon of Monmouth — Baderon fervently believed that the best way to ensure a lasting peace was by marrying his Norman daughters to powerful Welshmen, and it was a policy that seemed to work. Moreover, Isabella was a fine woman, and Gwgan seemed a gentler man in her presence.

William knew *he* should marry, too. He desperately needed an heir. Not only had he amassed a decent fortune, but there was his secret to consider, as well. It would be a pity for that to be lost, just for the want of children in whom he could confide. He supposed he could tell his brother Richard, but Richard was ruthless, hot-headed and volatile, and William was not sure how safe the secret would be in his hands.

So what manner of wife should he take? Not someone like Pulchria, the local butter-maker's wife — that was for certain! Pulchria was beautiful, it was true, but she was wanton. He had accepted her favours with alacrity when he had first arrived in Kermerdyn, but such behaviour had seemed inappropriate after he had discovered his secret. He winced when he recalled her fury at being rejected.

Then what about someone like Leah, who was married to Richard? She hailed from good Norman stock — kin to the Earl of Shrewsbury, no less — and was a wife worthy of any man. She was kind-hearted, dignified and soft-spoken, and, despite her apparent meekness, the one person in the world who could calm her husband's violent tendencies.

William sighed. Even with the perfect wife, it would be many years before any children were old enough to trust with his secret. Should he tell a friend instead? He had plenty – Sir Alberic and Sir Sear were his two favourite knights, and Abbot Mabon and Edward, Constable of nearby Kadweli Castle, were certainly men on whom he could rely. Then there was Cornald the butterer – Pulchria's husband – a man William had liked from the moment they had met.

William sighed again. He could not have explained why, but he was loath to divulge his secret to anyone who was not kin. It was so precious and delicate, and he *had* to be sure it was passed to the right person – his immortal soul might be imperilled if not. No, he decided, it could only be shared with a son – a boy he could mould for his own purposes.

He stared into the bailey, where his men were practising swordplay with some of Hywel's troops. The competition was good-natured, although there was an edge that was never present when the Normans trained alone. It was not a bad thing, he thought; he did not want his soldiers growing complacent just because the region was peaceful at the moment.

His musings came to an abrupt end when he felt an uncomfortable gnawing ache in his innards. He stood up straight, trying to stretch out the pain, but it grew worse. Clutching his middle, he sat down and gestured to one of the guards to fetch him some wine. Concerned, the captain of the watch – Sear that day – knelt next to him.

'Take deep breaths,' he suggested. 'You must have eaten something that disagreed with you last night. That butter probably. You have consumed rather a lot of it over the last few days, and it was rancid.'

'It was not!' snapped William. Sear disapproved of his friendship with Cornald and was always making disparaging remarks about his wares.

'It was,' countered Sear. 'And you were the only one who ate it. The rest of us declined, and the remainder was dumped in the midden immediately after dinner.'

'Pulchria sent it to me,' gasped William, face contorted with pain. 'And Richard brought it to Rhydygors, because he happened to be passing Cornald's shop when she was wrapping it.'

The ache was growing steadily worse. He was finding it difficult to breathe and began to fear that there might be something
seriously wrong with him. *Could* it have been the butter? Surely,
bad butter would just send a man racing to the latrines, not
double him up in agony?

Alarmed, Sear yelled to one of the guards to fetch a surgeon.
William was growing weaker, and there was darkness at the edges
of his vision. He was vaguely aware of Sear's strong arms carrying
him down the stairs to the chamber that served as bedroom, hall
and office. He felt a little better when he was lying down and
supposed he must have drowsed, because when he opened his
eyes, it was to find the room full of people.

Sear and Alberic were on one side; Abbot Mabon was praying
on the other, the monk Delwyn peering hawk-like over his
shoulder. Cornald and Constable Edward were at the end of the
bed, standing next to Richard and Leah. In the shadows, he
thought he could see Hywel and Gwgan, and Isabella too,
muttering to Bishop Wilfred. In fact, virtually everyone he knew
seemed to be there!

But Edward was away on business, while poor Leah was ill
and confined to her bed. New faces swam into focus, and William
knew he was hallucinating. He tried to grab Sear's sleeve, but the
knight had dissolved into Cornald. Then William saw his own
fingers. They were black and swollen, like those he had seen on
corpses kept too long from their grave.

He knew then that he was dying, and his mind returned to
his secret. *Someone* had to be told – and quickly. He looked around
at the assembled faces and made his decision. He would tell them
all. It was too great a burden for one to bear, but jointly . . .

He wondered why he had not thought of this before. In fact,
he wished he had been open from the start and told everyone
about the discovery when he had made it in Kermerdyn three
years before. People had certainly asked what had happened to
change him from a rather average man to one who was blessed
with an abundance of good fortune. He had always refused to
tell, and it had given rise to all manner of speculation. But there
was no time left for games now.

'I do not have long left for this world,' he announced. 'It is
time to tell you my secret.'

There was an immediate rush towards the bed, but William could not see faces. They shifted constantly around him, so he was unsure whether all his friends and family were there, or just one or two. Sensing time was of the essence, he began to speak anyway, but his eyes were now so dim that he could not even tell if they were listening.

When he had finished, he lay back, exhausted, feeling darkness begin to envelop him. Had he revealed his secret to a roomful of people, who would monitor each other and see it used wisely? Or had he confided to just one person? Or had he dreamt it all?

And had the butter killed him?

William took one last, shuddering breath. He would never know.

One

La Batailge, near Hastinges, early October 1103

Sir Geoffrey Mappestone did not like King Henry. He considered him devious and dangerous, and hated those occasions when he was summoned into the royal presence. Less worrisome, but equally annoying, was waiting around, kicking his heels, while the King determined that he might – or might not – see the knight.

Right now, Geoffrey was in just such a situation. He and his friend Sir Roger of Durham had recently helped thwart a minor rebellion and had finally been dismissed so that Geoffrey could return to his home in Goodrich on the Welsh borders. But within a day of leaving the abbey at La Batailge, they had been summoned back by a hard-riding messenger from the King. The two knights and their squires had then been forced to linger at the abbey until it was convenient for His Majesty to receive Geoffrey. The waiting was made even less tolerable because the one friend Geoffrey had made during his previous adventure – Wardard, an old Norman warrior turned monk – had evidently been sent 'on retreat' by the head of the abbey on the very day the knights had left. So Geoffrey could not even enjoy his company while waiting upon the King's whim.

The area around La Batailge was windswept and lonely, and Geoffrey often wondered what his father had thought of it when he had fought the Saxons there almost forty years before. If Geoffrey closed his eyes, it was easy to imagine the clamour of battle – the clash of weapons, the piercing whinnies of horses, the screams of the wounded and dying. The slaughter had been terrible, and, to ease his conscience, the Conqueror had founded an abbey on the site. The sound of Benedictine chants now filled the air, but Geoffrey thought the place a desolate one even so.

Three Norman monarchs had reigned since then. The first William had died twenty-one years after the Conquest, leaving

three ambitious sons. The oldest was Robert, Duke of Normandy,
under whom Geoffrey had trained to become a warrior. The next
was William Rufus, who had inherited the English throne and
had agreed with Robert that if one of them died, the other
should have his estates and titles. King William Rufus had been
dispatched by an arrow in the New Forest, and the youngest of
the Conqueror's sons, Henry, had raced to have himself crowned
before Robert could stop him.

Geoffrey thought Henry was wrong to have thus illicitly
grabbed the throne. But as his own estates were in England, and
Henry could easily take them away, he kept his thoughts private.
He had never sworn fealty to Henry – his oath of allegiance had
been to Tancred, Prince of Galilee, for whom he had fought most
of his adult life – but Henry held a certain sway over him.

Henry was holding court in the church, a typically Norman
building with a nave supported by thick pillars, and a clerestory
of round-headed windows. Geoffrey leaned against a pillar and
watched him conduct business. Henry had brought with him an
enormous retinue of clerks, scribes, servants and courtiers. The
clerks were the most numerous; Henry was wise enough to know
that the key to a successful reign was as much administration as
winning battles.

One clerk saw Geoffrey and walked towards him. He was a
pleasant-faced man with a cheerful smile, although there was
something about his eyes that suggested he was as devious as his
master. His name was Eudo, and he was Henry's most trusted
scribe.

'His Majesty has just told me that he will see you in a few
moments.'

'Thank you.' Geoffrey hesitated before continuing. 'Do you
know why? I do not think there is more to be discussed about
the recent events.'

Eudo inclined his head. 'I am sure His Majesty would agree.
It was a sordid business, and the less said the better.'

'Then why did he recall me?'

The court had taken every available berth in the abbey, and
Geoffrey and his companions had been reduced to sleeping behind
the stables, rolled in their cloaks. It was warm for the time of
year, and as a soldier he was used to uncomfortable conditions,

but it was still not pleasant. Moreover, the monks were struggling to find enough food for such large numbers, and Geoffrey could not leave to forage for his own lest the King demanded his presence.

'He has his reasons.' Eudo saw the look on Geoffrey's face and elaborated hastily: the knight was tall, strong and clearly not someone to be fobbed off with flippant responses. 'He wants to discuss it in person. But it involves some letters.'

'Letters?' echoed Geoffrey.

'You will find out soon enough,' replied Eudo. Then it was his turn to hesitate. 'I am sorry about Prince Tancred, by the way.'

'What about Tancred?' demanded Geoffrey.

Eudo looked at him warily. 'I am sorry you are no longer in his service. The King tells me that the two of you were as close as brothers, but he has recently dismissed you most rudely.'

That was one way of putting it, Geoffrey thought bitterly. Tancred had actually threatened to execute his former favourite if he ever saw him again. And it was Henry's fault – he had forced Geoffrey to remain in England, and Tancred had finally lost patience. Dismayed by Tancred's final missive, Geoffrey had known he would never rest easy until he had explained in person what had happened. Tancred might still be angry, but at least he would understand that the decision to dally had not been Geoffrey's.

'The King discusses my personal correspondence with clerks?' he asked coolly. 'I thought he would have better things to do.'

'He does,' replied Eudo, matching his tone. 'But, for some inexplicable reason, he likes you.'

Geoffrey seriously doubted it. Or perhaps Henry 'liked' him because he had a weakness – a sister of whom he was fond – and so was a suitable candidate for coercion. Henry had certainly exploited his knight's unwillingness to see Joan harmed in the past, and would doubtless do so again.

'Here is Sir Edward,' said Eudo, nodding to where a man in impractically fashionable clothes was approaching with fussy, mincing steps. Like many courtiers, his hair was long, flowing around his shoulders, and his beard had been carefully sculpted into an eye-catching fork. Geoffrey regarded the figure warily. The title suggested Edward was a knight, but Geoffrey could not imagine such a fellow on a battlefield.

'He is Constable of Kadweli Castle, in Wales,' continued Eudo. 'It is a prestigious post because Kadweli is strategically sited, and money has been set aside to build it in stone.'

'The King is ready for you now,' said Edward to Geoffrey. He looked the knight up and down, smothering a smirk. 'He will be pleased to see you have dressed appropriately.'

A tart rejoinder died in Geoffrey's throat when he glanced down at himself. His surcoat with its Crusader's cross was decidedly grimy, and although his mail tunic and leggings were in good repair – no sensible knight would allow them to be otherwise – they were plain and functional. He had not shaved in days, and his light brown hair, cut short in military fashion, had not seen a comb in weeks. Edward had a point.

'It is too late to change clothes now,' said Eudo, frowning. 'Go. He does not like to be kept waiting.'

Geoffrey was not pleased to find the King was not ready for him at all, but was leaning over his clerks as they scribbled feverishly at his directions. He dallied for so long that Geoffrey was tempted to walk away. But common sense reigned, and he forced himself to be patient. His dog, a savage back and white beast, also grew restless, and, foreseeing trouble if it bit someone, the knight told his squire to take it outside.

To pass the time, Geoffrey wandered to a table where building plans for the abbey had been laid out. He was impressed – it was going to be a massive foundation, housing upwards of a hundred Benedictines. The monks would have a huge cloister, dormitories, refectories, guesthouse, common rooms, fraters, kitchens, brewery, bakery, buttery and granaries.

'Is it convenient to speak to you now, or shall I arrange for an appointment?' came a caustic voice from behind him.

Geoffrey turned quickly, aware that he had been so engrossed that he had not realized the King was there.

'I am sorry, sire,' said Geoffrey. He gestured at the drawings. 'The abbey will be remarkable.'

'Expensive, too,' said Henry resentfully. 'But it cannot be helped. My father wanted to atone for the bloodshed that allowed him to conquer England, and I had better follow in his footsteps. There was that nasty rebellion on the Marches earlier this year, and now there is the one you have just quelled. It would be prudent to let God know that I am grateful that neither succeeded.'

'Yes, sire,' said Geoffrey, thinking the Almighty was unlikely to be impressed by acts of beneficence that were conducted with such obvious reluctance. He said no more and waited for Henry to speak.

On the surface, he and the King had much in common. Both were the youngest sons of powerful men, and neither had expected to inherit on the deaths of their fathers. But there the similarity ended, because Geoffrey had not wanted to accede to Goodrich Castle when his three older brothers had died, whereas Henry had seized *his* chance for land and property with considerable determination.

'Where is your dog?' asked Henry, looking around. 'I thought it never left your side.'

The dog was more than happy to leave Geoffrey's side if it thought its options were better elsewhere. Geoffrey frowned, wondering why the King should be interested in such an unappealing animal.

'I would not mind him servicing some of my bitches,' Henry went on before Geoffrey could reply. 'They seem to produce docile pups, and I want some with more fire.'

'You will not want him anywhere near them, sire,' said Geoffrey hastily. Henry's hounds were expensive, and his dog could not be trusted with them.

'You were on the verge of leaving my kingdom when your ship floundered and you were cast up on the coast here,' said Henry, changing the subject abruptly. 'You would have been well east by now, were it not for that storm.'

'Yes,' said Geoffrey, heartily wishing the weather had remained fine.

'You are my vassal by dint of your estates here, whether you like it or not,' Henry went on. 'I know you still consider yourself Tancred's man, but you owe me consideration.'

'Yes, sire,' said Geoffrey, as politely as he could; they had been through this before. 'But—'

'Yet you tried to slip away,' Henry continued, cutting across him. 'Without my permission.'

Geoffrey frowned. He had never understood why Henry

concerned himself with his comings and goings. The King was surrounded by able and loyal men, and did not need his services.

'But you *did* give me permission to go, sire,' he said. 'A year ago. You said I could leave as soon as the trouble on the Marches was quelled. And there is peace now.'

'Yes,' said Henry, regarding him rather dangerously for daring to contradict. 'But there is always the possibility that war might break out again, and Lord Baderon – your new father-in-law – will be incapable of subduing it.'

'I do not see how I can help with that,' said Geoffrey. He knew he was verging on the insolent, but he could not help it. 'He is—'

'I require reliable men in that turbulent region,' said Henry, interrupting again. 'Goodrich is small, but you are married to Baderon's eldest daughter, so you have some sway over him. He will need you if trouble erupts, and I know he will accept your advice, because I have told him to.'

'You have?' Baderon had mentioned no such discussion when Geoffrey had taken leave of him back in August, and he was inclined to suspect that the King either misremembered or was lying. Probably the latter.

'I have,' said Henry coldly, as though he had read Geoffrey's mistrust. 'Besides, I understand your wife was unhappy with you disappearing for what might be a very long time.'

That was an understatement: Hilde was older than Geoffrey and acutely aware that women could not bear children indefinitely; there was no sign of an heir, and she had not wanted him to leave until he had done his duty.

'And there is your sister,' Henry went on, when there was no reply. 'It was hardly fair to abandon your estates to her. And I doubt her husband will be much use: Joan and Hilde are twice the man that Sir Olivier will ever be.'

Geoffrey ignored the insult to his brother-in-law. It was true that his wife and sister were both formidable, quite capable of running the family estates and defending them against any enemies. He considered himself fortunate; it was not every lord of the manor who could disappear, confident that his property would still be in one piece when – if – he returned.

'The three of them work well together,' said Geoffrey, seeing some sort of answer was expected, 'whereas I know nothing of farming. Besides, I wanted to see Tancred.'

'Ah, yes,' said Henry. 'Tancred. Unfortunately, he does not want to see you. Indeed, I believe he offered to kill you, should you venture into his domains again.'

'Yes,' said Geoffrey, irritated by the King choosing to air sensitive topics.

Henry saw his dark expression and sighed with affected weariness. 'Tancred does not want you, Geoffrey. You should accept that.'

'It does not matter whether I accept it or not,' said Geoffrey, unable to keep the resentment from his voice, 'because I have sworn a vow never to visit the Holy Land again.'

'You have?' asked Henry, startled. 'Why in God's name did you do that?'

'Because the storms continued after the ship was wrecked. My companions said it was God's displeasure at my travels, and we would all die unless I took an oath to stay in England.'

'And did these tempests abate once you had made this vow?' asked Henry, wide-eyed.

'Eventually.' Geoffrey still did not believe the Almighty had produced inclement weather for his sole benefit, and felt the pledge had been extracted by underhand tactics. But what was done was done, and he was not a man to break a promise to God.

Henry regarded him appraisingly. 'I hope you are not expecting *me* to provide employment. You already declined such an offer in no uncertain terms, and I rarely extend the hand of friendship twice.'

'I do not want your friendship,' said Geoffrey before he could stop himself. He saw the monarch's eyebrows shoot up. 'I mean, I shall be happy to settle in Goodrich and learn how to farm.'

Henry laughed, although it was not a pleasant sound. 'You will be miserable,' he predicted. 'But I am happy with your plans, because they fit rather well with my own.'

So here it comes, thought Geoffrey: yet another errand to be run – of the kind that Henry would never ask his usual retainers to perform. His heart sank, as he saw he was going to be plunged into intrigue and deception yet again; with Henry, there *was* no other kind of task.

★　　★　　★

Eudo arrived at that moment with urgent documents to be signed. Henry turned his back on Geoffrey, leaning over the desk to give them his attention. The clerk winked encouragingly at the knight, no doubt thinking that the length of the audience was a good sign. Geoffrey merely wanted to go home. Goodrich might well prove dull, but it beckoned to him like an oasis in the desert while he was with Henry.

Several of Henry's barons approached when Eudo had finished, but Henry waved them away. Then he took Geoffrey's arm and steered him into the north transept, indicating with a haughty flick of his hand that he was not to be disturbed. Geoffrey did not miss the resentful looks that followed. There were many at court who would love to be taken into Henry's confidence, and they were jealous of the favour this unkempt, minor knight was shown.

'As you are riding west, there is something you can do for me along the way,' began Henry. 'I have received word that there may be trouble in Kermerdyn.'

Geoffrey regarded him blankly. 'Where?'

'In the south of Wales. About two thirds of the way towards the western seas.'

Geoffrey stared at him. 'But that is miles beyond Goodrich! It is not on the way at all.'

And, he thought, there was always going to be trouble with the Welsh, and he could hardly remain at Henry's beck and call until an entire nation was subdued. Secretly, Geoffrey thought the Welsh were right to fight for their independence from the acquisitive, ruthless and greedy Normans.

'It is still my country,' Henry pointed out. 'And I need a knight who can speak Welsh – preferably one who understands the politics of the region.'

'But I do *not* understand them,' objected Geoffrey. 'Not down there. They are not the same as around Goodrich. Moreover, the language is not the same either. It varies from region to region, and the people there will find me incomprehensible.'

'I am sure you will find a way around it,' said Henry dismissively. 'But, as it happens, my commission is very simple. I want you to deliver a letter that I hope will avert any trouble.'

'Deliver a letter?' echoed Geoffrey suspiciously. This was hardly work for a knight – kings had trained couriers for that sort of thing.

'Yes, and I am doing you a favour, because the recipient is your kin – the husband of your wife's sister Isabella.'

Geoffrey regarded him warily. He had never met Gwgan or Isabella, although his wife had mentioned them. He hoped his new relation was not the kind of man who indulged in rebellion.

'Is he accused of treason or some such crime? This letter is one he will not want to receive?'

Henry grimaced. 'Why must you always think the worst of me? It is hardly seemly, and there is only so long I can be expected to tolerate your insolence.'

'I am sorry, sire,' said Geoffrey. 'Recent weeks have been difficult, and I am overly tired.'

'You look tired,' conceded Henry, softening a little. 'Dirty, too. It seems suppressing revolts has left you scant time to wash.'

Geoffrey thought it best not to respond to such a remark.

'The letter to Gwgan is nothing to do with treason,' Henry went on. 'It is one he will be quite happy to receive, I assure you, loyal subject that he is. But its contents are sensitive nonetheless.'

'You mean you want it delivered with no one knowing about it?'

'Precisely! I shall write a missive to the local bishop, too – one that will involve a princely amount of money, and so warrants a knight to deliver it. And I shall include one to Abbot Mabon, for the same reason. They do not like each other, and I do not want Mabon to take offence because I wrote to Bishop Wilfred and ignored him.'

'Who is Abbot Mabon?' asked Geoffrey, a little bewildered.

'Head of Kermerdyn's abbey,' explained Henry. 'Mabon is Welsh, and Bishop Wilfred itches to replace him with a Norman. They bicker constantly and are always writing to me about it. Indeed, there is a messenger from Mabon here now.'

'Is there?' Henry's court was vast, and Geoffrey had not tried to work out who was who.

'A sly monk named Delwyn. Doubtless, he will want to travel with you when you go west, because it will be safer in a larger party.'

Geoffrey did not like the sound of that. But he made no comment and brought the subject back to Kermerdyn's religious squabbles.

'What will you do?' he asked. 'Back the Norman bishop who will have the support of the Church, or the Welsh abbot who will have the support of the people?'

'You see?' asked Henry with a wry smile. 'You *do* understand the politics! You show more insight by that question than my clerks have revealed in great discourses. And I, of course, want to be popular with both Church *and* people. So I shall resolve the matter by doing nothing.'

'I do not understand,' said Geoffrey, intrigued despite himself.

'One of them will emerge triumphant, and I shall back whoever it is,' explained Henry. 'I cannot be seen to be on the losing side, but the winner will be worthy of my approbation.'

'But the winner might not be a man you wish to own as an ally,' Geoffrey pointed out. The moment he spoke, he wished he had not, because a predatory smile suffused Henry's face.

'Then there is something else you can do for me – send me your impressions of these two churchmen, recommending which is more deserving of my support.'

'I am not suitable for such a delicate task, sire,' objected Geoffrey. 'I am a soldier, not a diplomat, and may inadvertently give you poor counsel.'

'You will not,' said Henry, making it sound more like a threat than a vote of confidence. 'And I shall be happy to have your views regardless. Besides, I am sure you are grateful for me giving you this opportunity to prove yourself.'

'To prove myself?' asked Geoffrey, bemused. Surely, he had done that by risking his life to prevent rebels from trying to take Henry's throne.

'I am in the process of exiling anyone affiliated with my brother, the Duke of Normandy – and you became a knight under his tutelage. However, I am willing to overlook that in return for this small service. Refuse me, and you lose Goodrich – and I am sure your sister will not be happy about that.'

Joan would be livid, and Henry knew it. Geoffrey felt his temper begin to rise. He was not one of Henry's creatures, to be ordered hither and thither, but a knight who had survived the

Crusade – his white surcoat with its red cross told all who saw it that he was a *Jerosolimitanus*, one who had liberated Jerusalem from the Infidel. He bitterly resented being manipulated.

'I have no allegiance to Robert, and neither does Joan,' he said shortly.

Henry nodded. 'Then you will do as I ask. You will deliver the letters to Abbot Mabon and Bishop Wilfred, and spend a little time in their company to provide me with impressions. And you will deliver my missive to Gwgan without anyone else knowing.'

'Yes, sire,' said Geoffrey, making no effort to keep the resentment from his voice.

The letters were not ready when Geoffrey went to collect them from the Chapter House – which had been commandeered by the King's clerks – and he sighed irritably when he saw he was going to be made to wait yet again. He was eager to be on his way now he had permission to leave. It was not yet noon – with good horses, he could be twenty miles away by nightfall.

'I am sorry,' said Eudo, not sounding at all contrite. 'But we have more pressing business to attend than yours.'

'I am sure you do,' said Geoffrey shortly. 'But it will not take you a moment to gather these letters together, and then I can be away to do the King's bidding.'

'I will do it as soon as I can,' snapped Eudo. 'But you looming over me will not expedite the matter, so go away. I shall summon you when they are ready.'

Infuriated that a mere clerk should try to dismiss him, Geoffrey promptly sat on a large chest and folded his arms.

'I would not like you to forget,' he said in a voice that carried considerable menace.

'I will not forget,' said Eudo, alarmed. Crusader knights had a reputation for ruthless ferocity, and Geoffrey's battle-stained armour and the compact strength of his body said he was a dangerous man.

'Good,' said Geoffrey, watching Eudo sort deeds into two neat piles with unsteady hands. He sighed, never easy with intimidation, and tried to engage Eudo in polite conversation instead, sensing friendliness might better serve his cause. 'What can you tell me about Kermerdyn?'

Eudo shrugged. 'Not much. It is under the dominion of a Welsh prince named Hywel. The King installed him there on the advice of influential nobles, because he helped quell the rebellion on the borders. But it was a mistake.'

'Why?'

'Because everyone likes him.'

'And that is a problem?'

'It is. He is powerful in his own right, and I doubt he will want to remain the King's vassal. He will rebel, and he will have a strong base, because we installed him in a fortress called Rhydygors.'

'But if Hywel has any sense, he will see that it is safer to live in harmony than to wage a war.'

'You would think so, but, in my experience, rebels are usually rather short on sense. Moreover, there is always the danger that he will encourage other Welsh princes to join him. Not everyone appreciates that the best rulers are Normans, and that we are acting for their own good when we subjugate a people.'

'Right,' said Geoffrey, amused.

'It is true!' declared Eudo. 'I know, from studying tax returns, that your father turned Goodrich into a highly profitable venture, whereas it was struggling under the Saxons.'

Geoffrey nodded. Godric Mappestone had been a ruthless tyrant, who had subdued his tenants with a fist of iron and had made up for any shortfalls by helping himself to his neighbours' resources and supplies.

'Is that all you know about Kermerdyn?' he asked. 'That its ruler is popular?'

'I do not waste time learning about distant outposts.' Eudo flinched as Geoffrey stood, although the knight had not intended to frighten him. 'But I can tell you that Hywel represents a threat to the stability of the entire region.'

'Really? But alliances have been made with marriages. My wife's sister, for example. Surely, these count for something?'

'They may keep *some* Welsh leaders from taking up arms,' acknowledged Eudo. 'But the longer I chat here with you, the longer it will be before your letters are ready. With your permission, I shall be about my duties.'

* * *

It was bad enough that Geoffrey had again been coerced into doing Henry's bidding, but to be forced to wait for scribes was outrageous. Tiredness exacerbated his irritation, and he was sufficiently annoyed that he did not trust himself to hunt out Sir Roger, who had been travelling with him to the Holy Land before the storm had intervened. Roger might react with violence if he felt Geoffrey was being insulted.

Instead, he went for a walk, his dog loping at his side. It galled him that Henry should manipulate him quite so readily, and it occurred to him to leave without waiting for the letters. But that would be a mistake: Henry was vengeful, and Geoffrey did not want Hilde and Joan to suffer the consequences.

It was difficult to find a place to be alone when the abbey was full of Henry's retainers, but a bell chimed to announce that a meal was ready, and the church emptied quickly. Geoffrey walked to the chancel, which was blessedly free of kings and clerks.

'Geoffrey! I had no idea you were still here,' came a cheerful voice from behind him.

Geoffrey spun around quickly, vexed that he was not to be permitted even a few moments of peace, but his pique faded when he found himself facing Maurice, the portly Bishop of London. Maurice was famous for his absolute loyalty to the King, his building of a magnificent cathedral, and his insistence that he suffered from a medical condition that necessitated regular frolics with pretty women. Geoffrey had worked with him in the past and liked him.

He smiled, feeling his bleak mood lighten. Maurice extended his be-ringed hand for the traditional episcopal kiss, but the moment the formal greeting was over, he gave the knight an affectionate hug.

'It is good to see you, my friend!' he cried. 'Bishop Giffard often asks for news of you in his letters and will be delighted when I can report that you are safe and well.'

'You look well, too,' said Geoffrey, meaning it. The prelate was rosy-cheeked and shone with health and vitality.

Maurice leaned close. 'I have just had a couple of *very* pretty damsels, and my humours are in perfect alignment. Of course, it will not last, and I shall have to find another one before long. I do not suppose *your* lady is with you, is she?'

'You mean my wife?' asked Geoffrey, sincerely hoping the lecherous prelate did not intend to put Hilde on his list of conquests.

'No,' whispered Maurice, looking around hopefully. 'Your other lady. The one who was with you last summer, whom I dubbed Angel Locks. She gave me such pleasure one night!'

'Oh, my squire,' said Geoffrey flatly. 'Durand.'

It was a sore point. With his flowing golden hair and mincing gait, Durand had often been mistaken for a woman from behind and had not minded at all. Geoffrey did not like to imagine what he had done with Maurice one dark evening to convince the prelate that he was a member of the fairer sex. He knew only that Maurice was keen to repeat the experience and that Durand had been paid extremely well.

'Is she here?' demanded Maurice eagerly.

'He is no longer with me,' replied Geoffrey shortly. 'I have another squire now. Bale.'

Maurice grimaced. 'I do not know why you persist with this charade of pretending she is a man, Geoffrey. There is no other woman like her.'

'We can agree on that,' said Geoffrey. He changed the subject. 'How is the construction of your cathedral in London?'

'St Paul's,' said Maurice with a fond smile. 'It proceeds apace, thank you. But I am surprised to see you here. I thought you would be in the Holy Land by now.'

'I took a vow not to go,' said Geoffrey unhappily. 'And the King has found a mission for me. Again. Will he never leave me alone?'

'Hush!' Maurice glanced around uneasily. 'Walls have ears, and so does His Majesty. Long ones. *I* do not want to be seen as a traitor, even if you do not seem to care what he thinks. But let us talk of happier matters. Tell me about your new wife. Is she pretty?'

'She has nice eyes,' said Geoffrey loyally. No one in his right mind would call Hilde pretty.

'Well, a man cannot be too fussy about his wife,' said Maurice. He saw Geoffrey's troubled expression, and his voice became kind. 'Henry really *has* upset you. What does he want? Is there more trouble on the Marches?'

'In Kermerdyn,' said Geoffrey. 'On the opposite side of the

country. It seems he expects me to keep the peace through all
of Wales, which is a lot more than he demands of his earls.'

'Geoffrey, please!' exclaimed Maurice, glancing around uneasily
again. He took the knight's arm and led him to an alcove. 'If you
have no care to keep your own head attached to your body, then
try to think of mine.'

'Sorry,' said Geoffrey, genuinely contrite this time.

'You mentioned Kermerdyn,' said the Bishop. 'There have been
rumours at court about Kermerdyn.'

'What rumours?' asked Geoffrey, hoping he was not about to
be sent into a situation that was more dangerous or complex than
Henry had led him to believe. 'Anything I should know?'

'It can do no harm,' said Maurice. 'And I have not forgotten
what you did for Giffard last year. Nor has he, and he made me
promise to watch out for you in return.'

'You mean escorting him out of the country after he defied
the King?' asked Geoffrey, wondering whether this had factored
into Henry's commission.

Maurice nodded. 'Henry was furious, and there are many who
would not hesitate to kill anyone who vexes their King – not
that Henry would condone an act of violence against the Church,
of course. But he surrounds himself with some very vicious men,
and poor Giffard will not be safe until Henry has forgiven him.'

'Does Henry know it was me who helped Giffard to the coast?'
asked Geoffrey.

'Yes, of course. Nothing happens in his kingdom without his
knowledge. Perhaps you will wipe the slate clean with this favour
you are about to perform.'

Geoffrey sincerely hoped so.

Geoffrey joined Maurice for a stroll in the abbey grounds, moving
away from the populated areas and walking down a hill to a series
of boggy fishponds. Because most of the court was still eating, it
was peaceful there, the only sounds the eerie calls of curlews and
the wind whispering in the reeds.

They discussed mutual acquaintances and the adventures they
had shared the previous year when they had worked hard to oust
the tyrant Robert de Bellême from Henry's domain. Maurice
talked about his cathedral, too, and Geoffrey wished he could see

how it had progressed. Unusually for a knight, he was literate and had once entertained hopes of attending the university in Paris. Philosophy was his first love, but he might have enjoyed a career in architecture, too.

'So what are these rumours about Kermerdyn?' he asked eventually, eager to learn about the place from a man whose opinions he trusted.

'Its castle – Rhydygors – was built some ten years ago by the Sheriff of Devonshire, one William fitz Baldwin,' Maurice began.

'Why would the Sheriff of Devonshire build a castle so far from his home?'

'He was ordered to by the last king. It was odd, though. William was not a very nice fellow when he lived in Devon – I found him extremely unpleasant. But in Kermerdyn, he changed – he became God-fearing, honest and good.'

'I believe Rhydygors has been given to Prince Hywel,' said Geoffrey, thinking of what Eudo had told him.

'It has. William died seven years ago, and Rhydygors reverted to the Crown; Hywel was awarded it last year. But there was said to be something odd about William's death. He died of a fever, although he was in his prime, not some old dotard to be felled by a passing sickness. And he had a secret.'

'A secret?'

Maurice nodded. 'One he believed brought him success and happiness, and made him a better man. It would certainly explain the transformation I observed.'

'Did he drink?' asked Geoffrey.

Maurice scowled. 'No, he did not! Some men *are* changed when they are touched by God, so do not look so sceptical.'

'You think he was touched by God?'

'Well, he was certainly touched by something. A number of his friends and kinsmen tried to learn the secret while he lay dying, but no one understood his delirious ravings. The secret was lost.'

It sounded like a lot of nonsense to Geoffrey. 'What happened to Rhydygors between William's death and it passing to Hywel?'

'A garrison was stationed there under William's brother Richard. But Henry appreciated Hywel's efforts against Bellême and wanted to show it. He appreciated *your* help, too.'

'He did not reward *me* with a castle.'

'You already have one – you would not have appreciated anything he gave you, anyway. And he is not a man to squander wealth.'

Geoffrey laughed, his good humour beginning to return. 'So he gave me nothing because he thought it was a waste of a prize?'

Maurice nodded earnestly. 'But he does not forget those who are good to him, which is why you have been allowed to wander freely after helping Giffard escape. He has a soft spot for you, because you are never afraid to speak your mind, and he is used to sycophants. Although a little more tact when dealing with him would not go amiss . . .'

'I shall bear it in mind. What else do you know about Kermerdyn?'

'Hywel was not the only man rewarded with a castle. At the same time, Henry gave a knight named Sear a fortress in a place called Pembroc.'

'I have never heard of Sear, although Pembroc is famous.'

'No one has heard of Sear, and it came as something of a surprise when Eudo was ordered to issue the relevant writ. Indeed, I recall there was speculation of a misunderstanding, and Eudo actually went to Henry and asked him to confirm Sear's name.'

'So who is Sear?'

Maurice shrugged. 'He is just a bold knight. There is nothing unusual or commendable about him, although you would not know it if you met him. He is arrogant and swaggers horribly. I do not like him at all.'

Geoffrey felt as though they were getting away from the point. 'Is there anything else about Kermerdyn that I should know before I go there?'

'I was one of those who advised the King to give Rhydygors to Hywel. But it was a mistake.'

'Because Hywel is popular?' asked Geoffrey.

Maurice's eyebrows shot up. 'We do not want popular leaders in Wales because the locals may prefer them to Henry.'

'Or they may see Henry as wise for appointing such men.'

'I doubt it,' said Maurice. 'And William's brother, Richard, cannot be happy about the situation – word is that he rather liked living in Rhydygors. Of course, he is wholly devoted to

Henry, so would never voice his disappointment openly. He is in Gloucester at the moment, swearing fealty to the Crown in a formal ceremony.'

'Does Henry not trust him to stay loyal without such an oath?'

'Henry does not trust anyone. Richard will return to Kermerdyn to resume control of the Norman garrison. Obviously, Henry will want good men on hand if there *is* trouble brewing.'

'Prince Hywel does not object to Norman soldiers in his lands?'

'He understands that he holds them from Henry, and is said to be quite content with the arrangement. People are happy with his rule, and the garrison is never needed to quell trouble. Richard is thought to be bored with the inactivity, but everyone else is satisfied.'

'How do you know all this?'

'Partly from listening to the King, and partly from letters I have received from Wilfred, Bishop of St David's. Kermerdyn is in his See.'

'I am supposed to take a letter to Bishop Wilfred.'

Maurice smiled. 'Then you must give him my blessings. He is involved in a dispute with Kermerdyn abbey at the moment. Apparently, its head constantly questions his authority.'

'I have never been that far inside Wales,' said Geoffrey, trying to look on the bright side of the commission. 'Perhaps it will be interesting.'

'I imagine it will,' said Maurice. 'But be careful. Any soldier can deliver letters, but Henry has chosen you. There will be a reason for that.'

Two

The letters were still not ready by that evening, and Geoffrey saw he would have to spend another night in La Batailge. When dusk brought with it a drenching drizzle, he decided he would no longer bed down behind the stables. He found a corner in the kitchens and was a good deal warmer than those of Henry's retainers who had been allocated quarters in the dorter and guest hall, the roofs of which leaked. It allowed him to secure a decent breakfast, too, by raiding the platters before they were carried to the refectory.

However, he did not fare as well as Roger and the squires, who had passed the night in a nearby tavern. He found them there mid-morning, enjoying the company of three whores and a veritable mountain of food. There was plenty of ale, too, although it was cloudy and tasted vaguely rotten. Geoffrey drank it anyway. As a soldier, he had never had the luxury of being fussy about food, except fish soup or raisins; he would rather starve than ingest those.

'Well?' asked Roger. 'What did Henry want? You were certainly with him long enough. We grew tired of waiting for you and came here.'

Roger was Geoffrey's closest friend, albeit an unlikely one. He was a giant of a man, with thick black hair and matching beard, both worn fashionably long. His father was the notoriously treacherous Bishop of Durham, and it had always amazed Geoffrey that Roger was proud of his infamous forebear. Roger was happiest when fighting, looting or frolicking with any woman willing to tolerate his clumsy advances, and he had a deep-rooted distrust of anyone who was literate. This sometimes included Geoffrey, whose scholarly tendencies he deplored.

'He wants me to deliver a letter to Kermerdyn,' explained Geoffrey. 'Although there is something odd about the affair, and you should not mention it to anyone else.'

'Where is Kermerdyn?' asked Roger, scratching his head. 'And

why would he order *you* to deliver a letter? Henry is a fool if
he thinks you are a lackey. You have always been your own man,
even when you were serving Tancred. It is what makes powerful
men eager to claim your allegiance.'

'Henry does not care about my allegiance. He makes no attempt
to earn it, and forces me to do his bidding by blackmail and
coercion.'

'Because that is the only way you will do what he wants,' said
Roger, uncharacteristically astute. 'I am sure he would rather you
obeyed him willingly, but that will never happen, so he is reduced
to other tactics. It is a pity you swore that vow never to visit the
Holy Land, because we could have jumped on a ship and been
gone before Henry realized.'

'You were the one who insisted I took it,' Geoffrey reminded
him, resentfully. 'Besides, it would leave Joan and Hilde to bear
the brunt of his ire. I will not do that.'

Roger sniffed. 'They can look after themselves. The Crusade
would not have lasted half as long if the army had been populated with the likes of Joan and Hilde. I have never encountered
such fierce women. They are true Normans!'

Geoffrey began to respond, but Roger continued. 'You can pay
a monk to release you from your promise, you know. You did
not *want* to take it, so God will not object when you renege.
Besides, you are a *Jerosolimitanus*, and all your sins have been
forgiven. You can do no wrong in God's eyes.'

Geoffrey laughed, amused by Roger's fluid approach to religion. 'Only past sins were forgiven for joining the Crusade, not
ones committed since. And I cannot break my vow, anyway.'

'Perhaps I should not have coerced you,' said Roger sheepishly. 'But I honestly thought we were going to die when that
storm struck – and *everyone* said it was God's disapproval of your
travels. But God will understand. And if He does not, you can
pay for a few masses in Jerusalem. That should take care of any
misunderstanding.'

'A misunderstanding with God,' mused Geoffrey, smiling at the
notion. 'No. There is nothing I would like more, but it cannot
be done.'

Roger grimaced. 'I cannot see Tancred staying angry with you
forever. You were like brothers in the Holy Land, and he valued

your counsel more than that of any other. He will forgive you, and then we shall be given the best opportunities for looting and fighting. It will be marvellous!'

His eyes shone. Looting and fighting were two activities very close to his heart.

'And my vow?'

'Well, then, I suppose we must stay here to deliver your letter instead,' said Roger stoically. 'Besides, life with you is never dull. You will find us a battle somewhere. You always do.'

Geoffrey sincerely hoped he was wrong.

Geoffrey went to the Chapter House at noon, wondering why there was such a delay. Even if the letters to Gwgan, Abbot Mabon and Bishop Wilfred had not been written when Henry had ordered Geoffrey to deliver them, it should not have taken long for one of Eudo's many scribes to dash them off.

He was not the only one waiting for the clerks, and the yard outside the Chapter House was full of courtiers and messengers, all kicking their heels while the ponderous wheels of administration turned at a slow, deliberate pace.

'Perhaps later today,' Eudo snapped when Geoffrey insisted on speaking to him. 'Or tomorrow. His Majesty's affairs cannot be rushed just because you are in a hurry.'

Geoffrey resisted the urge to grab him by the throat. 'I am eager to do what the King has asked of me before he thinks I do not intend to bother.'

'He will not notice whether you are here or not,' retorted Eudo, truthfully enough. 'He has far more important business to attend.'

The door was slammed with an abruptness that was rude and gave rise to an angry murmur from the people in the yard. Geoffrey studied them, noting that they included Bishop Maurice and several other high-ranking churchmen, along with two earls and a smattering of knights. If Eudo felt sufficiently secure to treat them with such insolent insouciance, then it showed the extent to which clerks now ruled Henry's kingdom.

'You are in good company,' came a voice at his ear. 'We are all at Eudo's mercy.'

Geoffrey turned to see it was Sir Edward, the foppish Constable of Kadweli. He was even more splendidly attired than before, and his flowing locks and beard had been crimped into crisp curls. His cloak was fastened with a jewelled clasp that was decidedly feminine, and his fashionable tunic was a delicate purple.

'I thought Henry was efficient,' muttered Geoffrey resentfully. 'It seems I was wrong.'

'Oh, he is efficient,' said Edward, smiling to reveal white, even teeth. 'If your message was urgent, it would have been penned within moments. But on lesser matters, his clerks like everyone to know who is in charge. And the more you agitate, the longer they will make you wait.'

'Then I shall not bother them again,' said Geoffrey. 'Or Henry may find he has one less clerk, because Eudo is asking for a sword in his gizzard.'

Edward laughed. 'Much as I would like to see the man's pomposity punctured, I cannot recommend that: Henry holds him in high esteem. But I understand you are lord of Goodrich, on the Welsh border. I shall travel west soon, too. Perhaps we could go together. There is safety in numbers, after all.'

'You are a knight – you do not need such protection.'

Geoffrey was reluctant to accept company. He was used to travelling fast and hard, using every moment of daylight, sleeping under hedges and trees if necessary. Edward did not look as though he would appreciate journeying under such conditions, and Geoffrey assumed he would slow him down. Of course, there was no particular urgency in Henry's quest, and he supposed it would not matter if he took longer to accomplish it. Yet old habits died hard, and the notion of dawdling when there was work to be done was anathema to him.

'I have a knighthood,' hedged Edward. 'But I am not sure I would call myself a knight.'

Geoffrey was puzzled. 'I do not understand.'

'At the risk of sounding immodest, I am an extremely able administrator. The King appointed me Constable of Kadweli several years ago, but knowing the garrison was unlikely to follow orders from a parchment-hound, he knighted me.'

Geoffrey regarded him askance. 'What happens when you need to deploy your troops? Surely, your lack of military experience will show?'

'I was trained in the basics, like all men of noble family, so I am not wholly without knowledge. But, more often than not, it is wiser to negotiate peaceful solutions – and, on the few occasions where it is not, my captains are competent.'

'I see,' said Geoffrey. He was inclined to think it was a foolish state of affairs, but then reconsidered. If Edward really *was* able to parley his way out of confrontations, then surely it was better for all concerned? Geoffrey had seen too often the havoc needless skirmishes could wreak.

Edward smiled again. 'So what do you say to my suggestion? I will be no trouble, I assure you. And I may even be of some use – I know the roads extremely well.'

Trapped, Geoffrey nodded reluctant agreement.

'Look at them!' exclaimed Edward suddenly, pointing to two knights who had pinned a monk against the wall. The monastic was cowering, hands over his head. 'I know Brother Delwyn is a dreadful little worm, but it is not kind to bully him.'

The two knights were strong and tall. Both wore plain white surcoats, and the swords at their sides were well-honed and functional. One was Geoffrey's age – mid-thirties – with dark hair and blue eyes. The other was older, larger and distinctly better-looking, with long auburn hair and a neat beard.

The monk was an unappealing specimen, with lank, greasy hair, eyes that went in slightly different directions, and a grubby habit. Geoffrey recalled that Bishop Maurice had mentioned a Brother Delwyn, sent by Kermerdyn's abbey with messages to the King. Maurice had deemed him sly, and, judging from his appearance, Geoffrey suspected he might be right.

'I will send you word the moment Eudo gives me the letters,' said Geoffrey, beginning to walk away. He did not want to become embroiled in squabbles that were none of his concern.

'Wait.' Edward gripped his arm. 'Sear and Alberic are violent men, and though my instincts clamour at me to leave well alone, my conscience will not let me walk away while a man of God is molested. Neither will yours, I am sure.'

With a resigned sigh, Geoffrey allowed himself to be led towards the trio, heartily cursing Eudo and his tardiness.

'What seems to be the matter?' asked Edward pleasantly. 'Brother Delwyn?'

'They say I smell,' squeaked the monk, raising a tear-stained face to his rescuer. 'And they are threatening to throw me in the fishponds.'

Geoffrey thought they had a point. He was not particularly devoted to hygiene himself, but he was a good deal more respectable than Delwyn.

'The same might be true of others around here, too,' said the larger of the knights. He did not look at Geoffrey, although the inference was clear. 'The court is letting its standards drop.'

'I could not agree more,' said Edward amiably, pulling a pomander from his purse and pressing it against his nose. 'It is quite disgraceful, and I am glad I shall soon be returning to Kadweli.'

'When will you go?' asked the younger knight, although he did not sound very interested in the answer, and Geoffrey was under the impression he spoke to prevent his companion from making another remark that might see them in a brawl. Henry disapproved of fighting among his retinue.

'As soon as Eudo gives me the necessary documentation to begin building Kadweli in stone,' replied Edward. He smiled at the older knight. 'And you, Sir Sear? How much longer will you remain in this godforsaken bog? Personally, if I had been the Conqueror, I would have taken one look at this place and sailed straight back for Normandy.'

So this was Sear, thought Geoffrey. He regarded the knight with interest, wondering what had possessed Henry to appoint Sear, who looked every inch a fighting man, to Pembroc, but Edward, who was more woman than knight, to Kadweli. The two could not have been more different, and made it seem as though Henry could not decide whether he wanted his domain ruled by warriors or clerks.

Sear regarded Edward with haughty indifference. 'My clerks made a mistake with Pembroc's taxes, so I was obliged to travel here, to tell Henry that they will be somewhat reduced in future. Now I am waiting for Eudo to confirm the arithmetic. When he does, Alberic and I ride west.'

'Was Henry not vexed?' asked Edward. Geoffrey was wondering the same: Henry was inordinately fond of money.

Sear smirked. 'Not when I told him he could keep the excess.'

'I am glad to hear it,' said Edward warmly. 'Pembroc and Kadweli have worked well together, and I am reassured to learn we shall continue to be neighbours.'

'Make them apologize, Sir Edward,' bleated Delwyn, cutting into the discussion. 'I am a monk, and they have no right to abuse me.'

'He asked for it,' growled Alberic sourly. 'He called us louts, expecting his habit to protect him from retribution. Well, he was wrong.'

'I did no such thing!' cried Delwyn, although Geoffrey could see from his furtive eyes that he probably had. 'I said *some* knights who haunt the King's court are louts. I did not mean you. Although, now I think about it—'

'Go,' interrupted Edward. 'Or *I* will toss you in the fishpond.'

'You would not,' sneered Sear. 'You would not want to soil your pretty white hands.'

At that moment, Eudo appeared with a sheaf of documents, and there was a concerted rush towards him, Edward, Sear and Delwyn included. Sear aimed a kick at Delwyn as he passed, but it was half-hearted, and the grubby monk did not see it. Certain *his* letters would not be among the pile, Geoffrey took the opportunity to escape.

The previous month, when the ship he was aboard sank, Geoffrey had lost everything except his armour and weapons, and a saddlebag containing writing equipment. He had no spare clothes and no money, but this was nothing compared to losing his horse. The animal had carried him into dozens of battles and skirmishes, and he missed it sorely. He still had his dog, but it was a sullen, vicious brute, which could not compare to his beloved destrier.

Fortunately, Roger – a true Norman in his love of wealth – had managed not only to save his purse from a watery end, but also to acquire a small fortune during their subsequent adventures. He had used some of it to purchase new mounts for Geoffrey and himself. Warhorses were not easily replaced. They had to be strong enough to carry a fully armoured knight into battle, fast enough to perform the intricate manoeuvres that made them so formidable, and brave enough not to flinch at slashing swords, raining arrows and jabbing lances. Needing to begin training his new horse to its duties, Geoffrey took him out that afternoon, welcoming the solitude after the busy abbey.

He rode towards the coast, giving the animal its head when they reached a long, sandy path, relishing the raw power thundering beneath him. It was larger than his previous one, a massive bay with a white sock. When it slowed, he took it through several exercises and was pleased with its responses. Would it conduct itself as well in combat? For the first time, it occurred to him that he was unlikely to find out if he returned to Goodrich. There would be skirmishes, certainly, but not the kind of pitched battle for which he had been trained. He was not disappointed. He had been fighting almost continuously since he was twelve, and twenty years of warfare was more than enough.

He turned back towards the abbey when the light began to fade, surprised to see his squire, Bale, riding to meet him. With his broad shoulders, muscular chest and baldly gleaming head, Bale looked every inch the killer. He had an unnatural fascination for sharp blades, and had been foisted on Geoffrey because the people in his village were afraid of him – they had decided that only a Crusader knight could keep his murderous instincts in check.

'I was worried about you, sir,' said Bale, grinning a greeting. 'The abbey is full of unpleasant types – men who can read – and you cannot trust *them* as far as you can see them.'

'I can read,' said Geoffrey unkindly, because he knew exactly how Bale would react.

He was not wrong. Bale's mouth fell open in horror when he realized what he had said. He had not been with Geoffrey long and was still trying to make a good impression, terrified that he would be ordered away from a life of glittering slaughter and back to the fields from whence he came. He was old to be a squire – older than Geoffrey himself – but had taken to the task with unrestrained enthusiasm and was thoroughly enjoying himself.

'But you are different,' he stammered uncomfortably.

'Am I?' asked Geoffrey wickedly. 'How?'

Bale flailed around for a reason. 'Well, you prefer fighting to writing,' he said eventually.

'That is untrue,' said Geoffrey, indicating that Bale was to ride at his side. 'Given the choice, I would far rather spend the day with a good book than on a battlefield.'

Bale regarded him uncertainly, then grinned. 'You are teasing me, sir!'

Geoffrey changed the subject, suspecting he would be unlikely to persuade his squire that he would be more than happy to hang up his spurs.

'What happened to Ulfrith?' he asked. 'I have not seen him today.'

Ulfrith was Roger's squire, a big, stupid Saxon prone to falling in love with unsuitable women.

'That is partly why I came to meet you. He has run away, and Sir Roger is vexed.'

Geoffrey was relieved, though. Ulfrith was a liability in a fight, because, unlike Bale, he did not possess the necessary aggression to become a soldier, and Geoffrey was constantly aware of the need to protect him. Moreover, he was by nature an honest, innocent lad, and Geoffrey did not like the fact that Roger was teaching him bad habits. Ulfrith would do better with another master – or, better still, by returning to his former life as a farmer.

Bale cleared his throat uncomfortably. 'I think he stole your dog, sir,' he began worriedly. 'Because he is nowhere to be found, either.'

Geoffrey did not think that likely: the dog was not pleasant company.

'Do you know why Ulfrith left?' he asked. The dog would appear in its own good time; he knew its habits too well to share Bale's concern.

Bale shrugged. 'Well, there was a girl in that group of pilgrims from Southampton who caught his eye. Perhaps he went after her.'

'Good,' said Geoffrey, kicking his horse into a gallop. 'He was far too gentle to be a soldier.'

'Not like me, then,' said Bale, trotting after him. 'I am not gentle.'

'No,' agreed Geoffrey under his breath. 'You are not.'

★　★　★

It was nearly three days before the King's letters were ready, during which time Geoffrey became increasingly irate with Eudo. Meanwhile, Roger fretted and fumed over Ulfrith's desertion.

'How dare he leave without so much as a word!' he snarled.

'Especially with my dog,' agreed Geoffrey. He found he missed the dog and wished Ulfrith had stolen something else.

'I doubt Ulfrith *chose* to take that thing,' said Roger disparagingly. 'I imagine it decided it would have a better life with Ulfrith, and that was the end of the matter. It was never loyal to you. Just like Ulfrith was not to me, it seems. Damn the boy! He swore to serve me.'

'Take Bale instead,' suggested Geoffrey hopefully. His tenants at Goodrich would not thank him for bringing the man home.

'I might,' snapped Roger. 'Because it is your fault we are still here. If we had slipped away on a ship as I suggested, we would be halfway to the Holy Land by now, Ulfrith with us.'

'I cannot go to the Holy Land,' said Geoffrey, becoming impatient in his turn. 'How many more times must I say it? I swore a vow.'

Roger opened his mouth to reply but was interrupted by the arrival of one of Eudo's scribes, who came to say that Geoffrey was to report immediately to the Chapter House. Not sorry to be free of his friend's testy company, Geoffrey walked there quickly, then sighed when he was ordered to wait because Eudo was out.

'The letters are ready,' said a portly Benedictine clerk named Pepin, pointing to a leather pouch on the table. 'But he told me not to let you have them until he returned. He promised to be back before sext, so I cannot imagine where he might be. He is not normally late.'

'Of course not,' said Geoffrey, suspecting he would soon be told to return the following morning. It had not escaped his attention that most of the other petitioners had left, and his commission was one of the last to be completed.

'No, really,' said Pepin earnestly. 'He is always extremely punctual, and it is not his fault you have been delayed. Indeed, he is anxious to get rid of this particular parcel.'

'Oh?' asked Geoffrey, instantly suspicious. 'Why? Does it contain anything dangerous for the carrier?'

Pepin reached out to finger the material of Geoffrey's surcoat. 'You are a *Jerosolimitanus*, so nothing will trouble you. I heard that only the most dedicated warriors returned alive.'

That was true, although more soldiers had died from disease, thirst and starvation than in skirmishes with enemies. Geoffrey was not proud of what the Crusaders had done in other lands, and had considered abandoning the surcoat. Unfortunately, he, like all Tancred's officers, had taken a vow to wear it whenever he donned armour.

'Look inside the pouch,' he suggested, when more time had passed and there was still no sign of Eudo. 'To ensure everything is there. It would be unfortunate if I were to arrive in Kermerdyn and find someone forgot to put one of the missives in.'

Pepin bristled. 'We may be slow, but we are not incompetent. I assure you, the package contains exactly what the King ordered us to include. No more and no less.'

'Show me,' ordered Geoffrey.

'I suppose I can oblige, although you cannot take them until Eudo arrives.'

'The letters,' prompted Geoffrey.

Pepin opened the pouch and removed the contents. 'There are five of them—'

'*Five?*' interrupted Geoffrey. 'The King told me there would be three.'

'He changed his mind,' said Pepin. 'There is no point sending a second messenger when you can take the other two as well. Here is the first. It is the thickest and is for Bishop Wilfred. It tells him that some of his parish churches now belong to La Batailge – that the tithes accruing from them will come to this abbey, rather than to his own coffers.'

'God's teeth!' muttered Geoffrey. 'No prelate will be happy to receive that sort of news.'

'No,' said Pepin smugly. 'I imagine he will be furious. But this endowment will make La Batailge the fifteenth richest house in England.'

'I am sure Wilfred will be delighted to hear it,' said Geoffrey acidly. 'Especially as his See is in Wales. He will not mind his resources leeched away to fund already-wealthy houses.'

'Has anyone ever told you that you have a caustic tongue?'

asked Pepin. 'And it is not becoming in a man who has set eyes on the holiness of Jerusalem.'

'Forgive me,' said Geoffrey sourly.

Pepin sketched a blessing at him. 'Very well, you are absolved, although you should bear in mind that God only forgives those whose penitence is genuine.'

'Where is the letter to Abbot Mabon?' asked Geoffrey.

Pepin held out a folded piece of parchment. 'I have drawn a small green circle on the bottom, so you can tell it apart from the others, because it would not do to confuse them. You will not mistake Wilfred's, because it is the thickest.'

'I can read,' said Geoffrey coolly. 'Your coloured circles are quite unnecessary.'

'Really?' asked Pepin in surprise. 'How curious! However, I would not attempt to digest *these* missives, if I were you. Even I do not know what is in some of them, because Eudo wrote them himself. The seals are special, too – tamper-proof. If you try to open them, they crack, and the recipient will know. Even *I* cannot bypass them, and God knows I have tried.'

'I see,' said Geoffrey. It had not occurred to him to interfere with the King's messages, and he was astonished that the scribe should have done so.

'So I am afraid you will have to carry them without knowing *exactly* what they say,' Pepin went on. 'But most messengers are in that position.'

'I suppose they are,' acknowledged Geoffrey.

'I know what is in Abbot Mabon's, though. It is not from the King, but from the Archbishop of Canterbury, and tells Mabon he must subjugate himself to Bishop Wilfred's rule and defer to him in all things.'

Geoffrey groaned. It would not be easy gaining the measure of the two churchmen when he was the bringer of such unwelcome news. Had Henry done it deliberately, to make the commission more difficult? Or was it to annoy them both to indiscretion, to make Geoffrey's task easier? Somehow, he suspected an agent's ease would not be uppermost in Henry's mind.

'One of Mabon's monks is here in La Batailge,' said Pepin. 'I imagine Brother Delwyn will ask to travel with you to Kermerdyn. The highways are not as dangerous as they were under King William Rufus, but it is a rash man who risks them alone.'

'Then why does *he* not deliver the letter to Mabon?' asked Geoffrey irritably.

'He is keen to do just that, but the King gave specific orders that you were to do it.' Pepin shrugged. 'I have no idea why, and neither does Eudo.'

Geoffrey rubbed his head. The quest was becoming less appealing by the moment. 'The next letter is to Gwgan,' he said, reading the name.

Pepin nodded. 'I understand he is the husband of your wife's sister.'

'News travels fast,' remarked Geoffrey.

'The King told me,' said Pepin. 'He also said that you can be trusted absolutely.'

'Good,' muttered Geoffrey, wondering whether he should bungle the mission, so Henry would be less inclined to ask for his help in future.

'Its contents are secret, so I cannot divulge what is in it,' said Pepin. Then he grimaced. 'Well, I could not even if I wanted to, because Eudo would not let me see it. The fourth letter is for Richard fitz Baldwin. Its contents are highly sensitive, too.'

'Richard fitz Baldwin,' said Geoffrey, frowning. 'He is the brother of the man who built Kermerdyn's castle – and then died of an inexplicable fever.'

Pepin nodded appreciatively. 'Taking the trouble to learn about the people there shows initiative. There were rumours that William fitz Baldwin was poisoned because he was believed to have acquired some kind of secret.'

'A secret that made him happy and successful.' Geoffrey was thoughtful. 'Perhaps he learned something that allowed him to blackmail someone in authority. *That* would bring him riches and promotion – and happiness would follow.'

Pepin was shocked. 'That is a terrible thing to say! There was not a malicious or greedy bone in his body. As I understand it, his secret had to do with something more . . . ethereal. He found a way to cover himself with holy blessings.'

'Right,' said Geoffrey, feeling he was wasting his time. He brought the discussion back on track. 'So I am to deliver a

message to this man's brother. I do not suppose its sensitive
contents pertain to what happened to William, do they?'

'I sincerely doubt it,' said Pepin scornfully. 'He died seven years
ago, and I cannot imagine anyone still being interested. Richard
runs the Kermerdyn garrison, so I imagine the message will be
about troops or supplies.'

'And the last letter?'

Pepin pursed his lips. 'That is to be delivered to Sear.'

'Sear? Of Pembroc?'

Pepin nodded with a disagreeable face. 'I cannot abide the
man. He is arrogant, condescending and ignorant. Moreover, he is
in La Batailge, so I do not know why the missive cannot be
passed to him here. The King's orders are explicit, however – you
can read them for yourself.'

Geoffrey was startled to recognize the King's own handwriting.
'It says that Sear's letter is not to be delivered to him until we
reach Kermerdyn. Why?'

Pepin scowled. 'As I said, I have no idea. But it must be
important, or Henry would not have gone to such trouble.'

It smacked of politics to Geoffrey, and he hated being part of
it. 'Why does Sear not carry these messages? He is here and is
due to travel to Wales anyway. Or Edward, for that matter? Or
Brother Delwyn. Why does Henry need me?'

'He can hardly ask Sear to deliver a letter to himself, can he?'
said Pepin with a shrug. 'However, it might be a good idea not
to let anyone know what you are charged to do. Tell anyone who
asks that you are delivering messages from Bishop Maurice instead.
He will not mind.'

Geoffrey had grown increasingly appalled as Pepin described what
Henry expected him to do, and he was annoyed that two more
letters had been added. Moreover, if Henry trusted Sear enough
to award him Pembroc Castle, then what was wrong with *him*
carrying the messages? He did not understand at all, but thought
the entire affair reeked of dark politics – the kind he tried to
steer well away from. He was racking his brains for an excuse
that would allow him to dodge the mission when the door opened
and Sear himself strode in.

'Sir Sear!' exclaimed Pepin, shoving the letters out of sight in a way that was distinctly furtive. The auburn-headed knight's eyes narrowed suspiciously. 'I was not expecting you today.'

'Well, you should have been,' growled Sear. 'I cannot leave for Kermerdyn until Eudo has checked my tax-collector's arithmetic, and I am tired of kicking my heels here. Where is he?'

'Out,' gulped Pepin, looking frightened.

'Out where?' demanded Sear, shoving past Geoffrey to grab Pepin by the front of his habit.

'Easy,' said Geoffrey, stepping forward to push him away. 'He does not know where Eudo is.'

Sear's expression was murderous, and his hand went to the hilt of his sword. Then he let it drop, although his posture said he had not relaxed his guard completely.

'I saw you three days ago,' he said. 'You are Sir Edward's friend.'

'Hardly!' exclaimed Geoffrey. 'I have only met him twice.'

'He is Sir Geoffrey Mappestone,' gabbled Pepin. 'Who will travel to Kermerdyn at first light tomorrow – or sooner, if Eudo signs the release for the messages he is to deliver.'

'Messages for Kermerdyn?' asked Sear incredulously. 'Then why not ask *me* to take them?'

'And there is Edward,' added Geoffrey. 'I imagine he would make a good courier, too.'

'Bishop Maurice is a law unto himself,' blustered Pepin. 'And if he says he wants Sir Geoffrey to take these messages, then it is not for me to question him. Is that not right, Sir Geoffrey?'

Geoffrey nodded reluctantly, loath to be drawn into lies. He hoped Sear would not storm up to Maurice and demand an explanation, because Maurice was certain to look confused, and Sear did not look like the kind of man Geoffrey wanted as an enemy.

'The King has intimated that he would like you all to travel together,' blurted Pepin. 'Brother Delwyn, Sir Edward, Sir Alberic and you two. He is fond of you all, and you will be safer in one big group.'

'I am quite capable of looking after myself,' said Geoffrey, becoming even less enamoured of the mission. Sear did not look pleased, either. 'And large parties travel more slowly than smaller ones. I will make better time alone.'

'You must do what the King suggests,' said Pepin unhappily. 'He does not like it when people ignore his requests.'

Geoffrey was ready to argue, but Sear spoke first. 'Well, I am not a man to question His Majesty. I shall be honoured to travel with a fellow knight, especially one who, like me, has the King's favour. I understand you fought on the borders last summer and helped to defeat Robert de Bellême.'

'I played a small part,' acknowledged Geoffrey cautiously.

Sear smirked. 'I heard you fought him in single combat – and would have won, but the King stopped you from killing him. It is a pity. The world will never be safe as long as he is in it.'

Once away from the Chapter House, Geoffrey set out to hunt down Eudo, so that the releases for the letters could be signed. He did not understand why Henry should insist he travel with others, and intended to dissuade him of the notion. Surely, he would want his messages delivered as quickly as possible and would see there was no sense in wasting time while others dallied? Unfortunately, Eudo was nowhere to be found, and his scribes were concerned, because they had important documents that needed his attention.

'I saw him with Brother Delwyn earlier,' said Maurice helpfully, after ushering two scullery maids from his quarters.

'I cannot see Delwyn being conducive company,' Geoffrey said, watching the women scurry away, all giggles and shining eyes. 'Especially for a man with elevated opinions of himself, like Eudo.'

'Eudo *is* a nasty fellow,' agreed Maurice. 'Still, he is better than Delwyn. The man brought complaints from his abbot about Bishop Wilfred, and I doubt Henry enjoyed hearing them – he is not interested in the Church's squabbles, or in emissaries who smell.'

'In Welsh, *del* means pretty and *ŵyn* means lamb. His parents were deluded!'

Laughing, Maurice indicated that Geoffrey was to step into his rooms and partake of a glass of wine. 'What is Welsh for "sly"? That is the word that suits him best. Far be it from me to malign a man I barely know, but he seems devious.'

'The King wants me to travel west with him,' said Geoffrey. 'But I will make better time alone.'

'You will go with Delwyn, if that is what Henry desires,' said Maurice severely. Then his expression softened. 'Please do not defy him, Geoffrey. I do not want to see you in trouble – I count you among my friends. And I do not have many.'

'But it is—'

'And think about it logically,' interrupted Maurice. 'These letters cannot be urgent, or you would have been on your way days ago. *Ergo*, it cannot matter whether you take two weeks or two months to travel to Kermerdyn. Do as Henry asks – there is nothing to be gained by flouting his wishes.'

Geoffrey knew he was right. He took the cup Maurice proffered and took a gulp.

'I am to travel with Sear, too,' he said gloomily.

'I have yet to gain his measure, although my instincts are to distrust him,' said Maurice. He frowned. 'However, Sear and Delwyn are paragons of virtue compared to Eudo. It is a pity he invented those tamper-proof seals, because I would like to open the letters you are to deliver.'

'You would read Henry's private correspondence?' Geoffrey was shocked.

The prelate winced. 'It is not something I indulge in regularly, but I distrust Eudo. It would not be the first time he has meddled in matters without the King's consent, and he has accrued altogether too much power. I am afraid of what he might have included in these messages.'

'Pepin said he was not permitted to see them, and that only Eudo knows their full contents.'

Maurice sighed. 'Well, there is nothing we can do about it, I suppose. I dare not meddle with the seals, because I do not want to be exiled like Giffard – or to see you hanged. You will have to deliver them as they are, but I advise caution.'

'I am always careful.'

'It might be wise not to mention them to anyone else. Delwyn will know about the one to his abbot, but that is from the Archbishop, not Henry.'

'Pepin told Sear I was delivering letters from you.'

Maurice beamed suddenly. 'What a splendid idea! I shall write some immediately. I promised Giffard I would look after you, and this will go some way to salving my conscience.'

Geoffrey regarded him doubtfully. 'Do you know anyone in Kermerdyn? If not, the lie may be unconvincing.'

'I know lots of people there,' declared Maurice, sitting at a table and reaching for pen and ink. 'First, there is Robert, the steward of Rhydygors. He is distant kin, so I can regale him with details about my cathedral in London. You will like him. He is very odd.'

Geoffrey regarded him askance. 'What do you mean?'

'He has a gift for seeing into the future. I have it, too, although to a lesser extent. It must run in the family.'

'And what do you see in mine?' asked Geoffrey gloomily. 'Death and danger?'

'Of course, but you are a warrior, so that is hardly surprising.'

'I will be a farmer when I have finished this errand. At Goodrich.'

Maurice reached up to pat his shoulder. 'Good. I shall visit you there, and you can arrange for me to spend another enchanted evening with Angel Locks. But back to the business in hand. I shall write to Bishop Wilfred, too – I will send him a copy of a rather beautiful prayer that Giffard wrote.'

It sounded contrived to Geoffrey. 'Can you not think of something else?'

'Nothing comes to mind,' said Maurice after a few moments of serious thought. 'I do not like Wilfred very much. But I met a Kermerdyn butter-maker called Cornald in Westminster last year; he seemed a nice fellow. I shall write to him, too, and send him a recipe for a lovely cheese I sampled in Winchester.'

Geoffrey groaned. No one was going to believe such matters required the services of a knight. It would be worse than folk thinking he carried missives from the King.

'These will be sealed, Geoffrey,' said Maurice, seeing what he was thinking. 'No one will know their contents are trivial until they are opened. And by that time, you will be in Kermerdyn. This ruse *will* serve to keep you safe.'

'Very well,' said Geoffrey. 'Although it still does not explain why the King ordered me to join Sear, Edward and Delwyn. If I am *your* messenger, my plans are none of his concern.'

Maurice chewed the end of his pen. 'Then we shall turn it about and say His Majesty is eager to ensure his constables arrive in one piece – that you are elected to protect Edward and Sear.'

Geoffrey regarded him in horror. 'I doubt Sear will appreciate that!'

Maurice waved a dismissive hand. 'Leave him to me. I think I shall pen a line to Isabella, your sister-in-law, too.'

Geoffrey's jaw dropped. 'You have not seduced . . .'

'No!' said Maurice hastily. Then he looked wistful. 'Although I would not have minded her help with my health. However, I tend to stay away from ladies with jealous husbands, and my message will give her the name of a London merchant who sells excellent raisins. I may even include a sample. You will not eat them, will you?'

'I will not,' said Geoffrey firmly.

Maurice set the pen on the table and regarded him thoughtfully. 'There is something else I should probably tell you, although I am not sure what it means. Before I do, will you promise not to leap to unfounded conclusions?'

'What?' Geoffrey had the distinct impression he was about to hear something he would not like. He saw the Bishop's pursed lips. 'Yes, I promise.'

Wordlessly, Maurice stood and unlocked a stout chest that stood near the window. He rummaged for a moment, then passed Geoffrey a piece of parchment. It was partially burned, but Geoffrey would have recognized the distinctive scrawl of Tancred's scribe anywhere. It was in Italian, his liege lord's mother tongue.

> *To my dear brother, Geoffrey, greetings, on Easter Sunday, the third since you left us. I trust your health is returned, and the brain-fever that led you to write such*

Geoffrey stared at it. It had been penned just five months earlier, and was dated *after* the one he had received threatening him with death if he ever returned. What did it mean?

Three

'I found it during the summer,' explained Maurice, as Geoffrey stared at the parchment in his hand. 'I was looking for Eudo one day in Westminster and saw documents burning in his hearth. The room was empty, so, out of simple curiosity, I poked one, to see what it said.'

'There were others?' asked Geoffrey, his mind whirling.

'A bundle, although they were too singed to allow me to say whether they were all in the same hand. Eudo is in the habit of destroying incriminating documents, and piles of ashes are commonplace in his lair, so they may have had nothing to do with you.'

'But you cannot say for certain,' pressed Geoffrey.

'No,' agreed Maurice. He looked down at his plump hands. 'The thing has plagued my mind ever since. Clearly, it is a letter to you from Tancred. Yet I suspect, from the expression on your face, that it was not one you received. You have never seen that letter before, have you?'

'No,' said Geoffrey. 'And the ones I did receive certainly did not call me "dear brother". They did when I first left the Holy Land, but the later ones addressed me as "treacherous serpent" or "disloyal vermin".'

'I have given it a good deal of thought,' said Maurice. 'And it seems to me that someone intercepted them, replacing ones of affectionate concern – Prince Tancred seems to think you are ill – with unpleasant ones that he never wrote. It would not be the first time an allegiance was destroyed by a clerk with a talent for forgery, and Eudo is rather good at it.'

'But why in God's name would he do that?' asked Geoffrey, bewildered. 'I had never met him before a few days ago. And do not say he did it for Henry, because I doubt even *he* would stoop that low.'

'No, he would not,' agreed Maurice. 'But someone has, and your friendship has been shattered. If Tancred thinks you were afflicted by a brain fever, then clearly someone sent him messages purporting to be from you that were uncharacteristically abusive or insolent.'

Geoffrey aimed for the door. 'Then I am going to the Holy Land. It is not—'

'You cannot,' said Maurice, jumping up and grabbing his shoulder with a hand that was surprisingly strong. 'First, you swore a vow to God. Second, you cannot neglect the King's business – not without serious consequences for your loved ones. And, third, this is all supposition. I may be wrong. Perhaps *this* is the forgery – someone hoped to make you think you were forgiven, so you would run directly into Tancred's noose. And yet . . .'

'Yet what?' asked Geoffrey heavily, knowing Maurice was right – not about Henry, whom he would defy in an instant, but about his promise to God.

'And yet oaths can be retracted under certain conditions. I, for example, can absolve you of it.'

'You can?' Geoffrey felt the stirrings of hope. He *wanted* to believe Maurice was right, that someone had tampered with the correspondence. 'And will you?'

'No.' Maurice raised his hand to quell the immediate objections. 'Because it is not in your best interests at the moment. Talk to Eudo – ask for an explanation – and then do Henry's bidding. After that, we shall discuss what might be done about your oath without imperilling your immortal soul.'

Geoffrey was silent, thinking about Maurice's advice – and about his own promise not to jump to conclusions. The Bishop was right: Geoffrey could not leave for the Holy Land now, any more than he could have done when Roger encouraged him to break his vow.

'Will you come with me to challenge Eudo?' he asked after a while. 'I am afraid that if he does admit to doing this, I will end his miserable existence. And then my soul really will be in peril.'

'Then how can I refuse?' asked Maurice with a smile. 'Besides, I dislike Eudo and would like to see him squirm. Then I shall report to the King, who will not be pleased to learn that his clerks dabble with his subjects' personal correspondence. No monarch likes to be tainted with scandal.'

They began a search of the abbey grounds, but Eudo remained

annoyingly elusive. Maurice was on the verge of giving up in order to take more of his medicine when there was a shout.

'Murder!' screeched Delwyn, racing towards the church from the direction of the fishponds, his filthy habit flying. 'Someone has murdered Eudo.'

'Well, at least you know it was not me,' said Geoffrey to the horrified Maurice.

Whoever had killed Eudo had chosen a lonely spot for his crime. To the south of the abbey, down a slope, was a boggy area that contained several fishponds. A line of trees effectively curtained it from the rest of the precinct. Geoffrey thought that if someone could not resist committing a murder in La Batailge, then these marshes were the best place for it. The abbey buildings and church were too crowded with members of Henry's court, and the grounds to the north were populated by Benedictines who had been ousted from their usual haunts.

Eudo lay face down in one of the ponds, a short distance from the bank, and there was a knife in the middle of his back. It was a cheap metal weapon – Geoffrey had seen dozens of them lying around in the kitchens. The killer was not going to be identified from it.

'Lord!' muttered Maurice, crossing himself fervently. 'Eudo is dead, and I have spent the last hour saying terrible things about him. God will not appreciate such behaviour!'

'Eudo was arrogant and devious,' said Geoffrey. 'Being dead does not change that.'

'You are a hard man, Geoffrey,' said Maurice, sketching a blessing at him. 'God forgive you.'

A number of people had responded to Delwyn's shrieks of alarm. They included Sear and Alberic, who stood together with impassive faces. Edward was near them, fanning his face with his hand to indicate the run down from the abbey had been strenuous for him; Geoffrey wondered how he managed to control a garrison when he was so patently unfit. Meanwhile, Delwyn was leading a large party towards the scene of the crime, skinny arms flapping wildly.

As no one seemed inclined to do more than stare, Geoffrey waded into the water and hauled the body out. By the time he had the clerk on the bank, a sizeable audience had gathered. It included a large number of scribes and courtiers, plus several monks, although most Benedictines were at their mid-morning prayers. There were also servants, both Henry's and lay-brothers from the abbey. They clustered around the King when he arrived, and several began to gabble at him.

'Eudo asked me if I knew of a quiet place, so I told him it is always peaceful here,' said Brother Ralph, the abbey's sacristan. His face was ashen. 'But I would never have suggested it, had I known . . .'

'Who would want to kill poor Eudo?' cried Pepin, appalled. 'He never harmed anyone.'

Geoffrey glanced up to see a number of courtiers shooting each other meaningful looks and shuffling uncomfortably.

'Who found him?' Henry demanded. His face was a shade paler than usual, and Geoffrey saw that the death of a trusted scribe had upset him.

'I did,' said Delwyn shakily. 'Do you remember me, sire? I am from the abbey in Kermerdyn; I delivered you some letters from Mabon.'

'How could I forget?' asked Henry dryly, looking him up and down. 'Well? What happened?'

'I came here for a quiet walk, because people keep picking on me when I loiter around the abbey.' Delwyn shot Sear and Alberic a reproachful glance.

'And what did you see?' prompted Henry.

'Eudo floating face-down in the water.' Delwyn shuddered. 'I am unused to violent death, and it was something of a shock. I am sorry if my agitated cries distressed you.'

'Oh, they did,' said Henry. 'Especially when I learned poor Eudo was the reason for them. So why was he down here? I thought he had plenty of work to keep him busy in the Chapter House. God knows, enough of my court have complained about delays and hitches.'

'He has been missing for several hours,' said Pepin, rather tearfully. 'We have been worried, because he never leaves us alone when there is important business to be done.'

'Well, obviously he does,' snapped Henry. 'Because here he is.'

'He spoke to me just after dawn,' said Ralph. He crouched

next to Geoffrey, peering into the dead man's face. Then he
reached out to touch it, although he withdrew his hand quickly
and immediately crossed himself. 'It is now mid-morning. It looks
to me as though he has been dead for two or three hours at
least.'

Geoffrey wondered how he could tell, although his own experience with corpses made him suspect the sacristan was right. Eudo
was cold, but not yet stiff, and he could not have been dead for
long – especially if he had been seen not long after dawn.

'Do any of *you* come down here?' asked Henry, gazing around
at the assembled mass. 'To escape the hurly-burly of court life?'

There was a chorus of denials and a lot of shaken heads.

'Then did you *see* anyone else setting off in this direction?'
pressed Henry. 'Think carefully, because Eudo was useful to me,
and I am not pleased by his untimely demise.'

'I may have seen him, sire,' said Sear in a low voice. 'At least,
I saw someone hurrying in the direction of the ponds, but it was
misty just after dawn, so I may have been mistaken.'

'And he was on his own?' demanded Henry.

Sear coloured. 'I am sorry, sire. As I said, it was misty. He may
have been alone, but he might equally well have been following
someone who was already invisible in the fog.'

Henry turned to Ralph. 'You seem to know about corpses.
Tell me how he died. Was the knife in his back fatal?'

'Well, it would not have done him any good,' hedged the
sacristan uncomfortably.

'He drowned,' said Geoffrey. He saw the King's raised eyebrows
and pointed to the foam that frothed from the clerk's mouth and
nose. 'Only drowned men ooze so, and the knife wound is not
in a place that would be instantly fatal.'

'You are right,' said Henry, leaning forward to look. 'It is too
high to have been mortal so quickly. So it seems he was stabbed
first and then pushed in the pond.'

'And churned mud and broken reeds suggest it happened there,'
said Ralph in an effort to redeem himself, as he pointed to a
spot some distance away. Geoffrey was inclined to believe him,
and went to look. Sear and Delwyn followed.

'This is not your affair, monk,' said Sear haughtily to Delwyn.
'Mind your own business.'

'It is not yours, either,' flashed Delwyn.

'It is — I am one of the King's favourites,' snapped Sear. 'He gave me Pembroc Castle, so he will be interested to hear my opinion on this matter.'

While they sniped at each other, Geoffrey knelt and inspected the ground. There were footprints, but they were too smudged to be of any use, and some were likely to be Eudo's anyway. There was also a smattering of blood on several reeds, which suggested that Eudo had indeed been stabbed first and then pushed in the pond to drown. Water had splashed into the footprints, and Geoffrey wondered whether the killer had followed Eudo into the pond and held him under until he was dead.

The only other thing was several silver pennies that had apparently been dropped during the struggle. Trailed by Sear and Delwyn, Geoffrey returned to the body, where a brief inspection indicated Eudo's purse was still firmly closed. The money had not been lost by him, but by his killer.

'What have you found?' demanded Henry.

It was Sear who replied, speaking loudly and importantly. 'The footprints are large ones. They were not made by an insignificant man, such as Delwyn here, but a bigger fellow, such as myself.'

'Are you telling us *you* are the culprit?' asked Delwyn archly. Several courtiers sniggered, and Sear flushed.

'Do not be stupid,' he snarled. He turned to the King. 'It is just an observation, sire, which may help to solve the crime.'

'Thank you, Sear,' said Henry, with what sounded to be genuine sincerity. 'Your observations are welcome.'

'Thank you,' said Sear smugly.

Henry smiled at him, and Geoffrey saw the knight was right when he claimed to be a royal favourite. Henry turned to Geoffrey.

'And you?' he asked. 'What can you tell me?'

'There were these,' said Geoffrey, showing Henry the coins he had found.

'Pennies from my mint in Pevenesel,' mused the King, taking them. He did not hand them back, and Geoffrey saw them disappear into the royal purse. 'Does it mean the killer is local?'

'I have Pevenesel pennies, too, sire,' said Geoffrey. 'And so will most of your courtiers by now. Nothing can be concluded from it, except one thing: the killer is unlikely to have been a servant, because he would not have abandoned such a princely sum.'

'A monk?' asked Sear. 'They are wealthy.' He included Delwyn in his scathing glance.

'I doubt a monk killed Eudo,' said Henry, looking around at the throng in a way that made several glance away uneasily. 'It must be a courtier. Or a knight.'

Because he did not like the notion of men standing around idly when they should be labouring on his behalf, Henry ordered everyone back to work, although he indicated that certain people were to stay. These included some of his favourites, the contingent from Wales, Pepin and several clerks, and Geoffrey. Maurice lingered, too, watching with narrowed eyes when the King caught Sear's arm and whispered something that made him smile.

'I do not understand what His Majesty sees in him,' the prelate muttered to Geoffrey. 'Oh, he is mannerly enough, and a bold warrior. But he is nothing unusual, and I do not see why the King makes a fuss of him.'

Geoffrey shrugged. 'Perhaps he just likes him. It does happen that men make friends.'

'That is not the King's way,' insisted Maurice. 'There is a reason for everything he does, and he does not dispense his goodwill lightly. But Eudo's death is a nuisance for you. Now you will never know what he was doing with Tancred's letter.'

Geoffrey nodded unhappily. 'Did he have a close friend? One he might have confided in?'

'No. Eudo was not a man for companions. Still, I am glad I gave you that letter *after* he was murdered – I dread to think what would have been said had you confronted him and hot words been exchanged.'

Geoffrey would not have cared, as long as he had been given answers. He was still shocked by Maurice's discovery, and now he was also frustrated that an explanation for Tancred's uncharacteristic threats should have been so tantalizingly close, only to be ripped away. He left Maurice and went to speak to Pepin, who was standing in a disconsolate huddle with his fellow clerks. He showed them the burned letter.

'Have any of you see this before?' he asked.

Pepin took it from him, then shook his head. 'I do not see how it can relate to Eudo's murder, because it is addressed to you. I thought you told me you could read.'

'Did you drop it in the fire by mistake?' asked another clerk. 'Eudo did that a lot – either he got flustered and consigned documents to the flames that should have been kept, or he fell asleep while reading by the fire and set them alight by accident.'

Pepin glared at him. 'It is unfair to reveal such matters to strangers, Justin. Do you *want* people to think badly of Eudo?'

'I want them to know the truth,' countered Justin. 'He was not the paragon you claim. He was not even very efficient. We were always helping him cover his mistakes.'

'The King trusted him,' cried Pepin, distressed. 'He dictated all his most secret letters to him.'

'Yes,' agreed a third clerk spitefully. 'Eudo certainly knew his share of secrets, and was as closed-mouthed as any man, I will grant him that. Of course, it made him dangerous, and I imagine there are dozens of men at court who will be delighted he is dead.'

'This letter,' said Geoffrey, not interested in Eudo's death. 'Are you sure none of you has seen it before. It is important.'

'Is it now?' asked Justin snidely.

Pepin examined it again. 'I am good at recognizing handwriting, but this style is unfamiliar. Besides, none of us knows Italian – we only use Latin and French.'

'Eudo knew Italian,' interposed Justin. 'He was the only one who did.'

Geoffrey watched them walk away, inclined to believe they were telling the truth: whatever Eudo had done had not involved them. But *what* had he done? And how was Geoffrey to find out now that he was dead and his colleagues were ignorant of the matter?

'Now I wish I had never given it to you,' said Maurice unhappily, coming to stand beside him. 'I would not have done, had Eudo's corpse been found earlier. All I have done is given you cause for distress, and it will make you restless to leave, too.'

'Leave where?' asked Henry, appearing suddenly behind them. 'La Batailge, to go and do my bidding in Kermerdyn?'

'Leave England, sire,' said Maurice, before Geoffrey could stop him. He took the letter from Geoffrey and showed it to the King. 'I found this several months ago. Eudo had burned it.'

'What does it say?' asked Henry. 'The language is unfamiliar to me.'

'It contains fond greetings from Prince Tancred, and was written at Easter,' explained Maurice, although Geoffrey wished he had kept his mouth shut. He did not want the King to know his business. 'It is either a forgery, to encourage Geoffrey to ride to his execution, or it is a real letter from Tancred, showing friendship and concern — meaning the hostile ones were false.'

Henry raised his eyebrows. 'And you believe Eudo was complicit in this affair? But why would he do such a thing? What did you do to earn his dislike, Geoffrey?'

'I met him for the first time a few days ago,' said Geoffrey. 'He had no reason to wrong me. The only explanation that makes sense is that someone paid him to do it.'

'An enemy,' mused Henry. 'I imagine your insolence has earned you plenty. In the meantime, this does not look good for you.' He looked pointedly at Eudo's body.

'Geoffrey knew nothing of this letter until I gave it to him a few moments ago,' said Maurice firmly. 'And then I helped him look for Eudo and did not leave his side for a moment. *He* did not slip away to murder your scribe. I will stake my life on it.'

'Then I shall believe you,' said Henry. 'Geoffrey does have a hot temper, though, and I have warned Sear to be on his guard as they ride west together. I am fond of Sear and do not want to lose him to a spat. But time is passing, and I have much to do.'

He flicked imperious fingers, and his people surged towards him, all eager to please. Sear and Alberic were the first to arrive. Edward followed more slowly, sighing theatrically when he saw that mud had stained the bottom of his fine cloak.

'We were discussing your journey west,' said Henry, smiling pleasantly at Sear. 'I know you and Alberic would rather go alone, but travelling together will be safer for everyone. My roads are freer of outlaws now than they were in my brother's reign, but you cannot be too careful.'

'Well, *I* am more than happy to be in a large party,' declared Edward. 'And when we reach Brechene, we shall have my garrison to accompany us, too. I did not bring them all the way here when I was summoned to see you, sire, because it was more economical to leave them in Wales.'

'Very practical,' said Henry, smothering a smile. 'How large a force is it?'

'Two dozen men, all well trained,' replied Edward. 'At least, that is what my captain tells me, and I am sure he is right. They certainly look the part – all oiled leather and gleaming weapons.'

'Good,' said Henry. 'You are all very dear to me, and I shall sleep happier knowing you will be in each other's company.'

Geoffrey was instantly on his guard, knowing *he* was not dear to Henry at all. Was Henry's insistence that the party ride together to protect Sear? Geoffrey did not think so – Sear looked perfectly capable of looking after himself, and so did Alberic. Was it Edward, then, who was unlikely to be much good in a fight? Or Delwyn? Geoffrey doubted the grubby monk would rate highly among Henry's friends and could only conclude that it was Edward he wanted to safeguard.

'It might be a good idea, sire,' began Maurice that evening, 'to rewrite the letters Geoffrey will carry tomorrow. Then we can be sure of their contents.'

They were in the Abbot's House. Henry was sprawled in front of the fire in a cushion-filled throne. There were several dogs at his feet, and he was devouring raisins at a rapid rate.

Geoffrey had been summoned to attend Henry at dusk, but had been kept waiting while the King looked over a horse, and then again while he ate his supper. By the time he had been admitted to the royal presence, he was tired, restless and irritable. Maurice had elected to accompany him, lest he say something to land himself in trouble.

Geoffrey's mind was not on the King's business, but on Tancred's letter. He had never broken a vow in his life, and it did not seem a good idea to start by reneging on one made to the Almighty. Yet he longed to resolve the misunderstanding with the man he loved as a brother. It occurred to him to write to Tancred, but how could he be sure that his message would not be intercepted and replaced by one that would make matters worse?

'But I *am* sure of their contents,' Henry was saying, his voice bringing Geoffrey back to the present. 'Eudo wrote them for me.'

'Quite,' said Maurice baldly, and Geoffrey held his breath, wondering whether the Bishop had overstepped the mark in criticizing His Majesty's favourite clerk. He was grateful to Maurice for trying to keep him safe, but did not want to see him in trouble. 'He had a tendency to include addendums. And they might be redundant now he is dead.'

'Explain,' ordered Henry, narrowing his eyes.

'Eudo was not honest,' said Maurice, meeting his gaze evenly. 'But he was loyal and always scheming to advance your interests. However, now that he is not here to see these plots through, they may miscarry, and—'

'No,' interrupted Henry. 'Kermerdyn is too distant an outpost to warrant Eudo meddling; you are worrying unnecessarily. Besides, there is no need to waste good parchment and wax, and these missives are already signed and sealed. Geoffrey will carry them as planned. Pepin!'

The door was flung open, and the scribe scurried in with the package he had shown Geoffrey earlier. 'Sire.'

'Give Sir Geoffrey the letters. Have you explained what I want him to do?'

'Yes, sire,' said Pepin. 'Five letters to be delivered. Four from you, and one from the Archbishop to Abbot Mabon. The ones to Richard fitz Baldwin and Gwgan are secret, and Sear is not to have his until everyone is safely in Kermerdyn. He will not be pleased, though – he will wonder why he was not given it by you, personally.'

'Because I do not want him to have it yet,' snapped Henry. He turned to Geoffrey. 'He doubtless *will* be vexed, but you must tell him not to question his King's wishes.'

Geoffrey said nothing but raised his eyebrows, feeling it was hardly his place to make such a remark to a fellow knight.

'Here are the letters,' said Pepin, passing them over. 'The green circle is for Abbot Mabon . . . but you can read so you do not need my devices. However, for your information, the red dagger is for Sear, because he is warlike, the diamond is for Richard fitz Baldwin, because he is hard, and the fancy cross is for Gwgan, because he is literate, like us.'

'And Wilfred's letter is the fat one,' finished Geoffrey, to show he had been listening earlier.

Pepin nodded. 'For God's sake, do not deliver them to the wrong people.'

'I think we can trust Sir Geoffrey to get it right,' said Henry dryly. He nodded to indicate Pepin was dismissed. The scribe shot out as quickly as he had entered.

'Is there no letter for Prince Hywel, sire?' asked Maurice. 'I imagine he will expect one, given that you are communicating with the two most powerful churchmen in his domain.'

Henry stretched. 'I do not pander to the sensitivities of vassals, Maurice. Besides, Hywel is too busy being popular to care what I think of him.'

'I imagine he *will* care,' said Maurice unhappily. 'And it is not pandering to sensitivities as much as acknowledging his continued loyalty. It is simple diplomacy.'

'Unnecessary diplomacy,' countered Henry. 'I have nothing to say at this time.'

While Henry and Maurice continued to debate, Geoffrey studied the letters carefully to assess whether they were the ones he had been shown earlier – he mistrusted everyone. Then Maurice took them, too, and held them to the light, as if he hoped to read what was written inside. The Bishop shook them, rubbed them against his cheek, and finally blessed them with great solemnity. Henry watched in astonishment.

'Are you finished?' he asked.

'I sense an evil in them,' explained Maurice. 'You know I have a knack for telling these things. I wish you would let me rewrite them, sire. I have a fair hand, and it will not take me long.'

'I cannot be bothered,' said Henry. 'It has been a long day; I am tired. And there is nothing important in them. They pertain to Kermerdyn, for God's sake – a place we could barely plot on a map.'

'Then why send Geoffrey to deliver them?' asked Maurice. 'Why not let Edward or Sear do it?'

Geoffrey winced. Maurice rarely questioned his King.

'Because it suits me to send *him*,' snapped Henry. 'Remember yourself, My Lord Bishop. Not even you have the right to question me.'

Maurice looked stricken. 'I meant no disrespect, sire! I was merely—'

'Merely poking your nose into matters that are none of your concern,' finished Henry. But he relented when he saw the prelate's distress. 'I am sending Geoffrey because one of these letters is for his kinsman – Gwgan. My Normans are not overly enamoured with the Welsh, and I would not like them to "forget" to deliver it, in order to see Gwgan in trouble.'

'I see,' said Maurice. He swallowed hard. 'Will you tell us what these messages contain? The recipients may have questions, and Geoffrey will look foolish if he cannot answer.'

'Very well,' said Henry with a bored sigh. 'The letter to Bishop Wilfred is about property, the one to Abbot Mabon is about clerical obedience, and the ones to Richard, Sear and Gwgan pertain to the routine deployments of troops. There is no reason to assume I am sending Geoffrey into danger. On the contrary, these messages could not be more innocuous.'

'I see,' said Maurice. 'Then why—'

'Besides, it will give him an opportunity to visit Goodrich en route, and warn his hapless wife and sister that they are about to have his company for the rest of his natural days. His ensuing excursion to Kermerdyn will give them the chance to get used to the idea.'

Geoffrey struggled not to gape, feeling it was hardly the King's place to meddle in his domestic arrangements. 'But Goodrich is *not* on the way to Kermerdyn. I will not go there first.'

'I insist you do,' said Henry. 'My letters are not urgent, and you must avail yourself of another opportunity to produce an heir. You do not have one in the making yet, I believe. We are similar in that respect, although neither of us has any trouble siring bastards.'

Geoffrey was not sure whether he was more taken aback by the bald order to impregnate his wife or the implication that he was the kind of man to leave women with unwanted offspring. With the exception of one lady – a duchess who still laid claim to his heart – he had never been in one place long enough to develop an enduring relationship, and the other women he had bedded tended to know how to avoid unwelcome pregnancies.

'I want Goodrich to have an heir,' Henry went on. 'Of course, my own wife is slow in that regard, despite strenuous efforts on my behalf, and I can hardly compel you to do what I cannot achieve myself. However, I would like you to try.'

Again, Geoffrey said nothing, thinking that what he did with Hilde behind closed doors was none of the King's damned business.

'Perhaps you should take your wife to Kermerdyn,' said Henry thoughtfully. 'She will be pleased to see her sister Isabella again, and I understand she knows how to wield a sword. She might even be useful to you, and you can make the heir along the way.'

'Sire!' exclaimed Maurice, glancing uneasily at Geoffrey and obviously worried about a tart response to the order. 'I hardly think this is a suitable—'

Henry laughed. 'Geoffrey does not object to me talking to him man to man. He is a soldier, for God's sake, and I know for a fact that they discuss little else when they are out on campaign.'

'I will put the matter to Hilde,' said Geoffrey cautiously.

'Oh, she will go,' predicted Henry. 'Besides, she may be in a position to help me, too. You see, William fitz Baldwin had a secret, and Isabella was one of those who was at his deathbed when he raved about it. She may have an inkling as to what it is. If so, you can find out for me.'

Geoffrey frowned. Now what was he being ordered to do?

Maurice was more forthright. 'Is that the real reason for you giving Geoffrey these letters, sire?' he asked uneasily. 'You want him to investigate another matter entirely?'

Henry raised his hands in a shrug. 'Well, why not? He will be in the area anyway.'

A messenger arrived with an urgent question from one of the King's barons at that point, and Henry ordered Geoffrey and Maurice to stand on the far side of the room while the man whispered to him and received his answer. Maurice's flabby face was unhappy.

'I do not like this,' he said. 'I wondered why you were selected to deliver these messages, and now we know: Henry wants William's secret.'

'You mentioned this secret before,' said Geoffrey. 'You said William had discovered a way to shower himself with blessings and make himself a better man.'

'And a richer one. At first, I assumed he was speaking metaphorically, but then it became clear that he had discovered some literal way of earning his good fortune.'

Geoffrey frowned. 'It sounds like superstition to me.'

'Perhaps. However, if you do discover some actual, physical thing that turned William into a saint, I strongly recommend you leave it in Kermerdyn.'

Geoffrey regarded him askance. 'But the King obviously wants it delivered to him.'

'Do not even *think* of meddling in such matters, Geoffrey,' said Maurice sternly, crossing himself. 'Whether this secret derives from God or from sorcery, you would be well advised to leave it alone. *I* would not tamper, and I am a bishop.'

'Not even for Henry?'

Maurice considered. 'No,' he said eventually, 'not even for him. Although he could make life unpleasant for me on Earth, that is nothing compared to the eternity that comes after. So investigate this matter and be ready to give the King an honest report. But if the secret does transpire to be something tangible, leave it where it is.'

'Very well.'

'I am serious, Geoffrey. I promised Giffard to keep you safe, and that vow extends to your soul. Do not interfere in matters beyond human understanding.'

'Come,' called Henry, beckoning them forward as the messenger bowed his way out. He yawned. 'Lord, I am weary! Have you two finished pestering me with silly questions?'

'William fitz Baldwin's secret,' said Maurice worriedly. 'You told Geoffrey to find out what it was, although I fear it may not be one you want to know.'

Henry's eyes narrowed. 'What do you mean?'

'Well, whatever it was did not protect William, because he died in suspicious circumstances. If my memory serves me correctly, there were rumours that he was poisoned. By rancid butter.'

Geoffrey could tell the information was not news to Henry, although the monarch did his best to feign astonishment.

'Are you saying one of my constables was *murdered*?' he asked. 'That is a grave crime and one that *must* be investigated. Take

Hilde with you, Geoffrey, and see what can be learned from Isabella about this secret. And if William *was* murdered, I want you to find the culprit.'

'But William died seven years ago, sire,' said Maurice, alarmed on Geoffrey's behalf. 'I doubt it will be possible to solve the case after so long.'

Henry smiled coldly. 'On the contrary, if William was dispatched to gain his secret, it is just a case of seeing who at his deathbed has been showered with blessings ever since. Besides, William really *did* become a different man after he built Rhydygors, and I want to know why. I cannot have inexplicable events occurring in my kingdom – it may lead to trouble.'

'Why look into the matter now?' pressed Maurice. 'Why not when it happened?'

'Because I was not king when it happened,' replied Henry shortly. 'I have only had my throne three years, and there have been other matters to occupy me – such as quelling rebellions. But now my enemies are crushed, I find myself with more time to explore different matters.'

Except *he* would not be doing the exploring, thought Geoffrey. *He* would be lounging in abbots' halls, eating raisins, while his hapless subjects trudged miles to distant castles to investigate incidents that had occurred far too long ago for any clues to remain.

'I shall do my best,' Geoffrey said unhappily, deciding that when he had completed this mission, nothing would keep him in England. Maurice would release him from his vow, and he would travel straight to Tancred.

'Meanwhile, Maurice can explore Eudo's death,' Henry went on. 'I want the culprit hanged.'

'*I* am not qualified to investigate such matters,' said Maurice, horrified.

'Then you will have to learn,' said Henry shortly. 'It is good for my bishops to develop a variety of skills. It is a pity Giffard was rebellious, because he would have done it.'

'Very well,' said Maurice. 'Like Geoffrey, I shall do my best.'

'Have you expunged the evil from my letters?' asked Henry, nodding that Maurice was still clutching them. 'Or shall I order a witch summoned to do it?'

'Please, sire,' said Maurice with quiet dignity. 'Do not jest about such matters.'

Henry ignored him and looked back at Geoffrey. 'And if you deliver my letters *and* send me William's secret, I shall forgive you for helping Giffard escape last year. Do not look surprised, man! You know perfectly well that I am still unhappy with you for it.'

'I accompanied him to the coast,' admitted Geoffrey. 'But I had nothing to do with his decision not to be consecrated. That was a matter between him and his conscience.'

'He should have mentioned his qualms *before* the ceremony started,' said Henry angrily. 'It was not polite to leave in the middle of it. Nor to enjoy the adulation of commoners afterwards – they cheered him for defying *me*. He is my enemy now, and his friends are my enemies.'

'In that case, perhaps you should entrust your mission to someone else,' said Geoffrey.

'How dare you!' snarled Henry, coming quickly to his feet. There was a dangerous light in his eyes, and Maurice signalled frantically behind his back for Geoffrey to recant. 'You are lucky Eudo is dead, or I would install you in my dungeons and send him instead.'

'Sear is—' began Geoffrey, ignoring Maurice's increasingly agitated gestures.

'How can I ask Sear to deliver a message to himself when he arrives in Kermerdyn?' raged Henry. 'He would do it, of course, honourable man that he is. But it is not for you to argue with me. Do it again and you will be sorrier than your darkest fears can imagine.'

'My apologies, sire,' said Geoffrey. His darkest fear was that Hilde and Joan would pay the price for his incautious tongue, and he was sure Henry knew it. 'I spoke out of turn.'

'Yes, you did,' snapped Henry. His voice became a sneer. 'You think someone tampered with Prince Tancred's letters and that he still feels affection for you, but you are wrong. He will not miss such an insolent rogue, and was certainly sincere in his offer to put a noose around your neck. Now get out of my sight before I do it for him.'

Before Geoffrey could make a rejoinder, Maurice bundled him out of the room.

'Are you insane?' the Bishop hissed as soon as they were out of Henry's hearing. 'Do you *want* him to execute you? Then what would I tell Giffard?'

Geoffrey sighed and rubbed his head, anger subsiding as quickly as it had risen. 'So the letters are a ruse, an excuse to take me to Kermerdyn and discover what turned an ordinary man into one who enjoyed wealth and success? And this same man died – possibly murdered with rancid butter – some seven years ago, and I am to discover how?'

'So it would seem,' said Maurice. His face was uncharacteristically bleak. 'However, do not dismiss those letters as inconsequential, because I have a *very* bad feeling about them. Be on your guard at all times, and tell no one – *no one* – what you have been charged to do. Go with God, Geoffrey – I suspect you will need Him.'

Four

The journey from La Batailge to Geoffrey's manor was one of the least pleasant he could remember. The weather turned sour on the first day out from the abbey and did not improve thereafter. Bitter winds and driving rain made riding miserable and turned the roads into boggy morasses, so progress was infuriatingly slow. The horses slipped and skidded constantly, and the knights, unwilling to risk injury to their expensive animals, walked more than they rode. Geoffrey had lost his cloak in the shipwreck, and the replacement that Roger had bought him did not keep him either warm or dry.

Furthermore, it was frequently impossible to find places to stay at night. Even Geoffrey, who had spent large portions of his life on campaign and was used to bedding down under hedges or in sheds, became tired of the discomfort, thinking it was one thing to sleep rough in the summer or in a desert, but another altogether in an English October.

Geoffrey and Roger also had to put up with Delwyn and Edward, who were poor travellers. Edward was an abysmal rider, incapable of making even half the distance the knights had expected. They might have abandoned him – and Delwyn, too – had Pepin not appeared as they were leaving and read a declaration from the King that commanded them to remain together until Kermerdyn. The order was unequivocal and made Sear responsible for ensuring it was so. Sear took his duties seriously, and although Geoffrey could have given him the slip, it did not seem a prudent move. The rest of the company left a lot to be desired, as well. It had not taken long for Geoffrey to come to dislike the arrogant, smug and condescending Sear, and Alberic was almost as bad.

Geoffrey also missed his dog. There had never been much true affection on either side, but he found himself constantly aware that it was not there. For the first few days, he thought it would reappear, as it had done in the past, but as days passed into weeks, he knew it was gone for good. Roger and Bale assured him that he was well rid of it, but he was astonished to learn he missed it as much as his previous horse.

Despite his lack of equestrian ability, Edward proved to be intelligent and amiable, and won almost everyone around with his unfailing cheerfulness. He encouraged Geoffrey to debate the philosophical texts they both had read in the past, although Sear and Alberic scoffed their disdain at such unmanly activities. However, they were all mystified by Edward's penchant for womanly gowns of an evening, and Geoffrey steadfastly refused to borrow one, preferring his own sodden clothes to Edward's flowing kirtles.

'They are warm, dry and comfortable,' Edward declared one evening, pulling a pair of pale purple gloves over his hands before stretching them towards the fire. 'I shall wake tomorrow refreshed and happy. You, on the other hand, will wake shivering and stiff – if you sleep at all.'

'It is not a good idea to remove your armour in a strange place,' Geoffrey cautioned.

'It is not a good idea to be uncomfortable all the time,' Edward shot back. 'Thank God *I* was not rash enough to have rallied to the Pope's call for a Crusade. I would have been miserable the entire time if it involved sitting around in damp clothes for weeks on end!'

'It involved a lot more than that,' Bale murmured, eyes gleaming. 'It involved killing, too.'

'Lord!' Edward shuddered. 'Worse and worse!'

Meanwhile, Delwyn endeared himself to no one with his constant litany of complaints. Geoffrey was not the only one who itched to knock him off his horse. And there were Geoffrey's saddlebags: someone rifled through them regularly. Geoffrey did not think the culprit was a fellow knight – although Roger did so on occasion – and Delwyn was the only likely culprit. The monk denied it vigorously, but Geoffrey suspected that Delwyn was looking for the letter intended for Abbot Mabon, which Pepin had inadvertently mentioned.

'I am Mabon's envoy!' Delwyn whined on a daily basis. 'What

will he think when I return empty-handed, but you carry a missive from the Archbishop?'

'I am sorry,' said Geoffrey shortly. 'But I am under orders to deliver it myself.'

'Then show me the letters you carry from Bishop Maurice instead,' wheedled Delwyn. 'I will study his handwriting and pen one from *him* to Mabon. Mabon will never know it is a forgery and will reward me for securing him such a powerful friend.'

'And what happens when Mabon replies?' asked Geoffrey. 'When Maurice receives the letter, he will write back in such a way that Mabon will know exactly what has happened.'

'He will not,' declared Delwyn, 'because I shall deliver it myself, amended accordingly. Do not look shocked. It is a clerk's prerogative to tamper with other men's correspondence.'

'Yes,' said Geoffrey, bitterly thinking of Tancred, 'so I have learned.'

Even Roger proved to be a mixed blessing. Geoffrey *was* glad of his companionship, but Roger needled Sear constantly. Geoffrey was obliged to prevent several fights with his sword, and Edward averted even more with his capacity for gentle diplomacy.

It felt like an age before the first familiar landmarks of home appeared on the horizon, and when they did, Geoffrey was so relieved that he no longer cared what Hilde and Joan would say when he rode into Goodrich's bailey with a party of men who were unlikely to be gracious guests.

Geoffrey itched to give his horse free rein as they rode along the wooded path on the final few miles. It was raining again, his armour chafed, and he longed to don dry clothes and sit by a fire. But the track was potholed and rutted, and some of the puddles were knee-deep. It would be a pity to ruin his horse, just because he was eager to be home. He pulled the destrier to a halt at the crest of a hill and waited for the others.

'What place is this?' asked Sear, looking disparagingly at the village on the slope below them.

'Rwirdin,' replied Geoffrey, supposing it did look dismal in the drizzle. Rain had turned its thatches brown, and the road was awash with mud. Moreover, there was not an open door or window in the entire settlement, although smoke said people were home. 'It belongs to Goodrich.'

'Then why have you not trained them to greet you with a welcoming cup?' demanded Sear. 'I would not tolerate such a display of insolence in Pembroc.'

'Because I have encouraged them to be wary of unidentified horsemen,' said Geoffrey tartly. 'Peace is fragile in this region, and incursions can be bloody.'

'Then crush such insurrection,' suggested Sear. 'Or step aside, so a stronger man can do it for you.'

'William fitz Baldwin would have stamped out rebellion,' added Alberic. 'He may have been a saint, but he was no weakling. I still miss him, even though he has been dead for seven years.'

'His spirit is still strong,' agreed Sear. 'And his secret lives on.'

'What secret?' asked Geoffrey innocently.

'The one that made him a great man and a powerful leader,' replied Sear. 'I am inclined to think it was a magical sword, like the one King Arthur owned. I think William found one just like it.'

'Do you have any idea where it might be?' asked Geoffrey with a sinking heart, thinking the King would certainly want to get his hands on such an object. Geoffrey would be expected to steal it, and he had never been comfortable with theft, not even on the Crusade, when looting was a way of life.

'He never told us,' replied Sear shortly, and Geoffrey saw that William's failure to confide had hurt his feelings. 'After he died, I looked in all the obvious places, but with no success. Perhaps it disappeared when William died, as these mystical objects are apt to do.'

Geoffrey wondered what Henry would say to that explanation. Feeling gloomy, he led the way through Rwirdin, towards where the River Wye was barely visible through the rain.

It was not long before Edward caught him up, flopping about in his saddle like a sack of grain, his friendly round face red from exertion.

'How much farther?' he asked, a hint of desperation in his voice. 'We have spent the last three nights in the open, and I hope there will not be a fourth.'

'So do I,' said Geoffrey fervently.

'Well,' said Edward with a sigh, 'at least our journey has been blessed with a lack of trouble from outlaws. It is Henry's doing, you know. The highways are much safer now. He is not called the Lion of Justice for nothing.'

'Is he called the Lion of Justice?' Geoffrey had never heard the title before, and it was certainly not one *he* would have chosen.

'You might want to lower your voice,' said Edward dryly. 'Sear will take umbrage if he hears the doubt in your voice. His loyalty to the King is absolute – I am faithful myself, but *I* do not feel the need to prove it every few moments.'

'No,' said Geoffrey, who never felt the need at all.

'And Delwyn does himself no favours with his incendiary remarks,' added Edward. 'He knows exactly how to aggravate Sear, Alberic *and* Roger. One of them will skewer him before long, and you and I may not be on hand to intervene.'

'Perhaps we should not try.' Geoffrey could hear Delwyn informing Roger that his facial hair was too long. Delwyn was playing with fire: Roger was proud of his beard.

'It is tempting,' said Edward wryly. 'He is as irritating as a marsh-fly, but that does not give knights the right to run him through.'

Personally, Geoffrey felt he and his fellow knights had shown admirable restraint, proven by the fact that Delwyn was not only still alive but as recklessly garrulous as ever.

Edward was silent for a moment, then began to chatter again. 'Talk of Delwyn reminds me of that last day at La Batailge. I heard the commotion when he came howling from the fishponds to tell us about Eudo. Who killed him, do you think?'

'I have no idea,' replied Geoffrey, startled by the question. 'And with hundreds of courtiers, clerks, servants, monks and lay-brothers, Bishop Maurice will not find it an easy case to solve.'

'Where were you when it happened?' asked Edward.

Geoffrey regarded him in surprise, and the thought flashed through his mind that Henry might have asked Edward to assess whether the culprit was in the Kermerdyn party, given that Maurice would be unable to do so. Henry would not have approached Sear or Alberic, because they were insufficiently clever, and Geoffrey doubted the King would put much faith in Delwyn.

'I was with Pepin and then Maurice,' he replied. 'And Roger was with Bale in a tavern all morning. Where were you?'

Edward smiled that the interrogation should be turned around.

'I was in the stables from dawn to noon, because my horse had a bout of colic. I may not be much of a soldier, but I love my faithful warhorse, and he likes me with him when he is unwell.'

Geoffrey liked horses, too, although he would not have described Edward's nag as a 'warhorse' and suspected the beast was more pet than fighting animal.

'Can anyone confirm it?' he asked. 'Not that there is any reason to doubt you, of course.'

Edward laughed openly. 'About twenty of the King's stable-boys, who were listening to me pontificate on matters equestrian. Feel free to verify my tale the next time you visit him.'

When they reached the ford, they found it swollen with rain. Geoffrey led the way across with no problem, but Edward's horse, alarmed by the surging water, bucked suddenly, causing its rider to slide off. It was not difficult to fish him out, but there was a delay on the other side when he insisted on divesting himself of his sopping clothes and donning a gown instead.

'You will ride into Goodrich dressed as a woman?' demanded Sear incredulously.

Edward tossed his wet cloak to Bale for wringing. 'Better than arriving dripping wet. I may stain the rugs, and that would be discourteous.'

'You are expecting rugs?' asked Geoffrey uneasily.

'This will not take a moment,' said Edward, shrugging out of his mail tunic, then selecting a long red kirtle with a fur trim. He began to primp fussily, which had Sear, Alberic and Roger fidgeting impatiently, all eager to be underway.

'I heard you asking Geoffrey about Eudo's murder earlier, Sir Edward,' said Delwyn. 'Are you trying to learn who murdered him?'

'I doubt anyone *here* is a killer,' said Edward. Geoffrey almost laughed. All knights were killers: it was what they were trained to do. 'But since you mention it, why not tell each other our whereabouts? Sear, perhaps you would oblige first?'

'What I was doing is none of your damned business,' retorted Sear haughtily. 'I decline to answer, and you can try to make me at your peril.'

'I do not mind answering on his behalf,' said Alberic. 'He was with me.'

'Actually, he was not,' countered Delwyn. '*You* were with a milkmaid all morning.'

Alberic gaped at him. 'How do you know? Were you spying on me, you little snake?'

'No,' replied Delwyn, although his face said he was lying. 'I was merely concerned for her well-being. Afterwards, I went for a walk by the fishponds to—'

Sear released one of his jeering, braying laughs. 'You cannot win a woman yourself, so you were reduced to watching others! What a miserable specimen you are!'

'I could win them if I wanted,' declared Delwyn angrily. 'Women like me greatly.'

'You are supposed to be celibate,' said Alberic in distaste.

'I do what I like,' flashed Delwyn. 'Especially when I am away from my abbey.'

'I think that should suffice,' said Edward loudly, straightening his finery and indicating he was ready to be helped back on to his horse. 'It will not be long now before we are all basking in front of a roaring fire with goblets of hot wine.'

The prospect of such luxury had Roger turning in the direction of Goodrich, and Sear and Alberic were quick to follow. Edward was next, leaving Geoffrey with Delwyn at the rear.

'*Sear* killed Eudo,' muttered Delwyn resentfully. 'He declines to tell us his whereabouts at the time of the murder, and he is jealous because the King chose you to take the Archbishop's message to Kermerdyn.'

'You are the only one who seems to be jealous of that,' Geoffrey pointed out. 'And why should it lead Sear to dispatch Eudo?'

'Probably because Eudo recommended you for the task in the first place,' replied Delwyn.

Geoffrey stared at him. 'I doubt that! I did not know him before Henry allocated me the task.'

'Well, you can think what you like, but it is true,' said Delwyn. 'Because I heard him tell Pepin so with my own ears.'

Geoffrey was thoughtful. *Was* it significant that Sear was unwilling to divulge his alibi? *Did* it mean he had killed Eudo? Or was the culprit Delwyn, eager to see someone else blamed, and who claimed he had stumbled across Eudo's body while out for a walk? Delwyn was puny, but it took no great strength to shove a blade in a man's back and hold his head underwater. These were sobering thoughts, and he decided he would not stay long in Goodrich – he did not want killers mingling with Hilde and Joan, no matter how warrior-like Roger claimed them to be.

When Goodrich Castle finally appeared through the trees, Geoffrey found his pleasure at seeing it went far deeper than the desire for dry clothes and a warm fire. There was something welcomingly familiar about its wooden walls, great ramparts and sturdy towers. He reined in to look at it, aware of an immediate rush of memories.

He had not been happy there as a child. His father had mocked his scholarly tendencies and his older siblings had bullied him until he had grown enough to hold his own. He had not enjoyed returning two decades later, either, when his father lay dying. But it was home, and it contained Joan and now Hilde. Goodrich had come to represent something far more pleasant than it had ever done in the past.

'Is that it?' asked Sear disparagingly. 'I was expecting something better. Pembroc is by far superior – and much better sited, too.'

'Geoffrey's home is extremely well sited,' argued Edward, fluffing up his hair. 'It is placed to guard the river, and three of its sides are protected by natural slopes. When its palisades are turned into stone walls, it will be virtually impregnable. Like Kadweli.'

'Kadweli is like Goodrich?' asked Geoffrey, pointedly acknowledging Edward's remark and ignoring Sear's.

'In many ways,' nodded Edward. 'My castle is also sited on a rocky bluff, although it is substantially larger, with facilities for a sizeable garrison.'

'The one you will collect in Brechene,' said Sear heavily. 'The one you tell us is the best fighting force in Wales.'

'The very same,' said Edward happily, declining to take offence at Sear's tone. He smiled at Geoffrey. 'But your castle has a cosy feel, which Kadweli lacks. I like it already.'

'Well, I do not,' said Sear sullenly. 'I would sooner have defensible than "cosy".'

'You can stay in the village, then,' said Roger. 'There is a rather shabby tavern that might lower itself to admit you.'

'You had better ride ahead, Geoffrey,' said Edward before Sear could respond. 'It is only polite to give your sister a little time to prepare for us, and I am incapable of riding fast after my dip in the river, anyway.'

'You had better tell her to get the rugs out, too,' muttered Sear.

'Go,' said Roger. 'I know the way from here, and I shall point out the sights as we ride. A man will want to know the whereabouts of willing lasses after such a long ride, and I doubt Joan has any at the castle.'

'*I* do not need to be shown such things,' announced Delwyn loftily. '*I* am a monk.'

'You can find your own loose women, can you?' asked Roger. He sniffed disdainfully. 'Then I hope you choose better than that poxy lass you cornered last week.'

'I did not "corner" her,' said Delwyn stiffly. 'We were discussing spiritual matters.'

'You can call it what you like,' said Roger with a wink. 'But bear in mind that Geoffrey's sister will not want you messing with anyone who is not willing. She runs a tight ship.'

Grateful to be away from his quarrelsome companions, Geoffrey spurred his way ahead, inhaling deeply as he went and relishing the clean scent of the forest and the river. He found himself wondering at the direction his life had taken since he had returned to the land of his birth. He had lost the master he truly respected, and was reduced to delivering letters and exploring nonsensical secrets for one he despised.

But he pushed such gloomy thoughts from his mind as he cantered through the village. People stopped to watch him pass, and one or two raised their hands in salute when they recognized him. Father Adrian stood from where he had been weeding his graveyard, but only crossed himself. He did not approve of warriors and firmly believed that Geoffrey was a ruthless slaughterer of unarmed women and children. Nothing Geoffrey said or did could convince him otherwise.

Geoffrey stopped to exchange greetings with Will Helbye, who had accompanied him to Normandy twenty years before and fought at his side. Helbye was too old for such antics now and had returned to Goodrich to retire with his wife and their collection of prize pigs. Delighted to meet his captain again, Helbye invited Geoffrey to share a jug of ale.

'I cannot, Will,' said Geoffrey. 'I need to warn Joan that she is about to be invaded.'

'My wife will do that,' said Helbye, grabbing the reins of Geoffrey's horse and indicating he should dismount. 'She will not mind.'

'Of course I will not,' said the large, comfortable woman who emerged from the house, wiping her hands on her apron. 'Go inside and sit down, Sir Geoffrey. I will speak to Lady Joan.'

'Invaded by whom?' asked Helbye, when she had gone, and Geoffrey had given a brief explanation as to why he was not halfway to the Holy Land.

'Two knights named Sear and Alberic, who have argued with Roger every step of the way, and another knight named Edward, who has managed to keep them from skewering each other. There is also a monk named Delwyn.'

'That is not too bad,' said Helbye, indicating he was to sit at the table. 'Joan can cope with those. She already has visitors, see. There was some sort of fealty-swearing ceremony in Gloucester, and these people have stopped off on the way home. They are bound for Kermerdyn.'

'Kermerdyn?' asked Geoffrey, startled. 'But that is where Henry has ordered me to go. What a curious coincidence!'

'Not so curious,' said Helbye soberly. 'Those at court will know about this ceremony, *and* they will know that its participants would return this way.'

'I doubt "those at court" anticipated that these fealty-swearers would stop at Goodrich.'

'Yes, they would,' countered Helbye. 'Because one of them – Cornald the butter-maker – is friends with Joan and Olivier. He *always* stops in Goodrich when he travels out of Wales, and I know for a fact that he has mentioned it to acquaintances in the King's retinue. Obviously, someone remembered and stored the information for future use.'

Geoffrey racked his brains for anyone who might have done such a thing. 'Bishop Maurice? He knows Cornald, because he has given me a letter for him.'

Helbye smiled. 'No, not Maurice. He is not treacherous, and he would never embroil you in anything devious. I imagine it was one of Henry's clerks. They can read, and – present company excepted – that means they cannot help being sly.'

Geoffrey stifled a sigh at such prejudice and changed the subject. 'Do I know anyone in this group from Gloucester? Or are they all strangers? I have never heard Joan or Olivier mention Cornald the butter-maker.'

'You have not spent two full months here since you were eleven, so that is not surprising. Cornald has been a friend of your family for years. He is a lovely man, very generous. Everyone likes him. But his wife . . .' Helbye shook his head, lips pursed.

'What about his wife?' asked Geoffrey.

'She is a walking brothel,' replied Helbye bluntly. 'My wife says she has never met a more wanton specimen.'

Geoffrey wondered whether she would extend her services to the new arrivals, thus sparing the hapless locals. 'Are Cornald and his wife the only visitors?'

Helbye rested his elbows on the table. 'No, and the others are an unsavoury crowd, so you should be on your guard. First, there is Richard fitz Baldwin, a vile creature with a vicious temper. He has already struck Father Adrian. Of course, I would not mind doing that myself at times, but it has done nothing to dispel Adrian's belief that all knights are louts.'

'Richard,' mused Geoffrey, thinking about the letter he carried inside his surcoat. It would be one less missive to deliver in Kermerdyn. Then he frowned. Adrian *was* sanctimonious, but he was a priest, so it went with the territory. 'I cannot imagine Joan allowed that to pass unremarked.'

'I thought she was going to hit him back,' said Helbye with a grin. 'But Olivier stopped her, so she settled for giving Richard a piece of her mind instead, which was probably worse. I felt sorry for his wife, Leah, who is a poor, sweet creature. She suffers from headaches, but it is probably Richard that gives them to her.'

Geoffrey winced. 'Please tell me they are the only ones.'

'I am afraid not. They are accompanied by a man named Gwgan, who is a high-ranking Welsh counsellor. He seems decent enough, although he can read, so you would be wise to be wary of him. He is your brother-in-law, married to Lady Hilde's sister.'

Geoffrey stared at him. Helbye was right: it could *not* be coincidence that two recipients for the King's letters should happen to be in Goodrich. Someone *had* arranged for them to be there when he arrived. Was that why Eudo had been so annoyingly tardy about producing the letters? To ensure he did not travel too quickly and so miss them?

'Finally, there is Kermerdyn's abbot – a man called Mabon. He is a curious devil; I have never met a monastic like him.'

Geoffrey put his head in his hands. Henry had given him missives for Sear, Richard, Gwgan, Mabon and Bishop Wilfred, and four of them were at Goodrich. What was Henry up to? Or was it Eudo's doing? As Maurice had said that Eudo was apt to scheme on the King's behalf, Geoffrey was inclined to believe the latter. So would the plot die now the clerk was not alive to see it through? Or would it stagger ahead, leading to danger for those unwittingly caught up in it?

No answers came, although Geoffrey made three decisions. First, he would give Richard, Gwgan and Mabon their letters that day, although he would still have to travel to Kermerdyn to deliver the ones to Sear and Bishop Wilfred. Second, he was not going to put his family in danger by staying at Goodrich; he would feed his guests, collect dry clothes, and be gone within the hour. And third, Hilde would not be going to Kermerdyn to wheedle secrets about William's secret from her sister. He did not want her embroiled in whatever sinister plan was unfolding.

'Why do you say Mabon is a curious devil?' he asked, raising his head to see that Helbye was regarding him worriedly. It would have been good to confide his fears and suspicions, but Helbye, with his deep distrust of the written word, was not the right candidate.

'You will understand when you meet him, and I do not have your way with words. But this subject has upset you, so let us talk of other matters. Would you like to see my new pig?'

It was tempting, but Geoffrey had already spent longer than he had intended with Helbye, and knew he should at least try to arrive at the castle before the others. He took his leave, promising to return later, when his guests were settled.

'Watch yourself, lad,' said Helbye, reaching up to grab his arm before he could ride away. 'None of us at the village likes Lady Joan's guests, and you will not, either.'

It had stopped raining by the time he left Helbye, and the clouds had rolled away to reveal a blue sky. The sun was shining for virtually the first time since La Batailge, and Geoffrey and his horse steamed in the sudden warmth. The rest of the day was going to be fine.

The bailey was busy as he trotted into it, full of horses and people. Some were servants, scurrying here and there with cloaks, boots and cups of hot wine. Others were richly dressed, and, since he did not know them, they were clearly the guests. In the middle of the hubbub was a small, neat man with a moustache but no beard – an odd fashion in England, when most men did it the other way around. He was giving orders to the servants, and a bird sat on his wrist, its head covered by a tiny leather helmet. Sir Olivier d'Alençon, Geoffrey's brother-in-law, was about to take his visitors hawking.

The clamour lessened when Geoffrey appeared, and people stopped talking to each other to see who was coming. Then a woman broke free of the cluster and ran towards him, her face an unrestrained beam of delight.

'So Mistress Helbye had *not* taken leave of her senses when she said she had seen you!' said Hilde. 'But you said you would be gone for months, if not years. What happened?'

'King Henry happened,' replied Geoffrey gloomily, dismounting and going to bow over her hand. They had not been married long enough to dispense with the formalities, and he did not want to embarrass her with a more affectionate greeting when there was an audience.

Hilde was a large, square-faced woman with a determined glint in her eye. She was older than Geoffrey by at least three years – she was coyly vague about specifics – and had been foisted on him because Goodrich had needed a politically expedient marriage. Fortunately, Geoffrey valued intelligence more highly than looks, and he had not been disappointed. Moreover, he had found himself blessed with a friend, as well as a wife.

'Is there more trouble brewing on the borders?' she asked in alarm. 'The last time he sent you here, we had a virtual war.'

'He has ordered me to Kermerdyn,' said Geoffrey. 'I leave in an hour.'

'An hour?' Hilde cried in dismay. 'Surely, you can rest here longer than that?'

'Best not.'

'Kermerdyn is where Isabella lives,' said Hilde. 'Gwgan – her husband, who is visiting us here at the moment – has offered to take me with him. But I would much rather travel with you.'

'No,' said Geoffrey, more sharply than he had intended. He hastened to explain. 'Henry told me to take you there, too, but there is something underhand about the whole affair, and I will not see you in danger.'

'If Henry issued you with a direct order, you must obey it,' said Hilde. 'You know what he is like when crossed, and I do not want to be the reason for you being in trouble.'

'He will never know.'

Hilde shook his arm gently. 'Of course he will know! Nothing happens in his kingdom without his knowledge. I would be sorry to lose Goodrich, and so would Joan, so we had better do as he says. Besides, I am no swooning maiden who must be coddled. I thought you understood that.'

'I do,' said Geoffrey. 'But—'

'No buts,' said Hilde, smiling. 'I was intending to make the journey anyway, because it has been too long since I saw Isabella. If I do not go with you, I will go with Gwgan.'

Before the discussion could become an argument, a second woman approached. It was Joan – tall, sturdily built and with a fierce face that told everyone who met her that she was not a woman to stand for nonsense. Middle years had made her thick around the middle, and her brown hair was now flecked with grey.

'I thought I recognized you,' she said gruffly, never one for unseemly displays of affection. 'What are you doing back so soon? And where is your horse?'

'Drowned,' said Geoffrey unhappily. 'And I have been ordered to travel west by the King.'

Joan's face hardened. 'Has that villain used Goodrich to force you into his service *again*? I am beginning to suspect that he plans to keep you at his beck and call for ever.'

'No,' said Geoffrey firmly. 'Because I will go to the Holy Land as soon as Bishop Maurice releases me from a vow I made never to return there. You see, I believe Tancred did not write the letters—'

'Stop!' ordered Joan. 'This is a complex tale and deserves to be heard properly. We shall have it as soon as we dispatch our guests for an afternoon of hawking with Olivier.'

And Geoffrey had three letters to deliver. He had not forgotten that Richard's and Gwgan's were secret, and would have to be handed over when the recipients were alone. And although no such stipulation had been attached to Mabon's, Geoffrey intended to be cautious anyway. The whole affair was too murky for him to risk doing otherwise.

It was not many moments before Geoffrey's travelling companions arrived, and he was made proud by the gracious welcome afforded by Joan and Hilde. Cups of welcoming wine were presented, and servants were waiting to take horses and see to baggage.

Even Sear could find no fault with their hospitality, although his eyebrows went up when he was introduced to Olivier. It was not difficult to read Sear's thoughts: Joan was twice the size of her diminutive husband, and they looked odd together. Although a knight, Olivier lied about his military achievements and was a liability in any kind of skirmish. But Joan loved him and he loved her, and Geoffrey had grown to respect the man's gentler qualities.

The newcomers knew the other guests, and Edward was unrestrained in his pleasure at seeing them. Geoffrey was slightly taken aback when Edward darted towards a tall, burly knight in black and treated him to a smacking kiss on the cheek. Both men immediately roared with laughter, although Sear grimaced his distaste and Alberic rolled his eyes.

'As the weather is fine, we have decided to go hawking,' said Olivier, beaming at the new arrivals. 'Perhaps you would care to join us? I can promise you a treat. Geoffrey, you will come?'

Geoffrey shook his head, not liking to imagine what Joan would say if he disappeared before explaining his sudden arrival. Besides, he had never really taken to the sport, although he knew that Olivier's birds were exceptional.

'He is probably too tired,' taunted Sear. 'After all, we must have ridden three hours today.'

'My husband has business to attend,' said Hilde coldly. 'And he always discharges his duties before taking his pleasure. Do you do things differently in Pembroc, sir?'

Sear opened his mouth, but seemed unable to think of a rejoinder, so he closed it again and stamped away, bawling to the servants to find him a fresh horse. Geoffrey grinned, gratified to see the man put so neatly in his place. He went to see his destrier settled in the stable, and it was not long before he was joined by Joan and Olivier.

'It is good to have you back, Geoff,' said Olivier, slapping a comradely arm around his shoulders. 'We feared we might never see you again, and Joan has not been herself since you left.'

'It was a summer cold,' said Joan stiffly. 'It had nothing to do with him.'

'You missed him,' countered Olivier. 'We all did. But tell us what has happened since you left. Or would you rather change first? You are soaking wet.'

'And dirty,' said Joan, looking him up and down disapprovingly. 'You always were a ruffian.'

Geoffrey was more inclined to ask questions than to answer them, at least until Joan thawed a little. And he needed time to think about what he was going to say, because he was certainly not going to give them details of Henry's orders, suspecting they would be safer kept in ignorance.

'Which one is Gwgan?' he asked, going to the door and looking across the milling bailey.

'The one with the black hair,' replied Olivier, pointing to a stocky man in fine but functional clothes. He lowered his voice. 'I know he is married to Hilde's favourite sister, but I cannot say I like the man. I always have the sense that he is laughing at me.'

'He would not dare laugh at you,' said Joan fiercely. 'Not in my hearing. But I suspect he does that to everyone, and he is not as bad as some of the others who are availing themselves of our hospitality. Richard fitz Baldwin, for example.'

'He is the one with a glower like thunder and the scar down his face,' supplied Olivier. 'I do not think he has smiled once since he arrived, although he has been polite enough. I would have ousted the miserable devil, but his wife seems frail, and Joan thought she needed the rest.'

Geoffrey saw a small, pale woman standing at Richard's side, dowdy in her unfashionable clothes and nondescript wimple.

'Her name is Leah, and she is kin to Robert de Bellême,' explained Joan. 'It was a good match originally, but now that Bellême is exiled, the association can do Richard no good. He is a surly brute, and if I were in Leah's shoes, I would knock some manners into him. Olivier is never sullen.'

Geoffrey was sure Olivier was not, because the small knight had a sense of self-preservation equal to none.

'Helbye told me Richard struck Father Adrian,' he said. 'And that you were going to hit him in return.'

'She was not!' declared Olivier. 'That would have been unlady-like, and we have standards. But not all members of the party have been objectionable. Cornald has been a delight.'

'He has, but I wish he had not brought his wife with him,' said Joan grimly. 'She is the one with the blonde hair and the come-hither smile. You will have to watch her, or she will be in your bed. And Hilde will not appreciate that, because she will have her own plans in that direction.'

'I will bear it in mind,' said Geoffrey, his eyes naturally drawn to the slender figure, flawless complexion and pale gold hair.

'Her name is Pulchria,' Joan went on, jabbing him in the ribs with her elbow when she saw him staring. 'Look at how she simpers at your friend Sear, fluttering her eyes at him while poor Cornald is forced to make polite conversation with that grubby little monk.'

'Sear is *not* my friend,' said Geoffrey firmly. 'And I will not inflict him on you for any longer than is necessary. I would have ridden to Kermerdyn today, but Olivier invited them hawking before I could stop him. We shall leave at first light tomorrow.'

'Is your business so urgent, then?' asked Olivier.

'No, but there is no point dallying.'

Joan took his arm tentatively, as if she was afraid he might jerk it away. 'Would it be too much to ask that you spend a few days with the family you see so rarely?'

'And you have unfinished business with Hilde,' said Olivier, rather primly. 'You did not leave her pregnant, you know, so she will want another stab at it.'

'Several stabs might be better,' recommended Joan practically. 'We all want an heir, and I am inclined to lock you up here until you provide us with one.'

'You could try,' muttered Geoffrey.

Joan's eyes narrowed when a familiar voice echoed across the courtyard. She released Geoffrey's arm abruptly. 'You brought that rogue Roger with you! Well, in that case, perhaps a shorter visit would be better. He caused a lot of trouble the last time he was here.'

'He also helped us fight off an army that was aiming to destroy us,' Olivier pointed out. 'And Roger and I love exchanging war stories.'

Roger had yet to realize that Olivier's stories were fiction and that he claimed to have taken part in wars that had been fought long before he was born. Like Geoffrey, Olivier could read, and his 'battle experiences' came from books.

'Well, in that case . . .' began Joan, her resolve weakening, as it always did when Olivier expressed an opinion. Geoffrey wondered whether he and Hilde would ever come to regard each other so highly; he hoped so.

'Who is the man that Edward kissed?' he asked, changing the subject.

'You mean the large fellow in the armour and the surcoat with the black cross?' asked Joan. 'That is Abbot Mabon.'

'But he is a knight,' said Geoffrey uncertainly.

'That is what *I* said,' replied Joan. 'But he informed me that God calls all sorts to His service, and I should not put too much store by appearances.'

'Do you think Cornald's party will leave when Geoffrey does?' asked Olivier, brightening suddenly. 'The road to Kermerdyn is fraught with danger, and they will be delighted to add another five knights and Bale to their number – although I doubt Edward will be up to much.'

'They might,' agreed Joan hopefully. 'Perhaps we *will* encourage you to make your stay brief, Geoff. The opportunity to be rid of them all is very appealing.'

'We will make it up to you when you return,' promised Olivier.

'First light tomorrow, then,' said Geoffrey.

Five

While Olivier and Joan went to oversee the final preparations for the hawking, Geoffrey lingered in the stable, rubbing his horse down with a piece of sacking. It was servants' work, but there was something soothing about seeing to the animal's needs. He was also content to be away from his travelling companions – and he had scant interest in meeting the new ones. Olivier and Joan had not painted a flattering picture of them, and he anticipated that the journey to Kermerdyn would be every bit as unpleasant as the one from La Batailge.

As he worked, he kept looking to see if Richard, Gwgan or Mabon might be approached discreetly. Unfortunately, Edward had cornered Mabon and was making him laugh with some tale, and Gwgan was chatting to Hilde. Richard was alone, slouching against a wall with a face as black as thunder, but there were too many servants nearby, and Geoffrey could not hope to deliver a letter without them seeing.

In the end, feeling he was shirking his responsibilities, he went to stand in the yard. It was not long before Sear spotted him. He was already wearing dry clothes, and his hands were full of food that had been set out on nearby trestle tables.

'Your brother-in-law had better not be exaggerating the quality of his birds,' he said coldly. 'The fact that you decline to join us may be an indication that I am wasting my time.'

'Olivier's birds are magnificent,' growled Roger, who had followed him. 'And the reason Geoff cannot come with us this afternoon is because he needs to impregnate his wife. It is a tricky business, this begetting of heirs.'

'Only if you do not know what you are doing,' said Sear. 'I would offer to show him, but his wife is hardly—'

He did not finish, because Geoffrey lunged suddenly, and the man found himself pressed against the wall with a dagger at his throat.

'Kill him, Geoff,' suggested Roger. 'Or cut out his tongue.'

'I was going to say that your wife is hardly the type to dispense favours like a common whore,' gasped Sear, trying without success to shake free. 'It was intended as a compliment.'

Geoffrey released him, thinking it was not much of one. 'My apologies,' he said flatly.

'Accepted,' said Sear, rubbing his neck. 'You are fortunate in your wife. You could have had a beauty, like Cornald, but Pulchria strays from the wedding bed, and everyone knows it except him. She has offered me a tumble later, when we return.'

'Me, too,' said Roger. 'You had better take her first, then, because she will not want anyone else once I have finished with her.'

'Go, or they will leave without you,' said Geoffrey shortly, nodding to where Olivier was sitting astride a small pony. 'And please do him the courtesy of not quarrelling with each other.'

'I have better things to do than spar with the likes of Sear when there is decent hawking,' said Roger. 'I shall be the perfect gentleman.'

Sear made no such promise, though, but within moments the party was gone, clattering out of the bailey. Delivering the letters would have to wait.

'Good,' said Joan when they had gone, and she was standing in a billow of dust with Hilde and Geoffrey. 'You two can retire to the bedchamber, while I organize tonight's meal.'

'I am not a performing bear,' said Geoffrey irritably, thinking that far too many people had ideas about what he should do with his wife.

'I am glad to hear it,' said Joan briskly. 'Because that would be no use to Goodrich. We need a performing husband. Now off you go.'

Hilde blushed scarlet, and to spare her more embarrassment – he could well imagine the smirks of the servants if they marched purposefully through the hall and up the stairs together – he indicated she should go without him. Gratefully, she sped away.

He returned to the stable to give her time to compose herself, and discovered a small nail embedded in his horse's hoof. His fingers were too thick to lay hold of it, and there was no convenient implement to hand. He grew exasperated, and released several colourful oaths that he never used in company. Then he became aware of someone behind him. He whipped around fast, reaching for his sword, but let his hand drop when he saw it was only the shy, grey creature who was Richard's wife. He struggled to remember her name. Leah. She looked, he thought, nothing like her violent kinsman Bellême.

'I was looking for Edward,' said Leah, backing away in alarm. 'We heard he has been granted permission to start building Kadweli in stone, and I wanted to congratulate him. He deserves the honour, because he is a good man.'

'He is not in here. May I escort you to the hall? You seem unwell.'

Leah smiled, an expression that transformed her face into something approaching prettiness. 'Just another of my headaches, but I can reach the hall on my own, thank you.'

Geoffrey felt he owed her some explanation for his bad language. 'There is a nail in my horse's foot, but I cannot tease it out. I am sorry—'

Leah stepped forward. 'Let me try. I know horses.'

Before he could stop her, she had lifted the hoof with deft efficiency and had grasped the nail in her tiny fingers. As if it sensed it was in the presence of someone who meant it no harm, the animal was unusually docile, and it was not long before Leah had extracted the offending sliver of metal.

'Will you stay in Goodrich long?' she asked before he could thank her. 'I imagine we shall all travel west together, but as you have only just arrived, you will want to linger for a few days. But I long to be back in Kermerdyn, although Richard has not been happy there since his brother died. I am so very homesick.'

'Tomorrow,' said Geoffrey, thinking he had never seen an expression of such sadness. 'There is no need to stay here any longer than that.'

'Thank you,' whispered Leah with a wan smile. And then she was gone.

Geoffrey lingered by the stable door, enjoying the smell of clean hay and the earthy scent of horse sweat and manure, wondering how long he should wait before advancing on Hilde. He saw Edward a few moments later, leading Leah to the well, where they sat talking. He was glad she had a friend, because she had seemed lonely and vulnerable, although her skill with horses made her more to Geoffrey than the shadowy nonentity Joan had described.

He was inspecting a fierce black stallion that he was sure could not belong to Olivier when a rustle in the straw made him turn quickly, hand moving automatically to his sword.

'He is a fine beast, do you not agree?' asked Abbot Mabon, striding towards him, his black surcoat billowing. He gave the animal a pat on the nose, and it snickered its appreciation.

'He seems spirited,' said Geoffrey.

'Very,' agreed Mabon proudly. 'I would have taken him out today, but I did not want to ruin him on rough tracks. I rode one of your sister's nags instead, but he turned lame before we were through the village, so I was forced to come back. Pity. I enjoy hawking.'

Close up, Mabon looked even less like an abbot than he had at a distance. He was an enormous man, and his black attire made him seem bigger. There was something of the pirate in his gap-toothed grin, and Geoffrey could not imagine him on his knees at an altar.

'I have a letter for you from the Archbishop,' said Geoffrey, grateful for the opportunity to discharge one of his tasks. He started to rummage for the package Pepin had given him, tucked well inside his shirt. 'It comes via the King.'

'Does it?' asked Mabon without enthusiasm. 'I doubt either of *them* has anything I want to hear. I cannot read anyway, so hang on to it until we reach Kermerdyn, where a scribe can tell me what it says.'

'Delwyn will oblige,' said Geoffrey. 'He has been trying to take charge of it ever since we left.'

'He would,' said Mabon disparagingly. 'But I would rather lose my sword arm than let *him* loose on my correspondence. We shall take it to Ywain when we reach Kermerdyn – he is my deputy and the man who will succeed me. He can read.'

'So can I,' said Geoffrey, unwilling to be lumbered with the responsibility of looking after the letter for longer than was necessary. 'And I will read it to you now, if you like.'

'Really?' asked Mabon, regarding him with disappointment. 'Why would a knight waste time on that?'

'That is an unusual stance for an abbot,' said Geoffrey.

Mabon laughed uproariously. 'I am an unusual abbot. But please keep the letter. I will only lose it, and then Ywain will be vexed. Besides, it is a lovely day and I do not want it sullied by unwelcome news – and *all* news that comes via that meddling usurper Henry is bad news. I cannot abide the man.'

Geoffrey warmed to Mabon. 'I understand you have a feud with Bishop Wilfred,' he said, supposing he may as well start one of his enquiries.

'That venomous Norman snake,' spat Mabon. 'Not that I have anything against Normans, of course, but they have no right to march into our country and award themselves all the best posts. *I* should have been Bishop of St David's.'

'The King does not know what he is missing,' said Geoffrey, suspecting Henry very much did, and that was why Wilfred had been appointed.

'Indeed!' agreed Mabon. 'It is a pity William fitz Baldwin died, because I did not mind *him* in a position of power. He was a lovely man, and I liked having him in Rhydygors.'

'You do not like Hywel?'

'Oh, yes – he is lovely, too, although he is Welsh, so that is to be expected. Of course, poor William was murdered. It was put about that he died of fever, but that was a lie. I was the one who first said he was poisoned, and I stand by my claim.'

'With what evidence?' Geoffrey felt his spirits sink. He had hoped to be able to report that William's death was natural and the tales about his secret no more than rumour.

'Evidence!' sneered Mabon. 'I do not need evidence when my gut screams foul play. Besides, his fingers were black.'

'Black?' asked Geoffrey, puzzled.

'Decayed, like a corpse. It was very peculiar. And there was a nasty scene around his deathbed. Of course, it was the butter that killed him.'

'Butter?' Geoffrey was bemused by the confidences.

'It was made by Cornald, was a gift from Pulchria, delivered by Richard. Then Delwyn was seen loitering around the kitchens where the stuff lay, talking to Bishop Wilfred. And Gwgan, Isabella, Hywel and Sear were at the meal after which William became ill. They are *all* suspects for the crime.'

'I see,' said Geoffrey. 'Where were you?'

'In my abbey, seeing to a sick horse, as my monks will attest. Edward was away at the salient time, too, while poor little Leah was ill and confined to her bed. We three are innocent, but the rest are guilty until proven innocent, as far as I am concerned.'

'What nasty scene happened at William's deathbed?'

'He took several days to die, and muttered and whispered almost the entire time. Little of it made sense, but we were all keen to hear as much as possible, lest he gave up his secret.'

'What secret?' asked Geoffrey, feigning innocence.

'The secret that turned him into the fine man he was, and gave him his fabulous luck,' replied Mabon. 'Surely, you have heard this tale? It is famous all over the *world*.'

'Enlighten me.'

Mabon grimaced. 'He would never say what the secret was, and even denied that he had one on occasion, although he was a poor liar. I happened to be alone with him at one point during his fever, and he told me he found the secret in the river.'

Geoffrey frowned. 'What do you think he meant?'

Mabon shrugged. 'It made no sense, but he was religious, and I know he liked to immerse himself in the water as though he were John the Baptist. Perhaps he had a vision. He certainly had great respect for the Blessed Virgin.'

'Many people do,' said Geoffrey. 'But—'

'I do not bother with her,' interrupted Mabon. 'When I want favours, I go straight to the top – to God the Father.'

'Oh,' said Geoffrey, feeling the discussion was blasphemous.

'But never mind all this religious claptrap. Let me see your destrier. There is no man in Wales who is a better judge of horse-flesh than me.'

Mabon was indeed knowledgeable and regaled Geoffrey with all manner of opinions about horses and weapons. He left eventually, and Geoffrey was about to go to Hilde when he sensed yet another presence. It was Pulchria, and her expression was predatory.

'The lord of Goodrich,' she crooned, mincing towards him. 'I was hoping for an opportunity to make your acquaintance. Joan and Olivier have been waxing lyrical about you.'

'Have they?' asked Geoffrey warily.

'Oh, yes,' whispered Pulchria, swaying closer. 'All the time. And my husband is very eager to meet you. He would like to learn the secret of your success.'

He could smell her heady perfume, and her eyes were dark with promise. Her beauty was rather dangerous, Geoffrey thought, taking a step back, and it would see him in trouble if he yielded to it.

'Secret?' he asked, struggling to keep his mind on the conversation. 'I have no secret – and I am not successful, either.'

'Of course you are. We both want to know how you turned Goodrich – an impoverished outpost – into the envy of the region.'

'That had nothing to do with me,' said Geoffrey, as she leaned closer still, treating him to a view of her bosom. 'Joan is the one who has done the transforming. Ask her.'

'I would rather talk to you,' breathed Pulchria. Her perfume was similar to that worn by his duchess, and he felt his heart begin to pound. He forced his thoughts to more practical matters.

'Abbot Mabon has been telling me about some butter William ate before his death,' he began.

Pulchria stepped away from him. 'You mean William fitz Baldwin?' she asked incredulously. 'He died seven years ago. I thought everyone had forgotten about those silly rumours. There was no truth in them – just gossip and spite.'

'Mabon said the butter was made by your husband and was a gift from you.'

'It was,' said Pulchria sullenly. 'And perhaps it *was* a little past its best – dairy produce spoils quickly – but it was certainly not rancid. And nor was it poisoned.'

'So you think William died of natural causes?'

Pulchria pouted. 'Of course! Half the town visited him on his deathbed, because he was considered such a saintly man, and when I went he had some sort of seizure – he shuddered and thrashed about, then went limp. Clearly, an ague killed him – perhaps one caught sitting by the river in the damp.'

'Mabon said he had black fingers.'

'I did not notice. To be frank, I was watching his face, to see whether he might whisper his secret. Unfortunately, all I could hear were prayers to the Blessed Virgin. What do you think of virgins, Sir Geoffrey? I consider them overrated.'

'I do not know many,' said Geoffrey, as she moved towards him again.

'Neither do I.' She gave a slow, smouldering smile that turned her eyes silvery black. 'Can you think of anything we might do to pass the time until the hawkers return?'

Geoffrey nodded as he stepped around her. 'Yes – see my wife.'

Despite his efforts to save Hilde's blushes, Geoffrey was still acutely aware of the grins and nudges of the servants as he crossed the hall and walked up the stairs. Trying to ignore them, he looked at the changes Joan had made since he had left.

During his childhood, the great hall had been a dark, forbidding place, with little in the way of comfort. Joan had changed it almost beyond recognition, with tapestries on the walls, clean rushes on the floor, and smart, well-polished furniture. A fire always blazed in the hearth, and he was amused to see there were even one or two rugs scattered around. Edward would be pleased.

He ran up the spiral steps and opened the door to the bedchamber. He was startled to find Hilde fast asleep, and supposed she had not required as much time to prepare as he had allowed her. She was lying on her back with her mouth open, and several bottles of unguents indicated she had gone to some trouble to render herself alluring. Touched that she should bother, he sat on the edge of the bed, which woke her.

'I thought you were not coming,' she said, rubbing her eyes drowsily. Then she shot him a sharp glance. 'Was my mouth open?'

'No,' lied Geoffrey. 'I was waylaid – first by Leah, then by Mabon, and then by Pulchria.'

'Pulchria,' muttered Hilde. 'She is a tremendous beauty, with her elegant figure and golden locks. Joan and I dislike being in the same room with her. She makes us feel fat and old.'

'You are both worth ten of her,' said Geoffrey gallantly.

Hilde's eyes narrowed. 'Did she make a play for you? I imagine she did, because she has been through every other man in the household. Except Olivier, who would not have her.'

'Neither would I. She has Roger and Sear lined up for later, so I hope they do not quarrel over times.'

'She will ensure they do not, lest one decides to find someone else instead, and she misses out. But never mind her. I have been thinking about Kermerdyn. You can order me to remain here, but I swore marriage vows in a church to stand with you in times of trouble. I do not intend to break them.'

It was a difficult stance to counter, given that Geoffrey took oaths seriously himself. He sighed, wishing he was in the Holy Land, fighting at Tancred's side. It would be a lot safer and less complicated.

'You can talk to me,' Hilde went on quietly. 'You will find me a good listener, and I can see you are troubled. Tell me what is happening.'

Geoffrey had not talked seriously to anyone since Bishop Maurice. He had confided in Roger to a certain extent, but the big knight was impatient with the mission's complexities and had again encouraged Geoffrey to abandon his responsibilities for the Holy Land. Geoffrey realized it would be a relief to tell someone about the worries that plagued him.

'Henry has set me three tasks,' he began. 'But the more I learn about them, the more I see he is sending me into some very troubled waters. First, I have five letters to deliver, four of them to men who are here in Goodrich. Sear is not to have his until we reach Kermerdyn, although Henry declined to tell me why. Richard and Gwgan can have theirs today, but I just tried to pass Abbot Mabon his, and he declined to take it.'

'He is not very interested in administrative matters,' said Hilde with a shrug. 'And he does not like the King, so I am not surprised he wants his deputy to deal with whatever it contains.'

'The last letter is to Bishop Wilfred. The second task is to assess whether Mabon or Wilfred is more deserving of the King's approbation. They dislike each other apparently, but he wants to know who will emerge victorious, so he can be sure of supporting the winning side.'

Hilde laughed without humour. 'And the last task?'

'To investigate a suspicious death that occurred seven years ago.'

Hilde sat up. 'Not William fitz Baldwin's?'

'You know about it?' asked Geoffrey, surprised.

'Yes, from Isabella. Apparently, he was just some sullen Norman when he arrived in Kermerdyn, but by the time he finished building Rhydygors, he had become good, kind and saintly. His luck improved, too, and everything he did was successful.'

'Except for the fact that he died before his time.'

'People were jealous of him, even his friends – Sear, Alberic, Mabon, Cornald, his brother. It was common knowledge that he had discovered a secret, which accounted for his transformation, but he would never say what it was to anyone, until he raved about it on his deathbed.'

'Did he rave enough to let anyone guess what it might be?'

'He gave snatches to different people. He told Isabella it was something to do with water.'

'He told Mabon it occurred in the river,' mused Geoffrey. 'A vision perhaps. Mabon is a curious man, do you not think? Rather irreligious for a monastic.'

Hilde laughed again. 'He has startled us all with his pagan remarks, and Joan will be glad to be rid of him.'

'What else do you know about William? Were there rumours regarding culprits for his murder?'

'Oh, yes. Isabella said everyone who attended his deathbed should be considered a suspect, because they were all so keen to have his secret – Sear, Alberic, Cornald and Pulchria, Bishop Wilfred and Abbot Mabon, Hywel, Gwgan, Richard and Leah, Edward, Delwyn. It will not be an easy case to solve, because none of them is likely to confess.'

'Mabon says he, Edward and Leah are innocent, because they had no contact with the butter that he believes killed William.'

'Isabella also mentioned the possibility that the butter was to blame, but she said it could not be substantiated, because the stuff was thrown away before it could be inspected. However, William had been eating it over several days.'

'Have any of these suspects inherited William's success? In other words did anyone acquire his secret?'

'Not to my knowledge.'

'Lord!' muttered Geoffrey, thinking again that Henry had burdened him with an impossible task. He said as much to Hilde and then he told her about Tancred's letters and Eudo's murder, and about the shipwreck and his vow never to return to the Holy Land.

'I am sorry,' he said eventually, realizing he had been speaking for a long time. 'You do not want to know all this.'

'Of course, I do,' said Hilde softly. 'Because now I will be able to help you when we travel to Kermerdyn – and I *am* going with you, Geoffrey. We shall discuss what you learn and make sense of it together. But we have talked enough today, and there are other matters to attend.'

She moved towards him with grim purpose.

It was late afternoon by the time Olivier brought his guests home, and, judging from the laughter around the bailey, a good time had been had by all, even Sear and Alberic, who gushed about Olivier's birds. Geoffrey tried to manoeuvre Richard and Gwgan into a position where he could speak to them alone, but there were too many people, and it would have looked suspicious had he persisted. Reluctantly, he decided to wait.

The party trooped into the hall, where Joan had prepared a feast fit for kings, with plenty of roasted meat, fresh bread, boiled eggs, fish, custard and even a small dish of cabbage for the rare few who liked a little greenery on their platters.

There was a raised table near the hearth, where the most important guests were seated. As lord of the manor, Geoffrey sat in the middle, with Hilde on one side, and Joan and Olivier on the other. Cornald and Pulchria sat next to Hilde, and Gwgan by Joan. Mabon, Sear, Alberic, Edward, Roger, Richard and Leah were opposite. Delwyn was relegated to the servants' table, much to his indignation.

'Ignore him,' boomed Mabon irritably, as the monk's whine buzzed around their ears like an annoying insect. 'He has ideas above his station.'

'Did you do much looting in the Holy Land, Sir Geoffrey?' asked Cornald conversationally. He looked exactly as a butterer should – portly, with a greasy face and soft hands. He smiled a lot and had rosy cheeks and shining eyes. Geoffrey immediately liked him and was sorry he was saddled with such a wanton wife. 'We heard great riches were there for the taking.'

'*I* did plenty,' said Roger, before Geoffrey could reply. '*I* returned a wealthy man.'

'It is easy to take from the weak,' declared Sear challengingly. 'But I have always considered it more noble to tackle those better able to defend themselves.'

'It is certainly more fun to remove treasure from a man who

puts up a decent fight,' agreed Abbot Mabon amiably. 'I have never enjoyed raiding peasants.'

'I am glad to hear it, My Lord Abbot,' said Gwgan softly. His intelligent face was alight with amusement, and it was clear he was enjoying himself. 'I doubt Prince Hywel would approve of you marauding those of his subjects who are helpless.'

'Not *his* subjects,' snapped Richard. 'The King's.'

'Hear, hear,' echoed Sear, while Alberic raised his cup in salute at the sentiment. Leah put a calming hand on her husband's arm, and he shot her what Geoffrey supposed was a smile.

'*I* would not have enjoyed the Crusade,' said Edward. 'I understand there were flies. I do not like flies.'

'You mean Saracens?' asked Roger, puzzled. 'There were plenty of those.'

'I mean *flies*,' said Edward with a fastidious shudder. 'Creatures that land on rotting meat and then buzz around your head afterwards. Dreadful things!'

'I kill them by the hundred,' said Richard. 'My brother made me a gift of a special implement with which to swat them. That was before his change, of course. Afterwards, he told me they are God's creations and so worthy of mercy. I ignored him.'

'Flies are not God's creations,' proclaimed Mabon authoritatively. 'They are the Devil's. So swat away.'

'Tell us more about your loot, Sir Roger,' invited Cornald. 'Did anyone try to stop you, or were you given free rein to take what you liked?'

'People *did* try to stop me,' admitted Roger. 'But I usually killed them.'

Hilde regarded him coolly. 'You had better not try to kill Geoffrey, should he ever attempt to instil a sense of honesty into you.'

'He knows better than to try,' said Roger carelessly. He turned to Sear. 'Why did you not volunteer for the Crusade? Was it beyond your martial skills?'

'Not everyone can jaunt off for pleasure when there is work to be done,' replied Sear tartly. 'I remained to tend to my responsibilities, like any decent man.'

'Tell us about *your* adventures in battle, Abbot Mabon,' said Olivier quickly.

'Later, perhaps.' Mabon raised a small phial and shook it jovially at the little knight. 'It is time to take my tonic, you see. This miraculous substance is what makes me the man I am.'

'Really?' asked Pulchria. She shot a speculative glance at her husband. 'Where do you buy it?'

'In Kermerdyn,' replied Mabon. 'The apothecary makes it for me.'

'It contains mandrake juice,' said Gwgan. 'And other ingredients to make a man feel invincible.'

'How do you know?' asked Edward. 'I appreciate that a counsellor is obliged to amass a wealth of knowledge if he is to serve his prince, but I would not have thought an intimacy with the contents of Abbot Mabon's medicine would be necessary.'

Gwgan laughed. 'My wife told me – she is interested in herb lore.'

'My sister Isabella,' nodded Hilde. 'She has always been fascinated by the medicinal properties of plants.'

'Well, I do not care what is in it, only that it does me a power of good,' declared Mabon. 'And not just me, either. Richard swears by it, too.'

Richard produced an identical pot. 'Three sips a day. But this expedition has taken longer than I expected, and I have run out. Give me some of yours, Mabon.'

'I certainly shall not,' said Mabon fervently. 'Because then I will not have enough to see me home, and I do not want to be found lacking by the ladies.'

Richard scowled, and Geoffrey braced himself to intervene when it looked as though he might take the potion by force. Roger's hand went to his dagger, giving the impression that he thought a brawl would round the evening off very nicely.

'Music!' declared Olivier quickly. 'Where is my lute?'

Without further ado, he began to sing a popular ballad about a lovelorn maiden. He had a beautiful voice and played well. Richard's scowl faded, Gwgan's mocking smile was replaced by something softer, Edward clapped his hands in girlish delight, and Mabon closed his eyes to listen.

'Look at Richard,' murmured Hilde in Geoffrey's ear. 'He will have Mabon's potion later, no doubt about it. I only hope they do not kill each other over it.'

So did Geoffrey — at least, not before he had given them the King's letters.

Warm and dry for the first time in weeks, Geoffrey allowed himself to relax. It was a mistake, because Hilde plied him with wine on one side and Joan from the other. By the time people began to withdraw to their sleeping quarters, he was decidedly unsteady on his feet. It also encouraged him to be reckless, and he decided he *would* deliver the letters to Richard and Gwgan that night.

He cornered Richard first, withdrawing the missive from inside his shirt, and checking that Richard's name and Pepin's diamond were on it before following him outside. It was a clear night, with masses of stars pricking the black sky. Had he been sober, he would have waited longer before grabbing Richard's shoulder and shoving the letter in his hand. Fortunately, Richard was drunk, too, and did not understand that it was Geoffrey's fault that he reeled and almost fell.

'That is from King Henry,' said Geoffrey in response to the questioning glance.

Richard regarded it warily. 'Does it contain orders? Or is it just from Eudo, telling me how much meat to feed my garrison? He is constantly pressing me with stupid instructions.'

'I am afraid neither of them confided its contents to me.'

Richard started to break the seal, but then stopped. 'I shall ask Gwgan to read it tomorrow. I doubt it is urgent.'

'I was sorry to learn about your brother,' said Geoffrey, taking the opportunity to question him. Then he winced. William had been dead seven years, so condolences were late, to say the least, and he realized he should leave his investigations until his wits were not floating in wine. Fortunately, Richard was drunker than he was, and it did not occur to him that sympathy for the death of a man so long in his grave was peculiar.

'Everyone liked William.' Richard's expression grew pained. 'I would have liked his secret, because I would not mind being popular myself.'

'You think his secret made him popular?'

Richard nodded so earnestly that he almost toppled over. 'He was like me before he found it — he had a temper and was disinclined to laugh at frivolous things. Then along came his secret, and he changed. He became kindly and tolerant, just and wise. And people loved him for it. I still grieve for him.'

'What was his secret?' asked Geoffrey tipsily.

'I wish I knew, but it was something to do with the Blessed Virgin. Mabon thinks it was connected to William's swims in the river, but he is wrong. It does not matter any more, though, because the secret is gone. He did not tell any of us enough on his deathbed to allow us to find it.'

'Are you sure?'

Richard nodded again. 'Yes. My brother was a saint, and no one else fits that description in Kermerdyn. If anyone did find his secret, then it did not have the same effect.'

'Was he murdered?' asked Geoffrey. The question was out before he realized he should have phrased it more tactfully.

Richard's scowl was back. 'No one would have killed William, although there were tales to the contrary. It was probably because his fingers turned black, but the physician said that can happen with many ailments. He was not murdered, and anyone who says otherwise is a liar.'

'I was only asking,' said Geoffrey, backing away with his hands in the air when Richard's dagger started to come out of its sheath. 'I meant no disrespect.'

'Good,' snarled Richard. 'Because I will kill anyone who speaks dishonourably about William. He was the best man who ever lived.'

'I see,' said Geoffrey, startled to see tears begin to flow.

He watched Richard stagger away and was inclined to believe his grief was genuine. It was difficult to feign emotions after swallowing so much wine, and there was no doubt that Richard had loved his brother dearly. Did that mean he would not have killed him? Geoffrey found he was not yet ready to say.

Six

When Richard had gone, Geoffrey looked for Gwgan, but the counsellor was in neither the hall nor the bailey. Then he remembered that he had letters from Maurice to deliver, as well as the ones from the King, and one of them was to Cornald. The others – to Bishop Wilfred, Isabella and Robert the steward – would have to wait until he reached Kermerdyn, but he could be rid of the one.

'Cornald went to the kitchen,' supplied Sear, when Geoffrey asked whether anyone had seen him. 'The ample feast your sister provided was not enough for him, so he has gone to see what more he can scavenge.'

Sear was dicing with Alberic and Roger by the fire. Edward was nearby, strumming Olivier's lute, and Geoffrey hoped he would suppress the inevitable quarrel that would arise when Roger's loaded dice came into play. Mabon lounged in Joan's favourite chair, while Delwyn sat at his feet, dozing restlessly.

'What about Gwgan?' Geoffrey asked. 'Where is he?'

'Probably with his horse,' replied Edward. 'It was lame earlier. But it is late and I am tired. We should all sleep now if you will insist on riding for Kermerdyn at dawn. Put up your dice, Roger.'

Geoffrey was surprised when Roger did as he was told, but supposed the big knight did look weary. So did Sear, Alberic and Edward, and Geoffrey saw the journey from La Batailge had taken its toll on them, too. Perhaps he was unreasonable to force them on so soon. Mulling over the notion of a respite, he walked to the kitchen block – a separate building to reduce the risk of fire.

Cornald was indeed raiding the pantries, and his cheeks bulged as he browsed along the shelves with a candle in hand. Pulchria was with him, and the unfriendly look she cast Geoffrey indicated she had not liked her advances being repelled earlier. He handed over the letter, with the brief explanation that it had been entrusted to him by the Bishop of London.

'From Maurice?' Pulchria asked wistfully, leaving Geoffrey in no doubt that she had helped the lecherous prelate with his medicine. 'How nice.'

Cornald scanned it quickly, his face alight with pleasure. 'He hopes we are both well, and confers blessings on us. What a lovely man! And he has included a recipe for cheese that he thinks might work well with Welsh milk. How thoughtful! Is he a friend of yours, Sir Geoffrey?'

Geoffrey nodded, then promptly forgot his resolve to leave his enquiries until his wits were sharper. 'He told me a lot about Kermerdyn, including an account of the death of William fitz Baldwin, whom he admired.'

'Everyone admired William,' said Cornald sadly. 'He was a wonderful man.'

'I preferred him when he was a sinner,' muttered Pulchria.

'You were at his deathbed,' said Geoffrey. 'And—'

'Not this again!' sighed Pulchria. 'I thought I had answered these questions already.'

'You did?' asked Cornald. 'When? You told me you spent all afternoon praying in the chapel.'

'I am about to go there again,' said Pulchria. The sultry look was back as she addressed Geoffrey. 'A night vigil always leaves me so refreshed. Perhaps you would care to join me?'

'No, thank you,' said Geoffrey. 'But I imagine Roger and Sear will oblige.'

'She is a pious lady,' said Cornald, placing an affectionate arm around her shoulders. 'She spends most nights and much of the day in prayer. Is that not true, dearest?'

'Yes,' said Pulchria. Geoffrey wondered how the butterer could be so blind.

'To return to William,' said Cornald, 'Pulchria and I were at his deathbed, and so was anyone of note in Kermerdyn. He had a secret, you see, and we all hoped he would reveal it. Not for our personal use, but so we could send it to His Majesty. Or even to the Archbishop, to be used for the glory of God.'

'Right,' said Geoffrey. 'Maurice told me a tale of poisoned butter—'

'No!' Cornald's voice was sharp and angry. 'There *was* a tale, but it was a lie. My butter is made from the finest ingredients, and even if it was a little past its best, it would not kill a man by turning his fingers black. It might drive him to the latrines, but nothing worse. William was *not* poisoned, Sir Geoffrey.'

'As I told you earlier,' added Pulchria irritably.

'You mentioned a secret,' said Geoffrey. 'What was—'

'William talked about it often,' said Cornald. 'He called it his "recipe for happiness". He was fond of fine food, and I believe he had stumbled across the perfect diet. *That* was his secret.'

Geoffrey regarded him warily. 'What?'

'A man is what he eats,' explained Cornald. 'I am in the business of creating victuals, so I know what I am talking about. Too much of one food or too little of another will cause imbalances in the body and lead to unhappiness. But I think William discovered the perfect harmony, and it was that which made him so good and kindly.'

'God's teeth!' muttered Geoffrey, not liking to imagine what Henry would say if presented with that theory.

'I do not agree,' said Pulchria. 'I believe he added something to his food – a herb of some kind that made him inclined to beneficence. I have read about such substances.'

Geoffrey had, too, and had seen them in action in the Holy Land. He supposed it was possible that William had dosed himself with powerful medicines. Indeed, it made a lot more sense than Cornald's hypothesis. And he would be more than happy to ply the King with herbs that might render him a better person. God knew, Henry needed them.

There was no more to be learned from Cornald and Pulchria, so Geoffrey went in search of Gwgan. He saw the discussion had spoiled the butterer's appetite, because Cornald followed him out of the pantry and disappeared into the bailey. Pulchria aimed for the wooden hut called the 'chapel', although it was rarely used and contained no altar or religious regalia.

When he reached the stables, still far from sober, he suddenly remembered that it was the place where one of his brothers had been murdered. He rarely thought about the incident and supposed too much wine had made him maudlin that night. He hesitated for a moment before putting his hand to the door, and it was that which saved him.

The crossbow bolt smacked into the place where his head

would have been, had he kept moving. Reacting instinctively, he dived behind a water butt, listening intently. The bailey was silent, but then he heard footsteps running away. He abandoned his cover and gave chase.

But it was hopeless – whoever it was had too great a lead and Goodrich contained too many outbuildings. Geoffrey looked around wildly. Alberic and Sear loitered by the chapel, and he saw Pulchria framed in the doorway there. All three seemed breathless, but Geoffrey could not tell whether it was anticipation or because they had been running. Meanwhile, Gwgan appeared from a direction that meant he had not been in the stables, and Edward was sitting on the hall steps. Cornald was chatting to Delwyn, and even shy Leah was hurrying from the latrines. Virtually everyone was out and might have taken a shot at their host.

Geoffrey retraced his steps and inspected the missile. It was one of Goodrich's own – distinctive, with a slight Saracen curve. Did it mean a servant was responsible? He did not think so, especially as he had not yet provided them with an heir. But which of the guests wanted him dead? Or had the culprit been aiming at someone else? The bailey was dark, and all knights tended to look similar in the clothes they wore when at leisure. Except Edward, of course.

Geoffrey stalked towards the Constable of Kadweli, who was taking deep breaths in an apparent effort to clear his head of wine fumes.

'Have you seen this before?' he asked, shoving the quarrel into Edward's hands.

Edward examined it in the faint light emanating from the hall. 'No, but it is a very peculiar shape. Why? Surely, you do not think we should have a shooting contest now? Wait until the morning, when we shall be able to see the targets.'

Geoffrey was about to press the matter further, when he saw Sear and Alberic coming towards them, aiming for the hall. They were speaking softly in low voices. As they passed, Edward addressed them.

'Look at this strange thing. Have you ever seen its like before?'

'No,' said Sear shortly. 'But then I have never bothered to make myself familiar with crossbows. I prefer a lance.

'And I prefer a proper bow,' added Alberic. 'I shall challenge you tomorrow, Geoffrey, because I warrant I am more accurate than you can be with this thing.'

'Do not be so sure about that,' said Cornald, making them all jump by approaching from behind. He held Pulchria by the hand. Her face was as black as thunder, and Geoffrey supposed he had decided against letting her keep her vigil. 'Sir Geoffrey will have had far more experience of weapons than any of us.'

'Not more than me,' said Sear. 'The King would not have appointed me Constable of Pembroc had I been a novice.'

'Well, I am hopeless with weapons,' said Cornald affably.

'Oh, fie!' said Pulchria. 'You are an excellent shot. When we were first married and were poor, you kept us alive with the rabbits you caught.'

'That was a long time ago,' said Cornald rather furtively.

'It is not something you forget,' persisted Pulchria sulkily. 'But then what do I know? I am a mere woman, after all—'

'You showed an aptitude for the bow, too,' said Cornald. The affable expression was gone from his round face, and something hard and angry had replaced it. 'When we first wed and were in love. I taught you how to shoot, and you took to it like a duck to water.'

Pulchria pulled a face at him, then smiled at Geoffrey. 'What has prompted these questions about weaponry? Is it to give us all nightmares, so we will seek solace in each other's company?'

'Someone just shot at me,' replied Geoffrey curtly, aware that Richard had just joined the little gathering. Gwgan was still some distance away. 'By the stable.'

'Unlikely,' said Sear with disdain. 'You are drunk and must have imagined it.'

'It was quite real,' said Geoffrey quietly. 'I am not that drunk.'

'You do not seem drunk at all now,' said Edward. 'It must have sobered you fast. I am sure it would have sobered me.'

Sear spat as he traipsed into the hall, making it clear he did not believe the tale. Richard shoved past Geoffrey without a word, a rough collision that almost took both men from their feet, although Geoffrey suspected it owed more to wine than hostility.

Richard turned when he reached the top of the steps. 'Look to

your servants for a culprit,' he suggested. 'Mine are always trying
to dispatch me.'

'How are you with a bow?' asked Geoffrey coolly.

Richard scowled. 'That is a question I decline to answer, and
if you want to see another dawn, you will not put it again. I do
not deal kindly with men who make unwarranted accusations.'

He staggered after the others. Sourly, Geoffrey thought that if
William had been anything like Richard, then it would have
needed a miracle to transform him into a saint.

Gwgan arrived at last, but forestalled his questions by taking
his hand and gripping it warmly. 'There has been no opportunity to become better acquainted today. Hilde tells me we shall
ride to Kermerdyn together, so I hope to converse more then.'

'If I survive the night,' muttered Geoffrey.

Gwgan took the quarrel from him and inspected it without
much interest. 'I have never had much use for crossbows. They
take too long to wind. Welshmen prefer simpler bows.'

'But you know how to use a crossbow?'

'Of course, but I have not had occasion to practise in a long
time. I am always willing to hone my skills, though. What do you
say to a competition tomorrow?'

'Only as long as I am not the target.'

Gwgan laughed uncertainly, then frowned. 'Are you saying
someone has just shot at you?'

Geoffrey nodded at the bolt. 'It missed me by a hand's breadth.'

Gwgan blew out his lips in a sigh. 'Well, it was not me! I make
a point of maintaining good relations with my kin, because I
might need their help one day. Wales is unstable, and only a fool
makes unnecessary enemies.'

Geoffrey was not sure what to think about anyone. He changed
the subject. 'It will be good to meet Isabella in Kermerdyn; Hilde
talks of her often.'

'She is a fine woman, although our union is yet to be blessed
with brats. I understand you are still waiting with Hilde, too. A
third sister has been wed seven years to a man with a dozen
bastards and no sign of a legal heir. I hope Baderon has not foisted
barren lasses on us.'

'I have not been home long enough for Hilde to—'

'Well, keep at it,' advised Gwgan. 'Fortunately, Welsh law sets scant store by legitimacy, and I have sons from previous liaisons. You will be under some pressure, though, being Norman.'

'I have been charged to hand you this,' said Geoffrey, feeling the discussion was disloyal to Hilde. He pulled the letter from his shirt, first checking it bore Gwgan's name and Pepin's elaborate cross. 'It is from the King.'

'Is it?' asked Gwgan, surprised. Then he shrugged. 'Then it is probably for Prince Hywel, but has been sent to me because I am his chief advisor. Hywel does not read, you see.'

'You can read?' asked Geoffrey. But of course he could. Gwgan's position demanded it, and Richard had already told him as much. He took a deep breath, wishing he had not drunk so much.

'Yes, and so can you. Hilde told me. She is very proud of you.'

'She is?' Geoffrey was pleased.

'And she will love you even more if you give her a son. So do not linger out here. Go to her!'

Grateful that two of the King's letters were now safely in the hands of the intended recipients, Geoffrey did as he was told.

Dawn the following day was pink and gold, and although Geoffrey's inclination was to leap out of bed and make preparations for leaving as soon as possible, Hilde persuaded him to linger, pointing out that no one else would be ready. All the guests had imbibed liberally the previous night, and even the vigorous Roger was drained by the journey from La Batailge. It would be a kindness – and good manners – to allow them a day to recover.

As they lay in bed, he told Hilde about the attack the previous night.

'Do you think it had to do with the letters?' she asked.

'Not the one from Maurice, certainly. It was a recipe for cheese.'

Hilde frowned. 'But Henry would not tell you what his missives contain. Perhaps someone does not want them delivered.'

'That means the culprit is someone who was already at Goodrich, because no attempts were made to harm me as we rode from La Batailge.'

'Not necessarily. You told me that none of your travelling companions – except Roger – knew about the King's letters. They believed you carried one from the Archbishop and several from Maurice. But then yesterday you started passing out missives from Henry. *Ergo*, it was only yesterday that they learned what you really carried.'

Geoffrey stared at her. Hilde was right. Then he shook his head. 'Sear, Alberic, Edward and Delwyn were trying companions, but none is the kind to loose crossbow bolts in the dark.'

'Then perhaps we are going about this the wrong way – looking for suspects before assessing the evidence,' said Hilde. 'Tell me exactly what happened. Who else was nearby?'

'Sear and Alberic were breathless shortly afterwards; they may have been running. So was Edward, who was sitting on the steps taking the air. Cornald claimed he could not shoot, but Pulchria contradicted him. Richard was aggressively defensive, and Gwgan invited me to challenge him in the butts.'

'And the women cannot be dismissed, either,' mused Hilde. 'I can use a crossbow.'

'I do not suspect you.'

'I should hope not! But where were Pulchria and Leah when all this was happening?'

'Leah was by the latrines, and Pulchria was near the chapel.'

'If my opinion counts for anything, I would say you can dismiss Leah and Cornald. Leah is too timid, and Cornald likes making friends, not killing them.'

Geoffrey was about to quiz her further when there was a sudden yowl from the bailey. He went to the window to see what was happening.

'Murder!' Delwyn was screeching, racing from the direction of the latrine. 'My abbot has been murdered!'

Geoffrey raced down the stairs in shirt and leggings, leaving Hilde to get dressed. The latrine was a thatched shed some distance from the other buildings. It comprised a seat that could accommodate three or four users simultaneously, separated by reed screens. It had been an evil place in Geoffrey's youth, but Joan saw it cleaned daily, and fresh soil was shovelled into the pit each night to reduce odours.

Mabon was sitting in the last stall, clutching a fistful of leaves. He was slumped to one side, eyes closed, as if he had fallen asleep. Geoffrey poked him, but there was no response.

'I have already done that,' said Joan. 'And there is no life-beat in his neck.'

'It is murder!' cried Delwyn.

'What has happened?' demanded Edward, thrusting his way forward. He stopped when he saw Mabon, and the blood drained from his face. 'Christ God! Is he *dead*? But he was hale and very hearty last night.'

The other guests arrived to express their horror, too – Richard, Sear and Alberic pushing past servants with unnecessary roughness; Gwgan entering more gently; Leah, hands to her mouth in mute horror; Pulchria, one eye on the abbot, and the other on the men in the crowd; Cornald white-faced next to her.

'Help me carry him outside,' ordered Geoffrey. 'It is not seemly to inspect him here.'

But Mabon was a large man, and his armour made him heavy. Sear and Richard helped, but Delwyn was useless, and Geoffrey was grateful when Roger elbowed the monk aside and lent his considerable strength to the procedure. Once they had manoeuvred Mabon out, they laid him on a bier and carried him to the chapel. Geoffrey ordered the servants back to work, but the guests lingered with Joan, Olivier and Hilde. Acutely aware of being watched by a sizeable audience, Geoffrey knelt to inspect the abbot.

Mabon was still slightly warm, so his death had not occurred long before, but there was nothing to say how he died. He was wearing mail and his black surcoat, but there were no breaches to indicate he had suffered a mortal blow, nor had he been struck on the head.

'He may have had a natural seizure,' Geoffrey said to Delwyn. 'There is nothing to suggest he was unlawfully slain.'

'Then it must be poison!' declared Delwyn. 'What other reason could there be for a healthy man to die so suddenly?'

Ignoring the murmurs of disgust from the onlookers, Geoffrey prised open the dead man's mouth and peered into it. He was horrified to see a bloody rawness within. Clearly, the bombastic abbot had ingested something caustic.

'You should not be doing that,' came a voice at his shoulder. It was Father Adrian, a priest with good Latin, but bound by ideas that betrayed an unworldly naiveté. 'It is not nice.'

'Neither is being poisoned,' retorted Geoffrey. 'And Delwyn is right: Mabon has swallowed something that seems to have seared his innards.'

There was a horrified gasp from the guests, and Adrian immediately began to pray. Edward, Hilde and Leah bowed their heads, but everyone else was looking at each other with expressions that ranged from shock to curiosity to disinterest.

'Did you *have* to announce that?' muttered Joan angrily. 'It will do our reputation as hosts no good at all.'

'Why would anyone harm Mabon?' asked Geoffrey, cutting through Adrian's petitions for the dead man's soul. The priest glared but Geoffrey ignored him.

There were a lot of shaken heads and shrugged shoulders. Edward made a sudden dive for the door. There followed the sound of him being violently sick.

'I am glad Kadweli is in such manly hands,' muttered Richard.

'It is a more honourable reaction than yours,' snapped Cornald, his cheerful face pale with shock. 'Cold indifference is never attractive.'

'Then it is a good thing you are not a soldier,' sneered Richard. 'And—'

'Why would anyone harm Mabon?' repeated Geoffrey, more forcefully. He did not want to listen to his guests sniping.

'Perhaps because he is not everyone's idea of an abbot,' suggested Delwyn, seeming more angry than distressed by the loss of his leader. 'But that is our business, and it is not for outsiders to interfere. Now we shall have Ywain foisted on us, and I am not sure we are ready for that.'

'That is a fine, compassionate attitude for a monk,' said Sear in distaste. 'And what do you mean exactly? Ready for what?'

'For the future,' snapped Delwyn. 'And the changes it will bring. But it is not me who should be interrogated here. *I* did not kill Mabon – I loved him like a father.'

'We can probably discount Delwyn as a culprit,' murmured Hilde in Geoffrey's ear. 'He would not want Mabon dead if Mabon will be succeeded by someone he dislikes.'

'Perhaps,' Geoffrey whispered back. 'However, Mabon despised Delwyn and refused to let him read the letter Henry sent. Delwyn lies when he says he loved Mabon.'

'What will you do with that particular missive now?' asked Hilde.

'Give it to Mabon's successor, I suppose. It contains orders to submit to the Bishop, so I imagine that applies as much to Ywain as Mabon.'

'You are no doubt thinking that Mabon's death means you are relieved of one of Henry's quests, but you are not. He will expect a report on Ywain instead and *his* relationship with Bishop Wilfred. I will help you write—'

Hilde stopped speaking when Delwyn sidled up to them.

'You had better give me the Archbishop's letter,' he said in a low voice. 'And any others intended for Kermerdyn. After all, someone *did* try to kill you last night.'

Geoffrey stared at him. 'Are you saying that Mabon's poisoner and the person who shot at me are one and the same? Why would you think that?'

Delwyn shrugged. 'No reason. I am merely concerned for your well-being. I am a monk, always alert for ways to protect my fellow creatures.'

'Sir Geoffrey had a valid question,' said Adrian when he had finished his prayers. Delwyn took the opportunity to slither away. 'Who did this terrible thing?'

Silence greeted his words, which came as no surprise to Geoffrey. The killer was not going to hold up his hand and admit responsibility.

'Then what manner of poison took him?' Adrian went on. He turned to Geoffrey. 'Return to the latrines and see if you can find a bottle or a packet.'

'I will help,' offered Sear, although Geoffrey would have preferred to work alone. He and Sear entered the building and began to poke unenthusiastically at the muddy floor. Joan followed.

'If there is a bottle or a packet, it is more likely to be down the pit,' she said practically. 'Here is a long pole with a hook, Geoff. Fish about and see what you can find.'

'You do it,' said Geoffrey in distaste. 'And why do you keep such a thing in here anyway?'

'Because people are always dropping things, and we often need to fetch them up,' explained Joan impatiently. 'Stand aside, then.'

'No, allow me,' said Sear, stepping forward and taking the stick. '*I* will not see a lady perform such a distasteful task.'

Geoffrey left abruptly, unwilling to witness such an operation – and hating the smile of startled gratitude Joan shot at the man he loathed. Sear was right – he should not have let his sister do something so ghastly – and it was shame that made Geoffrey angry. The pair appeared within moments, Joan holding a cloth in which lay a small phial.

'Here,' she said, holding it aloft. 'The poison must have come from this.'

'It is Mabon's tonic!' cried Delwyn, surging forward. 'He kept a pot of it with him at all times. He said it kept him vigorous.'

Adrian took it and smelled it tentatively. 'The contents of this would not have kept him vigorous. I am no alchemist, but it appears to have held wolf-tooth. I recognize the fishy stench.'

'Wolf-tooth?' asked Geoffrey, bemused.

Adrian shrugged. 'I know nothing about it, other than that it is poisonous.'

Cornald stepped forward and held out a smooth, plump white hand for the bottle. Adrian dropped it into his palm, and all watched the butterer take a careful sniff.

'Definitely wolf-tooth,' he declared. 'But there are other mysterious odours, too.'

'It is difficult to be certain,' said Gwgan, taking Cornald's wrist and using it to raise the bottle to his own nose. 'But I think there may be henbane, too – and that is certainly poisonous. I wish Isabella were here; she is very good at identifying scents.'

'Give it to me,' ordered Richard. He snatched the pot from Cornald and sniffed it hard. 'This is not the tonic that Mabon and I enjoyed. The priest, Cornald and Gwgan are right: it has been changed.'

Delwyn's eyes narrowed. 'Someone stole the bottle and replaced Mabon's remedy with poison. He was murdered, just as I thought!'

'What do you think about this Mabon business, Geoff?' Roger asked later that morning. The two were sitting at the far end of the hall, honing their weapons. The guests were clustered around the hearth, but Geoffrey had preferred to keep his distance.

Olivier was strumming his lute, and Sear was singing; Geoffrey was surprised that such a pleasant voice should emanate from so surly an individual. Edward and Leah were sitting together, clearly enjoying the music, although Richard only scowled at the flames. Delwyn was writing at the table, and Cornald and Joan were enjoying a good-natured discussion about cheese. Pulchria was making a play for Alberic, who did not mind at all, while Gwgan watched her antics.

'Someone definitely poisoned his tonic,' said Geoffrey. 'And the killer dropped the bottle down the pit afterwards, in the hope that his death might be passed off as natural.'

'But you thwarted that by looking in Mabon's mouth.'

'If I had not done it, Delwyn would have done. The killer stood no chance of masking his crime.'

'It is a pity,' said Roger. 'I rather liked Mabon. So who did it?'

Geoffrey gestured at the hearth. 'Everyone here had the opportunity. Mabon died at or near dawn, but the poison could have been added to his tonic at any time. Alibis mean nothing, because everyone spent a moment or two alone.'

'Then what about motive?' asked Roger. 'Who had a *reason* for wanting Mabon dead?'

'Who knows? Perhaps Delwyn was right, and someone did not like that he was more warrior than monastic. Mabon was unusual, and someone may have felt his antics were bringing Kermerdyn into disrepute – I cannot imagine he went unremarked at the oath-taking ceremony, for example.'

'And there were a lot of important people at that,' nodded Roger. 'So, can we narrow our suspects to those who were there?'

Geoffrey shook his head. 'We could be on the wrong track entirely, and Mabon's outspoken manners may have earned him enemies long before he came here. Sear and Alberic, for example, are easily offended.'

'Edward was fond of him, though,' said Roger. 'I saw the kiss they exchanged. But looking at motive and opportunity is getting us nowhere. We shall have to assess everyone individually. I hate to say it, but Sear cannot be the culprit, because he would not have fished the incriminating phial out of the latrine if he were – he would have left it there.'

'Not necessarily. Joan said he made a splash, which drove her back, and it was while she was distracted that he picked the bottle from the pit. It may have been coincidence; equally, he may have decided the phial was better "found" in the pit than among his own possessions.'

Roger grinned. 'Good! I would like him to swing for murder. But why would he kill Mabon?'

Geoffrey shrugged. 'Perhaps he disapproves of Mabon squabbling with Bishop Wilfred. Or perhaps Mabon is in the habit of giving him unwanted advice about his troops. Sear is sensitive to criticism.'

'What about Delwyn as a suspect?' asked Roger. 'I cannot abide that dirty little snake.'

'I am inclined to think he is innocent, because of his insistence that Mabon was murdered. If he were the killer, I think he would have stayed quiet. Of course, he certainly has a motive – Mabon made no effort to disguise his dislike of him.'

'I do not like Richard, either,' said Roger. 'Can you make a case against him?'

Geoffrey nodded. 'Yes – he asked for some of Mabon's tonic, but was refused. He may have taken the real tonic and exchanged it for wolf-tooth out of spite. And, as we are concentrating on men you do not like, we can include Alberic because Sear may have ordered him to do it.'

Roger rubbed his hands together, pleased. 'We can discount the ladies, though. Pulchria is more interested in seducing men than dispatching them, and Leah is too much of a mouse to contemplate doing something bold.'

'There may be more to Leah than you think, and Pulchria cannot be eliminated because I am sure she counted Mabon among her conquests. Perhaps he rejected her and she did not like it.'

'He *did* reject her.' Geoffrey regarded him in surprise. 'He told her that he could not oblige with Delwyn watching his every move. She was bitterly disappointed, so I showed her what real men are about, to take her mind off him.'

'Then perhaps Mabon was indiscreet about Pulchria's talents, and Cornald objected,' said Geoffrey. 'Cornald seems amiable, but no man likes the villain who seduces his wife.'

'It is her doing the seducing,' Roger pointed out. 'It is difficult to say no.'

'I managed,' said Geoffrey dryly. 'Several times.'

'You should,' said Roger primly. 'You are a married man, and I doubt Hilde would approve. However, if Pulchria *is* a poisoner, perhaps you should risk Hilde's ire and give in to her demands. We do not want *you* killed in a latrine, just for the sake of a few moments' work.'

'And finally, there is Gwgan,' said Geoffrey, ignoring the advice. 'He seems personable, but I cannot gain his measure at all.'

'Neither can I,' said Roger. 'But you should give him the benefit of the doubt, because he is a member of your family.'

'Unfortunately,' said Geoffrey soberly, 'that means nothing at all.'

Joan's eyes were hard when Geoffrey saw her in the kitchen, overseeing preparations for the next meal.

'You cannot leave today, Geoffrey,' she said curtly. 'Arrangements must be made to remove Mabon. That will take time, although I shall do my best to expedite matters, because I am not keen on entertaining murderers. Goodrich is a decent place, and now its reputation has been sullied.'

'I will leave – with Mabon – tomorrow,' said Geoffrey. 'And I will insist that everyone comes with me, so you and Olivier will be left in peace.'

Joan grimaced. 'Unfortunately, that brings its own set of anxieties – you being in company with a poisoner. I hope you do not intend to pry into such a dangerous matter.'

'That would not be as dangerous as pretending it did not happen,' said Geoffrey soberly. 'The best way to stay safe is to understand it.'

'No,' said Joan forcefully. 'An investigation will turn *everyone* against you. These are prickly people, and no one will appreciate you asking questions.'

'My diplomatic skills have been admired by kings and princes,' said Geoffrey flippantly. 'You need not worry about me. Besides, after more than two decades of fighting, I should be able to hold my own.'

'That is probably what Mabon thought,' said Joan soberly. 'But a sword is no use against poison. However, I see you have made up your mind, so I suppose I shall have to be content with a promise that you will be careful.'

'I am always careful.' That was certainly true: Geoffrey would have perished long ago if he had been reckless. 'What will you do with your guests today to keep them occupied? Do you want me to arrange a joust? Or sword practice?'

Joan gaped at him. 'No, I do not! Whoever shot at you last night might use it as an opportunity to finish the job, and the inevitable injuries would prevent half the competitors from leaving with you tomorrow. However, Gwgan suggested an archery contest, which should be safe enough. I will tell Father Adrian to officiate – a killer is unlikely to strike with a priest looking on.'

Geoffrey was not so sure about that, but he conceded that it would be difficult to stage an 'accident' if the competition was properly policed – and Adrian, with his visceral dislike of anything remotely martial, was the perfect man for the task.

'It will be a good opportunity for questions, too,' he said, more to himself than Joan.

'Geoffrey!' she cried, aghast. 'How can you think it is sensible to interrogate people when they are armed with bows?'

'They cannot shoot me in front of witnesses.'

'That depends on what you ask. I doubt Richard will stop to consider the consequences.'

'You think he is the culprit?'

'He is one of my suspects, certainly. You may think he is more likely to kill with a sword, but he is sly and dangerous.'

'Who are your other suspects?'

'Gwgan, because he has been here for days, and I still do not know him – he is an enigma. Besides, he is an extremely able politician, and we all know politicians are not to be trusted. The same goes for Edward. Then Sear and Alberic were out a lot last night, and so was Delwyn – possibly frolicking with Pulchria once Cornald was asleep, but possibly up to no good.'

'What about Cornald himself?' asked Geoffrey. 'Could he be a killer?'

'No. I have known him for years, and there is not a malicious bone in his body. Of course, I would not say the same about his wife. *She* would stop at nothing to have her own way.'

Seven

The Marches were an uneasy place, and border skirmishes were frequent and unpredictable. Geoffrey had left instructions that all Goodrich's tenants were regularly to practise their skills with the bow and crossbow, so permanent butts had been set up outside the bailey. Because Father Adrian was to be in attendance, Joan ordered the human-shaped targets to be replaced with simple bull's-eyes.

Word spread quickly, and people from the village came to watch, as did most of Goodrich's servants, many of whom intended to compete themselves. The prize was several gold pieces donated by Cornald, and guests and residents alike were determined to have them. Joan provided warm wine and cakes for the spectators, and there was a celebratory atmosphere in the air. If Mabon's death had cast a pall over the castle, it was not in evidence.

Richard was the first guest to compete and gained the highest score by a considerable margin. There was a sigh of disappointment from the servants, and Geoffrey saw the man's sullen manners had made him unpopular. Richard left the field scowling, just as he had entered it, taking no pleasure in his achievement.

'You did well,' said Geoffrey pleasantly. 'You may win.'

'Not with the crossbow you provided,' growled Richard. 'It is not fit for a peasant.'

'It was my father's,' said Geoffrey coolly. 'He used it at Hastinges.'

Neither statement was true, but they had the desired effect.

'My apologies,' said Richard stiffly. 'I did not mean to insult a family heirloom. And I should also say that I am sorry your house has been sullied by murder. Your sister and her husband have been hospitable, and if I learn who poisoned the abbot, I will kill him – to satisfy their honour.'

'But that would mean *two* murders under their roof,' Geoffrey pointed out. He saw Richard's puzzled look and decided nothing was to be gained by pursuing the matter. 'Do you have any idea who might have wanted to hurt Mabon?'

'Anyone,' replied Richard. 'I do not like *anyone* here, except Joan, Olivier and your wife. I am not very keen on you, either.'

'Why?' asked Geoffrey.

'Crusaders in general are—'

'I mean, why do you not like everyone else?'

'Because they are all vermin, and if I ever attain a position of power, I shall either execute them or throw them in my dungeons.'

Geoffrey raised his eyebrows and supposed the good people of Kermerdyn had better hope he was never promoted. 'Did you dislike Mabon?'

'Intensely – he was always trying to tell me how to run my garrison. But I did not kill him – I had hopes that he would relent and give me some of his tonic.'

'But now he is dead, you can take it all – you do not need to rely on his generosity.'

'Now he is poisoned, I shall eat and drink only what I am sure is safe – and nothing belonging to him will be. I did not kill Mabon, and if you accuse me, I will kill you.'

He could try, thought Geoffrey, regarding him with dislike. He turned to another matter. 'I understand you delivered some butter to your brother William just before he—'

Richard surged forward and took a handful of Geoffrey's surcoat, before slamming him against the palisade. He was strong and fast, but Geoffrey punched him away, sending him reeling, then whipped out his dagger, and it was Richard who found himself pressed against the fence.

'How dare you infer that I would harm my brother,' snarled Richard, uncaring of the blade that pricked his skin. 'I loved him and would give my life in an instant to see him alive again.'

'What are you doing?' came the querulous tones of Father Adrian from behind them. 'Sir Geoffrey! Put him down at once, or I shall have you doing penance for a week!'

Geoffrey released Richard, who took the opportunity to land a sly kick before stalking away.

'You deserved that,' said Adrian.

'A monk was poisoned last night,' snapped Geoffrey, rubbing his leg. 'And a good man was probably poisoned seven years ago, too. I was trying to bring them justice.'

'You mean William fitz Baldwin?' asked Adrian. He shrugged

at Geoffrey's surprise. 'It was the talk of the country when he died, because he was rumoured to be a saint. However, Richard did not kill him. I have heard his confessions, and his sins are not of that magnitude.'

'What are they, then?' asked Geoffrey.

'They are confidential, as you well know,' said Adrian sharply. 'However, I can tell you that they are nothing compared to yours. *Your* soul is stained black with the blood of the Crusade.'

'Do you think Richard capable of poisoning Mabon?'

'Of course – any knight is capable of murder. And Richard is the kind of man who goes around striking innocent priests.'

Geoffrey felt rather like hitting Adrian himself. 'Is that the only reason you—'

'Richard came to me for shriving yesterday – *after* Mabon's body was found – and would have mentioned such a foul deed. He is innocent. So are Leah and Edward, should you think to accuse them. All three came to confession, and murder was not among their sins.'

'And you are certain?' pressed Geoffrey. 'You would not lie, just because you dislike me?'

Adrian was offended. 'I never lie! Richard, Leah and Edward are innocent of Mabon's murder, I am sure of it. And I do not dislike you, Sir Geoffrey. I am just frightened of you.'

Discussions with Adrian often left Geoffrey with vague feelings of guilt and disquiet, so he hastened to put the priest from his mind by pursuing his enquiries. It was Cornald's turn to shoot. The butterer was putting on a display of being inept, but the way he held the weapon and the confident manner in which he inserted the bolt told Geoffrey it was an act. Nevertheless, all three of Cornald's shots went wide of the target. Pulchria went next and managed a considerably better score, although nowhere near high enough to threaten Richard.

'I am sorry about what happened to Mabon,' said Geoffrey, when they had finished. 'He will be a loss to Kermerdyn, I imagine.'

'A terrible loss,' agreed Cornald sadly. 'And wolf-tooth . . . well, it is a dreadful way to die.'

'You know about wolf-tooth?' pounced Geoffrey.

'I once used it – in very small amounts – for a personal ailment,' replied Cornald. 'However, I developed a violent aversion to it. Look at my hand. You see that redness? That is from simply holding Mabon's phial when you recovered it from the latrine. I no longer have anything to do with the stuff.'

'But there is some in the castle,' added Pulchria. 'Your sister keeps it for killing rats. Anyone could have taken some and given it to Mabon. It is a pity, because he was a fine man.'

'A very fine man,' agreed Cornald, either mistaking her meaning or ignoring it. 'I cannot imagine who would want to kill him. He was a little irreligious for a churchman, but I found that rather refreshing. And he had a wonderful sense of humour.'

'Could there have been wolf-tooth in the butter William fitz Baldwin ate?' asked Geoffrey.

'No,' said Cornald, amiability fading abruptly. 'As I told you last night, there was nothing wrong with that butter. It was perfect when it left my dairy. Of course, it was delivered to Rhydygors by Richard, and was a gift from my wife, but—'

'*I* did not poison it,' said Pulchria, shooting her husband an alarm-filled glance. 'Besides, dozens of people had access to it – Delwyn and Bishop Wilfred loitered by the kitchen, and had no explanation for why, and half of Kermerdyn was at William's last dinner—'

'But no one else had any butter,' pressed Geoffrey.

'No,' said Cornald coldly. 'It was a gift for William, not for general consumption. And he did not eat it all at once, anyway, but consumed it over several days. William was a lovely man, and we were all shocked when he was taken from us.'

Geoffrey turned to other matters. 'Why did you pretend to lack skill with the crossbow?'

'I was not pretending!' replied Cornald with an uneasy smile. 'It has been many years since I last touched one, and you, of all people, will know that military skills rust without practice.'

'Not to that extent,' said Geoffrey. 'You could have done better.'

'Yes, he could,' agreed Pulchria, shooting Cornald a cross glare. 'I wanted that gold back.'

'It would not have been polite to win the prize I provided,' said Cornald, seizing on the excuse with palpable relief. 'But my throat is parched after all the excitement, and I need some wine. Come, Pulchria. You can pour it for me.'

Geoffrey watched them go, exasperated. His questions had led nowhere, and neither Cornald nor Pulchria could be eliminated from either enquiry.

Some of the servants were selected to shoot next, giving Geoffrey time to observe Goodrich's guests. They were generally enjoying themselves, even Richard, and none looked to be suffering from a bad conscience. The only one looking miserable was Leah, who was sitting alone on a bale of straw, shivering.

'There is hot broth and a fire in the hall,' said Geoffrey, taking pity on her. 'It is not necessary to stay outside, especially as your husband has already had his turn.'

Leah smiled, and he thought it was a pity she did not do it more often. She held out a thin, white hand, so that he could help her to her feet. It was icy-cold to the touch, and the veins were blue against it. He released it as soon as it was polite.

'Will you walk with me to the gate?' she asked. 'I have another headache, and my eyesight is blurred. No, do not look concerned. It is an affliction I have had for a long time, and it will be gone in a while. All I need is warmth and quiet.'

'It sounds unpleasant,' said Geoffrey.

'It started just before William died,' Leah went on. 'Seven years ago. I had a violent ague that kept me in bed, and I have never fully recovered.'

Geoffrey sensed Richard glowering, but ignored him; he should have looked to his wife's comforts himself if he did not want others to do it for him. Then he stole a glance at Hilde, sheepishly aware that he had barely exchanged a word with her since the contest had started. But she was taking a turn in the butts, and appreciative applause from Goodrich's villagers indicated she was putting on a respectable show.

'Is that why you were not at William's deathbed?' he asked.

Leah nodded. 'Edward and Alberic were not there, either – they were patrolling the woods near Kadweli and visited me on their way home, which was nice. I had been abandoned to the servants, you see, because everyone was more worried about William.'

'Who do you think killed Mabon?' asked Geoffrey bluntly.

Leah blinked. 'I wish I knew, because I would urge him to go to your gentle parish priest and confess. That sort of deed is not good for the soul.'

'So you have no ideas?' pressed Geoffrey. 'No suspicions?'

'None. However, no one from Kermerdyn will be responsible – I have known them all for years. You will find the culprit is a Goodrich man. A lot of your servants were shocked by Mabon's irreligious views, and your sister makes no secret of the fact that she keeps a comprehensive store of medicinal herbs in the castle.'

'Really?' asked Geoffrey. Joan would not be pleased if it transpired that one of her own people was the guilty party.

'Look,' said Leah suddenly, pointing. 'It is Edward's turn to shoot. I shall watch him and then go to the hall. Would you mind waiting a moment?'

Edward sauntered up to the line with a good deal of confidence, then made a great show of setting his feet and taking aim. His first bolt whistled so wide of the target that it sent several onlookers ducking for cover.

'I am still not recovered from vomiting so violently yesterday,' he explained with an amiable grin. 'I am normally rather good at shooting. Give me another arrow.'

'Bolt,' corrected Sear, handing one over and then helping when Edward struggled to place it correctly. 'We call them crossbow *bolts.*'

'I knew that,' said Edward, hands on hips as Sear wound the weapon for him. He tried to take it before it was ready, restlessly impatient, like a child. His second shot was worse than his first, raising an indignant squeal from Adrian. But the third slammed neatly into the centre of the target, drawing an appreciative cheer from the onlookers.

'The luck of a beginner,' said Richard. 'That last shot was a fluke.'

'It was skill,' countered Edward indignantly. 'The first two were the flukes. This weapon pulls to the left and is horribly stiff for a man with delicate fingers.'

He danced a little jig, much to the crowd's appreciation, and then made a show of donning his pale purple gloves. Joan remarked politely that they were very fine, and was promptly rewarded with a complex description of how he had come to purchase them.

Bored, Geoffrey offered his arm to Leah, eager to see her to the hall so he could resume his enquiries.

'Where are you taking her?' demanded Richard. 'She is not well enough to be dragged all around the butts. Why do you think I found her a bale of straw to sit on?'

'I was escorting her to the hall,' replied Geoffrey shortly, hoping the man was not going to provoke another confrontation. 'She has a headache.'

Richard's face creased into concern. 'You should have told me, Leah,' he said, uncharacteristically gentle. 'You promised me you would.'

'I did not want to spoil your fun,' said Leah, leaning on his arm gratefully.

'You could never do that,' he whispered, kissing her lightly on the top of her head. He scowled when he saw Geoffrey was watching, and led her away.

It was not long before Edward came to stand next to Geoffrey, still preening from the praise lavished on his final shot. It would not see him win the competition, because his first two efforts would count against him, but it was certainly the best that day. His happy expression faded when he followed the direction of Geoffrey's gaze and saw Richard and Leah.

'I do not understand what she sees in him,' he said. 'Oh, he loves her well enough, but he is always so damn miserable. You would not know it to look at her, but she was a happy little creature as a girl. These days, her illness renders her as gloomy as him, and even I struggle to make her laugh. Of course, none of us has much to smile about today.'

'No?' asked Geoffrey. 'Why not?'

'Because of Mabon,' replied Edward. Geoffrey was horrified to see tears in his eyes. 'He was a good friend, and I shall miss him horribly.'

Geoffrey recalled the pleasure with which they had greeted each other the previous day, and knew he was telling the truth. Edward's distress at the abbot's death was genuine.

'When William died,' he began tentatively, 'you were out on patrol.'

'William fitz Baldwin?' asked Edward, startled. 'But he died seven years ago! Or are you thinking that if William was poisoned, then the same person might have murdered Mabon? It is certainly possible, I suppose, although I cannot imagine why someone would choose them as victims. They were so different.'

'Because William was a saint, and Mabon was irreligious?'

Edward's smile was pained. 'William had his faults, believe me. He was cloyingly pious for a start. However, Mabon was a fine man, and he *was* religious – he just did not allow himself to be confined by Church dogma. I admired him for that.'

'Your patrol,' prompted Geoffrey.

Edward sighed. 'Alberic and I were gone for almost two weeks, hunting a band of villains who were robbing travellers. It was dreadful work – hot, tiring and dirty. When we arrived in Kermerdyn, no one was home except Leah, who was ill. We availed ourselves of a bed in her home for the night and learned of William's death the next morning.'

'Do you believe he was poisoned?'

Edward was silent for a while, then nodded. 'Yes. I thought so at the time and I have no reason to revise my opinion. He said he had a secret, and a lot of people were eager to learn it. Of course, William dead meant it was lost for ever, so the killer made a grave mistake.'

'What was this secret?'

Edward sighed. 'I do not believe there was one. William may have been speaking figuratively – to explain his turn to goodness in a way he thought others would understand. But it killed him, because someone decided to take it from him.'

'Did anyone stand out to you as a suspect?'

Edward shrugged. 'Delwyn, Sear, Alberic, Cornald, Pulchria, Hywel, Bishop Wilfred, various servants. Not Richard, because he was devastated by his brother's death, and not Leah because she was too unwell. However, your silly shooting contest has been good for one thing.'

'And what is that?'

'You can cross me off your list of culprits for trying to kill you last night. I am a fine shot with a familiar weapon, but it takes me a while to get used to strange ones.'

He sauntered away, leaving Geoffrey not sure what to think.

★   ★   ★

When it was time for Sear and Alberic to demonstrate their skills, both did so with a careless confidence that demonstrated their superior ability. They beat Richard's score, and Sear was smugly aloof when Adrian declared him in the lead, with Alberic second.

'You will not do better,' Sear informed Roger. 'You and your friend will lose.'

'We will see about that,' growled Roger angrily, seizing the crossbow in his big hands 'Come on, Geoff.'

The crossbow was not Roger's forte, but pure bloody-mindedness led him to put three bolts in a neat triangle in the target. Unfortunately, they were all to one side, so although he scored more highly than Alberic, he was still behind Sear.

'I have been asking everyone about Mabon,' said Geoffrey to Sear and Alberic, while Roger wound the weapon for the next contender. 'Do *you* have any idea who might have killed him?'

'Richard,' said Sear immediately. 'And he probably shot at you, too, because he has more than ably demonstrated that he is skilled with a crossbow.'

'Why would he do either?' asked Geoffrey, not pointing out that Sear was highly skilled with a crossbow, too.

'Because he is that kind of man,' replied Sear shortly. 'Cruel, vicious and unfathomable.'

'Easy, Sear,' said Alberic softly. 'We have no evidence to make accusations.'

'Or else it was Delwyn,' Sear went on. 'He is sly enough to resort to poison, so he may have killed William all those years ago, too. I doubt he is much good with a crossbow, though.'

'I can shoot,' objected Delwyn, hearing the last part. He snatched the bow from Roger and demonstrated a respectable skill, although nothing to match that of the knights.

'Where did you learn to do that?' asked Alberic uneasily. 'Did Mabon teach you?'

'No,' said Delwyn haughtily, shoving the weapon back at Roger and beginning to stride away. 'I was not always a monk. And, for your information, you are *all* suspects for murdering Mabon in my eyes. The only one who is innocent is me, because I was praying at the time.'

'Your alibi is God?' asked Sear mockingly. 'I doubt that will convince Sir Geoffrey.'

'It will if he is not a heathen,' called Delwyn, stamping away.

'I have changed my mind,' said Sear, watching him. '*He* is the culprit. He probably killed William, too, because he was seen loitering in the kitchen near the butter.'

It was Geoffrey's turn to shoot, but Gwgan reached the crossbow first. Geoffrey had not known he had been standing so close, and realized uncomfortably that the Welshman possessed the ability to blend into the background. It was a trick he had seen other politicians employ, and it crossed his mind that Gwgan might be conducting his own enquiry into what happened to Mabon – not by asking questions, but by watching and listening. He decided to find out.

'What have you learned about Mabon's murder?'

Gwgan's eyebrows shot up. 'What makes you think I have been looking into it?'

'You are Prince Hywel's counsellor, and he will want to know what happened to Kermerdyn's abbot. Of course you have been exploring the matter.'

Gwgan smiled. 'You are right, although I have nothing to show for my efforts. Mabon had his eccentricities, but I do not see them as reasons to kill him. It was the same with William fitz Baldwin – most folk liked him, but it did not stop someone from feeding him poison.'

'You think the same person dispatched them both?'

Gwgan thought carefully. 'It is possible, although Mabon seems to have died almost instantly, whereas poor William lay ill for days, vomiting up anything he ate.'

'Mabon, Cornald and Richard noticed he had black fingers,' said Geoffrey. 'And Pulchria claimed he had seizures, too.'

Gwgan nodded, then shuddered. 'God save us all from such a terrible fate! He was out of his mind most of the time, babbling all sorts of rubbish.'

'About his secret?'

Gwgan waved a dismissive hand. 'The tales about his secret are nonsense. William *did* change when he arrived in Kermerdyn and started building a castle, but that was because he was in Wales. It brings out the goodness in people.'

Geoffrey did not think he would regale the King with that particular theory.

'Mabon thought it was something to do with a vision William had in the river.'

Gwgan shrugged. 'Then why did William keep it a secret? Why not tell everyone?'

It was a valid point, and Geoffrey barely noticed when Gwgan put three neat crossbow bolts into the centre of the target with a cool panache that indicated he was a warrior as well as a diplomat, thinking through the counsellor's claim. Adrian called out to announce that the score was equal to Sear's.

'Come on, Geoff lad,' said Roger, shoving the crossbow in his hands. 'It is your turn. You have to do better than Sear and Gwgan to win. You can do it.'

'It is discourteous to defeat your guests,' muttered Olivier in his other ear. 'And Goodrich is known for its good manners, so watch what you do.'

'Ignore him,' breathed Roger. 'There is more at stake here than your manor's reputation. That Sear needs to be taught a lesson.'

Geoffrey turned to Olivier. 'Does Joan keep wolf-tooth in the castle? For killing rats?'

'Of course not,' replied Olivier with a frown. 'There are far better substances than wolf-tooth for killing rats. However, I imagine it is readily available in the village. Why? Are you thinking that one of us might have made an end of Mabon? If so, you are wrong. He was a trying guest, but he was on the verge of leaving. We had no reason to dispatch him.'

'Never mind that,' snapped Roger. 'Concentrate on the task in hand. You *must* win.'

'Manners, Geoffrey,' warned Olivier.

'*You* should not be taking part in this contest,' said Adrian suddenly. 'Surely, you have had enough bloodshed and slaughter?'

Geoffrey regarded him askance. 'It is a straw target, Father. I doubt it will mind.'

'You imperil your immortal soul if you continue to hone these diabolical skills,' declared Adrian. 'And, as your household priest, I order you to desist.'

'Listen to him, Geoffrey,' said Joan.

'Then I declare the winners to be Sear and Gwgan,' announced Adrian loudly, before Geoffrey could tell Adrian what to do with his strictures. 'The gold will be divided between them. Unless they are good, decent men, who will donate it to the poor.'

'Why did you not tell him to go to the Devil?' demanded Roger, when the priest had flounced off with the purse without giving Sear and Gwgan an opportunity to object. 'You let Sear win.'

Geoffrey turned to Joan and started to laugh. 'Did you put Adrian up to that?'

Joan regarded him coolly. 'What if I did? You would have won, and it would not have been polite. I am *glad* Adrian is determined to save you from eternal damnation and so agreed to intervene.'

But Geoffrey was actually more concerned with the dangers on Earth, and determined that he would carefully watch what he, Hilde and Roger ate and drank on the trip to Kermerdyn. Especially butter or potions in small bottles.

Eight

Unlike the journey to Goodrich, the track into Wales was dry and hard, and made for excellent riding. Geoffrey's companions did not object to his rapid pace, although it still took longer than it should have done. Hilde and Pulchria did not slow them down, but Leah's debilitating headaches did, and concern for her well-being forced them to stop early nearly every day. The men did not object to the shorter journeys, happy that the presence of women meant the party tended to find shelter in inns and villages, rather than under hedges or in barns.

It was a large company – Richard and Cornald each had several servants – and an ostentatious one. All six knights – Geoffrey, Roger, Sear, Alberic, Richard and Edward – wore white surcoats, and so did Gwgan. Cornald, Pulchria and Leah dressed in a way that said they were people of substance, and, with such an overt display of affluence, Geoffrey expected them to be ambushed at every turn. Richard and Gwgan almost came to unfortunate ends when an unseen attacker threw knives at them, but otherwise there was no trouble, and Geoffrey supposed the presence of so many warriors deterred casual robbers.

Within the company, meanwhile, there were more feuds and factions than Geoffrey could number, and they seemed to alter with every mile. Sear and Alberic switched back and forth from being Richard's bosom friend to his bitter enemy with bewildering rapidity. Concurrently, Geoffrey and Edward were increasingly hard-pressed to prevent Sear and Roger from fighting. Throughout it all, Pulchria caused divisions with her assignations, and Cornald continued to give the impression that he was blithely unaware of her activities.

Delwyn annoyed everyone by complaining about the weather, the horses, the conversation and, most of all, the fact that Geoffrey had put him in charge of Abbot Mabon's body, which was being carried on a cart. Geoffrey was glad the weather had cooled, because Goodrich had no resident embalmer. Delwyn saw to the corpse on its cart each night, but his duties were perfunctory, and he gave no indication that he grieved.

Geoffrey was pleasantly surprised by Gwgan, who transpired to be intelligent and urbane. The Welshman was delighted to discover that Geoffrey spoke his language, and encouraged him to converse as often as possible. Geoffrey liked learning languages and was more than happy to oblige. He often sought out Gwgan's company and was even happier when Edward joined them in lively, intellectual discussions of the kind Geoffrey experienced too infrequently in his life as a soldier. They talked about Mabon's death, too.

'Did you ever reach any conclusions about who killed the abbot?' Edward asked Gwgan one day, as the three rode together. He spoke Latin, as they always did when they did not want the rest of the party to eavesdrop. 'I know you tried to investigate the matter for Prince Hywel.'

Gwgan grimaced. 'Unfortunately not. I am inclined to discount Richard, because he is too savage to use poison. Besides, he hates the notion of killing by toxins after the way William died.'

Edward shuddered. 'I was not at William's deathbed, but the affair sounded terrible.'

'It was,' agreed Gwgan. He crossed himself suddenly, something Geoffrey had not seen him do before. 'I was appalled by the length of time it took him to die.'

'Days,' said Edward, shaking his head.

Gwgan nodded slowly. 'If William was poisoned, then his killer is evil beyond words. I am no expert in the field, but I know there are substances that can end a man's life far more quickly and without the agonies poor William suffered.'

'What a grim discussion!' said Edward, after a reflective silence. 'I should never have raised the subject of murder. Forgive me. We shall talk about Socrates instead.'

'Only if we do not dwell on the fact that Socrates was poisoned, too,' said Geoffrey. 'Or the fact that he asked a lot of questions, but did not answer many.'

Gwgan laughed. 'It sounds safer to concentrate on his philosophy.'

'Then we shall debate a Socratic paradox,' determined Geoffrey. 'How about the notion that all virtue is knowledge?'

Roger disapproved of their discussions, especially as they were conducted in a language he did not understand. Meanwhile, Sear and Alberic mocked them incessantly, and Richard obviously itched to, but Leah had whispered something the first time he had started to make a disparaging remark, and he had desisted since. Geoffrey was grateful to Edward, who was blessed with a remarkable ability to keep the peace, which he achieved with unfailing cheerfulness and a battery of diplomatic interruptions.

Geoffrey enjoyed the company of Hilde and Leah, though. Leah kept Richard's surliness in check, and, though often ill, she was gentle and considerate with the servants. Hilde and Geoffrey grew closer as they spent more time together, and he looked forward to the evenings, when they were usually alone. Pulchria was a liability, though, especially at night, and she was the cause of several quarrels between Roger, Sear and Alberic.

'I am tempted to stay in Brechene and travel to Kermerdyn later with my garrison,' said Edward one day, having endured a lengthy tirade against knights who preferred discussing geometry to slaughter. 'I have had enough of this rabble.'

If the company had upset Edward's patient equanimity, then Geoffrey knew it was bad.

'Please stay with us, Sir Edward,' pleaded Hilde. 'We might never reach Kermerdyn if you are not here to help us keep these brutes from each other's throats. I would not care, but I do not want Geoffrey blamed when he and I are the only ones who arrive without slaughtering each other.'

'We will not have their company on the way home, thank God,' said Geoffrey.

'Will you stay in Kermerdyn long?' asked Edward. He smiled boyishly. 'I certainly hope so, because I would like you to see Kadweli. In fact, you should come with me directly, because it would be nicer and certainly safer.'

'You do not like Kermerdyn?' asked Geoffrey.

'Oh, it is lovely – it was an old Roman town, and the ancient walls can still be seen. I was thinking more of the inhabitants.'

'But my sister has always said there is no one more charming than a person from Kermerdyn,' said Hilde.

'And she is right,' said Edward. 'Especially now all the nasty folk are currently riding along behind us. It must be wonderful there at the moment. Kermerdyn does not deserve the likes of Sear and Richard. Or Alberic, who seems more pleasant than his touchy friend, but who is sly.'

It was the first time Edward had made disparaging remarks about their companions, and Geoffrey was inclined to listen.

'And Cornald?'

Edward was thoughtful. 'I like him, but can he really be so stupid as not to know what Pulchria does in her spare time? He is an astute businessman, so I do not see him lacking in wits.'

'You think he might harbour grudges behind his amiable façade?' asked Hilde.

Edward shrugged. 'It is not for me to say, but I cannot help but wonder.'

Geoffrey and Hilde exchanged a glance. Had Cornald lobbed the knives at Richard and Gwgan, and shot at Geoffrey in Goodrich? If so, then it was unfair, because none of *them* had accepted Pulchria's invitations – Geoffrey had Hilde, Richard had Leah, and Gwgan would not stray from the straight and narrow with his sister-in-law watching.

'Do you happen to know whether William enjoyed Pulchria's favours?' asked Geoffrey, thinking fast. 'Or Mabon?'

'William did regularly when he first arrived in Kermerdyn,' replied Edward. 'But not once he became a saint, which vexed her greatly. And Mabon would only take her when he was sure no one else would see. Well, you cannot blame him: he was an abbot, after all.'

Geoffrey and Hilde exchanged a second glance. Perhaps Cornald was innocent, and it was Pulchria who had the penchant for poison.

Edward sighed. 'I am glad we will soon be at Brechene. My knees ache today. It must be the cold weather.'

'And the fact that your saddle is on backwards,' said Geoffrey. 'It cannot be comfortable.'

'Is it?' Edward was astonished. 'Lord! That is what comes of rushing this morning. I was hoping Bale would help me, but he was busy with Pulchria.'

'Was he?' asked Geoffrey uneasily, glancing behind him to where the pair in question rode side by side. Bale was grinning rather inanely, and Pulchria seemed unusually content.

'Surely, you can saddle your own horse, Sir Edward,' said Hilde, laughing. 'You are a knight.'

'In name only, dear lady,' said Edward, unabashed. 'Although I do know horses. I bought this one in La Batailge and have been more than pleased with it.'

Geoffrey would not have been, because it was a poor animal that was easily winded. But he supposed it would suit someone like Edward, who was unlikely to push it too hard. He fell back to ride with Roger when he heard raised voices.

'My father is not a traitor,' the big knight was declaring hotly, while Sear's expression was vengeful. 'He is a godly, noble man.'

Geoffrey grabbed the reins of Roger's horse when it was not only Sear who started to laugh. The Bishop of Durham was one of the most unpopular men in the country, and Roger was alone in thinking he had virtues. Even Leah chuckled at the notion.

'Ride point with me,' he said, as Roger's hand dropped to the hilt of his dagger. 'Brechene cannot be far now, and it would be a pity to fall prey to an ambush.'

'What ambush?' snarled Roger. 'There has barely been a sniff of trouble since we left La Batailge, and I am disappointed, to tell you the truth. What is wrong with thieves these days, that they cannot stage a decent robbery? I itch to use my sword.'

'Yes,' said Geoffrey, suspecting he was about to use it on Sear. 'So we will let the others rest in Brechene, and we will spar a little.'

Roger nodded acquiescence and spurred his warhorse ahead of the main party. Fortunately, Edward was able to prevent Sear from following by initiating a conversation about hawks.

'How is your investigation?' asked Roger rather stiffly, when they were some distance ahead and could not be overheard.

'Only one thing is clear. If William did have a secret that turned him into a better person, it is not one he shared with anyone in this party.'

'Especially not Sear,' growled Roger.

Brechene was an impressive fortress under the command of an efficient Norman baron named Bernard de Neufmarché. It comprised a motte and bailey with enough outbuildings of wood and stone to house a substantial garrison. A short distance away was a Benedictine abbey, and the town was strewn between them. It was a pretty place, set in a gently wooded valley.

'I am not staying in another Benedictine house,' declared Roger. 'Not after La Batailge. We shall go to the castle.'

'It is not a good idea to take ladies into a fortress with a garrison,' said Geoffrey mildly. 'Although I imagine Pulchria would not mind.'

'I suspect she would, now she has Bale,' said Roger resentfully. 'God knows what they do of an evening, but she never has any energy for the rest of us.'

'God's teeth!' muttered Geoffrey. 'Does Cornald know?'

'He has not said anything. On the contrary, he has offered to show Bale how to make butter when we arrive in Kermerdyn, although we had better go with him, or he may "fall" inside some vile churning machinery and be chopped to pieces.'

'It would be no more than he deserves. What about an inn, then? That one looks reasonable.'

He pointed to a large, neat building with a thatched roof that looked big enough to house them all. It seemed respectable, with well-swept stables. Roger's eye strayed hopefully to the rather more dingy establishment opposite, where several scantily clad women hovered, eyeing passers-by with hungry speculation and shivering in the bitter wind that swept down from the hills.

'You can visit them later,' said Geoffrey. 'Take Bale with you. It may leave Pulchria free for her husband.'

Geoffrey's choice of inns did not meet with anyone's approval. Edward and Delwyn declared it too shabby; Sear, Alberic and Richard thought it too fancy; Gwgan sniffed that there were too many Englishmen; Cornald said it smelled of fish; and Pulchria was vexed because the landlord took one look at her and ordered her to behave herself on pain of eviction.

'The only one not complaining is Mabon,' said Geoffrey to Roger. 'And he is dead.'

'I am not complaining,' said Leah shyly. 'Ignore them, Sir Geoffrey. They would find fault with Nebuchadnezzar's Palace.'

'I have not been there,' said Roger, frowning. 'And I know

most of the Holy Land brothels. I am well acquainted with Abdul's Pleasure Palace, of course, which is—'

'You must be cold,' said Geoffrey, before Leah could be provided with details she would not want to hear. 'Let me escort you inside.'

The inn's main room was a pleasant place, with a clean floor, a high ceiling and a fire that did not smoke. It smelled comfortably of burning wood, new ale and damp wool. The landlord, a plump man in a white apron, offered them food. There was no meat on the menu because it was Friday; the choice was fish soup, pea pottage or bread with cheese.

'Fish soup!' exclaimed Richard, with an expression as close to pleasure as Geoffrey had yet seen. 'Excellent. We shall all have that.'

'We will not,' said Geoffrey firmly. He had never liked fish soup, but his aversion had intensified after someone had tried to poison him with some.

'Aye,' agreed Roger. 'We will have bread and cheese here, and then go across the road and see if they have any meat. That did not look like a place for silly Lenten customs.'

'And this from a son of a bishop,' murmured Gwgan. 'But I will have fish soup, landlord. Good and hot, if you please. I am chilled to the bone.'

The others ordered pea pottage, which transpired to be an unappetizing brown sludge. It was a considerable improvement on the fish soup, though, which reeked of ingredients past their best. Sear arrived just as everyone was finishing, because he had taken his horse to the stables. He ordered fish soup, and his face grew dark when he was told there was none left.

'You ate it all deliberately,' he said to Richard. 'You know it is my favourite.'

'I know nothing of the kind,' retorted Richard coldly. 'I have better things to do than recall your likes and dislikes. Besides, it was not very nice as it happens.'

'Well, I hope it makes you vomit,' said Sear.

Geoffrey braced himself to intervene, but Richard made no reply, indicating with a wave of his hand that he could not be bothered. He and Leah retired to their chamber shortly afterwards, and Sear and Alberic accompanied Roger to the brothel opposite. Cornald went to visit a fellow butterer in the town, Edward went to the castle to tell his garrison that they were to be ready to leave the following day, and Bale slipped away with Pulchria. Geoffrey heaved a sigh of relief, grateful to be rid of them all.

If Geoffrey had been hoping to enjoy some quiet time with Hilde, he was to be disappointed. She had no more started to tell him about the poor state of Goodrich's high summer pastures – not a subject that greatly interested him, but one that beckoned like paradise compared to the bickering of his companions – when Delwyn came to sit with them.

'I will share everything I know abut William fitz Baldwin's death if you let me give the Archbishop's letter to Ywain,' the monk said. 'He does not like me, but if I carry important documents from prelates, he cannot dismiss me as though I am nothing.'

'No,' said Geoffrey, tired of being asked. 'I have my orders.'

'Besides, I doubt you know anything of import about William, anyway,' said Hilde.

'Do I not?' bristled Delwyn. 'Well, you are wrong, because I know a lot. *I* was at his deathbed.'

'So was half of Kermerdyn,' goaded Hilde with calculated disdain. Geoffrey watched in astonishment; he knew exactly what she was doing and was amazed when the monk rose to the bait.

'I was there longer, because Abbot Mabon wanted a monk present, lest William needed spiritual comfort.' Delwyn sighed at her openly sceptical expression. 'All right, he left me there in case William mentioned his secret, and I have the sharpest ears in the monastery.'

'And what did your sharp ears tell you?' asked Geoffrey.

'That William most certainly *did* have a secret, and if anyone tells you otherwise, then he is lying or a fool. I heard it from his own lips that the secret was what made him good and holy. He wanted to tell his friends and family about it, so they could use it to the greater good. He said he had hidden it in a special place.'

'What special place?' demanded Hilde.

Delwyn's eyes flashed with annoyance at her tone. 'Unfortunately, I did not quite catch that part, although it must still be in Kermerdyn, because no one has become good and holy like him — and they would have done, had they claimed this secret for themselves.'

'Perhaps it does not work on everyone,' suggested Geoffrey.

'Oh, it will,' declared Delwyn with absolute conviction. 'Personally, I think it is something to do with the Blessed Virgin. Perhaps she gave him something. Regardless, I wish he had told *me* where he had put it. I would have—'

'Retrieved it and given it to your abbey?' asked Geoffrey mildly.

'Yes, of course,' said Delwyn unconvincingly. 'Or taken it to King Henry, who would have rewarded me.'

'I hardly think that information warrants my husband disobeying his King and giving you the Archbishop's letter,' said Hilde coolly. 'He already knew all this.'

'Then what about the fact that William *was* poisoned?' demanded Delwyn. 'And I know, because he told me so. I asked him whom he thought was responsible, and he said it was a dear friend. Well, his dear friends were Sear, Alberic, Edward, Mabon and Cornald. And his brother Richard, of course, whom he loved greatly.'

'Edward and Alberic were away when Richard died,' Geoffrey pointed out. 'They did not poison the butter.'

'Why assume the butter was responsible?' Delwyn shot back. 'Anyway, for all you know, the poison could have been left *before* they went on their patrol. William took days to die in sweating agony, so it was not a fast-acting substance. Now give me the letter.'

'No,' said Geoffrey curtly. 'You will have to find another way to worm yourself into Ywain's good graces.'

Delwyn's face hardened. 'You will be sorry you crossed me, Geoffrey Mappestone. I do not forget slights, and I will soon be in a position to do you serious harm.'

He scuttled away when Geoffrey started to come to his feet. Geoffrey could have caught him, but he was not worth the effort. Hilde shook her head in disgust.

'That did not help much,' said Geoffrey. 'I thought I had discounted Edward and Alberic as suspects, but Delwyn has just reinstated them on my list.'

'Not necessarily,' said Hilde. 'Think about it: no one else became ill from this poison, so it must have been in something eaten or drunk by William alone, and the butter still seems the obvious candidate. However, we *have* learned that the secret is probably real.'

'No,' said Geoffrey heavily. 'We have learned that William *thought* the secret was real, but he was raving, remember? I do not think I am capable of solving this case, Hilde. I only hope Henry does not vent his spleen on Goodrich when I tell him so.'

Hilde muttered soothing words, but Geoffrey could see she was concerned, too. They discussed the case until Gwgan came to join them, and although he felt they were going around in circles, it was good to have a trusted friend with whom to debate.

After a while, Gwgan persuaded Hilde to visit the market with him to buy homecoming gifts for Isabella, and Geoffrey asked the innkeeper where he might find a physician. He was directed to a house near the church, where a man named Huw plied his trade.

'You do not look as if you are in need of my services,' said Huw, a kindly, smiling man with a demeanour that inspired confidence. 'I have rarely seen a man more shining with health and vitality. Although I might recommend that you worry less and sleep more. You seem weary.'

Geoffrey suspected neither of those options was going to be available for a while. 'If I describe what I know of the death of a man who died before his time, could you give me a diagnosis?'

'No!' Huw laughed.

'Then will you be able to tell me whether poison might have played a part?'

Huw looked alarmed. 'Murder?'

Geoffrey told Huw all he had learned about William's demise, including the theory that butter might have been responsible. He described the days William had taken to die, during which he had been delirious. He also mentioned the seizures Pulchria had noted, the spells of vomiting observed by Gwgan, and the blackened fingers seen by Mabon, Richard and Cornald. When he had finished, Huw sat back thoughtfully.

'Vomiting, convulsions and blackening of the extremities are all signs of poisoning from bad grain. It is known by many names – ergot, fire-dance, wolf-tooth or rye-bane.'

'Wolf-tooth?' asked Geoffrey uneasily. 'There was wolf-tooth in a potion that killed another man recently, but he died very quickly.'

'Then something else was added to this potion, because wolf-tooth is not a rapid killer.'

Geoffrey thought about what Gwgan had said: that Mabon's tonic had included henbane, too. Did that mean the killer was someone skilled in the use of such substances – such as Gwgan? Or did it imply an amateur, who just added whatever deadly toxin was to hand?

'Is wolf-tooth ever used to kill rats?' asked Geoffrey, recalling what Pulchria had claimed about Joan's medical supplies – which Olivier had denied.

The apothecary's eyebrows went up. 'Not sensibly – there are far more effective substances for that.'

Geoffrey frowned. 'You said wolf-tooth is also called ergot. I was fed ergot not long ago, but my fingers did not turn black, nor did I have fits.'

'It depends how much was administered,' explained Huw. 'Clearly, yours was diluted, whereas your first victim was subjected to a much larger dose. Perhaps you are right, and it did reach him via butter – especially as no one else seems to have partaken of the stuff.'

'It was said to be rancid. The others must have tried a little or they would not have known.'

'A little might have had no discernible effect. Or perhaps the wolf-tooth was concentrated in one area – in the middle, perhaps – so that those paring off the edges were spared.'

'How would wolf-tooth come to be in the butter?'

Huw shrugged. 'It could have been added when the butter was churned, or later, when it was being delivered to your victim or while it sat unattended in the kitchen. Regardless, it is a vicious thing to have done, and I recommend you be on your guard if you are travelling with the person you suspect for this crime.'

Geoffrey had every intention of being careful. 'How easy is wolf-tooth to acquire?'

'Oh, very easy. You merely gather up the diseased grains. I do it myself; if applied properly, wolf-tooth can be a useful thera-peutic tool.'

'But such harvesting suggests the crime was premeditated.'

'Unquestionably. To collect and store wolf-tooth, then slip it into butter that might have been consumed by a large number of people . . . well, it suggests a callous ruthlessness.'

When Geoffrey returned to the inn, all his travelling companions except Richard and Edward were already there. Roger, Sear and Alberic were in high humour, the brothel having exceeded their expectations. Bale and Pulchria sat side by side with dreamy smiles on their faces, while Delwyn regaled them with complaints about the local abbey – they had taken one look at his filthy habit and declined to let him in. Gwgan appeared without a word and did not say where he had been, but his face was pale and he was in discomfort. Leah was lying down with a headache, and Cornald's tunic was spotted with crumbs from the repast he had enjoyed with his fellow butterer.

'You were right to avoid the fish soup,' said Richard, slumping down a few moments later, one arm across his middle. 'I think it was tainted. Trust you to select an inn that serves its guests rancid food, Geoffrey.'

Sear released a spiteful bray of laughter. 'Hah! Perhaps it is divine justice, because you failed to save me some. God struck you down for selfishness.'

'God had nothing to do with it,' said Gwgan in a quiet voice that was indicative of his own suffering. 'Neither did Geoffrey. Sometimes food is just bad.'

'I thought the soup smelled bad,' said Geoffrey. 'I was surprised you did not notice.'

'You let us eat rotten food?' snarled Richard. 'If I felt better, I would run you through!'

'I thought it smelled rotten, too,' said Delwyn smugly. 'But had I said so, you would have accused me of being girlish, so I held my tongue. Clearly, Sir Geoffrey and I have better noses for that kind of thing.'

He smiled ingratiatingly, which Geoffrey supposed was either a form of apology for his earlier threat or an effort to encourage him to lower his guard. Richard began to berate the landlord for providing putrid wares, although his diatribe came to an abrupt end when he was obliged to dash outside. Gwgan followed quickly, and Sear and Alberic sniggered at their discomfort.

'There was nothing wrong with my soup,' declared the innkeeper angrily. 'It was made from the finest trout giblets. Why do you think there was not much left? Because it is popular with my regulars, and they ate most of it before you arrived! None of *them* is ill.'

He stamped away, leaving Sear crowing about divine vengeance and Cornald defending the food industry by blaming the sickness on Richard and Gwgan drinking from streams. Then Edward arrived, his plump pink face a mask of consternation.

'We cannot linger in Brechene,' he said urgently, purple-gloved hands flapping in alarm. 'I have just been with Bernard de Neufmarché, and he tells me there is a contagion in the castle. Half my men have been affected, and he has ordered me to leave my whole garrison there, lest they carry the disease with them and spread it around the country.'

'What kind of contagion?' asked Delwyn uneasily, glancing to where Richard and Gwgan had just returned from the latrines.

'One that has the capacity to kill within hours,' said Edward. 'So I recommend we leave before we fall victim to it.'

Delwyn stood quickly, his face pale. 'Then let us go. I have heard about such agues, and I have no intention of succumbing to one myself. I will collect Abbot Mabon from the stable.'

'He is right,' said Richard, struggling to his feet. 'I do not want to be trapped here. I have been gone from Kermerdyn too long already. I never wanted to attend that silly ceremony in Gloucester – the King knows I am loyal; he does not require a scrap of parchment telling him so.'

'It gives him peace of mind to know he has loyal officers,' said Edward quietly. 'I am happy to sign and swear anything he likes.'

'He does not need anyone else when he has me,' declared Sear loftily. 'My loyalty is worth that of ten men, and I have never been asked to swear fealty. His Majesty knows it is not necessary.'

'You do not look well,' said Geoffrey to Richard and Gwgan, cutting across the argument he saw was about to begin. 'I have observed no signs of contagion in Brechene and see no harm in resting here until tomorrow.'

'I disagree,' said Cornald, crossing himself. 'We should all leave immediately, lest Bernard de Neufmarché decides to put the town under quarantine. We might be trapped here for weeks.'

'Then perhaps we *should* stay,' said Hilde quietly. She glanced at Richard and Gwgan. 'It would be unconscionable to carry a deadly disease to other parts of the country.'

'Gwgan and Richard do not have what had afflicted my men,' said Edward, crossing himself soberly. '*They* are completely covered in bleeding red blotches.'

Geoffrey had never seen his companions move so quickly, and whereas he and Roger were usually the first to be ready of a morning, they were last that day. Even Leah was there before them, her face pale and beaded with perspiration from the agony of her headache.

'This is not a good idea,' said Geoffrey, regarding her with concern. 'We should wait.'

'Do not worry about me,' whispered Leah, giving him a wan smile. 'I am used to these pains, and they will pass whether I lie in bed or sit astride a horse. It makes no difference.'

'Your husband should rest, too,' said Hilde. 'Or at least not stray too far from a—'

'He can manage,' interrupted Sear briskly. 'And so can Gwgan. They are both warriors and used to discomfort. We are not talking about monks here.'

Without further ado, Sear led them at a brisk canter out of Brechene, following a track that ran along the side of a wide, shallow river. Once clear of the town, he slackened the pace; the road was rutted and he did not want to spoil his horse. Geoffrey and Roger brought up the rear.

The first Geoffrey knew of trouble was a yell from Alberic, followed by a sudden hail of arrows. The path was narrow at that point, hemmed in by trees on one side and the river on the other, and there was scant room for manoeuvre. Sear and Alberic immediately raised their shields and prepared to ride towards the point of attack. Geoffrey opened his mouth to stop them – woods were no place for horsemen, and they would be killed by hidden archers – but they saw the danger for themselves, and his warning was unnecessary.

An arrow bounced off Geoffrey's shield and told him attackers were behind, as well as in front. Unfortunately, those in the middle of the convoy, which comprised servants, the women and Cornald, stopped dead in hopeless confusion. So far, the attack had focussed on the two ends of the cavalcade, where the knights were able to defend themselves with their shields, but Geoffrey sensed that would not last, and staying still would see them all shot.

'Ride on!' he yelled.

Fortunately, Sear and Alberic understood the reasons behind his orders and galloped forward to clear the way. Richard followed, although Gwgan took time to control his prancing horse, putting Hilde directly in the line of fire. Geoffrey watched in horror, certain the Welshman's ineptitude was going to see his wife dead. Then Edward spurred forward, placing himself and his shield between Hilde and the point of attack, and escorted her out of danger.

Delwyn and Pulchria screamed in terror, although Leah gamely put her head down and kicked her horse after her husband's. Delwyn's fear transmitted itself to his nag, which reared and threw him. With Roger howling like a Saracen behind him, Geoffrey grabbed the monk by the back of his habit and hauled him across his saddle, vaguely aware that Cornald had produced a small bow and was returning fire in a manner that suggested his paltry efforts at the competition had been a front.

Once safely away from the hail of arrows, Geoffrey threw Delwyn to the ground and galloped back towards the woods, aware of the attackers scattering before him. Roger was at his heels, and they almost succeeded in laying hold of one of the villains, but the fellow dived through a thicket of brambles, a place where Geoffrey had no intention of taking his horse.

'Shall we track them?' asked Roger, breathing hard from his exertions. He glanced around as Sear, Alberic, Bale and Edward joined them, ready to help. Richard and Gwgan were behind, although the pallor of their faces said they would not be much assistance.

Geoffrey shook his head. 'That might be what they are hoping for – leaving the baggage cart unattended.'

'But there is nothing on it except Abbot Mabon,' Sear pointed out.

'Yes, but they do not know that,' explained Geoffrey. 'It would not be the first time a coffin was used to transport riches, and I do not want to leave Hilde and the other women without protection.'

He expected Sear to argue, but the older knight merely inclined his head in acknowledgement and trotted away, taking Alberic with him. Bale looked disappointed that there was to be no bloodshed, but obediently trotted back to see whether Pulchria needed any comfort.

'I saw what you did,' said Geoffrey gratefully to Edward. 'Thank you for protecting Hilde.'

Edward smiled, but his unsteady seat in the saddle suggested he was already suffering from the weakness that often followed such incidents for those unused to them. Geoffrey handed him a flask that contained medicinal wine, and watched the colour seep back into the man's cheeks. Then he rode back and reorganized the column, with him and Roger at the front, and Sear and Alberic bringing up the rear.

'Sear and Alberic gave a good account of themselves,' said Roger begrudgingly, as they led the way out of the wood, alert for more trouble. 'I would not have expected it. Richard and Gwgan did not, though.'

'They are both unwell. It is unfair to judge them today,' said Geoffrey. 'Cornald reacted well, too. He began shooting at the robbers almost instantly.'

'I saw,' said Roger with a grin. 'Cunning old Cornald, hiding his talents! Do you think we should turn back? We escaped harm, by and large, but it will be dark soon.'

'There are lights ahead,' said Geoffrey. 'Let us hope the villagers are friendly.'

The villagers were not friendly, but Cornald's heavy purse encouraged them to let the travellers use a large barn, in which there was plenty of clean straw. Gwgan, Richard and Leah lay down immediately, and Roger lit a fire and began to prepare a basic meal. Geoffrey, Edward, Cornald, Sear and Alberic sat with him, recounting the relatively easy way they had defeated the ambush.

'Wisely, they concentrated their attack on us,' said Roger. 'They shot at the knights at the front and rear of the column, intending to dispatch the warriors first. Then, with us dead or incapacitated, they would have moved in on the cart and the women.'

'White surcoats,' said Alberic. 'We all wear white surcoats, which makes us easy targets.'

'Mine has a red Crusader's cross,' said Roger proudly. 'And so does Geoff's. We are different.'

'Not that different,' said Cornald. 'They are both rather grubby, and the crosses do not stand out as well as they did when we left Goodrich.'

'Perhaps we should don something else, then,' suggested Edward nervously. 'I have enough gowns for everyone. Perhaps if we wore no surcoats, the next attack would not be so fierce. I have a lovely red one that will suit you, Sear.'

'There will not be another ambush,' predicted Roger confidently, as Geoffrey struggled not to laugh at the image of Sear in a womanly kirtle. 'We saw the last one off with ease, and the villains will not risk a second one.'

'I do not want to think about it,' said Edward, accepting a bowl of soup from Roger with hands that still shook. 'I will not sleep a wink tonight.'

Geoffrey was just returning from a foray outside, on which he had circled the barn three times to ensure all was in order, when he saw Bale and Pulchria exchange a smouldering look, then aim for the shadows at the back of the building.

'Bale,' he said sharply, unwilling to stand by while his squire insulted the butterer quite so flagrantly. 'Sit with Roger.'

'But there is something I want him to do,' said Pulchria.

'I am sure there is,' said Geoffrey coolly. 'But he is not available.'

He nodded curtly to Bale, who looked from master to lover in dismay, but did as he was told, bald head well down so he would not have to see the disappointment in Pulchria's eyes.

'You have no right to interfere,' Pulchria hissed to Geoffrey, coming close so she would not be overheard. 'You declined my services in favour of your hag of a wife, but—'

'You would be advised to say no more, madam,' snapped Geoffrey with barely controlled anger. 'Or we both might regret it.'

The expression on his face told Pulchria she would be wise to back away, although she continued to glower. He glanced to where Hilde was talking to the servants, calming their uneasiness with her easy confidence. He felt a surge of affection for her, feeling he was much more fortunate in his spouse than Cornald was.

Restlessly, he went to stand in the doorway, scanning the darkness outside. He wished he still had his dog, knowing it would have growled to warn him of danger. He was not alone for long, though, because Delwyn came to join him.

'The next time you save me, perhaps you would do it a little more gently,' he said. 'I have a bruise where you grabbed me.'

'My apologies,' said Geoffrey caustically. 'If there is a next time, perhaps I shall not bother.'

'There is no need for that sort of talk.' Delwyn stepped closer. 'You are vexed, because I made a remark to you in anger earlier today, but I did not mean it. I would never harm you.'

'I am glad to hear it.'

'And to prove it, I have been considering William's murder for you. Would you like to hear my conclusions?'

'Only if they do not come accompanied with another demand for the Archbishop's letter.'

Delwyn grimaced. 'I think you should not confine your suspicions to the people in this barn – or the ones who are still alive. Do not dismiss Abbot Mabon from your musings, or Bishop Wilfred and Prince Hywel.'

'Right,' said Geoffrey tiredly.

Delwyn leaned closer still. 'And also bear in mind that Hywel is something of a saint, too. He is not as goodly as William was, but everyone likes him.'

'Was he "something of a saint" before William died?'

'I suppose he was, but you should not dismiss the possibility that he killed William for his secret and is now reaping the benefits.'

'Or perhaps he is just a decent man. They do occur from time to time.'

'Not in my experience,' said Delwyn. 'Of course, if Hywel *is* naturally godly, then it means William hid his secret well. I have searched Rhydygors thoroughly and found no sign of it.'

It was distasteful listening to the gossip of such a man, and Geoffrey cursed the King for obliging him to do so.

'Tell me who visited William when he was dying,' he instructed.

'Virtually the entire town. Most doubtless came to pay their respects to a fine man, and there was certainly a lot of weeping. They included Robert the steward, Osmund the stationer . . .'

The list continued for some time, and Geoffrey began to despair of ever finding the culprit, when his list of suspects was expanding into the dozens.

'The only people not there were Alberic and Edward, who were out on patrol – and they really did leave Kermerdyn, because twenty soldiers were able to confirm their alibi. I checked.'

'You suspected them?'

'I suspect everyone. The other person who cannot be a suspect is Leah. She had a fever and could not leave her bed. Her physician confirms the tale, and so does her health – she has never fully recovered and remains frail.'

'Tell me about the day William was taken ill. You were talking to the Bishop in the kitchens where the rancid butter was. Why? I thought your abbey was at war with Wilfred.'

'*Mabon* was at war with the Bishop,' replied Delwyn. 'If you must know, I was offering Wilfred information about the abbey in an attempt to bring Mabon down. It is not healthy for the Church to indulge in internal squabbles. I acted as my conscience dictated.'

'You betrayed the man you said you loved as a father?' asked Geoffrey.

Delwyn's face creased into a sneer. 'I *did* love him like a father – it just so happens that I hated my sire, damn his evil soul.'

'Go away, Delwyn,' said Geoffrey in distaste. 'You cannot speak without lying and scheming, and I am sick of it. Stand back!'

'I stand where I like,' declared Delwyn. 'It is not for you to—'

The rest of his sentence was lost as Geoffrey shoved him in the chest, bowling him from his feet and dropping into a fighting stance as he did so, sword in one hand and dagger in the other. Seeing him, Roger kicked out his fire and flew to his side. Sear and Alberic were not far behind, and Edward leapt to his feet with an uneasy whimper. Cornald grabbed his bow.

'What is it?' whispered Roger, silencing Delwyn's outraged spluttering with a glare.

'Someone is out there,' replied Geoffrey softly.

Sear relaxed. 'It will be one of the villagers checking on their animals – or checking we are not stealing their wretched pigs. You saw how unwilling they were to house us—'

He stopped speaking when an arrow thudded into the door above his head.

With a wild cry, Sear launched himself into the night, Roger and Alberic at his heels. Geoffrey was more concerned with defence than attack: the arrow was alight, and the intention was clearly to set the barn ablaze and incinerate everyone within. He raced for the bucket of water the villagers had provided, and dashed it over the flames, but they had no more sizzled out before another fire-arrow took its place.

'There!' said Hilde, stabbing a finger in the direction from which the missile had sailed. 'Go and stop him, Geoff. I will deal with the fire.'

Geoffrey did not waste time arguing. He sped across the darkened yard, jerking back when another flaming arrow passed so close to him that he felt its heat sear his face. Then he was among a pile of broken barrels, and two shadows, both carrying bows, were running away. He hared after them, but they were fleet-footed and terrified, and mail-clad Norman knights were not built for speed. He managed to jab one with his outstretched sword, but his companion whipped around with his bow. Geoffrey staggered as it caught him in the face, and lost momentum, which was just enough time for the pair to escape into the surrounding woods.

'They were too fast for us,' said Roger, coming to join him a moment later. 'But they were soldiers of a sort – they wore leather jerkins, or at least two of them would be dead.'

'Three,' said Geoffrey. Armour explained why his jab had done so little damage.

'Sear and Alberic are scouting the woods,' said Roger. 'We should help them.'

Geoffrey obliged, and by the time they converged to report that the attackers had gone, Hilde had doused the flames and was kneeling next to Edward, whose face was contorted with pain.

'It is not serious,' she was saying. 'The arrow has just scored a furrow in your arm. Clean water and a little salve will see it right in a day or two.'

'Well, it hurts,' said Edward weakly. 'I was not built for this kind of thing.'

'And I was not built to be knocked around by bullying knights,' said Delwyn to Geoffrey. 'You did not have to shove me quite so hard. I shall have *another* bruise tomorrow.'

'He should not have shoved you at all,' said Cornald, his face uncharacteristically cool. 'And then you might be lying here instead of Edward.'

'This would not have happened if my troops had been here,' said Edward. 'We would have posted guards, and robbers would have come nowhere near us.'

'Your rabble?' asked Richard unpleasantly. 'I doubt they would have made any difference. They are not as good as *my* men.'

'You were very brave, Edward,' said Pulchria kindly. 'Your quick thinking in shutting the door saved us all; those archers would have had arrows in us otherwise.'

'It is true, sir,' said Bale to Geoffrey. 'Several bowmen appeared near the door when you dashed after the others, and I ran towards them, but Sir Edward shoved the door closed, so they could not fire in on us. They would have killed me, Richard, Gwgan *and* the ladies, and he took an arrow protecting us.'

'Were they the same ones who ambushed us earlier?' asked Cornald.

'I could not tell,' said Gwgan. His face was white, and he looked as though he might be sick. 'They were just shadows. I am sorry I was useless, Geoffrey. These pains in my innards make it difficult to stand, let alone fight.'

'What did they want?' asked Edward shakily. 'Burning down the barn was not sensible; anything of value would have been consumed in the flames, along with us.'

'Not if we dashed outside to escape, carrying our fortunes with us,' Roger pointed out. 'I imagine the aim was to have us all silhouetted by the flames, so we could be picked off.'

'Strange,' mused Gwgan. 'Surely, they would have questioned the villagers first and learned that we carry a dead abbot in the coffin, not treasure. Unless they are interested in the butter-making equipment Cornald bought in Brechene.'

'They might be,' said Cornald. 'It was expensive. And do not deceive yourself that robbers are only interested in gold and jewellery. Our country is poor, and even a decent cloak is a worthy prize to many men.'

'*Were* they the same men?' asked Roger in an undertone to Geoffrey.

Geoffrey nodded. 'Yes, I think so.'

'I was bored travelling between La Batailge and Brechene,' said Roger with a rather diabolical grin. 'But things are definitely picking up. I love a decent skirmish.'

'Well, I hope it is not going to happen every few hours,' said Geoffrey tiredly. 'Because it will be a very long journey, if so.'

'Aye lad,' said Roger. 'But what fun!'

Nine

It was the end of another glorious day. The setting sun was a glowing amber ball in a haze of blue sky and salmon-tinged clouds, which presaged well for the morning. A blackbird sang somewhere in the forest, its voice a clear, clean trill above the lower murmur of the river, and the air was rich with the scent of damp earth and fallen leaves. Geoffrey breathed in deeply, feeling the satisfaction of having travelled a decent distance that day.

It had been two days since the last attack, although he was too experienced a traveller to assume their assailants had given up. He still had no idea what led the motley band to harry them with such dogged determination – another six skirmishes ensued after the incident in the barn – and he could only conclude that one of his companions had done something seriously wrong in Brechene. But no one would admit it, and he had other matters to occupy his thoughts.

He had concluded that William fitz Baldwin *had* been murdered seven years before, and the poison had almost certainly been in the butter. Despite Delwyn's efforts to make him think otherwise, he strongly suspected that the killer was from a pool of Delwyn, Sear, Gwgan, Cornald and Pulchria. He had discounted Edward, Alberic, Leah and Richard – the first three because they had either been away or confined to bed when William had become ill, and Richard because it was clear he had loved his brother far too deeply to have harmed him.

Geoffrey had reached no firm conclusions about William's secret, however. Sear and Alberic thought it was a mystical weapon; Mabon had believed it was something that had happened in the river, perhaps a vision; Pulchria still maintained William had discovered a potent herb; and Delwyn said it was a gift from the Virgin Mary. Richard also thought the Blessed Virgin was involved, and Cornald continued to claim that William had learned how to eat himself happy. Edward was firm in his conviction that there was no secret, and Gwgan laughingly asserted that William's saintliness was all to do with him being in Wales.

As regards Mabon's murder, Geoffrey's suspects were Sear, Gwgan, Cornald, Pulchria and Alberic. He was inclined to dismiss Richard, Edward and Leah on the grounds of Father Adrian's testimony, and Delwyn had too much to lose by his abbot's death.

He was also convinced that Eudo had indeed tampered with his letters to Tancred, and he was now even more determined to travel to the Holy Land and set matters right – the moment Maurice released him from his vow. He had mulled over Eudo's untimely demise, too, and thought it not entirely impossible that Eudo's killer was among his travelling companions. One of them had killed William and Mabon, so why not Eudo?

The party was quiet that day, each longing for the journey to end. Roger, riding at the front next to him, had enjoyed a late night in a brothel and was still suffering from an excess of wine. So were Sear and Alberic, who were bringing up the rear.

In the middle, Edward was entertaining Pulchria and Leah with an amusing story, while Richard slouched next to him. Gwgan was with Hilde, listening to embarrassing revelations about Isabella's childhood with an indulgent smile. Behind them, Delwyn was gabbling at Cornald, who was pretending to be asleep.

'I have enjoyed the journey from Brechene,' said Roger eventually. 'I like a decent skirmish.'

'I do not – not when my wife is with me.'

'Eight separate incidents,' said Roger. 'Each one fiercer and more determined than the last.'

'It is a pity Edward's soldiers were ill,' said Geoffrey. 'They would have been useful.'

'Not if they fight like him,' said Roger scathingly. 'Although I suppose his quick thinking did prevent Hilde and the others from being cut down in the barn.'

'And he saved her in the first attack,' added Geoffrey. 'He may not be a warrior, but there is no question of his courage.'

'Aye,' acknowledged Roger reluctantly. 'And Sear, Alberic and Richard cannot be faulted in that respect, either. Gwgan has proved himself useful, too. He may not be a knight, but he is better in a fight than any other politician I have met.'

'He might not have survived the journey, had he not been,' said Geoffrey. 'Every one of the ambushes has concentrated on dispatching anyone in a white surcoat first.'

'I noticed that, too. So I told him to wear something else, but he pointed out that it would be mean more arrows for the rest of us – that it would be numerically safer if the attacks were aimed at seven men, rather than six.'

'I hope they do not harry us on the way home,' said Geoffrey.

'There will be no trouble going home,' said Roger with utter conviction. 'Because *you* will not have the letters. I have been thinking about it for several days now, and I am sure I am right.'

Geoffrey blinked. 'What are you talking about? Robbers are not interested in what Henry has to say to vassals. Or do you think they are interested in preventing Maurice from telling Isabella where to buy raisins?'

Roger shot him an unpleasant look. 'It is obvious from our baggage that we carry little of value – unless you happen to have a penchant for rotting corpses.'

'I told you – they probably see the coffin as a ruse.'

'But they have been nowhere near the coffin – they aimed for *us*. Besides, how many robbers do you know who wear armour? They are soldiers, not outlaws, and they were after the letters.'

'That is not possible, Roger. No one but you and Hilde knows I have them.'

'Delwyn found out about the one to his abbot, and you gave missives to Gwgan and Richard in Goodrich. I would say it is obvious that you have more. Why else would you be going to Kermerdyn?'

Geoffrey gazed at him. Was he right? But ambushing a cavalcade of six knights seemed an extreme way to prevent them from being delivered – and they had had no trouble at all between La Batailge and Brechene. Or did that explain why the attacks had concentrated on the knights, rather than the baggage cart; the intention was to kill the King's messenger, but all knights tended to look alike, so the villains were obliged to target them all?

'Do you still have them?' asked Roger. 'They have not fallen out?'

'No,' replied Geoffrey shortly.

It was not the first time Roger had posed the question, and it was beginning to make him nervous: he found himself constantly checking they were still there. He was not overly concerned about the one to Mabon's successor, but he suspected Henry would be furious if Wilfred's was lost, given that it involved money. And he was beginning to suspect that Sear's was important, too, or Henry would not have issued such peculiar instructions for its delivery.

'Good,' said Roger. 'The moment you have handed them over, we shall take the first ship we can find. Tancred will forgive you for any misunderstandings and will welcome us into his service. And then you will never have to accept a commission from Henry again.'

'And what about my wife?' asked Geoffrey. 'Do I abandon her in Kermerdyn?'

Roger shrugged. 'From our experiences so far, I would suggest she is safer without you. Or perhaps Tancred will find her a post. With a few women like Hilde in his army, he would not need the likes of us.'

It was not long before the forest track emerged into more open countryside, where farmers had cleared away trees for crops. It was good land, made fertile by the meandering River Tywi, and the stubble indicated the harvest had been good that year.

'Lanothni,' said Hilde, pointing along the track to where a huddle of houses clustered around a simple little church. 'I remember it from when I last visited my sister. The beds were clean, although the food left something to be desired.'

She urged her horse forward to lead the way. People came out of their houses to stare, unused to such large parties. Geoffrey saw recognition flash in the eyes of several when they settled on Hilde, and supposed she had said or done something to be remembered. He braced himself for trouble – she could be sharp-tongued when something displeased her. Unerringly, she rode towards the handsome building that stood next to the church. It was neat, clean, and had a tiled roof. A man emerged to see what was going on.

'Lady Hilde,' he said, his face falling. He swallowed audibly. 'What a . . . a nice surprise.'

Hilde inclined her head. 'And your name is Fychan.'

'Yes,' said the man uneasily. 'Landlord of this fine inn. Will you be wanting to stay again? Despite all the complaints you levied last time?'

'I imagine you have rectified those,' said Hilde loftily. 'You have had two years.'

Fychan gulped again, then shouted for boys to come and tend to the horses. The travellers dismounted and followed him into a low-ceilinged chamber, full of wood-smoke and the scent of roasting meat. There were fresh rushes on the floor, and the dogs that lounged near the fire were clean and sleek. It was far nicer than anywhere else they had stopped, and Geoffrey felt hopeful it would meet his wife's exacting demands.

Hilde looked around appraisingly. 'Yes,' she said eventually. 'It will suffice.'

Villagers were ousted from the tables nearest the hearth to make room for the newcomers, although Geoffrey would have preferred a seat by the door. It was warm in the room, and he knew he would quickly become uncomfortable in armour and padded surcoat. Politely, Edward saw the ladies and Delwyn settled, then claimed the next best seat for himself, quickly divesting himself of what little armour he wore and exchanging it for a long robe that matched his gloves.

'You have been here before, too, sir,' said Fychan, addressing Sear as he served his guests with a platter of roasted meat, bread and a peculiar mash of boiled vegetables that Geoffrey suspected had been prepared for the pigs. 'I recognize your fine warhorse.'

'The King gave it to me,' replied Sear smugly. 'I am one of his favourites. Which is why it is strange that Geoffrey was entrusted with the business His Majesty wanted done in Kermerdyn. There was no need for him to have made this journey.'

'Well, I am glad he did,' said Hilde mildly. 'It has been two years since I saw Isabella, and I am eager to know how she fares.'

'Is she anything like you?' asked Roger, a little warily.

'No,' replied Hilde shortly. 'She is thinner.'

'She shares your love of cleanliness, though,' said Alberic. 'Gwgan's home is always spotless. And your love of water has certainly rendered Geoffrey more congenial company, Lady Hilde. He let himself grow filthy between La Batailge and Goodrich, but now he wears clean clothes, shaves, and even washes on occasion.'

This was certainly true – Hilde's fastidiousness extended to her husband as well as taverns – but Geoffrey did not think it was polite of Alberic to remark on it.

'Then you could do with a wife, too,' said Hilde frostily, before her husband could respond. 'Do not criticize Geoffrey when you leave rather a lot to be desired yourself.'

'Nonsense!' cried Alberic, stung. 'I washed just a week ago. Geoffrey, on the other hand, would probably not have seen a bowl of water since he left the Holy Land, were it not for you.'

'Well, he is perfectly tidy now, and we should say no more on the matter,' said Edward, ever tactful. 'I should like to visit the Holy Land. Will you tell us about it, Geoffrey?'

'*I* will,' offered Roger eagerly. 'It is a lovely place, full of willing whores and fabulous brothels. What are the brothels like in Kermerdyn? Are they worth visiting?'

'I would not know,' said Edward in distaste. 'I do not frequent such places.'

'I do,' said Sear. 'The one by the church is better than the one in the market.'

'Is it?' asked Richard, startled. 'I always thought it was the other way around. Of course, I have not visited a brothel in years – not since I was married. You should take a wife, Roger. You will find they are cheaper than whores. I would not be without mine.'

'I imagine that rather depends on the wife,' said Delwyn, lips pursed.

'And the whores,' drawled Gwgan, smothering a smile.

Talk of whores reminded Geoffrey of Pulchria, and he looked for her, but she was not in the tavern. Bale was still outside seeing to the horses, and Geoffrey stifled a sigh, knowing the woman was taking advantage of the situation. Cornald had not seemed to have noticed her absence and was stretching his plump hands towards the fire, humming to himself.

'Richard knows as much about brothels as he does about soldiering,' said Sear unpleasantly. 'You want to listen to me, Roger. *I* know what I am talking about.'

'I have a headache,' said Leah quickly, as Richard surged to his feet, sword half out of its scabbard. 'Will you take me upstairs, husband? I need to rest.'

Richard obliged, although he did so reluctantly; it was clear he would much rather have challenged Sear. Geoffrey thought Leah was right to distract him: Richard was competent, but Sear would chop him into pieces.

'Is there anything in the Holy Land besides brothels?' asked Cornald pleasantly. 'There must be plenty of churches.'

'Churches?' echoed Roger in disbelief. 'You do not want to hear about those! But do you remember Abdul's Pleasure Palace, Geoff?'

Because they had stopped early, a long evening lay ahead of them. Geoffrey's descriptions of Jerusalem's churches had intrigued Gwgan, who responded about some in Wales. Edward added several intelligent observations, and the three of them were soon deep into a complex analysis of flying buttresses and crown posts. The others quickly grew bored.

Cornald berated Delwyn for leaving Abbot Mabon in the yard when there was a church to hand, and Delwyn responded with a snipe about Cornald not being in a position to offer advice about how to look after others when he was so patently bad at it himself. Cornald looked bewildered, although it gave Roger an idea. He jumped to his feet and made a feeble excuse about taking the air. Moments later, Bale appeared, rumpled and sullen. Sear and Alberic settled to a game of dice, and Richard joined them when he returned from settling Leah. The atmosphere around the three of them was tense and icy, and Geoffrey suspected it would not be long before there was a fight.

'You will be pleased to see Hywel, I warrant,' said Edward amiably to Gwgan. 'I am sure you will want to know what has been happening in your absence.'

Gwgan smiled. 'I *will* be glad to see him. He is like a brother to me, and I am proud to serve as his counsellor. But he does not require constant monitoring. He is wise, just and good, and there is no man I trust more to rule a kingdom.'

'William was the same,' said Edward, nodding. 'Perhaps living at Rhydygors brings out the best in people.'

'Or Hywel has inherited William's secret,' probed Geoffrey.

'There is no secret,' said Edward. 'I have told you this already
– it is a silly tale invented by foolishly gullible minds to explain
something they cannot understand. Namely that some men *do*
suddenly reflect on their past lives and decide it is time to turn
over a new leaf.'

Gwgan agreed. 'And if there *is* a secret, then it lies in the fact
that this is Wales. Hywel is a good man, but he was decent long
before he was given Rhydygors.'

'He did not undergo some miraculous change, then?' asked
Geoffrey. 'Like William?'

'Oh, no,' said Gwgan. 'Hywel has always been decent.'

'In what way?' asked Geoffrey.

'Well, his men admire him and will follow him into any battle
– as you will have heard last summer, when he fought on the
Marches for Henry. He inspires confidence and respect, and he has
an affable, likable disposition. He is compassionate to those less
fortunate than himself, he is devout, and he exudes an aura of fair-
ness that tells men he will deal honestly with them.'

'It is true,' agreed Edward. 'You will like him, Geoffrey. Indeed,
I would go as far to say that there is no man – Norman, English
or Welsh – that I would sooner have as a neighbour. But it is
getting late, and my wound still pains me. I shall bid you good-
night.'

Gwgan stood and stretched, too. 'I am weary, too. But I have
friends in the village, so will stay with them tonight. This tavern
is too small for all of us, and I am tired of sharing a chamber
with Sear and Alberic. They both snore.'

'So does Leah,' said Richard, overhearing. 'Especially when she
has taken her medicines. I will join you.'

As they opened the door to leave, Roger stepped inside, straightening his surcoat and pulling straw from his hair. Immediately,
Bale aimed for the door, but Geoffrey was disinclined to stop
him. If Cornald chose to be blind to his wife's antics, then that
was his affair.

'I heard what Gwgan and Edward were telling you about
Hywel,' said Alberic, looking up from his dice. 'It is true: he *is* a
fine man.'

'He is,' agreed Sear. 'He was awarded Rhydygors at the same
time I was granted Pembroc, so we travelled to Westminster

together. It gave us time to get to know each other. He is brave, as well as noble. Like me, he fought courageously on the Marches. You two were there, too, I understand.'

The implication was that Roger and Geoffrey had not performed well enough to have been rewarded. Roger immediately bristled, but Geoffrey laid a calming hand on his shoulder.

'It is very warm in here,' he said, to change the subject. 'I am surprised you think it necessary to have such an enormous blaze, Master Fychan.'

Fychan glared at Hilde. 'Yes, but, unfortunately, I have been told by *visitors* that a welcoming fire makes an important first impression. And I dare not disagree.'

'That was because I was here in winter,' said Hilde with a sigh. 'And a dead hearth is not something a traveller wants to see when she arrives cold and wet.'

She and Fychan began to argue about the proper heights for fires at various times of year, and when Sear and Roger added their opinions, the conversation quickly grew acrimonious. Geoffrey did not join in. Now they were almost at their destination – Kermerdyn was no more than eight miles distant – he found himself pondering yet again about the tasks the King had set him. He let the angry voices wash over him, abrogating responsibility to Hilde to prevent spillages of blood.

Eventually, when he could stand the heat and the bickering no longer, Geoffrey rose, muttering about checking his destrier. He stood outside, breathing in deeply of the smoke-scented air, which carried with it a hint of frost in the offing as daylight faded to dusk. Then he went to the stable, reaching for his dagger when he saw two figures lurking in an empty stall.

'Go inside, Bale,' he ordered curtly, not liking to imagine what would have been said if it had been Cornald coming to look at the horses.

Head down so he would not have to meet his master's eyes, Bale scuttled away. Pulchria was less easily intimidated, though.

'You have no right to interfere,' she hissed.

'I have every right: Bale is my squire. But it is cold and dark out here, so I recommend you go inside, too. Doubtless your husband will be pleased to see you.'

He treated her hate-filled glower with the contempt it deserved, turning his back on her and giving his attention to his horse. A moment later, he heard her stamp towards the door. He spent a little while with the animal, rubbing its nose and checking its legs for signs of damage, but the raised voices from the inn were distracting. Craving silence, he walked towards the river.

The Tywi was wide and shallow, with golden stones littering its bottom and the occasional waving frond of green weed. It wound across a wide valley, much of which was cultivated, although he suspected it was prone to flood, when it would lose its gentleness and become a raging torrent. Two uprooted trees nearby indicated it probably happened frequently.

He thought about Roger's contention that the attacks they had suffered since leaving Brechene were connected to the King's letters. Roger had been concerned from the first ambush that the attack had concentrated on the knights, but Geoffrey had argued it was because their assailants wanted to eliminate the warriors before turning to the easier business of dealing with the women, servants, Cornald and Delwyn. But did Roger have a point?

Delwyn was sloppy in his care of Mabon's coffin, and it would have been easy for thieves to make off with it at night, assuming – as Geoffrey believed – that they thought it was filled with treasure. Yet they had never bothered. Did it mean the ambushers *were* after something else? But, surely, no one could be interested in a letter to Wilfred about the transfer of property or an order telling Mabon to obey the Bishop, or in whatever was written in the missive to Sear?

Geoffrey sighed. More urgent was the fact that he was almost in Kermerdyn, and although he had spent weeks in company with people he suspected had killed William, Mabon and possibly Eudo, he was no nearer finding the truth. Soon they would part company, and he would never have answers for the King.

As he stared at the river, he became aware that one of the stones was an odd shape. He leaned down to retrieve it, plunging his arm up to the elbow in cold water. He was startled to find it was a small statue. He had seen similar ones in Italy, carved by the Romans, and he recalled Gwgan telling him that Romans had visited Kermerdyn and established a fort there. He gazed at the little sculpture, awed to be holding something that had been crafted hundreds of years before.

It was a pretty piece, and he recognized in it Aphrodite's alluring beauty. It was made of marble, and when he rubbed it on his surcoat, the algae came off to reveal the white underneath. It was not very big, although too large to close his fingers around. He decided to keep it and present it to Hilde at some opportune moment. Perhaps this pagan charm would help her conceive, given that prayers in churches did not seem to be working.

He was about to return to the tavern when he saw Delwyn walking towards him. The monk was pulling uncomfortably at his habit, and his face was red. Geoffrey was not the only one who had found the room unpleasantly close.

'Your return to Kermerdyn tomorrow will be tainted by sadness,' said Geoffrey, thinking he had better remind Delwyn that he was sorry Mabon had died while a guest in his home. He did not want the abbey being told he did not care, so they could complain to the King about him. 'I wish that we had brought his killer to justice.'

'It would have been good to string the villain up,' agreed Delwyn. 'He condemned me to a miserable journey, because it has not been pleasant, toting a rotting corpse around.'

Geoffrey tried to conceal his distaste for the man's selfishness. 'It will be a sad homecoming, regardless of odours. I imagine Mabon was popular.'

'Then you would be wrong. He was rather worldly, and most of my brethren will be delighted to learn he is no longer with us. Especially Ywain.' Delwyn looked concerned. 'I hope he does not think *I* killed Mabon.'

'Why would he think that?'

'Because I was always complaining about the fact that Mabon would insist on aggravating Wilfred. But he *was* wrong to annoy the Bishop — it is no way to ensure we are left alone.'

'Left alone?' asked Geoffrey, puzzled

'Allowed to exist,' elaborated Delwyn. 'Without Normans coming along and trying to turn us into Benedictines or Cistercians. We are happy as we are, but Mabon's belligerence was a danger.'

'Will Ywain be less confrontational?'

'Oh, yes,' said Delwyn bitterly. 'He is no brash fool. But I would like to impress him anyway. *Please* give me the letter from the Archbishop, Sir Geoffrey. He will be much more kindly disposed towards me if he sees the King trusted me with it.'

'I cannot,' said Geoffrey shortly. He did not want yet another debate on the subject.

'Do you have any more?' asked Delwyn rather desperately. 'You *must* have a missive for Hywel. He is the most important man in this region, after all. Give me the one for him.'

Geoffrey shook his head, hoping Hywel would not be offended when he learned that Henry had not deigned to acknowledge him.

Delwyn sighed heavily. 'You are a hard man, Sir Geoffrey. I can only pray that it will not count against you when your sins are weighed on Judgement Day. And that may come sooner than you think, given the way that you court danger.'

'I do not court danger,' said Geoffrey, wondering whether he was being threatened.

Delwyn regarded him haughtily. 'Then you have nothing to worry about.'

And, with that enigmatic remark, he sauntered away.

Hilde had obtained four separate chambers on the upper floor, with hay-filled stable lofts for the servants. Geoffrey was uncomfortable when Hilde confided that the one for them was the landlord's own, but she assured him that Fychan had not minded going to sleep in the kitchen.

Privacy was rare while travelling, and it was not often they had the luxury of a separate room. Usually, Roger and Bale were with them, which Geoffrey did not mind – it was safer with three of them listening for signs of trouble as they slept – although Hilde was less sanguine about the arrangement and preferred nights when they could be alone.

'I shall be glad when Roger leaves,' she remarked, as she doused the candle and slid into the bed, in the now pitch-black room. 'God save us, Geoffrey! You are still wearing boots and full armour! We will not make an heir with fifty pounds of steel and leather between us.'

'You want me to take them off?' asked Geoffrey uneasily. He rarely divested himself of his mail when travelling.

'If you would not mind. Besides, I am cold, and snuggling up to metal is hardly pleasant.'

'I would not know,' muttered Geoffrey, prising himself out of the bed to oblige. It did not take long, although he felt cold and strangely naked without his mail, and shivered as he climbed back into the bed. Then he winced. 'Are you still wearing a dagger?'

'I like one readily available on a journey,' she replied, placing an ice-cold hand on his stomach. He was hard-pressed not to fling it off, and strongly suspected the gesture was more to warm it up than for affection.

'Why will you be glad when Roger leaves?' he asked.

Hilde sighed. 'I know you have been through many battles together and saved each other's lives more often than you can count, but I cannot take to him. He is uncouth, greedy, dishonest and ruthless. Did you know that he regularly rifles through your saddlebags?'

'Yes.' It was a habit Roger had acquired in the Holy Land. Geoffrey did not care, because he rarely had anything that Roger coveted, but Hilde objected to her possessions being mauled. 'However, he is not doing the searching now – it is Delwyn, although he denies it.'

'Roger is always saying that your literacy is a skill learned from the Devil,' Hilde went on, declining to be sidetracked. 'And Bale said that, in Brechene, he even paid a witch for a spell to make you forget how to read. He thinks that if you are stupid, Henry will leave you alone.'

'Then he will want his money back,' said Geoffrey, laughing. 'Because the spell did not work.'

'Spells are dangerous,' said Hilde angrily. 'I shall never forgive him if you are turned into a drooling idiot.'

There was not much to be said to such a remark, so Geoffrey closed his eyes and waited for sleep to take him. Hilde had other ideas.

'Are you comfortable with *him* releasing you from your vow?'

'What?' asked Geoffrey, wondering whether he had dropped off and missed some vital part of the conversation. 'Roger?'

'Bishop Maurice,' said Hilde impatiently. 'From what I hear, he is rather worldly, and God may not accept his intervention. You may bring His wrath down on yourself. Or on Goodrich.'

Geoffrey rubbed his chin. 'I know. I have never broken a vow before – it is why I keep wearing my Crusader's surcoat, when common sense urges anonymity. I did not know sacred oaths *could* be retracted until Maurice told me it was possible.'

'Well, you did swear it against your will. But you must be sure that Maurice *does* possess the authority to absolve you, because if you make a mistake, you might have to undertake another Crusade to make up for it. And I would miss you.'

He could tell from her voice that she was smiling, and wished he could see her face, because it was an expressive one. He found himself wanting to know whether she was smiling fondly, or whether she was teasing him and rather liked the idea of an absent husband. He moved towards her, then wished he had not when her dagger jabbed him a second time.

'Perhaps I should make you promise not to leave me until we have an heir,' she said. 'That would keep you safely in England, especially as it seems a somewhat lengthy process.'

'We could try again now,' he suggested.

Immediately, there came the sound of laces being unfastened and brooches being unsnapped. While he waited, Geoffrey listened to the other sounds of the night – an owl in the distance, the wind in the eaves. Roger, Alberic and Sear were still in the room below; their voices were loud, and he could tell they were drunk. Out in the stables, a horse whinnied suddenly, and he supposed Bale and Pulchria were using the stable again.

He thought a floorboard creaked outside their door, but Hilde hurled some garment to the floor at the same time, and he could not be sure. He sat up abruptly, straining to hear, then flopped back again when his head cracked against Hilde's in the darkness.

'What are you doing?' she demanded angrily. 'That really hurt.'

Geoffrey signalled for her to be quiet, but she did not see him and continued to berate him in a voice that made it difficult to hear anything else.

'Hush!' he snapped. 'I thought I heard something.'

At that moment, there was a cheer from downstairs, followed by a lot of jeering. Roger had won something – no great surprise, given that he always cheated.

'I really will be glad when he is no longer with us,' Hilde muttered.

Geoffrey sat up a second time when the merest of draughts touched his cheek; he knew the door was open. Reacting instinctively, he grabbed Hilde and hauled her off the bed, snatching the dagger from her belt as he did so. At the same time, he heard something thud into the mattress. Most other women would have screeched indignantly about being hurled around in the dark, but Hilde was blessedly silent. There was an advantage to marrying a woman who was a warrior.

Geoffrey was also silent. Then he heard the creak of a floorboard, this time to his left. He stabbed with the dagger, thinking that if someone was coming to rob them, then any injuries were the culprit's own fault.

He heard a grunt as the blade connected, although he could not tell whether it had done any harm. He stepped forward, to place himself between the invader and Hilde. There was another creak, and he lunged again. This time, the dagger met thin air, but something crashed into his shoulder, making him stagger. He went on the offensive, suspecting he might not survive if he confined himself to defensive manoeuvres. He struck out wildly, moving towards the door as he did so, aiming to haul it open and yell for Roger.

Then something cracked into his head, and he saw stars. He lunged again, but he was disoriented, and the blow lacked the vigour of the previous ones. He had his attackers on the run, though, because he could hear footsteps moving away. He tried to estimate how many sets of feet, but it was difficult to be sure.

He sensed rather than saw someone flail at him, and fought by instinct, predicting which way the blows would come and parrying them with his forearm as he jabbed with the dagger. There was a howl and a curse, and then more footsteps. He became aware of Hilde next to him. She grabbed his arm, and he felt his sword shoved into his hand.

Howling his Saracen battle cry, he charged forward and saw at least three shadows in the hallway. How many were there, given that several had already fled? He swiped wildly, but he was dizzy and blood dripped into his eyes. He brushed it away impatiently, then whipped around when he heard someone behind him. A blow across the shoulders drove him to his knees.

He was not sure what happened next. He tried to tell Roger

to give chase, but he could not make himself heard over the racket. He attempted to go himself, but his legs would not support him. He thought he heard Sear and Alberic coming to report that the culprits had disappeared, and was also aware of Pulchria regarding him in a distinctly unfriendly manner. Surely, she had not organized the attack, because she had objected to him depriving her of Bale?

He rubbed his head, knowing his wits were not working clearly. However, he was not so muddled as to miss the fact that the attackers had ignored everyone else in the tavern and come after him. Perhaps Roger's theory about the letters was not so wild after all, and what he had feared from the first was coming to pass: that there was more danger in the King's errand than Henry had led him to believe.

Ten

As the following day dawned bright and clear, Geoffrey and Roger explored the tavern and its surroundings, hunting for evidence that would identify who had invaded the bedchamber. There was nothing, however, except a few footprints outside the window and those might have been there for days.

'Do you accept now that I was right?' Roger asked. 'The villains went after *you* last night – no one else. They wanted Henry's letters. Once again, the King has ordered you down a dangerous road and has not bothered to explain why.'

'He certainly has not,' agreed Geoffrey tiredly. His mind was frustratingly fuzzy, and there was a nagging ache behind his eyes. His shoulder hurt, too, and he hoped it would not incapacitate him, should he be obliged to fight again.

'Then admit I am right,' said Roger. 'I want to hear it.'

'You *may* be right,' said Geoffrey, loath to give the big knight reason to gloat. 'However, there is more to Henry's orders than delivering letters. Perhaps someone does not like the fact that I have been asking questions about William and his secret. Or perhaps someone does not want me to report to Henry about the Bishop's war with Kermerdyn's abbey.'

'I suppose there is Abbot Mabon's murder, too,' conceded Roger. 'You were discussing it with Richard and Gwgan yesterday. *And* you asked Sear what he thought about Eudo, and it was obvious to me that you had him in mind as Eudo's killer.'

'Well, I hope it was not obvious to Sear,' said Geoffrey wryly, 'because I was *not* accusing him. I was merely trying to learn whether Eudo had ever tampered with his correspondence.'

'I imagine he did,' said Roger carelessly. 'Men who read are not noted for their integrity. And Sear almost certainly *did* kill Eudo. I told you the first time we met him that he was a villain.'

'Yes,' said Geoffrey, too tired to argue.

Roger nodded smugly. 'So pay attention to what I say in future, because I am always right. Still, it is a good thing you had Hilde in bed with you last night, and not Pulchria. I imagine she would have screeched and howled and got in the way of the fighting. Hilde located your sword and handed it to you, but sensibly stayed out of the way.'

'Thank God she was not hurt,' said Geoffrey. 'I wish I had not brought her. Do you think the King knew she would be thrown in the way of danger?'

He rubbed his head. Of course Henry would not want Hilde harmed. The Baderon clan was a powerful ally, and it would suit him to have one at Goodrich – he would not want Geoffrey marrying someone else. Unless, of course, the King had heard the rumours that Hilde – like her sisters, apparently – was barren and unable to produce the desired heir. But why would Henry concern himself with such an insignificant part of his realm?

'You say you believe these men were the same as the ones who attacked us after Brechene?' Roger asked, changing the focus of the subject. 'That is unsettling. It means they have followed us here. But who are they? Are you sure you can remember nothing to let us identify them?'

'It was pitch black, so I could not see. And they were silent, so I could not tell whether they were Welsh, English or Norman. But I am glad you arrived when you did.'

'You had already ousted them, lad,' said Roger. 'They had gone by the time I arrived, more is the pity. How many of them were there?'

'At least six, judging by the number of footsteps.' Geoffrey hesitated. 'I was too befuddled to notice last night, but what were our companions doing?'

'You think it was them?' asked Roger. He stroked his beard. 'Delwyn, Edward and Cornald emerged from their room fairly quickly, all in a state of undress, and they *did* look as though they had been sleeping. Sear and Alberic were with me, but their men were later found to be missing. Gwgan and Richard were staying with friends in the village.'

'What about Pulchria?'

'You think she arranged it?' Roger considered. 'Well, she certainly resents the fact that you make it difficult for Bale to service her, and she is wealthy enough to hire villains. But I do not see this as the work of women, Geoff. And lest you think to ask, Leah was asleep, too – I could hear her snoring from the corridor.'

Geoffrey scrubbed hard at his face. 'I must still be addled: of course none of them is responsible, not if the attack was by the same band that has harried us along the way. All our companions fought back when we were ambushed, which they would not have done if it was against their own hirelings.'

'Delwyn and the women did not fight back,' said Roger.

Geoffrey dismissed that notion. 'Bear in mind that I may not be the only one carrying messages from the King. Sear is Henry's favourite, Richard ranks more highly than me, and Edward is the Constable of Kadweli. Henry may have given them letters, too.'

'I suppose it could have been a case of mistaken identity,' said Roger doubtfully. 'The raiders could not have known who was in which chamber. There was no moon, and the inn's window shutters are very secure.'

Geoffrey did not know what to think.

'Come to the church,' said Roger, after more fruitless hunting for clues. 'Fychan arranged for the body to be taken there last night. If we look at it in daylight, something might spring out at you.'

'What body?' asked Geoffrey, bewildered.

'The body of the villain you killed, of course,' snapped Roger. 'What is wrong with you? Surely, you remember? And judging from the blood on the stairs, you injured at least two more. It was not a bad tally, under the circumstances.'

Geoffrey knew that some of his wild swings with dagger and sword had struck home, but his memories were distinctly hazy. Moreover, he doubted that looking at a corpse would advance his enquiries. But it would do no harm, either, so he followed Roger.

The church was a circular building with a sod roof and mud-brick walls. It was a poor structure for a village that appeared to be prosperous, although a pile of cut stones in one corner of the churchyard indicated something grander was planned.

Roger pushed open the door and wrinkled his nose. The place reeked of damp, and droppings on the floor said birds had made themselves at home. Attempts had been made to repair the roof and shore up the listing walls, but the building was losing its battle with gravity. It was clearly loved, though, because flowers had been placed on the windowsills, and the chancel had been swept clean.

The corpse had been set before the altar, and Geoffrey felt a surge of guilt at seeing one of his victims in a holy place. He crossed himself, wondering whether it would discourage Maurice from releasing him from his vow. Bale was already there, looming over the body like some massive carrion bird, head gleaming in the faint light from the window. Knowing the squire's penchant for stealing from the dead, Geoffrey wondered uncomfortably what he had been doing.

'Looking for clues to tell us who he was, sir,' Bale replied in a sibilant whisper when Geoffrey put the question. 'Sir Roger gave me permission.'

'And have you found any?' he asked.

'No,' said Bale, although his failure did not seem to have detracted from his enjoyment of the task. 'I brought Fychan here at first light, but he said he did not know the villain, either. And I know he was telling the truth, because I said I would slit his throat if he lied.'

There were times when Geoffrey felt unequal to dealing with Bale, and that morning was one of them. 'You should not have said that,' he said rather feebly.

'No,' agreed Roger. 'Especially as poor Fychan was a victim himself – also knocked on the head. And, worse yet, relieved of all his money. Obviously, *he* was not complicit in the attack.'

'What are you talking about?' asked Geoffrey. 'Fychan was attacked?'

Roger regarded him askance. 'Yes. I told you about it last night. Sear and Alberic found him when they were conducting their search. He had been sitting in his kitchen, counting his money, and the villains burst in, punched him senseless and stole his gold.'

'I do not remember,' said Geoffrey. 'But surely this puts a different complexion on matters? If he was assaulted, too, then—'

'It means they saw a man counting his money and decided to earn themselves a little extra,' interrupted Roger firmly. He walked to the body and pulled away the blanket that covered it. 'It changes nothing. Now look carefully. Do you recognize him?'

Geoffrey stared at the unfamiliar features. The body was that of a man in his forties, heavily built with an oddly scarred nose. He wore leather leggings and a mail jerkin, and the sword at his side was in excellent repair. There was no question that he was a professional soldier. But was he one who had turned outlaw, robbing with a gang of like-minded men for his own benefit? Or was he a mercenary, who had sold his services to someone who wanted dirty work done?

'I have never seen him before,' said Geoffrey. 'I would have remembered the nose.'

'So would I,' agreed Roger. 'Are you sure there is nothing to identify him, Bale?'

Bale nodded. 'He did not even have any jewellery. Whoever he was, robbery did not make him wealthy. Perhaps he was not very good at it.'

'Or he was not paid much,' said Roger. 'But we cannot waste more time on this business. We should round up our companions and be on our way. Who knows? Perhaps when you deliver the letters, these attacks will stop.'

Geoffrey sincerely hoped so, but he had a bad feeling their arrival in Kermerdyn would just make matters worse.

They started to walk towards the door, but it opened suddenly, and both knights' hands dropped to the hilts of their swords, and Bale drew one of his sharp little knives. The priest who entered cried out in alarm and took several steps backwards.

'Sorry, Father,' called Geoffrey hastily. 'We came to see whether we could identify this man.'

'I see,' said the priest, advancing cautiously. He was in his fifties with a sizeable paunch and grey hair that clung in greasy wisps around the back and sides of his head. 'And can you? This is a peaceful village; we cannot imagine why anyone should sully it with so foul a deed.'

'You do not know him, then?' Geoffrey asked.

The priest came to look at the body, and an expression of compassion filled his face. 'No, but I am sorry circumstances brought him to this. I am Ninian, vicar of this parish. Who are you?'

Roger made the introductions, and Geoffrey was not surprised when Ninian was unimpressed by the big knight's ecclesiastical connections.

'Fychan told me what had happened last night,' Ninian said, speaking good Norman-French. 'He is distraught.'

Geoffrey nodded sympathetically. 'I imagine it is not every day that a man dies under his roof.'

'Or that innocent travellers are attacked under it,' added Roger.

Ninian shook his head wryly. 'It is not that − it is that all his money was stolen. The felons invaded while he was counting it − as he likes to do each night − and did not leave him so much as a penny. He has been amassing that hoard for years, and its loss is a serious blow to him. And to my church, too.'

'Why to your church?' asked Geoffrey.

'Because he was going to pay for a new one,' explained Ninian. He gestured around him. 'As you can see, we need it desperately. This building will not survive the winter, and we shall be reduced to saying our devotions under a tree if we do not raise another soon.'

Geoffrey frowned. 'But this church looks as though it has been in decline for years, and the stones in the graveyard have been left long enough to gather moss. If Fychan was wealthy, why has the new church not been built already?'

Ninian grimaced. 'You touch on a sore point. Fychan says we can only have the gold when he is dead. Counting it gives him so much pleasure that he wants to keep it for as long as possible.'

'Sensible man,' said Roger approvingly.

Geoffrey was staring at the priest, his mind working furiously. 'Does anyone else know he counts it so often?'

Ninian nodded. 'Oh yes. He is the wealthiest man in the village, so we are all interested in the state of his finances. He is not generous with it, but we live in hope.'

Geoffrey was relieved. 'The attack had nothing to do with us,' he said to Roger. 'If Fychan is in the habit of poring over his money each night, and the whole village knows it, then it is hardly surprising that robbers visited his tavern.'

'No,' countered Ninian immediately. 'We have never had any trouble before. Prince Hywel keeps good order in these parts, fine ruler that he is. *You* must have attracted them.'

'Attracted them?' demanded Roger, although he had said as

much to Geoffrey not long before. 'Only fools attack a company with several knights.'

'Several knights with a baggage cart,' said Ninian. 'Although I understand that most of it is taken up by poor Mabon. Still, outlaws will not know that. You cannot blame thieves for chancing their hand. Of course, it was rash to tackle six Norman knights, even if you *were* all drunk.'

'None of us was drunk,' declared Roger indignantly. 'Sear, Alberic and I were enjoying a quiet game of dice, Geoffrey and Edward were asleep, and Richard had gone to stay with friends. So had Gwgan, although he is not a Norman knight.'

'Gwgan,' said Ninian fondly. 'A fine man, and a wise counsellor for Prince Hywel.'

'I thought the fighting made a lot of noise,' said Geoffrey to Roger. 'Yet it took an age for anyone else to come and help me.'

'Well, perhaps our dicing was a little rowdy,' admitted Roger. Then his face hardened and he lowered his voice. 'Or are you saying that Sear and Alberic made a racket deliberately, so I would not hear you yelling? Or even that Richard and Gwgan were not visiting friends at all, but were directing assassins in the middle of the night?'

'I do not know,' said Geoffrey. 'But Delwyn, Edward and Cornald were not carousing *or* visiting friends. Why did they not come?'

'You should be glad Edward and Delwyn stayed out of the way,' said Roger. 'They are hopeless in a fight. Meanwhile, Cornald is a mystery to me. Perhaps he wanted to pay us back for sleeping with his wife.'

'*I* have not slept with his wife.'

'Did either of you kill this man?' asked Ninian, breaking into their muttered discussion. 'Because, if so, the culprit had better kneel in front of my altar and allow me to bless him. Murder is not good for the soul. Of course, I see you are *Jerosolimitani*, so I imagine this death is but just one of many.'

'Oh, yes,' said Roger, taking it as a compliment. 'But Geoff here is responsible for this one.'

'He was trying to kill me,' said Geoffrey defensively. 'And my wife was in the room.'

'Well, God will decide who was in the right,' said Ninian. 'Kneel and let me do my duty.'

Geoffrey did as he was ordered, feeling he needed all the blessing he could get.

When Ninian pronounced himself satisfied, Geoffrey left the church and returned to the inn, Roger in tow, hoping Fychan was not so stricken by his loss that he would be unable to provide breakfast. The inn's main room was cold and empty. The fire had not been lit, the place reeked of spilled ale, and there was no sign of any of their companions. Fychan was there, sitting at a table with his head in his hands, eyes red-rimmed and puffy.

'They took everything,' he whispered brokenly. 'Every single penny. I am *glad* you killed one of them. I hope he burns in Hell!'

'Were you saving the money for a reason?' asked Geoffrey. 'Ninian told us that you intend to donate some for a new church—'

'I saved it because I loved it,' interrupted Fychan. 'Now it has gone, and I have nothing.'

'You have your life,' Geoffrey pointed out. 'They could have killed you.'

'I wish they had,' said Fychan bitterly. 'They have deprived me of my reason for living.'

'Aye,' said Roger, gruffly sympathetic. 'It must be a terrible blow.'

'It is like having your soul ripped out,' said Fychan. 'Much worse than when my wife died.'

'Did you see anything that might allow us to identify them?' asked Geoffrey, trying to mask his bemusement.

'No!' wailed Fychan. 'If I had, I would have told you last night. You promised to take word to Prince Hywel today. He is a good man, who will see my distress and do what he can to get my money back. I would go out hunting the villains myself, but I am too ill with shock.'

'Have there been rumours of thieves in the area?' asked Geoffrey.

Fychan shook his head. 'None at all. This is a decent place, with law-abiding people, and Prince Hywel keeps everything in order. Indeed, were it not for the fact that you were a victim, too, I might have assumed one of your party was the culprit.'

'Now, just a moment,' began Roger dangerously. 'We had no

idea that you had a hoard of coins for the taking. Only locals would know that sort of thing.'

He made it sound as though he *would* have launched an assault on Fychan's hoard, had he known about it in advance. But there was no more to be learned from the distraught Fychan, so Geoffrey asked him to provide breakfast.

By the time it was ready, the others had joined them. Cornald and Edward were yawning and rubbing their eyes, as if the incident had not prevented them from having a good night's sleep. Sear and Alberic were slightly green about the gills, and Geoffrey wondered whether Fychan had plied them with ale past its best once they had become too inebriated to notice. Gwgan and Richard also seemed quiet, both claiming they had enjoyed boisterous welcomes from friends.

Delwyn was aggravatingly spry, though, and talked in a deliberately loud voice that had most of the party wincing. Leah was the only one who demonstrated any concern for Geoffrey, coming to take his hands and peer into his face.

'He is pale,' she said to Hilde. 'And the cut on his head is nasty. Perhaps we should not leave today.'

'He *should* stay and regain his strength,' said Delwyn immediately. 'But the rest of us should proceed to Kermerdyn. Give me the Archbishop's letter; I shall see it delivered today.'

'We leave within the hour,' said Geoffrey shortly. 'Anyone not ready can travel on his own.'

'We will be ready,' said Gwgan quietly. 'I must ensure Hywel hears of last night's outrage as soon possible. I am sorry I was not here to help you. I should have known better than to lodge elsewhere. But we are in Hywel's domain, and I thought we would be safe.'

The wry gleam that usually danced in his eyes was gone, and Geoffrey saw the apology was genuine. He knew that Welshmen took family ties seriously; Gwgan probably *was* angry that he had not been there to defend a kinsman.

Hilde looked hard at Edward and Cornald. 'But *you* were not lodging elsewhere. Are you sure you heard nothing? The skirmish started quietly enough, but when my husband attacked back, he issued some very blood-curdling yells.'

'They woke me immediately,' replied Edward. 'Unfortunately,

this inn is inordinately dark, and I could not find my sword. There was no point dashing into an affray unarmed.'

'I tried to light a candle,' added Cornald. 'But Edward was screeching at me to hurry, and it flustered me. By the time I managed, the villains had escaped.'

'I heard nothing until it was too late,' said Sear offhandedly. 'And I would not have come to the rescue if I had. You should have been able to manage a few outlaws by yourself, Geoffrey.'

'*I* would have come, had I known what was happening,' said Alberic quietly, as Geoffrey grabbed Roger's shoulder to prevent him from reacting. 'But we were making too much noise, and by the time we realized something was amiss, the villains had fled.'

'I heard a lot of clashing weapons, then yelling,' said Pulchria. 'And I saw at least a dozen shadows haring off into the night afterwards. I told Sir Sear the direction they had taken.'

'Into the woods,' said Sear. 'It was pitch black and impossible to follow, especially as it took us a moment to arm ourselves, which gave them a good start.'

'They looked as though they knew where they were going,' said Pulchria. 'But if they are the same rogues who have pestered us since Brechene, then I am wrong.'

'I woke when I heard Sir Geoffrey shout,' said Delwyn. 'But I have learned to crawl under the bed when those sorts of things are screeched in the hours of darkness. I hid and stayed hidden until I was sure it was safe to come out. Which was this morning.'

'You stayed under the bed all night?' asked Roger incredulously.

Delwyn nodded. 'And I slept like a baby. I did not even hear Sear and Alberic return.'

'*I* did not return,' said Sear. 'I decided to stay on alert, lest the villains attempted anything else. They made off with Fychan's money, but I am not sure whether that was what they really wanted.'

'What do you mean?' asked Edward. 'What else could they have been after?'

'They would not have looked in a bedchamber for him,' said Sear scathingly. 'Personally, I suspect they intended to rob *us*, not the innkeeper. Six knights travelling together is unusual and has aroused interest; the King was wrong to think it would render us safer. It has made us a target, because greedy thieves have assumed we are protecting something important.'

'I disagree,' said Hilde. 'The first thing they did when they opened the door was to shoot a crossbow bolt into the bed. They were more than simple robbers. Moreover, as Geoffrey fought them, I had the distinct feeling they knew their way around – they did not stumble about blindly, like him. It gave them a huge advantage.'

'So, they are locals, then,' surmised Roger.

'Or strangers who had taken the time to explore the place,' said Geoffrey.

It was another clear day as the travellers rode the last few miles to Kermerdyn. It was a pleasant journey, along a path that followed the river. Fishermen bobbed about in leather-skinned coracles and raised their hands in greeting as the riders passed. Gwgan waved back and greeted several by name. They seemed pleased to see him return.

Now they were in home territory, Sear, Alberic and Richard took the lead, while Geoffrey and Roger brought up the rear. They were making good time, showing how eager everyone was to reach their destination.

'They grow complacent,' remarked Roger disparagingly. 'They think we are safe now, but I have not forgotten last night so quickly.'

'There is Kermerdyn,' said Geoffrey, pointing. 'It is a fair-sized settlement, so they probably *are* safe. I doubt Hywel will permit outlaws to come too close to his seat of power.'

Roger sniffed. 'Do you think we shall have the same problems on the way home? Or have you accepted my conclusion that all this is related to some business of that villain Henry?'

'God knows,' muttered Geoffrey. 'Last night's trouble may have been an attack by local thieves on a man known to be rich – Hilde and Pulchria both said the culprits seemed to know their way around. Yet I have had a bad feeling about this mission from the start. I wish I had not brought you, Bale or Hilde.'

'Rubbish,' declared Roger. 'You need us. Besides, I have enjoyed myself. Moreover, I relieved Sear and Alberic of a considerable amount of money last night. It will more than pay for our journey home, which is just as well, because the funds Henry provided barely saw us out of Sussex.'

'Unfortunately, now we are at Kermerdyn, the opportunity to solve the murders of William and Mabon is over,' said Geoffrey. 'Our companions will go their separate ways and will take their secrets with them. I shall have to tell Henry that I have no idea who killed them, and he may give me another commission to make up for it.'

'He might,' agreed Roger. 'So perhaps we had better invent something, because I have set my heart on being in the Holy Land by spring. Tell him Sear is the culprit. It is probably true, so justice will have been served. And if it is not, well, he is a vile specimen and it serves him right.'

Geoffrey laughed, then became serious again. 'I wish I could have learned who murdered Mabon. It happened in my own home, and it feels as if a challenge was issued – one I failed to answer. Besides, there was something refreshing about a monastic with original ideas about religion.'

'His sword would have been useful on the journey, too,' said Roger. 'I am sure—'

He ducked suddenly, and both men raised their shields when they heard the unmistakeable sound of an arrow hissing through the air. The first struck Geoffrey's saddle. Others thudded into his shield, telling him he would certainly have been dead had his instincts not been so finely honed.

'Not again!' muttered Roger. 'I like a fight, but this is beginning to be tiresome.'

Eleven

'Shields!' yelled Geoffrey at the top of his voice. Like the warriors they were, Sear, Alberic and Richard heeded the warning without hesitation, which saved the lives of all as a hail of missiles came towards them. Geoffrey spurred his horse forward, aiming to put himself between the attackers and Hilde.

It was a mark of the frequency of the ambushes that the company knew exactly what to do. Hilde took charge of Pulchria, Leah, Delwyn and the servants, hauling them behind Mabon's cart. Cornald joined them, crossbow at the ready, and he began to return fire as quickly as it could be wound. Sear, Alberic and Richard formed a tight cluster, using their shields to protect each other and themselves, and Gwgan galloped to join Geoffrey. Edward was the only one who dithered, looking back and forth like a trapped rat as he assessed which way to run.

'Here!' yelled Geoffrey, seeing he was going to be shot if he stayed where he was. 'Now!'

Edward's horse heard the urgency in Geoffrey's voice, even if its rider was slow to obey, and cantered towards him. Edward gripped the pommel of his saddle to prevent himself from falling off, and a distant part of Geoffrey's mind wondered how the King could have knighted a man with such dismal equestrian skills.

'There!' shouted Roger, stabbing a finger towards a thickly wooded copse. 'Half are lurking there, and the rest are by the bend in the track.'

'Attack!' roared Sear, spurring his way towards the corner. 'We have reacted defensively for long enough.'

Geoffrey was sure it was proximity to Kermerdyn that induced Sear to make such a rash decision. He was drawing breath to order him back when Roger broke formation and galloped towards the wood. Alberic and Richard tore after Sear, so Geoffrey had no choice but to support his friend. He was aware of Gwgan behind him, armed with a short stabbing sword.

Cursing under his breath – a wood was no place for mounted

warriors, and the ambushers held all the advantages – Geoffrey plunged into the trees. He cursed even more when he became aware that the ground was thick with fallen leaves, hiding ruts and roots that were likely to see the horses stumble and their riders thrown. He began to howl his Saracen battle-cry, hoping that its strangeness would unsettle the attackers. The ploy worked, and several promptly turned and crashed through the under-growth ahead in a bid to escape.

Unfortunately, rather more remained, and the continued hail of arrows indicated they were not about to give up. Geoffrey's horse whinnied in pain as one scored a furrow across its chest; another glanced off his helmet. When he reached a section where the trees grew more thickly, hampering him further still, men poured out to do battle with him, hacking at his destrier and his legs in equal measure.

It was unlike the other attacks, when the action had been broken off relatively quickly. This time, there was a grim deter-mination – desperation even – among the men who surged forward against him. But even without being able to manoeuvre, his horse gave him height, and he was devastating with his sword, slashing and chopping at anyone rash enough to come within his reach. His destrier, too, had been well trained and began to flail with its front hoofs at those who pressed around it.

Gradually, the ambushers began to fall back, although one continued a frenzy of blows. He howled furiously at his retreating comrades, and several returned to help him. Geoffrey launched another assault that scattered them, then concentrated on the man he was sure was the leader. He lunged with his sword, and when the man was off balance, followed it with a kick that took him in the chest. The fellow flew through the air and landed awkwardly, gasping for breath. Ignoring any knight's cardinal rule – never to dismount in battle – Geoffrey leapt off his destrier and ran to press his sword against the man's throat.

'Who are you?' he demanded. 'Speak, and I will let you live.'

'Go to hell,' snarled the man, although Geoffrey could see fear in his eyes. He pressed down on the sword.

'I will ask you once more. Who are you?'

'I am—'

But the rest of his sentence was lost in a cry of agony as an arrow thumped into the man's neck. Blood sprayed, and Geoffrey knew the fellow would not be revealing any deathbed secrets. He whipped around, scanning the trees, shield held in front of him. Had one of the man's own comrades killed him to ensure he did not betray them? Or, he thought grimly, as a quarrel pounded into his shield, had they made a mistake and actually been aiming at him?

The fight had isolated him from his companions, although he could hear sounds of battle to his left. Keeping his shield raised, he ran towards it, unwilling to stay pinned down. He exploded into a clearing with another howl, and the sight of him caused several men to break from where they had been skirmishing with Roger and run for their lives.

Geoffrey's horse had followed him, so he mounted it quickly and rode to his friend's side. Roger was breathing hard and held his arm awkwardly.

'Arrow,' he muttered.

'Go back to Hilde,' ordered Geoffrey. 'I will find the others.'

Roger wheeled around and was gone, leaving Geoffrey to penetrate farther into the woods. He was angry. It was foolish for experienced knights to let themselves be lured into such terrain, and he wondered what Sear, Alberic and Richard thought they were doing.

He found Sear first. One of the attackers lay dead at his horse's feet, although he looked to have been shot, whereas Sear only carried a sword. It was curious, but there was no time for questions as more ambushers suddenly poured through the trees.

'Back!' yelled Sear. 'Towards the road.'

He turned and thundered away, leaving Geoffrey with no choice but to follow: there were too many for him to tackle alone. Sear burst into another clearing, where Richard was heavily besieged. Most ran away when they saw reinforcements arrive.

They encountered Edward next, sword drawn and bloody, but his face pale. Gwgan materialized suddenly on foot, leading his horse. He was breathless but unhurt.

'My horse bolted,' he gasped. 'I always considered him a steady beast, and he has never baulked at a battle before. I cannot imagine what—'

'Back to the road,' Geoffrey ordered urgently, wondering

whether they had been enticed into the woods on purpose, so as to leave the cart unattended.

But he need not have worried. The cart was unscathed and so was Hilde. Roger was sitting on it as she and Leah tended his arm, although he had refused to relinquish either sword or shield while they did so. He relaxed his guard when Geoffrey appeared.

'It is just a scratch,' he said.

'Where are Cornald, Pulchria and Delwyn?' asked Geoffrey, dismounting and inspecting Roger's wound.

'Here,' said Delwyn, arriving suddenly enough to make Geoffrey jump. 'I told you: I tend to hide at the first sign of trouble. And thank God I did. That attack was the most vicious yet.'

'It was,' agreed Roger soberly. He glanced over Geoffrey's shoulder. 'And here comes our brave butterer. It does not look as though he dispatched many bolts after we rode into the forest, and God alone knows what Pulchria was doing.'

Geoffrey spoke in a low voice, so only Roger and Hilde could hear. 'One of the attackers was about to tell me all, but he was shot before he could speak. It may have been an arrow intended for me, but, equally, one of our companions may have loosed it. Sear, Richard and Gwgan were all behaving oddly when I found them, and now Cornald and Pulchria . . .'

'What about Edward?' asked Roger. 'What was *he* doing?'

'He is the one man who *cannot* be behind these attacks,' said Hilde. 'He was wounded outside Brechene – if he had ordered these ambushes, he would have been safe from stray arrows.'

'What about Delwyn?' asked Roger. 'He is sly enough to organize raids on his fellow travellers, and he is desperate to lay his hands on the Archbishop's letter.'

'I agree,' said Hilde. 'However, I do not trust *any* of them except Edward. And that includes Alberic, who is missing still. So is Bale.'

'You had better go and find them,' said Roger to Geoffrey. 'We cannot leave until you do, and every moment here is another moment for those villains to regroup and come at us again.'

Aware that Gwgan, Richard and Sear were following, Geoffrey rode back into the trees. Roger had been right to fear another assault, because Geoffrey encountered a group of men who were massing for a second attempt almost immediately. He tore into them, wounding three with his first set of manoeuvres. He was surprised when they did not scatter, and was then hard-pressed to hold his own when they came at him *en masse*. He was aware of Gwgan at his back, although he had no idea what Richard and Sear were doing.

But none of the attackers was equal to his level of skill, and it was not long before his superior talents began to tell. One man dropped his weapon and ran, and then suddenly it was a rout. Another paused long enough to lob a dagger, which would have hit Gwgan, had Geoffrey not deflected it with his shield.

'Thank you,' gasped Gwgan. 'It would have been a pity to die so close to home.'

As the knifeman had come very close to killing Gwgan, Geoffrey suspected the counsellor was innocent of hiring the men. He was glad. He liked Gwgan and had enjoyed his company. He was pleased Edward was exonerated from suspicion, too, and supposed that if the ambushers *were* under the command of one of their companions, the only remaining suspects were Sear, Alberic, Cornald and Pulchria. And Delwyn, of course, who had ensured he did not suffer injury by hiding.

Sear and Richard arrived at last, and the remaining attackers fled at the sight of them. A sudden crashing in the undergrowth behind them made Geoffrey whip around with his sword raised, but it was only Bale. Cornald appeared from another direction.

'The villains have all escaped, sir,' reported Bale apologetically. 'I tried to question one, but he declined to answer, so I cut his throat.'

'And he was definitely not talking after that,' said Gwgan dryly. 'I tried to get one to talk, too, but Cornald shot him just as he was opening his mouth to reply.'

'I shot him because he had a knife,' declared Cornald. 'He was beckoning you towards him so he could stab you. I saved your life.'

'Did you also shoot the one I was talking to?' Geoffrey asked him.

Cornald shrugged. 'I may have done. It is difficult to recall what happened – it was all very fast and very nasty. I know I hit several, although I do not think I killed any others. All I can say is thank God we are almost home.'

'Did I see you leap off your horse earlier, Geoffrey?' asked Sear smugly. 'You are lucky to be alive.'

'I was trying to get answers,' Geoffrey replied curtly. 'Like Gwgan and Bale. I imagine we will all be safer once we know who these men are and what they want.'

'They are just local felons,' said Edward, coming to join them. 'They cannot be the same ones who assaulted us before. Why would they follow us so far? It makes no sense.'

'Unless one of us is involved in something nasty,' said Richard, looking at no one in particular. 'The attacks began in Brechene, so perhaps some bad business was conducted there. It was not me, because I was unwell. So was Gwgan. We had eaten that putrid fish soup.'

'It was not me, either,' said Sear. 'I am not involved in anything unsavoury, because the King would expect better of me. Where is Alberic?'

They separated to look for the lost knight, and it was Richard who found him. Alberic was dead, his eyes gazing sightlessly towards the sky.

Sear accepted the death of his friend with no more emotion than a grimace, although he nodded his thanks when Geoffrey and Gwgan helped him put Alberic on the cart with Mabon. Afterwards, they all stood silently for a moment, until Roger reminded them that it would be unwise to linger longer than necessary. His warning galvanized them into action. Geoffrey, Roger and Gwgan reclaimed their horses, Leah packed away her medical supplies, and Hilde rounded up the frightened servants.

'I say it again,' said Edward, looking around with a shudder. 'This would not have happened if my soldiers had been to hand. It was bad business that they were detained in Brechene.'

'They would have made no difference,' said Gwgan quietly. 'These attacks have been ambushes, not frontal assaults. Your men would have done no more than provide additional targets for these archers to shoot at.'

'You might want to talk less and ride more,' said Richard sharply. 'There is no more room on the cart for anyone else.'

It was good, if callous, advice. Geoffrey took up station between

Roger and Hilde, ready to protect them again. The big knight was pale and quiet, a sure sign that they needed to find an inn where he could rest.

'Did you see any of what happened?' Geoffrey asked of Hilde.

'Unfortunately, Leah was sobbing so loudly that I was afraid she would draw attention to us,' said Hilde. 'Most of my attention was on trying to keep her quiet. However, what little I did see told me that there was a desperation in them that was not present on previous occasions.'

Geoffrey looked at her. 'I thought the same. Do you believe they were the same ones?'

Hilde nodded. 'Yes, I do, and I would suggest their remit today was to ensure we did not reach Kermerdyn alive. They were also determined not to answer questions. One let Bale kill him rather than speak; another was too badly injured to move, and was clubbed to death by his fellows.'

'Cornald shot a man Gwgan was trying to question,' said Geoffrey uncomfortably. 'And someone killed the one I was interrogating, too.'

'It was a mess,' said Hilde quietly. 'It was difficult to tell what was happening, and all the time you were fighting, arrows were raining down from the trees. However, I suspect they could have dispatched Delwyn, Leah, Pulchria and me, had they really wanted. They focussed on you.'

'On me, specifically?' asked Geoffrey, supposing that Roger's contention had been right that morning, and the trouble they had experienced since Brechene was connected to the letters. Or perhaps his orders to explore William's murder and provide the King with a culprit and William's secret.

Hilde shook her head. 'No – on all the knights. Did you not notice that they withdrew quickly once Alberic fell?'

'Did they?' Geoffrey was not sure how long the skirmish had lasted, nor did he have any notion of when Alberic had died.

Hilde lowered her voice. 'Sear did not seem overly distressed by his friend's death, did he?'

'It is hardly manly to wail and carry on.'

'I imagine you would have shown more emotion, had it been Roger. You would not shed tears, perhaps, but there would be anger and vows of revenge.'

'Not in this company,' said Geoffrey. 'I would keep my thoughts to myself.'

Hilde shrugged. 'Well, let us hope we do not have to put it to the test. And if it was Alberic they came for, perhaps we shall be safe from now on.'

Geoffrey nodded to where a bridge lay ahead of them. 'Fortunately, it does not matter any longer, because we have arrived.'

Kermerdyn nestled near a bend in the River Tywi. It comprised an ancient settlement on a rise, protected by a series of walls and ramparts. Geoffrey supposed they had been built the last time an invading army had foisted itself on the locals, which meant they were several hundred years old.

South of the town was a wharf with several piers, and Geoffrey could tell from the salty smell of the river that it was tidal to the sea. Several substantial ships were moored, indicating Kermerdyn was an important trading centre – there was certainly a bustle about the place that suggested money being made.

A second settlement was springing up in the shadow of the first, ranged along the river, and comprising warehouses and merchants' homes. There was a wooden bridge across the river, with a tollhouse at its far end. The number of carts trundling across it suggested that the revenues from it alone would be substantial, further enriching the little town.

Just to the east was a walled enclosure dominated by a pretty church, and Geoffrey saw Delwyn cross himself when he saw it. He could only suppose it was Kermerdyn's abbey, which he would visit when he delivered the Archbishop's letter to Mabon's successor.

He usually reserved judgement about the places he visited until he had had time to explore them, but there was something about Kermerdyn that appealed to him instantly. Perhaps it was the fine weather, which bathed it in a welcoming glow, or the warm grey stone from which its houses were built. Or perhaps he was just grateful to have arrived in one piece. Regardless, he found he was eager to look around it and hoped there would be time for leisure once he had finished his work.

'Personally, I would have built my castle there,' said Richard, pointing to the ridge above the river, just to the west of the town. 'I think my brother made a mistake when he raised Rhydygors.'

'Where *is* Rhydygors?' asked Geoffrey, realizing it was nowhere to be seen.

Richard gestured to the east, where a third settlement had sprung up. It was some way down the river and apparently protected a ford across it. All that could be seen from that distance was a motte with a wooden tower on top of it, and a few houses scattered among the nearby trees. Some were large, and he supposed it was where Hywel's people lived, so they would be close to hand if needed.

'Well, your brother was a Norman,' said Delwyn sneeringly. 'What do you expect?'

'What do you mean by that?' demanded Richard, swinging around to glower at him.

'That a Welshman would have put a fortress nearer the town,' replied Delwyn, unmoved by his anger. 'There is no point protecting a ford when there is a perfectly good bridge a mile away. We always thought it was odd. But, then, William was odd when he first arrived.'

'Odd?' asked Geoffrey.

'He was a good man,' declared Richard hotly. 'No one should say anything bad about my brother, God rest his sainted soul.'

Delwyn crossed himself. 'He *was* a good man, but only after he discovered his secret.'

'There was no secret,' said Edward. 'He invented it to explain his change in character, because none of you would believe he just woke up one day and decided to become a better man.'

'There *is* a secret,' declared Richard fervently. 'And I would not mind having it – I would be honoured if the Blessed Virgin appeared to *me*. Moreover, if I learn any of you had a hand in his death, I will kill you.'

'You will do nothing of the kind,' said Sear. 'Because I will be there before you. But his secret will never be found because, as I have said all along, it was a holy sword, and he was the only one on this Earth good enough to hold it. It disappeared when he died, and will not reappear until another man is born who is his equal.'

'Rubbish,' declared Cornald. 'He was a new man because he ate properly. You may all have noticed that *I* am a happy fellow, too, despite the trials and tribulations that beset me.' Here he shot an unreadable glance towards his wife. 'The secret to true happiness is food.'

'Potions,' countered Pulchria. 'Some herb grows near Kermerdyn that made him what he was, and I still intend to find it. That sort of popularity will be very useful for a woman like me.'

'If there is a secret, then it just goes along with being the master of Rhydygors Castle,' said Gwgan dismissively. 'Hywel has goodness in abundance. It is all to do with being in Wales.'

'Yes, but Hywel's is a different kind of goodness,' said Edward. 'He *does* have it in abundance, but William was saintly. They are not really comparable.'

They fell silent, pondering the matter. So, there they were, thought Geoffrey, regarding them one by one: his suspects – all of whom would exploit William's secret, should it ever be revealed.

He turned his thoughts back to the latest skirmish, realizing that he had seen none of his companions actually engage the enemy – Richard's encounter had been uncharacteristically lacklustre, and the others had only appeared once most of the ambushers were on the run. Did that mean one of them *had* hired mercenaries to do battle with the travellers? Was Roger right, and Geoffrey and his friends would be safe only once the remaining messages were in the hands of their intended recipients?

With a sigh, he led the way towards the bridge.

They arrived to find Kermerdyn a busy, bustling place that smelled of cows and fish. Cattle were being driven from every direction to the market, and there was a thriving fishing industry, the stalls on the riverside well stocked with silvery wares from both river and sea.

The market stood on the open ground near the bridge, and there was a staggering array of goods, ranging from livestock and foodstuffs, to cloth, building materials and pots. It seemed to Geoffrey that anything a person could possibly want was on offer in Kermerdyn, and he supposed he would not have to worry about Hilde becoming bored there.

Their companions did not linger once they had paid their toll to cross the bridge. Sear was the first to break away. He snapped his fingers at two passing soldiers and ordered them to help him carry Alberic to the church.

'I cannot tote him to Pembroc, so I am going to bury him here,' he said.

'Alberic will understand,' said Edward kindly. 'St Peter's is a pretty church with a spacious graveyard, and I will undertake to pay the priest to say masses for Alberic's soul whenever I pass through the town.'

'Thank you,' said Sear gruffly. 'I shall stay here until it is done, and then ride to Pembroc. Richard will lend me an escort.'

He rode away before Richard could say whether he would or not. Geoffrey fingered the letter in his shirt. Henry had ordered it delivered on arrival in Kermerdyn, but it seemed callous to do it when Sear was about to bury his friend. He decided to leave it until the next day.

Suddenly, Richard spat a colourful oath and surged towards a gaggle of men who were inspecting a display of ironware. When he reached them, he began to berate them for their slovenly appearances. They immediately tried to smarten themselves, and Geoffrey saw he was the kind of leader to rule by fear and bullying. Richard disappeared with them eventually, without so much as a backward glance towards his erstwhile companions.

Delwyn wasted no time with pleasantries, either. He ordered the servant driving the cart to follow him to the abbey, and also departed with no word of farewell or thanks.

'I shall see you home, Leah,' said Edward solicitously. 'The journey has been arduous, and we should both rest. But I must bathe first. Just look at the state of me! God grant me a speedy return to the peace of Kadweli, where I can rule with pen and parchment; I was not built for charging around the country and engaging in battles.'

'Thank you,' said Leah to Geoffrey. 'You have been kind and patient, and you kept my husband from killing anyone, for which I am grateful. He would have been sorry afterwards, and I am glad you spared him that.'

Geoffrey was not quite sure how to reply and left Hilde to murmur some suitably tactful remarks.

'If you want any butter, you know where to come,' said Cornald, smiling politely, although it was clear his mind was already on his home and business. 'Travelling with you has been a pleasure, and I am grateful to you for keeping us all alive.'

'It *has* been a pleasure,' agreed Pulchria, smirking meaningfully at Bale before following her husband. Pointedly, she ignored Geoffrey.

Soon, only Gwgan was left. He sat on his horse, breathing in deeply of the familiar scents of home. Geoffrey knew how he felt, and wished he was back in Goodrich.

'Where now?' asked Roger, forcing a smile. 'Shall I come with you to deliver the letters?'

'No,' said Geoffrey. He nodded to an inn called the Trout. It appeared respectable enough, with a smart thatch and clean white walls. 'We shall rest there for a while first.'

Roger did not object when Geoffrey hired a room and ordered him to lie down. Geoffrey helped him drink some broth, then assisted Hilde as she bathed and dressed the wound properly. Gwgan stayed downstairs talking to the innkeeper and using his influence to ensure Roger was provided with the best possible care.

'Stay with him, Bale,' ordered Geoffrey. 'No leaving to frolic with Pulchria.'

'I will frolic with her here, then,' said Bale practically. 'Sir Roger will not mind.'

'Actually, I will mind,' countered Roger. 'Sit by the window and sharpen your knives – quietly, if possible. And you go about your business, Geoff lad. I cannot sleep with you looming over me like an anxious vulture. It is making me nervous.'

'He is right,' whispered Hilde, tugging on Geoffrey's sleeve to pull him out of the room. 'Leave him in peace. I suspect he will be safer once you have discharged your duties, anyway. Where will you start?'

'Not with the abbey,' said Geoffrey. 'I should give them time to deal with Mabon. The same goes for Sear with Alberic. That leaves Bishop Wilfred.'

'You cannot meet a prelate looking as though you have just fought a battle,' said Hilde. 'You are splattered with blood and filth. You should wash and don suitable attire first. No, do not disturb Roger by invading his chamber again! Let the man rest. We shall find somewhere else to make you respectable.'

Geoffrey groaned, thinking it was a waste of time. 'Then perhaps I should start asking questions about William instead. Perhaps the townsfolk have ideas about who killed him and what his secret might have been.'

'Again, you are unlikely to secure their cooperation if you descend on them looking like a killer. You will frighten them and learn nothing.'

'Then I shall start my hunt for William's secret without their help,' said Geoffrey, exasperated. 'He lived in Rhydygors, so that seems a good place to begin. And if I have no luck there, I will search the abbey and the church, because William was said to be devout, and those are places he may have trusted.'

'Rhydygors, then,' said Hilde. 'My sister spends a lot of time there, and she is sure to have hot water to hand. We shall just have to hope we do not meet Prince Hywel before I have been at you with a brush.'

Geoffrey was not sure he liked the sound of that, but acknowledged that the skirmish had left him somewhat soiled. He followed her down the stairs, carrying the saddlebag she handed him, in which were some of his clothes, laundered and neatly folded. They met Gwgan at the door, and he smiled when Hilde informed him that she wanted to see her sister.

'Good. Isabella will skin me alive if she learns you are in Kermerdyn and that I failed to take you straight to her. She will be at Rhydygors; she always stays there when I am away. There is no man I trust more than Prince Hywel to look after my wife.'

They climbed on their horses, and Gwgan led the way back over the bridge and along a track across the marshes. The castle loomed in front of them.

'Hywel will want to meet a friend of the King,' said Gwgan as they went. 'And I am sure His Majesty has messages for him, just as he sent one to me.'

'Just verbal greetings,' said Geoffrey, hoping Henry's carelessness was not going to land him in trouble. 'Besides, you said the letter he wrote to you would really have been for the Prince.'

'Yes, it was, but that was all rather cold and businesslike,' said

Gwgan. 'Pertaining to taxes and who owns the advowsons of various churches. There was nothing personal in it for Hywel.'

'What about in Richard's?' asked Geoffrey. 'He told me he was going to ask you to read it to him.'

'His message was even briefer than mine.' Gwgan's rueful smile indicated that the sullen knight had not been best pleased when he had heard it. 'It just ordered him to patrol the river, because Irish pirates have been at large.'

'River patrols sound tedious,' said Hilde. 'Was he disappointed that the King did not ask him to do something more significant?'

Gwgan laughed. 'He was livid! I suspect the instruction was Eudo's, not Henry's. But there is not much for Richard to do in this area. Hywel is more than capable of keeping the peace and does not need Norman help. Personally, I was hoping the letter would be an order to deploy elsewhere. So was he – he is wasted here.'

'No wonder he has been surly all the way from Goodrich,' said Hilde. Then she shrugged. 'Of course, he was surly *before* he had his letter.'

'Let us not spoil our day with talk of that black-faced villain,' said Gwgan, spurring his pony into a trot. 'We are almost home, and Isabella will be delighted to see you.'

Twelve

Rhydygors was a typical Norman castle, with a wooden tower atop a large mound. It afforded excellent views of the river, and although Geoffrey would have located it nearer the town, the site chosen by William fitz Baldwin had its advantages. Its garrison would be able to react sooner to an invasion by water, and the marshes that surrounded it conferred their own line of defence.

Besides the motte and bailey, there was also the usual jumble of outbuildings – halls for sleeping and eating, stables, kitchens and huts for storage. Hywel was in the process of rebuilding some of them in stone, and Geoffrey imagined that, in ten years or so, it would be as stalwart a bastion as any he had seen. He wondered how he was going to search it for William's secret without anyone guessing what he was doing.

Isabella's face split into a delighted grin when she saw Hilde, and Geoffrey saw immediately the resemblance between them – both had honey-brown eyes and thick hair – although Isabella had been rather more fortunate with her looks. She was exceptionally beautiful, and Geoffrey found himself uncharacteristically tongue-tied when Gwgan introduced her.

'You have made my sister very happy,' she said, smiling at him. 'We had all despaired of her finding a man she considered worthy.'

'She was given no choice in the matter, I am afraid,' said Geoffrey, acutely aware of his filthy surcoat, battle-stained armour and grimy hands. He wished he had followed Hilde's suggestion and washed in the river along the way. It had been wilful obstinacy that had led him to decline – a stubborn refusal to acknowledge that she was right.

Isabella shook his arm, releasing it quickly and surreptitiously wiping her hand on her gown. 'You are wrong. She refused plenty of suitors before you came along, and our father could not have made her marry a man she did not like. She *chose* you.'

'Oh,' said Geoffrey uncomfortably.

'Here is Prince Hywel,' said Isabella, indicating with a graceful sweep of her hand a man walking down the stairs from the tower and heading towards them. 'He will want to meet my sister *and* the man who captured her heart.'

'Christ!' muttered Geoffrey, wondering whether anyone would notice if he grabbed Hilde's cloak and used it to conceal the worst of the mess.

Hywel ap Gronw looked every inch a Welsh prince. He had jet black hair and blue eyes, and was tall, handsome and strong. He wore a plain but elegant tunic of blue, and there was gold thread in his cloak. He carried himself with a light grace, and there was none of the arrogant swagger affected by Normans. His people smiled and nodded at him as he passed, and it was clear they served him for love, not like the frightened minions in Richard's service.

He embraced Gwgan like a brother, his eyes shining with boyish delight at the return of his friend and most trusted counsellor.

'I have missed you,' he said in Welsh. 'You have been gone too long. There is much we must discuss, but not now: today belongs to your wife.'

'You shall come to my home tomorrow night, then,' said Gwgan. 'We shall prepare a feast and talk until the cockerels announce dawn. I have much to tell you.'

'You have brought guests,' said Hywel, turning his smile on Geoffrey and Hilde, and speaking Norman-French. 'Your wife's sister, I believe? And a *Jerosolimitanus*?'

'Sir Geoffrey Mappestone,' explained Gwgan. His eyes gleamed with wry humour as he continued to speak Welsh, knowing perfectly well Hilde would not understand a word of it. 'He went to some trouble to make himself presentable, as you can see. But do not judge him by his surcoat. He speaks passable Welsh, which more than compensates for his wild appearance.'

Hywel laughed. 'I hope you do not mind Gwgan's mordant sense of humour, Sir Geoffrey. But he is your kin now, so you will have to forgive his liberties.'

He indicated they were to follow him to the hall, where food had been prepared. He led, his arm thrown around Gwgan's shoulders, and Isabella and Hilde followed. Geoffrey brought up the rear, a little chagrined when a servant stepped forward to offer him a bowl of water. Once he had scrubbed his face and hands and had exchanged his stained surcoat for a clean one Hilde had to hand, he felt considerably more presentable.

The food was plain, but fresh and plentiful, and it was not long before someone began to play a harp. Isabella and Hilde sat together at one end of the table, talking incessantly, while the men took the other. Politely, Hywel enquired after their journey.

'You might not have seen me, had Geoffrey not been with us,' said Gwgan soberly. 'He saved me this morning. We were ambushed constantly by outlaws after Brechene, and we are fortunate to reach Kermerdyn alive.'

'Outlaws?' asked Hywel, frowning. 'But we have had no such trouble since Bellême's louts were ousted last year.'

'Well, we were plagued by them,' said Gwgan firmly. 'Alberic was killed today, and another knight wounded. Edward was injured just outside Brechene, and Geoffrey was knocked half-senseless last night in Lanothni. I have never known a journey like it; there was no trouble on the way to Gloucester.'

'This is worrying news,' said Hywel sombrely. 'I had better send some patrols to find them. I cannot have my territories infected by law-breakers.'

'They stole money from the taverner in Lanothni, too,' Gwgan went on. 'He is famous locally for having a lot of it, apparently. Foolish man! He should have kept it quiet.'

'There should have been no need to keep it quiet,' said Hywel sternly. 'Every man has the right to keep what he has honestly earned. I shall see to it immediately.'

He started to rise, but Gwgan waved him back down. 'I will do it. You can entertain our guests.'

After Gwgan left, Hywel began to tell Geoffrey about his plans for the region. The knight found him easy company, and he had an engaging, infectious laugh that made it impossible not to like him. How different it would be, Geoffrey thought, if Hywel, not Henry, had been King. Geoffrey would not have minded serving a man like the Prince.

After a while, Hywel stood and indicated Geoffrey was to walk with him outside. Like many military men, the Prince quickly grew restless sitting and preferred to be active.

'Gwgan tells me you carried a letter to him from the King, about taxes and advowsons,' he said. 'I assume there is a personal message for me, too?'

He held out his hand.

'It was a verbal one, My Lord,' said Geoffrey, silently cursing Henry for his shabby manners. 'He sends you his felicitations as a fellow prince and trusts he finds you well and strong.'

Hywel smiled wryly. 'I suspect he forgot, and you are being tactful. But I appreciate your thoughtfulness in not wanting me to feel neglected. However, whereas other men might feel slighted, peace is important to me – to this region – and I shall not let Henry's lack of grace spoil it.'

It was an admirable stance, and Geoffrey thought Henry could learn much from Hywel.

'This is a fine castle,' he said, trying to decide how best to assess it for William's secret without making Rhydygors' residents think him unacceptably nosy – or that Isabella's sister had married a man not quite in control of his wits.

Hywel glanced around. 'It will be, once it is finished in stone, although I wish William fitz Baldwin had sited it nearer the town. But I am always pleased to show guests my domain. Come. I shall take you around every nook and cranny.'

He was as good as his word, and, as he was willing to provide detailed information, it was easy for Geoffrey to identify which buildings had been extant in William's time and which had been raised since. Hywel was proud of his little fortress, and Geoffrey might have found the extensive tour tedious had he not been assessing every inch of it for potential hiding places.

Unfortunately, there was nothing to find, because William's buildings had been simple and functional, and there was little storage space. Geoffrey assessed the walls for hidden recesses, looked up the chimneys, and stamped across the floors to assess whether something might be buried underneath, but it was all to no avail. Moreover, it was obvious that William's retainers would have noticed if their master had started digging holes or hacking at the walls.

Geoffrey suppressed a sigh when, once finished with the buildings, Hywel led him on an exhaustive expedition around the grounds. Again, there was nowhere William could have buried something he did not want anyone else to find, and Geoffrey was forced to conclude that whatever he was looking for was not in Rhydygors. He would have to look in the abbey and church.

When Gwgan had finished briefing Hywel's troops about the outlaws, the Prince excused himself from Geoffrey to spend time with his counsellor. Geoffrey retrieved his horse from the stables and mounted up, intending to return to Kermerdyn to check on Roger. Hilde and Isabella came to intercept him.

'Where are you going?' asked Hilde worriedly. 'It will be dark soon, and it is not wise to ride out alone, given what happened earlier today.'

'Please stay,' begged Isabella. 'I have not thanked you for saving my husband's life. He told me how you knocked away the knife that would have killed him today.'

'There is no need to thank me,' said Geoffrey. 'But I have a letter for you, as it happens. From Bishop Maurice.'

'Bishop Maurice?' asked Isabella, startled. 'Why would he write to me? I barely know him.'

Geoffrey could hardly say it was in order to disguise the fact that he was delivering more contentious letters from the King, so he said nothing and merely held it out to her, along with the now battered packet that contained the raisins.

'Read it to her,' instructed Hilde, taking the raisins and opening them. She began to eat them. 'Or Isabella will have to wait for a clerk to become available, and I imagine she is impatient to know what it says.'

'I *am* curious,' admitted Isabella.

Geoffrey did not want to do it. 'It might be personal,' he hedged, suspecting they would all be embarrassed by its sentiments. Maurice had an unerring eye for beautiful women, and he would certainly have noticed Isabella.

'It will not!' laughed Isabella. 'I did not help him with his unbalanced humours, if that is what you are thinking, so it can contain nothing to shock us. Besides, I am a married woman.'

Geoffrey broke the seal, forbearing to remark that a woman's marital status was neither here nor there to Maurice when his humours were awry. He scanned the letter quickly, ready to omit anything indelicate. The first section contained some rather bald and inappropriate statements about her fine figure and alluring eyes, but the rest was, as Maurice had claimed, information about a place where good raisins might be bought. Geoffrey paraphrased the first part to render it innocuous, and read the second verbatim, while Hilde made inroads into the raisins.

'Well,' said Isabella, bemused. 'It is good of him to remember me, but I am not sure why I should warrant such attention. Perhaps you will help me compose a suitable reply, Geoffrey?'

'He did not send many of these raisins,' said Hilde, shaking the packet to see whether there were any left. 'You would think he would have been a little more generous. They cannot be easy to come by here.'

'Oh, you can buy them readily in Kermerdyn,' said Isabella. 'We shall purchase some tomorrow, and Geoffrey will take them to Maurice as a gift when he returns to the court.'

'So I am a raisin courier now?' asked Geoffrey, wondering to what depths he would have to plummet before his duties to the King were complete.

'We will buy *you* some, too,' promised Isabella. 'As payment.'

'Please do not,' said Geoffrey with a shudder. He took up his reins and prepared to leave, thinking he had abandoned Roger quite long enough.

'Wait – I will come with you,' said Hilde. She sounded disappointed that her reunion with her sister was going to be cut short.

Geoffrey smiled. 'Stay. You and Isabella will have much to discuss.' And, he thought but did not say, Hilde would be considerably safer in Hywel's stronghold than in town.

He rode to Kermerdyn alone, alert for trouble. He thought about Hywel as he went, and decided it was not surprising that there was speculation that he had discovered William's secret, because the man certainly possessed abilities and virtues in abundance. In fact, Geoffrey wondered whether that in itself would work against Hywel. There were men who would be jealous of such easy amiability, including King Henry.

When he arrived at the Trout, Geoffrey found Roger much improved and in the middle of consuming a gargantuan meal with Bale. He laughed when Geoffrey told him how Hywel had helped him search Rhydygors for William's secret.

'Let us hope he never learns the real reason for your interest in his domain,' he said. 'Incidentally, I have not been totally useless while you have been gone. I have done some investigating on your behalf.'

'Have you?' asked Geoffrey in alarm.

Roger grinned at his reaction. 'Nothing to cause you trouble, so do not worry. I asked the landlord whether he knew where the Bishop might be, and he said we are fortunate, because Wilfred is in Kermerdyn this month. He spends a lot of time travelling, apparently.'

'A few days' rest will put Sir Roger back on his feet,' said Bale, although Geoffrey could see the big knight would not need that long and suspected it was self-interest that prompted Bale's remark. Pulchria lived in Kermerdyn, and Bale did not find it easy to recruit female admirers.

They talked a while longer, but Roger was tired and sleep soon claimed him again. Geoffrey lay on a pallet that he had placed against the door – anyone invading would have to move him first – and stared at the ceiling as he thought of all he would have to do the following day. At first light, he would visit the abbey, and deliver the Archbishop's letter to Mabon's successor. He would have to apologize for the fact that Mabon had died in his home, too, and then assess the new abbot for his report to Henry. He would also try to search the place for William's secret.

When he finished that, he would deliver Henry's letter to Bishop Wilfred and hope to spend long enough in his company to gather sufficient information for the second half of his report. That done, he would set about exploring the church. And if those places did not reveal William's secret – and he had scant hope they would – he decided that he would tell Henry that a religious vision had turned William into a saint.

And William's murderer? Geoffrey would just have to tell His Majesty that too much time had passed to allow him to investigate the matter properly. He was loath to pass on his list of suspects – now down to Delwyn, Sear, Gwgan, Cornald and Pulchria – lest royal retribution followed and four innocents paid the price for one guilty party. He would also admit that there was insufficient evidence to trap Mabon's killer, and hoped the King would overlook the matter on the grounds that Mabon's successor was likely to be more malleable and less likely to fight with the Bishop.

It took a long time for him to fall asleep. His rest was plagued by concerns that Henry was going to be less than satisfied with his performance and might demand another favour to compensate. He dreamed about Tancred, too, and the clerks whose poisonous pens had destroyed their friendship. One disturbing nightmare had Eudo rising from his grave to stab Bishop Maurice with a quill, for failing to lay hold of *his* killer. All in all, Geoffrey was relieved when the first glimmer of grey showed morning was approaching.

Although Roger claimed he was fully recovered, Geoffrey could tell by the stiff way he held his arm that he was not. Roger did not argue when Geoffrey declined his company; he seemed more than happy to spend the day in the tavern, getting to know the locals and treating them to a session with his loaded dice. Geoffrey left Bale with strict instructions to keep him out of trouble.

Supposing he should at least try to make himself presentable when visiting two high-ranking churchmen, he washed in water from the well, shaved, donned a fresh shirt and leggings, and set Bale to cleaning his armour. He even raked his fingers through his hair to remove the mud and bits of vegetation that had collected in it since leaving Goodrich. Eventually, feeling he was as respectable as a travelling knight could make himself, he left, electing to walk so that his horse would be rested should he need it for a later journey.

It was not fully light as he walked up the hill from the quay, past where little fishermen's cottages hugged the side of the road. Eventually, he reached a gate in the ancient walls, which signalled the entrance to the town proper. He found the settlement was larger than he had thought, extending for some distance on its plateau. The walls were taller, too, and the houses inside were in good repair.

Just inside the gate was the church. As he passed it, he saw Sear in its graveyard with a tall, fierce-looking priest. Twenty or so soldiers were with them, all wearing conical metal helmets emblazoned with a small red castle. Geoffrey supposed the emblem represented Pembroc, and these were men Sear had left in Kermerdyn while he had travelled to Henry.

Geoffrey started to join them, to pay his own respects to Alberic, but Sear looked up with such a black scowl that he had second thoughts and continued on his way.

The monastery lay at the far end of the town, reached by means of a long, straight road that cut the settlement in two. He exited through the town walls by a second gate, and the abbey lay to his right. It was surprisingly grand, and the sturdy wall that ran around its entire circumference suggested its occupants thought it worth protecting. There was a large, stone-built church in the middle, as well as a dorter, refectory, stables and kitchens. It was considerably more luxurious than the castle, and rich aromas wafted from the bakery; the monks apparently enjoyed good food, as well as pleasant accommodation.

Geoffrey knocked on the gate and asked for an audience with Mabon's successor. The lay-brother took one look at the Crusader's cross on Geoffrey's surcoat and asked whether he would mind waiting outside while he went to see whether Ywain was available. Fortunately, Delwyn happened to be passing.

'It is all right,' he told the lay-brother. 'It is the King's messenger – the one who was ordered to escort me safely home. Follow me, Sir Geoffrey. I shall conduct you to Ywain.'

'How did your monastery receive the news about the death of Abbot Mabon?' asked Geoffrey as they went, to gauge the level of the apology he would have to offer.

Delwyn shrugged. 'Well, they were vexed at having to buy a coffin – the one you provided is now too full of arrow holes to go in our vault – but one of the lay-brothers offered to run us up a cheap one, so the expense will not be too great.'

Geoffrey was not sure how to reply to such an observation and said nothing.

'Ywain is praying over the corpse,' Delwyn went on. 'But he will be glad of an excuse to do something else for a while, so do not feel you are intruding on his grief.'

He was right: Ywain leapt to his feet when Delwyn introduced Geoffrey, and shot out of the church with indecent haste. He was a short man with a shock of white hair. Delwyn was unimpressed when Ywain ordered him to take his place by Mabon's bier.

'But I have been minding the thing for days,' he objected. 'I have no prayers left!'

'Then you will have to use your imagination,' said Ywain tartly. 'I am Abbot now, and you must do as I say.'

He was gleeful as Delwyn stalked inside the chapel with a face as black as thunder.

'I cannot abide that man, and he will not have the liberties he enjoyed when Mabon was in power. I shall see to that.'

'I am sorry Mabon is dead,' began Geoffrey. 'Especially as he died in my home.'

'Delwyn said he was poisoned,' said Ywain. 'Nasty stuff, poison. Very indiscriminate. I doubt anyone would have wanted to murder Mabon, so you should ask yourself whether it was a case of mistaken identity.'

Geoffrey stared at him. Could he be right? *Had* the poison been intended for someone else?

'Sit with me on this wall,' ordered Ywain, after he had instructed the lay-brother to bring them cups of warmed ale. 'I feel the need for fresh air after being closeted with that reeking corpse, and you do not look like a man who objects to being outside.'

When they were seated, Geoffrey handed him the letter, careful to ensure it was the one bearing Mabon's name and the green circle.

'I am sure Delwyn told you about this,' he said. 'Mabon declined to take it when I tried to pass it to him at Goodrich, and then he died . . .'

'Mabon was not a man for reading,' said Ywain, breaking the seal. 'I dealt with all his correspondence, which is why I was elected his successor. Delwyn thought the honour should fall to him, but none of us likes the man. But what is this? This epistle is not addressed to Mabon – it is for that scoundrel Bishop Wilfred!'

'Mabon's name is on the outside,' said Geoffrey, after a brief moment of panic. And there was the green circle that Eudo had drawn to represent Mabon; Wilfred's epistle was the fat one.

Ywain grimaced. 'Yes, it is, but obviously the King's clerk made an error, because it is addressed to Wilfred on the *inside*. It is about St Peter's Church and says that, from now on, all tithes and benefits will go to La Batailge instead of to him! Hah! The old devil will be livid. You had better make sure he gets it.'

'God's teeth!' muttered Geoffrey, a quick glance telling him that

Ywain was right. He could not imagine the Bishop would be pleased that his enemy should have perused it first.

'If you have one for Wilfred, too, then you had better give it to me,' said Ywain gleefully. 'The clerk will have confused them – so that the one for him will actually be for us.'

Geoffrey was unwilling to risk it. 'It is more likely that Eudo forgot to include yours at all.'

Ywain scowled. 'If you do give the other letter to Wilfred, and it *does* transpire to be to me, I shall not be amused. In fact, I shall write to the King and order you boiled in oil.'

'Please do not,' said Geoffrey tiredly. 'He might do it.'

Ywain made an impatient gesture. 'Eudo is not very efficient. He is one of those men who has risen higher than his abilities should have allowed, and he has made mistakes before. Do you know the kind of fellow?'

'Oh, yes,' said Geoffrey.

'The court is full of them,' Ywain went on bitterly. 'All Normans, who itch to see an end to Welsh foundations like this one, and want a Benedictine or Cistercian house established here instead. With a *Norman* abbot. Our days are numbered.'

'What will you do?' asked Geoffrey.

Ywain shrugged. 'Delwyn thinks we should ingratiate ourselves with the King – he went to court to try – but it was a waste of time. Our only hope is to support Hywel in all things, because *he* will not let a Welsh monastery be supplanted by Normans.'

'He seems a good man.'

'He is an *excellent* man – even better than William, and *he* was a saint. William was inclined to think nice things about people, whereas Hywel is more realistic and knows that people have human failings. We are safer with Hywel than we were with William.'

'Do you know anything about William's secret?' asked Geoffrey.

'I do, as a matter of fact,' replied Ywain. 'He mentioned it to me when it first happened to him – he needed to consult a priest, you see, and I was the best one available. But it pleased me to see all those greedy Normans scrabbling around for it, so I have never confided in anyone else.'

'Will you tell me?'

'No,' said Ywain. 'Why should I?'

Geoffrey hesitated.

'Oh, all right, then,' said Ywain, giving him a playful jab in the ribs. 'Your surcoat says you are a *Jerosolimitanus*, so you must be a decent soul.'

Geoffrey was bemused by the Abbot's capitulation. He wondered whether he was about to be regaled with a story that would make him look silly when he investigated it.

'And now you will not believe me,' said Ywain, reading his thoughts. 'Perhaps I *should* keep it to myself then, as I have done for the past seven years. It has been great fun watching everyone scrabble to learn the secret, but I am bored with the spectacle now. It would give me great satisfaction to share it.'

Geoffrey regarded him uncertainly. 'Does anyone else know you have it?'

'Of course not; the likes of Richard, Sear, Edward, Delwyn, and Pulchria would have used violence to make me tell.'

'Almost certainly,' agreed Geoffrey. He thought about what Mabon had believed. 'Did William have a vision? When he was near the river?'

'Yes,' said Ywain emphatically. 'Of the Blessed Virgin. And when she had gone, she left a statue of herself behind. William never showed it to me, but he said he had put it in a safe place.'

'And that was his secret?' asked Geoffrey. 'A statue?'

'A statue from the hands of Our Holy Mother herself,' corrected Ywain. 'A big one.'

'As a priest, you must have been interested in seeing it?' asked Geoffrey, not sure he believed him.

Ywain screwed up his face. 'Well, I considered asking for a peek, but William became rather holy after he set eyes on it, and I did not want the same thing to happen to me. I was tempted to tell Wilfred, though, because I would not mind seeing *him* cursed with sanctity. But it was more amusing to keep the tale to myself.'

'So why tell me?'

'Because, as a *Jerosolimitanus*, you have set eyes on the holiest sites in the world, and if *they* have not turned you religious, then neither will William's statue. I do not want any more saintly people wandering around Kermerdyn. It makes the rest of us look bad.'

'Where is this statue now?'

'Ah, there I cannot help you. William never told anyone.'

'May I look around your abbey?'

Ywain laughed. 'You think it is here? It is not – I have looked, believe me – but go ahead. No one will disturb you. And it is not in the church, either. If it had been, I would have found it, because I looked very carefully several times.'

Geoffrey took him at his word and explored every inch of the abbey, Ywain at his heels. But the Abbot was right: there was nothing to find.

Thoughts whirling, Geoffrey left the monastery. He knew he had been right to search the abbey, though, because William would not have shoved a gift from the Blessed Virgin somewhere profane – he would have placed it on hallowed ground. He trudged towards the church, not holding much hope of finding it there, either – it was more public than the monastery, and he suspected Ywain had been more thorough than he could ever be.

As he approached, he saw that Sear and his men were no longer in the graveyard, and the place where Alberic's coffin had lain was now a mound of cold soil. The priest with the fierce face was just locking the door as he arrived, using one of the largest keys Geoffrey had ever seen.

'Hah!' The priest jabbed the key challengingly at him. His robes were thin and threadbare, and he was wearing sandals, despite the nip of winter in the air. 'I want a word with you.'

'Do you indeed?' replied Geoffrey coolly. 'And who might you be?'

'Bishop Wilfred,' replied the priest. He waved an arm in a vigorous swinging motion, although Geoffrey was not sure what the gesture was meant to convey. 'And *this* is my See.'

'You do not look like a bishop,' said Geoffrey, wondering whether the priest was short of a few wits and in the habit of waylaying strangers with wild claims.

'And you do not look like a *Jerosolimitanus*,' retorted Wilfred. 'Far too clean by half. Not that I have met many, of course. They are rare in Wales. But why do you say I do not look like a bishop? Am I not regal enough for you?'

'Your manner is certainly regal,' said Geoffrey tartly. 'But most bishops I have met dress rather more grandly. Well, Giffard does not, but he is exceptional.'

Wilfred's manner softened. 'You know Giffard? He is a fine man, and it is a wicked shame that he was exiled for obeying his conscience. The Archbishop of York should *not* consecrate us. Only Canterbury can do that, and Giffard was right to reject York's blessing.'

'King Henry does not think so.'

Wilfred grimaced. 'No, I imagine not. But do not judge me on my working clothes, if you would be so kind. I have been painting, and I can hardly wear my finery for menial work, can I? Would you like to admire my masterpiece?'

It was an odd invitation, but it suited Geoffrey's purposes. He watched Wilfred unlock the door and followed him inside the church. The moment his eyes had grown accustomed to the gloom, his heart sank.

St Peter's was a large building, comprising a long nave, two aisles and an enormous chancel. Every available patch of wall was graced with an alcove in which stood a statue. Some were small, some were large, some finely wrought, others crude. Most were of St Peter and Mary, with a few local saints thrown in. He wondered if he would be able to determine which was William's. Or should he merely pick one and present it to Henry, knowing His Majesty would never be able to tell the difference?

'I have letters for you from the King,' he said, reaching inside his shirt for the thick packet and the one Ywain had opened. He handed them over; he now only had Sear's left to deliver.

Wilfred snatched them. 'Yes! That was why I wanted a word with you. That rodent Delwyn hinted there might be something coming my way from His Majesty.' He grinned gleefully. 'I antici-pate that I shall be the richer at the end of it. Not that I have any great love of wealth, of course.'

Geoffrey took a step away, knowing Wilfred was going to be disappointed. He was not wrong. As the bishop read what was written, his face went from pleasure to rage.

'What is this?' he cried. 'I am to give seven of my churches to foundations in England! My taxes are raised, too. And why is the seal broken? It is addressed to Mabon on the outside, but me inside. Did you give it to the Abbot to read first?'

'I am afraid so,' admitted Geoffrey. 'A clerical error, and not my fault.'

'But it says I am to give the tithes and benefits of St Peter's to La Batailge!' shouted Wilfred, his furious voice ringing down the nave. 'And it is my favourite church in the whole See!'

'I am sorry,' said Geoffrey quietly.

'And Abbot Ywain knows about it?' yelled Wilfred. 'Damn you for a scoundrel, man!'

'It was not deliberate,' said Geoffrey, beginning to edge away. He stopped when a sly expression crossed Wilfred's face.

'Hah! Come and see this! You have made two errors, because here is a parchment that is addressed to me on the *outside*, but Mabon on the *inside*. It says the abbey is to obey me in all things. This is excellent news! I shall deliver it immediately. Better still, you can do it. They will be livid!'

'Then I decline the honour.'

'Ah, but wait,' said Wilfred, frowning as he continued reading. 'It says that, in compensation, Ywain can claim one hundred marks from the treasury. That is not fair! I am deprived of money, but he is given a fortune! I had better see what can be done to eliminate this final paragraph, and just give Ywain the first half of the letter. You can deliver the revised edition tomorrow.'

Geoffrey regarded him with distaste, feeling he had learned all he needed to know about the characters of Bishop Wilfred and the Abbot. 'I will not do it.'

'I do not blame you,' said Wilfred, patting his shoulder. 'I do not like visiting the abbey myself. But it cannot be helped; you will just have to grit your teeth and know you are earning your reward in Heaven.'

'There is just one more missive,' said Geoffrey, declining to debate the matter. 'From Bishop Maurice of London.'

'Dear old Maurice,' mused Wilfred fondly, taking the letter and breaking the seal. 'How is his medical condition? It must be a wretched nuisance to be so afflicted, and I admire him for overcoming adversity and continuing with his sacred work.'

'He is a good man,' said Geoffrey pointedly. 'Not prone to cheating the abbeys in his See.'

'It is a prayer. How thoughtful! And by Giffard, too. Actually, it is rather beautiful.' Wilfred became sombre suddenly. 'It is about

forgiveness, compassion and kindness – virtues Giffard has in
abundance, but not ones that come readily to me. Maurice is
wise to remind me of them.'

Geoffrey read it. It was one he had heard Giffard use before,
and reminded him that his friend was a deeply devout man, unlike
most of the clerics he knew.

'It is beautiful,' he said, admiring the simple poetry of the
words. 'And you are right: he should not be exiled for following
his conscience.'

For a while, both men were silent. Wilfred took the prayer and
read it again, while Geoffrey stared towards the high altar, aware
of the peace and stillness. It was a lovely building.

'But I brought you here to admire my work,' said Wilfred
suddenly, making Geoffrey jump. 'Not to stand here praying.
Come with me.'

He led the way down the nave towards the rood screen, against
which leaned a precarious piece of scaffolding. Pots and brushes
were arranged neatly on a table nearby, and sheets had been spread
across the floor.

'It is a depiction of Judgement Day,' explained Wilfred. 'And
to make it more terrifying for my flock, I have included local
features. You can see Rhydygors at the top, being burned by a
fire-breathing dragon, and the abbey is at the bottom, inviting
the Devil in.'

'*Mabon* is inviting the Devil in,' corrected Geoffrey.

Wilfred rubbed his chin. 'So he is. I had better wash him off
and insert Ywain instead. It is one thing attacking the living, but
it is unfair to tackle the dead, who are not in a position to appreciate it. Do you recognize any familiar faces among the souls
burning in Hell at the bottom?'

'God's teeth!' muttered Geoffrey, as several jumped out at him.
'Is that legal?'

Wilfred sniggered. 'What are they going to do about it? Besides,
I am doing them a favour. They *should* be thinking of their
immortal souls, and I am reminding them of what will be in
store if they do not do what the Church – me, in other words
– demands.'

'Is that William?' asked Geoffrey, pointing to a bright figure that was winging its way upwards, away from the rest of Kermerdyn's hapless residents.

Wilfred nodded. 'He was a holy man, and it was a pity he died young. Still, we have Hywel now, who is just as valiant and honourable. I have been blessed with those at Rhydygors.'

'I understand William had a vision,' probed Geoffrey.

Wilfred nodded. 'He was always rather cagey about it, although I did inform him he should tell *me* about the experience, because I am a bishop.'

'And did he oblige?' asked Geoffrey.

Wilfred grimaced. 'Only on his deathbed, when he was not in control of his wits – and then I was obliged to listen for days before I had the full story from him. He claimed it happened when he was bathing in the river, and that it entailed the Blessed Virgin.'

'He told Abbot Mabon much the same.'

Wilfred's expression hardened. 'Did he? Well, he went further with me. He claimed she said some very nice things about Wales, and that she was carrying a sword – although I may have misheard the last bit. She also advised him to eat wisely and stay away from mandrake juice, which has a tendency to make men see things that are not there.'

Geoffrey stared at him. Wilfred's testimony contained elements of all the theories that had been repeated to him on the journey from England. He could only suppose that the Bishop had been more assiduous at listening to a dying man's ravings than the others and had come away with a more complete picture.

'Did he ever mention a statue?' he asked.

'Not to me, although he did have a penchant for them. He donated every one of the carvings you can see in this church.'

Clever William, thought Geoffrey, looking around in awe. The man had known that concealing his secret might mean it could be lost for ever, so he had hidden it in plain sight – among the scores of other icons he had bought to keep it company.

'I do not suppose he had a favourite, did he?'

Wilfred seemed startled by the question. 'Well, yes, he did, as a matter of fact, although no one has ever asked me about it before. Would you like me to show you?'

Geoffrey nodded, and the Bishop led him to the Lady Chapel.

It was a small, intimate place, and the worn stones on the floor suggested it was also a popular one. Geoffrey understood why. It exuded an aura of tranquillity and felt sacred, even to a man normally immune to such sensations.

'That one, in the niche above the sedilla,' whispered Wilfred, pointing upwards. 'He was always in here praying to it. Well, it is of the Virgin, so I suppose it was not surprising.'

Geoffrey stared at one of the most beautiful carvings he had ever seen. It showed a woman in flowing robes of purest alabaster; the only colour was the sapphires of her eyes.

Geoffrey gazed at the statue for a long time before he spoke. In his imagination, he could almost see William kneeling by the altar, lifting his eyes towards it.

'William's secret,' he whispered.

'What are you talking about?' demanded Wilfred irritably. 'Have you been listening to local gossip? There was a tale that William had acquired a secret that made him turn his back on his sinful ways to live a godly life, but it was nonsense. It was his *vision* that changed him.'

'You seem very sure.'

'I *am* sure! A *vision* is religion, but a *secret* is superstition. Surely, you see the difference?'

'Not really.'

'Of course,' Wilfred went on, not interested in his reply, 'this was one of the first statues he brought to us, and he insisted on carrying it here himself, despite the fact that it is heavy. The others were delivered by his soldiers.'

'Did this happen soon after his vision?'

'Very soon.' Wilfred gaped at him. 'Are you saying those tales were right? That the Blessed Virgin *did* give him something to remember her by, and it was this statue? But it is a worldly thing, and when I came to clean it, there were bits of river weed behind her eyes.'

'I suspect what happened was that William went swimming and he saw this statue in the water,' explained Geoffrey. 'We will never know whether it really spoke to him, but he certainly believed it did, and it changed him. He brought it here, of course; what better place for something he believed to be holy?'

'But if you are right, then why did he not tell everyone his secret was this statue? Why stay silent and let all those silly rumours take hold?'

Geoffrey shrugged. 'I cannot answer that.'

'But I can,' said Wilfred thoughtfully. 'People gave him a lot of cloying attention once they thought he was holy, and he hated it. If this carving really is the essence of his vision, then he may well have wanted to protect her from self-serving petitioning.'

It seemed as reasonable an explanation as any.

'This statue has never performed any miracles, though,' Wilfred went on. 'And she has been in here for nigh on ten years.'

'Well, there is a good reason for that,' said Geoffrey. 'Namely that it is not the Blessed Virgin.'

Wilfred gaped at him a second time. 'How do you know?'

'My liege lord, Tancred, hails from Italy, and I lived there for several years. I know the carvings of the ancient Romans. This is Aphrodite, the goddess of beauty.'

'Are you sure?' asked Wilfred dubiously. 'She looks like the Blessed Virgin to me.'

'Quite sure. There are several just like it in Rome. Moreover, I think you will find that blessed virgins do not smile in quite such an alluring manner.' Geoffrey produced the little statue he had found in Lanothni. 'Here is another.'

'You carry them around with you?' breathed Wilfred, shocked. 'What are you — a heathen?'

'I found it two days ago,' explained Geoffrey. 'Kermerdyn was a thriving Roman settlement once — they would not have invested in such enormous walls had it been small and insignificant — so it is not surprising that their treasures appear from time to time.'

Wilfred took it from him. 'They are identical! It is a pity you were not here seven years ago. You could have confounded all these silly tales and prevented needless speculation. You might even have saved a good man's life, because I am sure William was murdered.'

'I do not suppose you know by whom?' asked Geoffrey hopefully.

'No, although I have plenty of suspects. Top of the list is Sear, the man whose dearest friend I laid in the earth today. He did not shed a single tear.'

'That does not mean he did not care,' said Geoffrey. 'But why do you think he killed William?'

'Because I do not like him,' replied Wilfred, as if that was all that needed to be said. 'And his clerks made an error when calculating the taxes owed by his Pembroc subjects – but he still insisted on claiming the higher amount, even when the mistake was exposed. It makes him a thief.'

'Doubtless the King did not mind,' said Geoffrey.

'Oh, *he* was very happy. But Sear could not keep collecting it, because it was turning Pembroc destitute. That was why he went to La Batailge – to explain in person why the King would be getting less in future. I did not envy him that task, because His Majesty is partial to revenue and would not have been pleased by the news.'

Geoffrey wondered whether Sear had decided not to do it at the last minute; he had detected no cooling in the relationship between monarch and subject. And Wilfred was right: Henry would not have been pleased to learn he was losing a source of income.

'Who else is on your list of suspects for killing William?' he asked.

'Anyone who was jealous of William's success,' replied Wilfred. 'And that includes all of Kermerdyn and half the surrounding villages. Why? Do you intend to solve that mystery, too? If so, I wager it will take you a good deal longer than it did to identify his secret.'

Thirteen

Geoffrey left the church pleased with his progress. He had identified William's secret and delivered all the King's letters, except Sear's. He also knew what he was going to write in his report about the warring churchmen. Moreover, the germ of a solution had begun to grow regarding William's murder: he was fairly sure he knew who had committed the crime. The answer to one question would tell him for certain, and he intended to ask it immediately.

There was an apothecary's shop near the church, but it was closed. Geoffrey waited outside, thinking that it was mid-morning, late for merchants to open. He was about to give up when the owner arrived, rubbing his hands together in greedy anticipation when he saw a customer waiting.

'I am unusually late, because of the news,' he explained as he unlocked the door. 'So please forgive my tardiness.'

'What news?' asked Geoffrey.

'Richard fitz Baldwin's home was attacked last night. He escaped harm, but fled the town, saying he is not going to wait here for another attempt on his life. At first, folk said it was his own soldiers who staged the assault – he is not popular – but two of them were killed in the incident.'

'Killed by Richard?'

'Killed by whoever broke into his home with knives and crossbows. From what I gather, it was fortunate more were not slaughtered, although word is that they were aiming for Richard, not his minions.'

'Was Leah harmed?' asked Geoffrey, concerned.

The apothecary lowered his voice confidentially. 'It pains me to say something nice about such a rank villain, but Richard does love his wife. He protected her bravely last night, then gave her to Abbot Ywain this morning, hoping she will be safe inside a holy place.'

'Where has Richard gone?'

The apothecary waved his hand. 'The forests that surround us will keep a man hidden for as long as he pleases, and the marshes are lonely and abandoned. He might have gone anywhere. Personally I hope he stays away, because he is not good for Kermerdyn with his brutality and pent-up fury. It is a pity he is not like his brother.'

Geoffrey asked the apothecary his question. When he had the answer, he knew, beyond the shadow of a doubt, what had happened to William. He thanked the man and retraced his steps to the abbey. The monks were in their chapel, praying for Mabon, but Leah was sitting on the wall where Geoffrey and Ywain had talked earlier. Her eyes were red, and she was pale and wan.

'You heard what happened?' she whispered when Geoffrey approached. Tears began to fall. 'Men broke into our home, and would have killed us if Richard had not fought like the Devil. Now he has fled, and I am left here in the hope that Abbot Ywain can protect me.'

'I doubt anyone will harm you,' said Geoffrey gently.

'I was worried about our travelling companions, too,' sobbed Leah. Geoffrey perched next to her. 'So I sent our apprentices to find out whether they were attacked. Gwgan was ambushed as he walked home last night, but everyone else is safe, thank God.'

'Gwgan fought them off?'

'He had just dispatched a unit of men to hunt for the outlaws, but, luckily, they heard the clash of arms and galloped back. The villains escaped, though; Gwgan said they knew the area.'

Geoffrey was thoughtful. He had delivered royal letters to Gwgan and Richard. Could it be that the ambushes since Brechene were aimed at *them*? He wondered whether Sear would become a target when given his letter. But such ponderings would have to wait. He turned to Leah.

'I did not come here to talk about ambushes,' he said. 'I came to ask why you killed William.'

There was silence, and Geoffrey was aware of chaffinches twittering as they squabbled for the crumbs that had been brushed outside the kitchen door. He could hear the river, too, a soft gurgle as it flowed towards the sea. It was peaceful and idyllic, and it was difficult to believe he was sitting next to a poisoner.

Leah gaped at him. 'But I am one of few people who could *not* have killed William: I was ill in bed when he died. Anyone will confirm my tale *and* tell you that my ailment was genuine, because I have never fully recovered my health.'

'No,' agreed Geoffrey. 'But that is because you were either careless with what is a very potent substance or unsure how to use it. You put it in the butter that your husband brought for his brother from Pulchria, but you did not need to be present when your victim ate it.'

'What are you saying?' cried Leah in horror. 'These are terrible accusations!'

'I am saying that I allowed myself to be misled by your alibi. Your whereabouts when William became ill and died are irrelevant – the poison could have been sent ages before he actually consumed it. But I imagine you did select Cornald's butter as the way to get rid of him. And it was a perfect choice – a lot of people had access to it.'

'Yes, they did,' said Leah, white with shock. 'It was a gift from Pulchria, and she is a much more likely candidate for murder than me – she was terribly bitter when William rejected her. And you know for a fact that she dislikes being repelled, because she threatened you, too.'

'She did, but it was all hot air. Besides, she thought Joan kept wolf-tooth for killing rats, but it is never used for that purpose. Her knowledge of poisons is deficient. I know she did not kill Mabon for the same reason.'

'But Cornald's knowledge is not deficient,' said Leah. 'And *he* made the butter.'

'Cornald has an aversion to wolf-tooth and would not have used it. I know he is telling the truth, because of the rash he developed after touching the phial that killed Mabon. Besides, he has been Joan's friend for years, and I trust her judgement.'

'Then what about Delwyn?' asked Leah desperately. 'Or Bishop Wilfred? Both were lurking in the kitchen where the butter was stored.'

'Neither would have risked meddling with poisons while the other was there – abbey and Bishop hate each other, and any suspicious behaviour would have been exposed with glee.'

'But there are others,' insisted Leah. 'Sear—'

'Sear's grief was genuine. He did not kill his friend. The same goes for Richard.'

'Hywel and Gwgan had access to Rhydygors, too. And Hywel inherited the castle . . .'

'Hywel could not have known seven years ago that he would be awarded Rhydygors for fighting Bellême on the Marches. And Gwgan has learned enough about poisons from Isabella not to inflict a lingering death on his victim. If he had been the killer, he would have used something quicker. He was appalled by William's suffering.'

'But there were servants . . .'

'Yes, the list of suspects is enormous,' acknowledged Geoffrey. 'And you must have been delighted by the way events unfolded, with everyone accusing everyone else. The only problem was that *you* were affected by the poison, too, and almost lost your life over it. Of course, it did mean you were the last person anyone would ever suspect.'

'That is because I am innocent,' protested Leah.

'William told Delwyn that he had been killed by a dear friend. I imagine he considered you – the wife of his beloved brother – a dear friend.'

'Well, yes, he did, but why would I kill a man everyone loved? Besides, Richard was heartbroken when William died.'

'Yes, he did love his brother. Perhaps more than you realized, because I doubt you intended to cause him so much pain. You killed William because you knew that, as long as he lived, Richard would never have anything. William was the better man in all respects—'

'No!' cried Leah. 'William was *never* the better man! His sickly saintliness was ridiculous, and I hated the way everyone kept comparing the two and finding Richard lacking. It was unfair.'

She flushed in horror when she saw her outburst was effectively an admission of guilt. Then she closed her eyes and slumped in defeat. 'All right. How did you guess?'

'The apothecary has just told me that you regularly buy herbs to make remedies for the headaches that plague you. About the time William died, you started using wolf-tooth. It is beneficial in small quantities, and you have no doubt learned to use it properly since. But seven years ago, you shoved some in William's butter and subjected him to a terrible death.'

'You cannot prove it,' said Leah, with a spark of defiance. 'So what if I buy wolf-tooth? You cannot prove it was my supply that killed him – or even that he was poisoned at all. If you dig him up, he will be nothing but bones and dust. And people will never believe what you are saying. They all think I am too feeble.'

'You are not feeble,' said Geoffrey. 'You are kin to Robert de Bellême, the great tyrant. I guessed the first time we met that there was more to you than you let anyone see, and I was right. Did you poison Mabon, too?'

'No,' said Leah firmly. 'You will probably accuse me of it, because some of my wolf-tooth did go missing at Goodrich, but I swear to you, on Richard's life, that I did not kill Mabon.'

Geoffrey recalled Father Adrian's testimony – that Leah, Richard and Edward had sought absolution the morning Mabon had died, and murder had not been among the sins they had confessed. Moreover, Leah would not risk the life of the man she loved by swearing lies on it. Reluctantly, he accepted that she was not the culprit, although he was not about to say so.

'Why did you not mention this theft immediately?' he demanded.

'Because you might have accused *me* of the crime,' said Leah. 'It was safer to say nothing.'

'Was any other toxin missing?' asked Geoffrey. 'Or just wolf-tooth?'

'I do not have any other toxins,' Leah snapped. 'Wolf-tooth is not a poison anyway. It is—'

'Who took it?'

'It might have been anyone staying at your nasty little castle,' she hissed, voice full of spite. 'Gwgan, perhaps; you have just said that he knows all about fast-acting poisons.'

'Gwgan had no reason to kill Mabon. Indeed, I imagine he would rather Mabon was alive, because he was a strong man, who would have kept the abbey Welsh. Ywain is not his equal and will be unable to keep it from being overrun by Normans.'

'Then it was someone else,' she snarled. 'Including your wife and sister, so do not think you can level accusations at *me* without them being dragged into the matter. If you charge me publicly, I will see they will suffer, too.'

Geoffrey regarded her contemptuously. 'You would harm the innocent to save yourself?'

Leah returned his glare in kind. 'Yes, if you leave me no other choice. I *did* do a wicked thing seven years ago, but I have paid the price by not being well since. And I did not mean to kill William, anyway.'

'No?' asked Geoffrey coldly. 'What then?'

'I meant to make him ill, to shake him from his smug conviction that he was touched by God. I thought a fright might instil some humility into him. But he died, and Richard did not inherit—'

'And there is your real motive,' pounced Geoffrey. 'You wanted Richard in Rhydygors, taking William's place.'

'No!' cried Leah. 'Well, yes. I suppose so. I did it for Richard, because I thought he would be happier if his brother was not so saintly. There is no reason for you to believe me, but murder was *not* my intention. I was young and foolish, and blinded by love for an unhappy man.'

'What will he say when he learns what you have done?'

'He will never know,' said Leah. There was something cold and hard in her eyes that was definitely redolent of Bellême. 'Because I will not tell him, and neither will you. If you do, you will be more sorry than you can imagine.'

Geoffrey took his leave of Leah, stopping only to ask Ywain to make sure she did not leave the abbey. He was not sure what to do about her and decided to ask Hilde's opinion. Roger would doubtless recommend hanging her, but Hilde would offer sensible advice.

When he arrived at the inn, he found Roger surrounded by townsfolk as he regaled them with lies about the Crusade. His face was flushed from the amount of ale he had consumed, and he shook his head at Geoffrey to say that he did not want to be interrupted. Geoffrey went to the stable, collected his horse and set out towards Rhydygors.

But when he reached the castle, he was told that Hilde had gone out with Isabella to buy raisins. Laughingly, Prince Hywel informed Geoffrey that he would be unlikely to see his wife before sunset.

'And do not even think of trying to hunt her down,' he added. 'It will be like looking for a needle in a haystack.'

Geoffrey nodded, although his attention was taken by Gwgan, who had the entire garrison assembled in the bailey. They wore travelling packs and were being issued with enough rations to suggest they might be gone for some time. Clearly, Hywel was taking seriously the presence of outlaws in his domain and was doing all he could to round them up.

'I heard Gwgan was ambushed last night,' said Geoffrey.

'We are fortunate our men heard the clash of weapons and raced back to help him,' said Hywel grimly. 'There is no question that he would have been killed otherwise, and I would have lost my trusted counsellor and most beloved friend.'

'Richard was attacked last night, too, and has fled the town.'

Hywel shook his head slowly. 'These villains are bold and reckless to stage an assault within sight of the castle. Gwgan recommended that we send every available man out to track them, and he is right. My only regret is that pressing business will keep me here until tomorrow.'

'But then you will go?' asked Geoffrey.

'At first light,' said Hywel. He smiled. 'And any knight who would like to join me will be welcome. Especially one who speaks Welsh.'

Geoffrey nodded agreement. 'But is it wise to send *all* your soldiers? You will not consider keeping some in reserve, lest the town is attacked again?'

It was not his place to question the tactics of another commander, especially one who was the ruler of vast tracts of land, but the questions were out before he could stop himself.

Fortunately, Hywel did not seem to mind. 'Richard's men can defend the town, and Gwgan's personal guard are more than capable of manning the castle. We have no choice, anyway: what would my people say if I sat safe and secure in Rhydygors, while they cannot ride my highways unmolested?'

Geoffrey made no reply, although his soldier's instincts warned him that Hywel's plan was not a good one. He wondered whether he should take Hilde somewhere else. But where?

'Stay here with Hilde tonight,' said Hywel, reading his mind. 'She will be safe enough, but I can see you would prefer to see to her well-being yourself.'

'You will not be here?' asked Geoffrey.

'I am dining with Gwgan in his home.' Hywel waved his hand towards the nearby hamlet, its rooftops just visible through the trees. 'There is much to discuss after his visit to Gloucester, but we have no peace here. We will work twice as quickly in his house, and then nothing will stop me riding out after these outlaws tomorrow.'

Geoffrey had two more letters to hand over before his delivery duties were complete, and he decided to be rid of them as soon as possible. Unfortunately, Sear had taken his Pembroc soldiers to hunt for the outlaws and was not expected back until evening. Robert the steward was at work in an office, though, and snatched the letter eagerly when it was presented.

'It is all about Maurice's new cathedral,' he cried in disappointment. 'I thought it would be something useful – something I could use to avert the trouble I sense is brewing.'

'What trouble?' asked Geoffrey.

'The trouble that started the moment you and your companions rode into our town with tales of outlaws. It was peaceful when Sear and Richard were away, but the instant they return, we are thrown into turmoil.'

'Bishop Maurice merely heard I was travelling west and used the opportunity to write to distant kin,' said Geoffrey. 'He knows nothing of—'

'I do not like the fact that Richard has disappeared,' interrupted Robert. 'It bodes ill.'

'You cannot blame him for not wanting to be in a place where he is in danger,' said Geoffrey. 'We were ambushed nine times between here and Brechene, and he might have been the target.'

'Nevertheless,' said Robert, 'I sense evil in the air.'

'Oh,' said Geoffrey, unsure what to make of such a claim. 'Perhaps you should see a priest.'

'They cannot help,' said Robert scornfully. 'The kind of wickedness I sense is the earthly kind, which can only be defeated by stout men with swords. You look sceptical, but I have a talent for predicting this kind of misfortune. It runs in the family – just ask Maurice.'

'He does claim an ability to sense evil,' acknowledged Geoffrey, recalling Maurice's unhappiness over Henry's letters and the way he had rubbed them and blessed them.

'Well, so do I,' said Robert. 'And I sense it now, with every fibre of my being.'

Geoffrey regarded him uncertainly. 'Then tell Gwgan or Hywel.'

'I have, but they will not listen. But I *know* Richard is up to something. There was a cant to his eyes when he reported the attack this morning, and he took all his men with him when he left Kermerdyn. Something is badly wrong, and you must stop it.'

'Me?' asked Geoffrey, startled. 'How? I am a stranger to the area.'

'That does not matter,' cried Robert, agitated. 'You must try.'

'It might help if you were more specific—'

'I cannot be more specific!' snapped Robert. 'I only know that you must be on your guard, and you must protect others who are not in a position to do so themselves.'

'Do you mean my wife?' asked Geoffrey in alarm, wondering whether he should ignore Hywel's advice and try to find her.

'I do not *know* what I mean!' shouted Robert in frustration. 'You will just have to use your imagination. Maurice writes that you are intelligent, so use the wits God gave you.'

It was hardly helpful advice, and Geoffrey left him in a troubled frame of mind.

The first thing Geoffrey wanted to do was to warn Roger to be on his guard. The next was to find Hilde. He collected his horse and was about to ride back to Kermerdyn when he saw Gwgan. The counsellor's face was pale and worried.

'We *must* catch these villains,' he said, when Geoffrey reined in next to him. 'They attacked Richard, as well as me, last night, and it is not to be countenanced. Not in Hywel's domain.'

'It is unwise to leave the castle so depleted of soldiers,' said Geoffrey, knowing Gwgan would not object to him speaking his mind. 'Robert is right: something untoward *is* afoot.'

Gwgan groaned. 'Robert and his stupid premonitions! I did not expect *you* to be unsettled by his ravings, though – I had taken you for a steady man. Our steward is a silly old woman; I do not know why Hywel does not replace him.'

'Perhaps so, but it is unwise to take Hywel away from the castle tonight,' persisted Geoffrey. 'He might be needed to defend it. And so might you.'

'My house is not far,' said Gwgan impatiently. 'We can be back in moments, should the need arise – which it will not. But there is daylight left, and I intend to use it. My guards and I will scour the marshes until dusk. Will you come with us? Another pair of eyes would be useful.'

'My first duty is to Hilde and Roger, but I will ride with you and Hywel tomorrow.'

'The best way to protect your wife and friend is to help me today,' said Gwgan. 'Besides, you will never find Hilde if Isabella has taken her shopping.'

'I will not rest easy until I try,' said Geoffrey. 'I will ride after you later.'

Gwgan nodded his thanks and climbed on to a Welsh pony. He raised his hand to indicate he was ready, then trotted out of the bailey with his men at his heels. Geoffrey followed and was almost at the gate when Edward entered, flopping about on his nag like a sack of grain.

'Something nasty is happening in this town,' he declared without preamble. 'If I were you, I would leave. Take Hilde with you. She is too fine a person to be caught up in anything foul.'

'She is shopping,' said Geoffrey, alarmed. 'And I am told she will not be found.'

'Nonsense,' said Edward. 'They will be in Pedrog's warehouse on the wharf. All women go there around noon, because that is when Pedrog exhibits his newest wares.'

'Thank you,' said Geoffrey gratefully. 'What will you do?'

'My men arrived this morning from Brechene – minus the six or so who died from the contagion. They made better time than us, probably because they were not hindered by women. I intend to take them and leave Kermerdyn.'

'You will ride away when Hywel might need your assistance?' asked Geoffrey, shocked.

'He has plenty of good men, and this threat may extend to Kadweli. I am duty-bound to return there with all possible speed.

I repeat: collect your wife and your loutish friend and leave while you can.'

Geoffrey nodded. It was sound advice, and he fully intended to spirit Roger and Hilde to safety. Then he would return to Kermerdyn and help Hywel, as he had promised. Sear's letter could be delivered at the same time, and if Henry was piqued that his missive was not in his henchman's hands soon enough, then that was too bad.

It was not difficult to locate Pedrog's warehouse, because it was the building that had a steady stream of women walking in and out. Inside, Geoffrey was immediately aware of the musty scent of imported cloth, spices and other exotic goods. He found Hilde cooing over a stall filled with different kinds of raisins, Isabella standing smugly behind her.

'We have to go,' said Geoffrey, grabbing Hilde's hand and pulling her towards the door.

'No!' exclaimed Isabella in dismay. 'We have not explored the silks yet.'

Once again, Geoffrey gave thanks for his choice of wife when Hilde took one look at him and followed without demur, dragging her sister along.

'What is wrong?' she asked as they walked briskly towards the Trout. 'Where are we going?'

'Anywhere but here,' said Geoffrey. 'It is not safe.'

'I have enough money with me to keep us for a week,' said Hilde. 'We can send for our belongings later. Should Isabella come with us?'

'Yes,' said Geoffrey. He felt something akin to love for Hilde at that moment – she did not regale him with questions, but rather turned her considerable intelligence to deciding how best to help him. Isabella, however, was far more vocal, and Geoffrey saw she was going to be a problem.

'I am not going anywhere until you explain what is happening,' she declared. 'This is my home and . . . Oh, look! There is Sir Sear. That is odd! He told my husband he was going to hunt for outlaws.'

'He is going into the Trout,' said Hilde worriedly. 'Roger was well on the way to being drunk there not long ago. I hope they do not fight.'

Geoffrey abandoned the women and his horse and ran towards the inn. He flung open the door and found the main room almost empty, its regulars driven away by Roger's tales – enjoyable and even believable at first, but degenerating into absurdity as the ale flowed. Bale was still there, lying on a bench with his mouth open, and Roger was slumped across a table. Sear was leaning over him. Geoffrey hurtled forward and shoved the older knight away.

'Easy!' yelled Sear angrily, staggering. 'I was only making sure he was not dead. He does not usually drink himself into unconsciousness, and I was concerned.'

Hand on the hilt of his dagger, Geoffrey felt for a life-beat in Roger's neck. It was strong, but sluggish. He crossed to Bale and did the same, although the squire stirred at his touch and opened bleary eyes.

'God's nails!' Bale swore, struggling to sit. 'That last brew was potent! I only had a gulp, and it made me reel like a virgin. That Richard certainly knows his claret!'

Geoffrey stared at him. 'Richard sent you claret?'

Bale waved a hand, the gesture almost unseating him. 'It is on the table. Richard's message said it was for both of you, and I doubt Sir Roger has finished it. I will fetch you a clean cup.'

He tried to stand but slumped back down again, holding his head in his hands and moaning. Sear released one of his harsh brays of laughter.

'They are *both* drunk! I heard men gossiping in the street that they had been at the ale since dawn, and the claret proved too much for them. I hope they have not drunk the place dry, because I have been out doing a man's work and I am thirsty.'

'They are not drunk,' said Geoffrey, his stomach churning as he darted to the table and grabbed the jug. Was it Leah's doing, in revenge for his discovery of her dark secret? She had threatened to make him sorry, but he had not anticipated she would strike quite so soon.

The door opened, and the taverner arrived. Behind him was the apothecary Geoffrey had spoken to that morning. Hilde and Isabella crowded in behind them.

'There you are,' said the taverner, relieved. 'Good. When your friend flopped across the table and resisted my attempts to wake him, I thought I had better fetch help, but I am glad you are here, because *you* can put him to bed. He is a too heavy for me to haul upstairs.'

The apothecary examined Roger briefly, then turned his attention to the wine jug Geoffrey shoved into his hands, first sniffing cautiously at its contents and then taking a tentative sip.

'Something has been added,' he announced. 'A soporific. And from the flavour, I would say it is the one I prescribe for over-feisty horses.'

'Have you sold any to Leah recently?' asked Geoffrey, watching Hilde manoeuvre Roger into a position where he would not choke.

'Not Leah,' replied the apothecary, going to Bale and assessing him, too. 'But Richard was having trouble with a nag last night and came to me for the remedy. This was before he was attacked, of course. Surely, you cannot suspect *he* had anything to do with this?'

'The wine came from him,' insisted Bale, finally managing to stand. 'Ask the landlord.'

'It is true,' agreed the landlord. 'Richard delivered it last night. He ordered me to give it to you at noon and to make sure you both enjoyed it. I thought it was an odd request – he is not usually a generous man – but I did as I was told.'

'You should have refused,' said the apothecary sternly. 'Any fool could see the instruction was sinister, and now we have two men poisoned. But do not worry, Sir Geoffrey. Your friend has not swallowed enough of it to be dangerous, and your squire is already rallying. They will both be recovered tomorrow.'

'I knew Richard did not like you,' said Sear wonderingly. 'But I did not think he would stoop to poison. It is a shameful way to eliminate enemies, even for a villain like him.'

Geoffrey was in an agony of guilt. It was *his* fault Roger was laid low. He had brought his friend to Kermerdyn, knowing Henry's mission was dangerous, and first Roger was shot and now he was poisoned. He wished with all his heart that he had left him and Hilde at Goodrich.

'What are you going to do?' asked Sear with professional interest. 'Hunt Richard down and challenge him to fight? I would, in your position. He will cheat, though, so watch him.'

'No,' said Hilde urgently, grabbing Geoffrey's arm. 'Think! There is something odd about this whole business. Richard wanted you incapacitated at a specific time. Why? It all reeks of intrigue, and you should stay here until you understand what is happening.'

'Actually, that is good advice,' said Sear soberly. 'Heed her, Geoffrey.'

Geoffrey decided he would make up his own mind what to do about Richard, although he stayed long enough to help Bale carry Roger to the chamber upstairs, where they saw him comfortably installed. The apothecary assured him again that his friend would make a complete recovery, and Hilde settled at the bedside to monitor him for as long as was necessary. Isabella had disappeared, but returned not long afterwards with three burly men who, she said, hired their services to anyone needing stalwart guards.

'They have repelled Richard before,' she said. 'They do not like him.'

'Good,' said Geoffrey. 'Because they will protect you, Hilde *and* Roger tonight. They will be paid double what you offered if they succeed, but if they fail, I will hunt them out and kill them.'

The men met his gaze steadily as they nodded agreement to his terms. It was a reassuring reaction, but he would not be easy in his mind until he had tackled Richard and was back in the tavern watching over his wife and friend.

'You plan to challenge him?' asked Hilde in alarm, as Geoffrey grabbed his helmet and buckled on the heavier of his two swords. He also tucked an extra dagger in his boot.

'Yes,' said Geoffrey shortly. 'Keep the door locked, and do not answer it to anyone.'

Sear was still in the main chamber when Geoffrey stalked through it. The older knight was about to make a quip about Roger's stupidity in imbibing wine sent from such a dangerous man, but stopped when he saw the expression on Geoffrey's face.

'The King ordered me to give you this when we arrived in Kermerdyn,' said Geoffrey, handing him the last letter. 'Do not ask why he told me to wait, because I do not know.'

He strode into the yard and yelled to one of the taverner's sons to fetch his horse. The lad started to roll his eyes – Hilde had ordered him to unsaddle and stable it only moments before – but a hard stare sent him scurrying off to oblige. Geoffrey was aware that Sear had followed him outside and had broken the seal of his letter to gaze uncomprehendingly at the words.

'Damn!' he muttered. 'Henry probably sent this because I told him he would not be getting such high taxes from Pembroc in the future. I thought reprisal would not be long in coming.'

'That is what happens when you serve a master who loves money above all else,' said Geoffrey, angry enough with Richard to speak recklessly.

'Henry is a good man,' declared Sear hotly.

'Right,' said Geoffrey, controlling his temper; it would be foolish to waste time and energy arguing with Sear.

'My clerks made an error in their calculations,' Sear went on, apparently feeling an explanation was in order. 'It resulted in people being charged too much, and I could not, in all conscience, let it continue. I went to tell him what had happened.'

Geoffrey did not reply. He was wondering where to begin his hunt for Richard.

Sear cleared his throat uncomfortably. 'Will you read it to me? I would rather not take it to the abbey, because they do not like me and will probably make me wait until morning.'

'No,' said Geoffrey. The King's letters had caused him enough trouble already.

'Damn it, man! Will you make me beg?' Then Sear's face took on a cunning expression. 'Or shall we make a bargain? You read me the letter, and I will tell you where Richard is likely to be hiding.'

'Where?'

'Do we have an agreement?'

Geoffrey nodded impatiently.

'There is an abandoned village about two miles south of Rhydygors,' began Sear. 'You cannot miss it if you follow the river path. It is where he and Leah courted, so it has special significance for him. Now read me the letter.'

Geoffrey took it from him and scanned it quickly. It was short, blunt, and its tone was cold and unfriendly. He handed it back. 'You will not want to hear this, and I have no time to accept challenges from you. Ask Bishop Wilfred. He will not make you wait.'

'No, tell me,' said Sear softly. 'I have been expecting something dire ever since I saw the flash in Henry's eyes when I explained about the taxes, and I feared his continued affection for me was a sham. Read it, Geoffrey. I swear we will not come to blows.'

'You are dismissed from Pembroc Castle and ordered to

hand over command to someone called Gerald of Windsor.'

'Gerald of Windsor,' mused Sear. 'A ruthless, greedy man who will have every last penny out of the hapless souls at Pembroc. Is that all?'

'No. As you are in Kermerdyn and have troops here, you are ordered to put them and yourself under Richard's authority and do whatever he says.'

'You lie!' yelled Sear, whipping out his sword.

Geoffrey drew his own weapon, finding he was more than ready to fight a man he had never liked. It would limber him up for when he met Richard. But it was not Geoffrey who was at the end of Sear's blade, but Cornald, who had just entered the yard and walked towards them.

'It is true!' squeaked Cornald. 'I swear!'

He tried to back away, but Sear clutched a handful of his tunic and gripped him so his feet barely touched the ground. Cornald was holding a purple glove that Geoffrey recognized as Edward's. Bemused, Geoffrey looked from one to the other, wondering what was happening.

'If you are lying, I will cut out your tongue,' snarled Sear.

'I swear to you, on holy William's soul, that this is the "evidence" from Lanothni,' gulped Cornald. 'It proves the attack was ordered by Edward.'

'What are you taking about?' demanded Geoffrey, lowering his sword.

'We had word from Fychan that he had discovered a clue to the identity of the raiders who attacked his inn,' explained Sear tersely. 'Having lost so much, he was rather more painstaking in his hunt for evidence than we were.'

'I still do not understand,' said Geoffrey.

'There was a witness – a villager saw and heard the raiders' leader giving them orders. This villager also saw the leader drop something on the ground by accident as he turned to leave. Cornald offered to return to Lanothni today, to collect it.'

'It was the least I could do,' said Cornald, freeing himself from Sear's grasp. He scowled. 'Although I would not have obliged, had I known I would be manhandled on my return.'

'My apologies,' said Sear stiffly. 'It was the shock.'

Geoffrey struggled to follow what they were saying. 'But Edward was injured in one of those attacks. He would hardly order—'

'Not very seriously injured,' interrupted Cornald. 'Moreover, another group of travellers arrived from Brechene last night. They told me they had not been attacked once on the road, nor was there any contagion in Brechene Castle.'

Geoffrey was bewildered. 'So Edward lied about his men being sick, and, instead of accompanying us, they harried us every inch of the way? But why?'

'I have no idea,' said Sear grimly. 'But your wife *and* Pulchria said the men who attacked you in Lanothni knew their way around in the dark – and Edward's men are mostly local. It would explain why Alberic and I were unable to catch them after you drove them off. I sense something evil is unfolding here, and Edward and Richard seem to be at the heart of it.'

Geoffrey tried to rally his reeling thoughts. 'I delivered two letters in Goodrich: one to Gwgan and one to Richard. All the ambushes concentrated on us knights – in our white surcoats, we doubtless look much the same to soldiers who do not know us. And it was Gwgan and Richard who were targeted last night. Perhaps . . .'

'Perhaps what?' demanded Sear impatiently.

'Perhaps Gwgan and Richard have been ordered to do something of which Edward disapproves,' finished Geoffrey.

'Something like what?'

Geoffrey shook his head slowly. 'Gwgan lied about the contents of his letter. He said it was about taxes and advowsons, but that sort of thing is complex, and his missive comprised a few sentences on one page – I saw it. It was much more likely to have contained an order.'

'Yes, but *what*?' demanded Cornald. 'And why send the order to him, not Hywel? The Prince is in charge of the region, and it is for him to carry out royal commands, not his counsellor.'

Hywel! Suddenly, the answer snapped into Geoffrey's mind, and it was so obvious he wondered why he had not seen it before.

'Everyone acknowledges that Hywel is a good and popular leader, and I know Henry resents it. He told me so in La Batailge. Eudo went further and said putting Hywel in power was a mistake. It is unwise for a vassal to outshine the King, but Hywel does, and it has not gone unnoticed.'

'You think Hywel will be ousted?' whispered Cornald, aghast. 'And that Richard and Gwgan will do it? But how? The people will not stand for a coup. They will support Hywel.'

'I doubt a coup is what they have in mind,' said Geoffrey soberly. 'The only way to eliminate the threat Hywel has become is to kill him.'

Cornald and Sear gaped at him. 'And how will they do that?' demanded Sear in disbelief. 'Hywel is safely inside Rhydygors, surrounded by a garrison that would die to protect him.'

'He will not be inside Rhydygors tonight,' said Geoffrey. 'He will be at the house of his trusted friend and counsellor. Alone, so they can do business together. And Hywel's troops – to the last man – have been sent out to round up these so-called outlaws.'

'Except Gwgan's personal guard,' said Cornald, aghast. 'They have been held back. When the garrison returns, Hywel will be dead and Richard will sit in his place. Or will it be Gwgan?'

'Richard,' replied Geoffrey. 'Henry will not want another Welshman in charge.'

'But Gwgan is Hywel's friend!' objected Cornald. 'They are like brothers. Why would he betray him?'

Geoffrey had no answer.

'So this is why I am ordered to serve Richard,' mused Sear. 'He will be the new lord, and I am expected to help him quell any resulting rebellions. Henry did not want me to know until we arrived in Kermerdyn, lest I took umbrage and disappeared home to Normandy.'

'Listen to what we are saying!' said Cornald, shaking his head. 'We are accusing the King of cold-blooded murder.'

'The evidence *is* compelling,' said Sear.

'Eudo,' said Geoffrey softly. 'Bishop Maurice said he schemed on the King's behalf. Moreover, he wrote the letters to Gwgan and Richard himself, and refused to let his deputies see what was in them. He even sealed them in such a way that they could not be opened.'

'So the King probably has no idea of what has been planned for Hywel,' said Cornald in relief. 'And all this treachery is the work of a clerk with misguided notions of loyalty.'

'But Eudo was murdered in La Batailge,' said Sear, frowning. 'Who . . .'

'Edward,' said Geoffrey, the last pieces of the puzzle falling into place. 'He must have discovered what was in the offing, and decided to stop it.'

'Why would he do that?' asked Cornald. He shrugged. 'His devotion to Henry is absolute, and though we may disapprove of Hywel's murder, no one can deny that it is in Henry's best interests.'

'No, it is not,' said Geoffrey. 'Henry will be glad to be rid of a popular rival, but the taint of murder will damage him badly. Edward will want to protect him from that.'

'So Edward killed Eudo to prevent him from sending these letters?' asked Cornald.

Geoffrey nodded. 'But he was too late – the letters had already been written and handed to Pepin. Edward stabbed Eudo, then drowned him when the blow was ineffective – I should have seen that such a messy death was the work of a man unused to killing.'

'He dropped silver pennies as they struggled,' mused Sear. 'You said at the time that they meant the culprit was a wealthy man. But this makes no sense – Edward has an alibi. He was in the stables when Eudo died, lecturing twenty stable-boys on horses.'

'Edward knows nothing about horses – he can barely ride,' snapped Geoffrey. 'And the nag he bought in La Batailge is a miserable specimen. Moreover, he saddled the thing back to front the other day. No self-respecting stable-boy would have listened to him. He lied.'

'But I thought he was looking into Eudo's murder for the King,' said Sear. 'He certainly gave us that impression as we were riding towards Goodrich.'

'Yes, he did,' agreed Geoffrey. 'Very cleverly, because we were less likely to suspect him.'

'There cannot be *two* cold-blooded murderers in our company,' said Cornald. 'So it stands to reason that Edward killed Mabon, as well as Eudo. But why?'

'Because he was aiming at Richard,' explained Geoffrey. 'Richard is selfish, and Edward predicted he would steal Mabon's tonic. I assumed the same. Edward must have decided it was safer to poison him than to fight. He stole wolf-tooth from Leah, who keeps some for her headaches . . .'

'But Richard must have been too drunk to steal,' finished

Cornald. 'You were not exactly sober yourself, Geoffrey – your sister and Olivier know how to ply the wine.'

'Edward was horrified when Mabon died,' said Geoffrey. 'I remember his face. Of course, it did not stop him from using poison a second time. In Brechene.'

'No one died in Brechene,' said Sear, bewildered.

'No, but two men became very sick after eating fish soup – the fish soup that was enjoyed by the locals with no ill effects.'

'Richard and Gwgan!' exclaimed Cornald. 'The recipients of the letters.'

'But although he used too much on Mabon – enough to leave evidence that screamed murder – he used too little in Brechene,' Geoffrey went on. 'Mabon's fate made him overly cautious.'

'What shall we do?' asked Cornald, frightened. 'Who is in the right? Richard and Gwgan, who believe they are under the King's orders? Or Edward, who is almost certainly acting alone?'

'We cannot look the other way while murder is committed,' said Geoffrey, snatching his horse's bridle from the stable-boy.

'But that is what Edward is doing,' said Sear. 'And I imagine it is why he left Kermerdyn earlier today – I doubt he has gone to Kadweli, as he claimed. We should leave it to him and not become embroiled in such unholy matters.'

'He will fail,' said Geoffrey, climbing into the saddle. 'As he has failed so far.'

'Do as he says, Sear,' said Cornald urgently. 'The King will *not* want Hywel murdered, because *he* will be accused of ordering it. Besides, if you thwart Richard, he may give you the Kermerdyn garrison in his place. It is not Pembroc, but it is better than being second in command.'

'Very well,' replied Sear reluctantly. 'I shall summon my men.'

'And I will hire messengers to fetch Hywel's soldiers back,' determined Cornald. 'You will be heavily outnumbered, even if you do join forces with Edward, because Gwgan has his personal guards and Richard has his garrison.'

Geoffrey nodded his thanks, but he knew any such help would arrive far too late.

Fourteen

Geoffrey fought down his impatience as Sear saddled his horse and summoned his men. He was itching to be away, but common sense prevailed – he could not defeat Gwgan's guards and Richard's troops single-handed, and there was no point in squandering his life on futile heroics, especially when the addition of Sear's force might make a difference.

His agitation was transmitted to his horse, which pawed and wheeled restlessly. Geoffrey's attention was more on the problems that loomed ahead than on keeping it in line, so he was startled when he heard an indignant squeal from near its feet.

'If you cannot control that thing, do not ride it!' It was Delwyn, his dirty face pinched with anger.

'What do you want?' asked Geoffrey curtly.

'Ywain sent me with a message. Leah fled the abbey this morning and ran to Edward, who she said was her only friend, but he returned her. She was furious and spat some terrible curses. I could scarce believe she was the same woman.'

Geoffrey was about to tell Delwyn to warn Ywain to be wary of a second escape attempt, when Sear surged towards the monk and grabbed him by the throat.

'You knew about this business,' he snarled. 'You are too sly to be innocent. The King knew it, too, which is why he gave Mabon's letter to Geoffrey. He did not trust *you.*'

'What business?' squeaked Delwyn in alarm. 'Leave me be! I am a monk, a man of God.'

'A monk, perhaps,' said Geoffrey with distaste. 'But no man of God. You are Eudo's helpmeet.'

'What?' exclaimed Sear. A dagger appeared in his hand.

'Do not kill him,' warned Geoffrey. 'We need him as a witness. Besides, he is not worth hanging for.'

'What do you mean?' demanded Delwyn indignantly. 'I am worth a great deal. But you cannot blame me for what Eudo and his cronies did. I am no organizer of murders'

'And there is your confession,' said Geoffrey to Sear. 'How could he know what Eudo planned unless he was party to it? He has been spying on us ever since we left La Batailge. Or, rather, spying on me, to ensure I delivered Eudo's deadly missives.'

'Lies!' cried Delwyn, alarmed. 'You do not—'

'I enjoyed Edward's company, and you became worried that I might tell him I was carrying letters for Richard and Gwgan. I wondered why you kept asking for Mabon's, but I understand now: you wanted to see where I kept it, so you could steal the others and deliver them yourself.'

'Where did you keep them?' asked Delwyn sullenly. 'Not in your saddle—'

'No, not in the saddlebags that you searched so assiduously,' said Geoffrey, glaring at him. 'But you need not have worried. I am not in the habit of blathering about the missions I am ordered to complete.'

'But *I* did not know that,' said Delwyn. 'Knights tend to be braggarts, not known for their discretion. I was constantly worried that Edward would have it out of you.'

'I kept my counsel,' said Geoffrey coolly. 'Besides, Edward did not ask, because he believed that killing Eudo was the end of the matter.'

'Yes – but Eudo wrote the letters and passed them to Pepin *before* he was killed,' said Delwyn. 'Do not wave that knife at me, Sir Sear. *I* have done nothing wrong. I was asked, by men loyal to the King, to ensure two messages were delivered. And that is what I did.'

'Except you failed,' said Geoffrey. 'You have no idea whether I delivered the letters or not.'

'I assume you did it here,' said Delwyn. 'After you visited the abbey. Are you telling me you have not done it yet? For God's sake, man! It has been two days!'

'I did it in Goodrich,' said Geoffrey.

'Did you?' asked Delwyn, startled. 'I did not see. Of course, I only have your word that you did it. You made a mistake with Wilfred's and Mabon's, I understand.'

'The mistake was Eudo's,' said Geoffrey curtly. 'I can only assume he was a little more careful with the ones he deemed more important. But you are a monk. How can you condone murder, especially of a man like Hywel – a decent man and a fellow countryman?'

'I have my price,' Delwyn flashed back. 'And so do you – you carried these letters because you want to protect your family. You are no different from me.'

'And what was your price?' asked Geoffrey coldly.

'My abbey,' replied Delwyn. 'It comprises Welsh monks serving a Welsh saint. But there are plans to turn it into a Norman foundation. I was promised that if I helped get the messages delivered, the abbey would stay Welsh.'

Geoffrey regarded him in surprise; he had assumed Delwyn had been paid in coins. And there was something else, too: he had assumed Eudo had acted alone, but Delwyn's claims suggested there was a wider conspiracy.

'Who made you this promise?' he asked.

'I cannot say,' said Delwyn. 'But he is powerful and ruthless, and if you ever challenge him, he will ensure you never live to tell the tale.'

'Then I definitely need to know,' argued Geoffrey, 'because I cannot live the rest of my life suspecting everyone I meet. Tell me.'

'I shall not,' said Delywn defiantly. 'And you cannot make me. So let me go before I tell my abbot that you have been manhandling me and he complains to the King.'

'The King would pay no heed to grumbles made by you,' said Sear in disdain.

'Take your hands off me, you ignorant, stupid Norman,' snarled Delwyn. 'Your loutish—'

Geoffrey leapt from his horse when he saw what was going to happen, but he was too late. Sear was not the kind of man to tolerate abuse from someone like Delwyn. There was a brief flash of steel, and Delwyn sank slowly to the ground, staring in disbelief. Geoffrey tried to stem the bleeding, but it was not many moments before Delwyn's eyes closed in death. Geoffrey gazed up at Sear in horror, appalled that he should kill an unarmed monk.

'He asked for it,' said Sear defensively. 'Indeed, he is lucky I did not skewer him a good deal sooner; he has been an aggravation ever since La Batailge.'

'We needed him alive,' said Geoffrey angrily. 'Now we may never know who really ordered Hywel's murder.'

'The King will find out,' said Sear dismissively. 'But do not waste any more time. If we are to save Hywel, and rescue the King from the accusations that will follow, we must hurry.'

*　　*　　*

A week before, Geoffrey would never have envisaged riding side by side with Sear to save the life of a man he barely knew. Sear's men were behind them, although they were an undisciplined rabble, and he did not think they would be much help in a skirmish. He hoped, although he knew it was unrealistic, that Cornald's messengers would be successful, and Hywel's own troops would come to the rescue.

It was not far to the castle, but dusk was falling, and the track between town and Rhydygors was rutted and uneven. To gallop along it risked tumbles for the horses. Sear slowed to an amble, and Geoffrey had no choice but to match his pace, although he chafed furiously at the lost time.

'What is your plan?' asked Sear, still clearly unhappy with the whole business.

'Go straight to Rhydygors to warn Hywel. If he is not there, we will go to Gwgan's home. Then we will stay with him until his own garrison arrives to protect him. It could be a long night.'

'It could,' agreed Sear. 'Even with my men, we will be heavily outnumbered. We will be lucky to survive. I suppose Edward and his creatures may come to our assistance, but, given their bumbling attempts at ambushing, I do not think our chances will be very much improved.'

Geoffrey said nothing, because Sear's concerns were valid.

'I hope you are right about this,' muttered Sear after a moment. 'Because it is going to be very embarrassing if you are wrong, and we burst in on a friendly dinner.'

'I am right,' said Geoffrey. 'It is obvious now we have all the pieces.'

'But Gwgan,' persisted Sear worriedly. 'He is Hywel's closest friend. I admire him.'

'So do I,' said Geoffrey, not liking to think of what Isabella would say. 'But Richard cannot do this without Gwgan. Hywel will dine with him in his house tonight, and Richard will ambush him there. That is why Richard left Kermerdyn – not because he is afraid of being attacked, but so he will be ready to strike.'

'Did you believe Delwyn?' asked Sear uneasily. 'About Eudo being under orders from someone else? Or do you think he was just trying to make himself seem more important?'

'We may never know,' said Geoffrey coldly, still angry about the killing. 'However, at least I know why Eudo took so many days to prepare the letters. I doubt they contained blunt orders to kill, but were couched in terms that could be denied later, should they fall into the wrong hands.'

And, he thought, the King may have wanted to vet them, too. The fact that he had declined to let Bishop Maurice rewrite them after Eudo's death was testament to the fact that there was something untoward afoot. Maurice had been right when he said he sensed evil in them.

And if the King *was* aware of what was happening, it explained his rather casual attitude to Eudo's death. The murder was to his advantage: whether the plot succeeded or failed, Henry could blame it on a rogue clerk who dabbled in dark affairs, and Eudo would not be in a position to deny it. Of course, Geoffrey could confide none of this to Sear, because the man was likely to withdraw his support if he thought Hywel's murder was what Henry wanted. Sear was nothing if not loyal.

'Gwgan is clever,' Sear was saying. 'He will understand ambiguous commands. And he can read, so there will be no need to involve clerks or scribes. Any message will stay between him and the sender.'

Geoffrey nodded. 'And he read Richard's for him too. Doubtless that was also anticipated.'

'I received some devious messages from Eudo myself, and it was fortunate Alberic knew how to interpret them, because I did not see their real meaning at all.' Sear glanced at Geoffrey. 'But I am still uneasy with all this. Supposing we thwart Richard, and the King is angry, because *he* told Eudo what to write?'

Geoffrey tried to conceal his alarm at the notion that Sear might decide to join Richard and Gwgan instead. He thought fast.

'Hywel's murder will throw the entire region into chaos, and Henry told me personally that he does not want trouble here. He will not condone the murder of a popular prince when it will cause untold problems among the people.'

'The people will have to be suppressed if Hywel's death *is* what the King wants.'

'He will learn it is *not* what he wants,' argued Geoffrey. 'Welsh princes will not rally to his side if he arranges to have them killed after a couple of years. Hywel's death will cause immeasurable damage, and the King will *not* want that.'

'But his letter said I am now under Richard's orders,' argued Sear. 'And if Richard is going to kill Hywel, then it is my duty to help him.'

'But—'

Geoffrey felt the mace swinging towards his head. He ducked, but it caught him on the shoulder, and the blow was powerful enough to dislodge him from his saddle. He cursed himself for joining forces with such a man – a fool, so devoted to his King that he could not bring himself to act against him even after he had been dismissed in a demeaning manner. Did he have no pride?

Geoffrey landed heavily, then put his hands over his head to protect it when his tumble put him directly in the path of the horses behind. One hoof struck his leg and another his arm.

'Leave him,' yelled Sear, when one or two men reined in. 'Dead or alive, he is irrelevant now.'

For the first time since leaving Kermerdyn, Sear urged his horse into a canter, and Geoffrey saw he had dawdled deliberately, to give his new master a chance to do what he had been ordered.

Geoffrey staggered to his feet, heartily wishing Roger was with him. Or Hilde, for that matter. His horse had gone with the others, and his left arm and leg throbbed painfully. It was dark, and he was not sure where Gwgan's house lay. He saw the vague shape of Rhydygors to his right, with lamps lit in the tower. He began to limp towards it.

It was not easy staggering in full armour along an unfamiliar track in the dark, and Geoffrey made poor time. His breath came in gasps, but every time he looked up, the castle seemed no closer. Then he heard the thunder of hoofs.

He looked around for somewhere to hide, but the stretch of road was open, without so much as a bush to crouch behind. He braced himself to fight. He still had his sword and a dagger, but his shield had been attached to his saddle, and was gone.

It was Edward, a number of rough looking men riding behind him. Geoffrey recognized several from the ambushes. Edward reined in when he saw Geoffrey.

'You *know*,' he said, peering down in the darkness. 'You must, or you would not be out here, unhorsed and alone. You know Gwgan and Richard mean to murder Hywel tonight.'

Geoffrey nodded. 'And you have been doing all in your power to stop them.'

Edward flicked his fingers. One of his men dismounted and offered Geoffrey the reins of his horse. Geoffrey did not need to be invited twice. He grabbed the bridle and climbed into the saddle, then turned towards Rhydygors again, kicking the animal into a gallop.

'What else do you know?' asked Edward, as he struggled to keep up with him. 'Slow down, man! We will be no use to Hywel if we break our necks.'

'I know you killed Mabon,' said Geoffrey. He knew it was unwise to make reckless remarks to killers, but he was too agitated to care.

'Mabon was a mistake,' said Edward softly. 'I was aiming for Richard.'

'And you were so convinced of your own moral rectitude that when you made your confession to Father Adrian, you did not mention the sin of murder.' Geoffrey was disgusted.

'Poisoning Richard would not have been a sin, because it would avert a greater evil,' replied Edward. 'You understand what a disaster Hywel's death will be, or you would not be here now, so you know I am right. But I am sorry if I have offended your religious sensibilities.'

'And what about your attempt to murder me?' asked Geoffrey coolly. 'You loosed a crossbow bolt in an effort to ensure I did not deliver Henry's letter to Gwgan. Was that not a sin, either?'

'No, because my heart was not in it. Unfortunately, the bolt came closer to you than I anticipated, telling me I am rather more deadly when I am *not* aiming to kill than when I am. It must have been that peculiar Saracen curve on the arrow.'

'You tried to kill Richard and Gwgan after we left Goodrich – you lobbed daggers at them, but missed, and you added poison to their fish soup. I should have known then that they were the targets, because others ate it with no ill effects. And you hurried them away from Brechene when they should have rested, so they would be more vulnerable to ambushes.'

'If I had succeeded, we would not be here now,' said Edward bitterly, 'chasing around in the dark and likely to face insurmountable odds.'

'You could have taken me into your confidence,' said Geoffrey, exasperated. 'Told me that I was about to deliver letters that would lead to a good man's murder.'

'I would have done, had I known what you carried. But you kept it secret, and the first I knew of it was when I saw you give a letter to Richard in Goodrich. I was horrified, and the poison and the crossbow were desperate measures that I now regret. The ambushes were more rational.'

'Rational, but ineffective,' said Geoffrey scathingly. 'They almost killed me in Lanothni.'

'All knights look alike in the dark. Why do you think I barred my door and took my time coming to your rescue? I did not want to be skewered by mistake. Where are you going?'

'Rhydygors,' replied Geoffrey shortly. 'To stop Hywel from accepting Gwgan's invitation.'

'The invitation was for sunset.' Edward laughed mirthlessly. 'Gwgan said he did not want Hywel walking about after dark, lest some harm befell him. Hywel is already in Gwgan's lair.'

Without a word, Geoffrey aimed towards the huddle of houses where he thought Gwgan lived. Edward followed, using the opportunity to talk, although Geoffrey was setting a rapid pace.

'There were whispers in La Batailge about a plan to replace Hywel with Richard. Hywel is a decent man, but Richard is harsh and uncompromising. Hywel is better for Wales.'

'And better for you,' said Geoffrey acidly. 'As Constable of Kadweli, you will be obliged to work with whoever rules here, and there is no question that Hywel will be more reasonable. But I heard no such rumours at La Batailge. I suspect you overheard Eudo himself.'

Edward shot him a sideways glance. 'You are certainly very astute. Yes, I heard Eudo tell the King how much safer the region would be if Hywel was dead. So I slipped into his office later, to explore the chest where he kept his secret correspondence.'

'You saw the letters to Richard and Gwgan?'

'No! Eudo was not a fool; he knew better than to leave a parchment trail. What I found were copies of letters to powerful barons in the area, asking for their assessment of Hywel. I knew then a plot was afoot to unseat him.'

'You murdered Eudo, but you were too late. He had already written his letters.'

Edward made no effort to deny the accusation. 'Pepin lied when he told me you were only to deliver a letter from the Archbishop to Mabon. I should have known not to trust him. And Eudo lied when he swore – on his immortal soul – that he had not embarked on any plot to kill Hywel.'

'Then why did you kill him?'

'To ensure he did not write any such missives in the future.'

Geoffrey suddenly felt very tired, appalled by the mire of intrigue that had been created, and by the devious minds – on both sides – that had dreamt it up.

'Well, I am glad you are here,' said Edward, when Geoffrey made no reply. 'Eudo chose well when he recommended that you should be the King's courier.'

'*Eudo* recommended me?' asked Geoffrey, startled. 'Why? He did not know me.'

'No, but he knew *of* you. He had read letters sent to you from Tancred. Your Holy Land prince is not a man who is easily impressed, but his missives showed he respects and trusts you. Of course Eudo would want to secure such a man for our King.'

Geoffrey thought fast. 'Then the burned letter Maurice gave me *was* an original, and the ones I received threatening me with execution are forgeries. I *knew* Tancred would not take against me so violently! He remained loyal, despite someone's efforts to sabotage our friendship.'

'Eudo did it,' said Edward. 'It would not be the first time he has intercepted letters. I imagine his intention was to keep you in England, because the King finds you useful.'

Maurice would have to release him from his vow now, Geoffrey thought. But it was no time to plan for the future, because they had arrived at the hamlet, where lights blazing from the largest of the houses indicated something was happening within.

'Are you working alone?' he asked suddenly. 'Or are you in the pay of someone else?'

'The King, of course,' replied Edward. '*He* ordered me to stop Richard and Gwgan. Why do you think he insisted Sear, Alberic and you travelled with me from la Batailge? To ensure I reached Kermerdyn alive to do his bidding.'

Clever Henry, thought Geoffrey bitterly. He had looked the other way while Eudo organized a murder, but had hired a man to prevent it. He would emerge well from the affair, however it ended.

Taking charge, Geoffrey indicated that three men were to go around the back with Edward, while the rest should stay with him at the front. Even as he issued the orders, he was aware that the house was oddly silent, and wondered whether they were already too late.

'I must have been wrong,' said Edward in a strangled whisper. 'Hywel is still in Rhydygors. We had better—'

'No!' Geoffrey stabbed his finger to where he could see shadows approaching. It was a dark night, with no moon, but light filtered from the windows of Gwgan's house, affording a little illumination. 'That is Richard's garrison.'

'Oh, Christ!' breathed Edward, frightened when he saw how many men Richard had brought. 'I am an administrator, not a warrior. Perhaps we should retreat and tell Henry the task was beyond us. He will understand.'

'For God's sake, do not run,' hissed Geoffrey. 'Or your soldiers will follow, and Hywel will die for certain. Take those three men and go around the back of the house. Get Hywel out and take him to Rhydygors. Lock yourselves in the tower.'

'And what will you be doing while I am risking my life?' demanded Edward.

'Engaging Richard's troops at the front with the rest of your men. The longer we hold out, the longer you will have to escape. Now go. Hurry!'

'But you will all die!' breathed Edward. 'There are too many of them!'

'Go!' snarled Geoffrey.

When Edward had gone, Geoffrey quickly issued some basic instructions to the remaining men, orders that would have been unnecessary to skilled soldiers. Then he waited out of sight, hoping their horses would not give them away with snickers or whinnies and lose them the element of surprise.

Meanwhile, Richard assembled his own warriors, intent on a headlong assault on the house, to kill Hywel before he had a chance to fight back.

He made certain his men were ready, then raised his sword

and issued a bloodcurdling howl as he began to gallop towards the house, his men keeping pace. Immediately, Geoffrey spurred forward with a battle cry of his own, relieved when some of Edward's men followed.

Richard faltered when he saw horsemen converging on him, and his howl ended in a gulp. His men scattered in confusion, then all was noise and chaos. Geoffrey saw Richard's distinctive profile and aimed for him, wielding his sword. Several men went down, and others retreated. The clash of arms was deafening, and so were the screams of the wounded. Geoffrey closed his mind to them, concentrating only on the rise and fall of his sword.

Then there was a sudden flash of light behind him, and Geoffrey saw the door had opened. Hywel had heard the noise of battle and come to investigate. Even a brief glimpse told Geoffrey he was unarmed – doubtless Gwgan's doing.

'Go back!' Geoffrey bellowed, aware that Hywel's silhouette made a perfect target for archers. 'There is murder afoot.'

He thought Hywel had ducked away, but there was no time to check, because the sight of their quarry had heartened Richard's troops, and they surged forward. Geoffrey's line was hard-pressed to hold them, and he felt it beginning to give way.

Then there was another yell, and Geoffrey glanced up to see more horsemen racing to join the affray. It was Sear's party. Geoffrey's little force was already retreating, forced back by sheer weight of numbers, and Sear's arrival would eliminate any small chance they might have had. Sure enough, the man who had been fighting at his side turned and fled. Others followed. Geoffrey battled on, his muscles burning with fatigue as he desperately tried to reach Richard in the hope that the plan would falter when deprived of its leader.

It was difficult to see who was who in the darkness, and Geoffrey was sure some of Sear's men were battling Richard's. It was a pitiful business. Only a handful of Edward's men stood between Richard and Gwgan's door now, and Geoffrey was aware of soldiers slipping around him. He could not prevent them from entering the house while on horseback, so he leapt off. He slapped the animal hard, driving it forward into the advancing men.

But it was only a temporary respite, and they soon came forward again. Richard, also on foot, put three men in front of him and ordered them to advance as a unit.

'Give up,' shouted Richard from behind them. 'You cannot win. You are virtually alone.'

It was true, but Geoffrey was not about to surrender. He fought on, but then became aware of another danger. Sear had seen what Geoffrey was doing, and was bearing down on him. The knight stood in his saddle and aimed blow after blow at Geoffrey, who, having no shield, was obliged to parry them with his sword. The clangs as metal met metal made his ears ring.

He could not fight Sear and guard the door at the same time, and he knew soldiers were cutting around behind him, Richard one of them. Geoffrey aimed a vicious jab at Sear that scored a deep cut in the man's thigh, then turned, aiming to stop Richard, but Sear did not baulk at a wound that would have made most men swoon. He came at Geoffrey in earnest, sword whirling, forcing him to retreat.

Geoffrey ducked under one blow intended to decapitate him, and, when Sear was off-balance, threw his dagger. It was an unorthodox move, but effective. Sear made a curious gagging sound, scrabbling at his throat. Geoffrey did not wait to see his end, but barged into Gwgan's house.

He had taken no more than a few steps before Gwgan stepped in front of him. The counsellor was wearing a rich tunic and no armour, and there was blood from a cut on his left arm. He was holding a dagger, and Geoffrey suspected he had wounded himself, so he could later claim he had been injured in the attack, thereby denying complicity in the murder of his friend.

'Geoffrey, stop,' he said quietly in Welsh. 'What has been set in motion cannot be stopped. Stand back and do not interfere.'

Breathing hard, Geoffrey thrust past Gwgan, lest Edward had not managed to spirit Hywel away, and was besieged inside. Gwgan lashed out with his dagger, and Geoffrey felt pain blaze through his shoulder.

'I do not want to fight you,' Gwgan said, although he grabbed a sword. 'Stand down, Geoffrey. This is not your concern.'

Geoffrey tried to pass him a second time, parrying the next slash with his sword. When he saw the knight was not going to do as he was asked, Gwgan began to fight in earnest.

'I did my best to keep you out of it,' he hissed. 'But you

would not listen, so now you must pay the price for your meddling.'

'I suppose you would have killed me, had I ridden into the marshes with you this afternoon,' snarled Geoffrey, backing away. 'And I imagine it was you who told Richard to send drugged wine to the tavern, too. He is too stupid to have thought of it himself.'

'I wanted you and Roger sound asleep until morning,' snapped Gwgan. 'And if you had come with me to the marshes, I would have knocked you out and blamed it on outlaws. You are kin. I never intended to kill you.'

'Then stop fighting me and do what is right,' shouted Geoffrey. 'End this mad scheme. No one else has to die.'

'You do, I am afraid,' said Gwgan, coming at Geoffrey with another series of slashes. 'Which is a damned shame, because I like you. But you will tell everyone about my role in this affair, and I cannot allow that.'

Geoffrey gaped at him. 'You think you can keep this secret? When Sear, Edward and Richard *and* their men know what you have done? You will be branded as a traitor.'

Gwgan launched himself at Geoffrey, who normally would have had no trouble defeating the man, but the wound in his shoulder hurt enough to make him dizzy and was sapping his strength. Nevertheless, he outlasted the counsellor's offensive, and then, drawing on his own last reserves, went after Gwgan with a series of vicious swipes, determined that if he was to die that night, then Gwgan was going to perish with him. He pressed his advantage relentlessly, driving the man back and into the main chamber.

Richard was already there with three other men, and he reacted instinctively to the sounds of a skirmish behind him. He whipped his sword around fast, catching Gwgan in the neck and killing him instantly.

'Damn!' muttered Richard. Then he shrugged. 'Well, we would have had to dispatch him anyway. He was a traitor, and his people would have taken his life. I have saved them the trouble.'

'Hywel,' demanded Geoffrey. 'Where is he?'

Richard stepped aside, and Geoffrey closed his eyes when he saw the prince's body. The attack had been ruthless and determined, and there were dozens of wounds.

At that moment, Edward entered the room at a run, his three

men at his heels. All were dishevelled and two were bleeding, indicating they had at least tried to carry out their orders. Edward faltered when he saw Hywel.

'Richard had posted men at the back of the house, too,' he explained to Geoffrey. 'We could not reach . . .'

'You have lost this battle,' said Richard. 'I am lord of Rhydygors now. My appointment will be confirmed as soon as news of Hywel's death reaches the King. It was in the letter you brought me, Geoffrey.'

'Then I suppose we shall have to work together,' said Edward with a sigh of resignation. 'Kadweli will support you, should there be any unpleasantness arising from this incident.'

'That is it?' breathed Geoffrey, aghast. 'You will transfer your allegiance to this—'

'Be careful what you say, Geoffrey,' interrupted Richard sharply. 'I am the King's appointed representative. If you malign me, you malign him.'

'He is right,' said Edward. 'What is done is done, and we must all make the best of it.'

He left without another word. Geoffrey watched helplessly as Richard ordered his men to carry Hywel's body to the castle. Gwgan was left like so much rubbish.

'Your brother would not have condoned this,' said Geoffrey.

'No,' agreed Richard. 'But we cannot choose the way that power comes to us – he had holy visions, and I have letters from court. I am tempted to kill you, too, and nothing would give me greater pleasure, I assure you, but the letter also said I was to send you back with a report of what happened. So I cannot stab you – not now Edward has seen you alive.'

'Why would the King want a report from me?'

'I do not know. But an order is an order, and I know better than to flout one. You will tell the King what happened here.'

'How? I do not understand any of it.'

Richard smiled. 'I suspect none of us does – not me, you, Edward, Gwgan or Sear. And probably not Eudo, either. Between you and me, I suspect the only man who really knows is the King, but I would not advise quizzing him about it.'

'No,' agreed Geoffrey softly. 'I doubt that would be wise.'

Epilogue

Reddinges, November 1103

It did not take Geoffrey long to recover from the skirmish, and he set off towards England the moment he was able to ride. Hilde insisted it was too soon, but Geoffrey wanted his interview with the King concluded as soon as possible. There were no ambushes as they rode, and Hilde was safely deposited at Goodrich, along with her widowed sister.

Then Geoffrey, Roger and Bale rode fast and hard to Reddinges, a place for which Henry held an unaccountable affection. There were rumours that he intended to found an abbey there, to atone for his sins. Geoffrey wondered whether Hywel's murder would be among them, because as he travelled and had time to reflect on all that had happened, he decided it would have been all but impossible for the King not to have known what was in Eudo's letters.

Before leaving Kermerdyn, Bishop Wilfred had given him William's statue, claiming he did not want a pagan goddess in his church. It was, he said, a gift to the King.

When they arrived at Reddinges, they found it full of the customary bustle associated with the royal presence, with clerks and scribes everywhere. They met Pepin, who informed them that he had been promoted to Eudo's post, but was finding it a trial, and Geoffrey suspected he would soon be relieved of the position. Pepin was no Eudo, and Henry would be looking for someone more devious.

While they waited to be summoned, Geoffrey sat in the parish church, reading. It was not long before Roger came to sit next to him. He rarely strayed far from his friend's side now, mortified that he had missed a battle that had nearly claimed Geoffrey's life.

'What is that?' he asked.

'A letter from Giffard,' replied Geoffrey. 'I told him about William's secret, and he writes that we are wrong to assume that a statue, or even a vision, can turn a man into a saint. He says goodness comes from within and is ignited by the hand of God.'

'Well, he *is* a bishop,' said Roger dismissively. 'He *would* claim that sort of thing.'

'What do you believe?' asked Geoffrey, although he suspected he would be better not knowing.

Roger shook his head. 'Not that the statue has any particular powers. I touched it several times, but it did not make me feel holy. But perhaps I am holy enough already, what with having been on the Crusade.'

'Perhaps,' said Geoffrey. 'But William believed it.'

They were silent for a moment, listening to the coo of a dove somewhere in the rafters.

'Tell me again what happened,' said Roger. 'I did not pay much attention back in Kermerdyn, and the King might ask for my views. I will look foolish if I do not understand it all.'

'I am not sure *I* understand it,' said Geoffrey, amused by the notion that Henry would ask Roger's opinion on so complex a matter.

Roger cleared his throat. 'It began when Eudo decided it would be better for Henry if a Norman held the castle in Kermerdyn, because Hywel was too popular. He was afraid Hywel would think he had better things to do than swear allegiance to a Norman king and might make trouble.'

Geoffrey nodded. 'He thought Richard fitz Baldwin would be a better choice, and told me himself that he thought Henry was wrong to have given Rhydygors to Hywel.'

'So Eudo wrote letters to Richard and Gwgan arranging Hywel's murder,' said Roger. 'And he hoped that the "secret" that made William and Hywel decent would act on the surly Richard, too.'

'Yes. But Edward overheard Eudo and managed to gain access to his strongbox, where his suspicions were confirmed. He tackled Eudo by the pond at La Batailge. Eudo told him that no letters had been written, and, rather stupidly, Edward believed him.'

'And then Edward killed him,' said Roger.

'Edward thought that Hywel was safe, but Eudo had already written the letters.'

'And Henry gave them to you,' said Roger.

'Yes, he did, and refused to let Maurice rewrite them. That may imply Henry knew what they contained and thought he had nothing to lose by letting the plot run its course – he could always deny culpability, and Eudo could not contradict him. But, equally, he might have not thought it worth the bother of inspecting the work of a trusted scribe.'

'Which do you think?' asked Roger.

'That Henry is innocent,' lied Geoffrey, unwilling for his friend to know the truth, lest he blurted it out at some inopportune moment.

Roger continued the tale. 'So Edward rode west, thinking the plot was thwarted, and was appalled when he saw you deliver a message to Richard. He tried to kill you before you gave Gwgan his, then tried to kill Richard with poison, but Abbot Mabon took it by mistake.'

'It horrified him, so he left the business of dispatching Gwgan and Richard to his troops after that, telling them that they should not reach Kermerdyn alive.'

'But their efforts failed, and Richard and Gwgan murdered Hywel. Delwyn had already been hired, too, ready to step in and deliver the letters, should anything happen to you.'

'Delwyn lost more than his life,' said Geoffrey. 'His abbey will soon be under a Norman.'

'That is a pity, because you had brokered a sort of peace between Wilfred and the abbey.'

'Giffard's prayer of kindness, compassion and forgiveness did that; it had nothing to do with me.'

'Well, at least you forced Edward's men to return the money they stole from Fychan at Lanothni. However, it was unkind to insist that a portion went directly towards a new church. It was Fychan's money; you had no right to tell him what he could do with it.'

Geoffrey shrugged. 'I liked Lanothni's priest, and the money will do more good with him than with Fychan, who would just sit counting it until someone else decided to rob him.'

'Incidentally, did I tell you that I spoke to Pepin about the two letters that were confused?' asked Roger. 'Mabon's epistle sent to Wilfred, and vice versa?'

'What did he say,' asked Geoffrey.

Roger smirked. 'That he was very, very careful about what went where, because he had made mistakes before. He is certain he made no errors. But he left them for the King to seal.'

'It was Henry who exchanged them?' asked Geoffrey, shocked.

Of course it was, he thought. Henry wanted a report on the two churchmen, and what better way to test them than to arrange a 'mistake'? He would not need Geoffrey's report, because their reactions would tell him all he needed to know. La Batailge would receive St Peter's tithes if Ywain was trustworthy and passed the letter to its intended recipient, and if Wilfred was honest, Ywain would write to Henry to claim the promised hundred marks.

'But La Batailge *did* get the tithes,' said Roger in confusion, when Geoffrey explained it to him. 'And Ywain did *not* get the hundred marks. So why suppress the abbey? It was Ywain who was honest, not Wilfred.'

'Quite. And an honest man is likely to lose in the long run. Or perhaps Henry appreciated the fact that Wilfred ensured a claim was not made on the treasury. Regardless, he prefers Wilfred, and my recommendation to let them find their own resolution was ignored.'

'Leah will not be pleased,' said Roger. 'She vowed to stay in that abbey until she received a sign from God to say she is forgiven for murdering William.'

'Perhaps she will think that *is* the sign,' said Geoffrey. 'Richard has agreed to take her back, so I imagine she will be looking for the first portent that appears. And she might pass Pulchria going the other way when she leaves the protection of the Church, because I understand that Cornald has finally been forced to recognize his wife's illicit behaviour and is considering sending her to a nunnery. It would be appropriate justice.'

Roger nodded, then looked at Geoffrey's dog lying contentedly at his feet. 'Are you really pleased to have that thing back?'

'Of course I am pleased,' said Geoffrey, leaning down to ruffle the animal's fur. It growled softly. 'I missed him – more than you missed Ulfrith, I suspect.'

'The King has a lot to answer for,' said Roger grimly. 'He had no right to poach Ulfrith from me, or to steal your dog. Still, he soon learned he made a mistake, because neither suited his plans – Ulfrith looks strong and competent, but he is too stupid to be a decent soldier, and your dog did rather a lot of damage to several prize bitches.'

Geoffrey laughed. The failure of Ulfrith and the dog to live up to Henry's expectations had been one small gleam of victory in a dark and murky affair.

'Well,' sighed Roger, nodding to where the box with the statue was sitting with some of the King's other recently acquired possessions. 'Perhaps we should hope that goddess does bring out the goodness in people, because if there is one man who *could* do with some, it is Henry.'

The meeting with the King went better than Geoffrey had anticipated. News had come of trouble in Normandy, and Henry was little interested in events in Wales. He listened absently while Geoffrey gave a carefully worded account of all that had happened.

'Pity,' he said, when the knight had finished. 'Hywel was a good man.'

'Yes,' said Geoffrey quietly. 'He *was* a good man. And a good ruler, too.'

'But justice has been served,' Henry went on. 'Gwgan is dead.'

'Richard is not,' said Geoffrey. 'He has won himself Rhydygors.'

'He should have had it anyway,' said Henry. 'Seven years ago, when his brother was killed. I do not know what Eudo was thinking when he advised me to hand the place to a Welshman. Rhydygors was built by a Norman and should have stayed in Norman hands.'

'Yes, sire,' said Geoffrey, deciding not to point out that this interpretation of events was somewhat at variance with the facts.

'I shall need you to stay here for a few days, by the way,' said Henry, as Geoffrey bowed and prepared to leave. 'One of my ministers has been murdered, and I want you to find the culprit. But I shall tell you about it some other time, because I am busy now. You are dismissed.'

Seething, both at the King's manners and because his departure for Tancred was going to be delayed yet again, Geoffrey went in search of Maurice. He had raisins to deliver from Hilde. He found the Bishop ushering a giggling serving wench from his rooms. Maurice looked well, and Geoffrey saw he was enjoying life as one of the most powerful men in the court.

'So I was right,' said Maurice, indicating that Geoffrey was to
enter and sit by the fire. It was a cold day, and rain was pattering
against the window shutters. 'Those letters *were* evil, although
there is nothing to say the King knew what was included in
them.'

'No,' said Geoffrey noncommittally.

'He would never condone murder,' continued Maurice. 'Eudo
obviously acted alone.'

'Not entirely,' said Geoffrey. 'Someone appointed Delwyn to
ensure the letters reached their destination. Eudo could not have
done that, because he did not know his plan had been exposed
until Edward confronted him, and he was killed before he could
do anything about it.'

'What are you saying?' asked Maurice nervously. 'That Eudo
had an accomplice?'

'We both know he did,' said Geoffrey. 'You knew exactly what
he had done, although you grew worried after his murder and
begged Henry to let you rewrite them.'

'Geoffrey!' cried Maurice, shocked. 'How can you say such
things?'

'Because they are true. You did not dare break the seals on the
letters to see whether Eudo had set the plan in motion, but you
were desperate to know. You hired Delwyn to report back to you
– and to make sure the letters were delivered if something
happened to me along the way.'

'No,' said Maurice. 'If you recall, I told you he was devious.
Why would I hire such a man?'

'Probably to ensure I did not associate him with you. Or to
ensure I would not believe him if he ever told me the truth. And
you were right to worry, because he *was* going to tell me the
name of his master. Luckily for you, Sear killed him before he
could.'

'But I have no reason to dabble in such deadly affairs!' claimed
Maurice.

'Yes, you do. You are loyal and devoted, and foresaw problems
for the King with a popular Welsh leader in Kermerdyn. There
is no reason for a proud, independent prince to subject himself
to Norman rule, and Hywel probably would have rebelled in
time.'

'I am not a fool, Geoffrey. Putting Richard in Hywel's place will be a disaster. He is likely to provoke a rebellion by dint of his unpleasant character.'

'And that is why you encouraged me to find William's secret but told me to leave it in Kermerdyn. You hoped it would make Richard as decent as Hywel and William.'

'Rubbish!' cried Maurice. 'This is all rank superstition, and I am a bishop!'

'It was not superstition as long as there was a possibility that the Blessed Virgin was involved. It was religion. And that *is* your business.'

'The secret is a carving of a pagan goddess,' said Maurice angrily. 'It is not even Christian.'

'But you did not know that at the time,' pressed Geoffrey. 'You had no idea what it entailed; only that it could be put to good use.'

'You have no evidence,' said Maurice, and for the first time since Geoffrey had known him, his face held something dangerous. Geoffrey realized that it took strength, ruthlessness and cunning to rise so high in King Henry's realm; Maurice would not have been promoted to such a powerful post if he was a bumbling fool.

'I have this,' said Geoffrey, holding up the remains of the letter from Tancred. 'Eudo was too wily to have left half-burned papers in his hearth. No, you caught him burning the documents and demanded an explanation. He gave you one, because you and he had an understanding.'

Maurice's lips tightened into a firm line. 'Very well, I admit that I know more of that matter than I admitted. Roger gave Eudo these letters – he had some tale about taking them from a squire of yours who is now dead. The squire made the forgeries, not Eudo.'

'Durand,' said Geoffrey heavily.

'The one you claim is Angel Locks? I doubt she would have done anything so cruel.'

'Why did you not tell me sooner?' demanded Geoffrey coldly.

Maurice smiled. 'Because it suited me to keep you confused and uncertain. And do not loom in a way that suggests you mean violence, because we both know you will not harm me. I am an unarmed bishop, and your principles will not let you. Besides, the King would kill you if you did.'

'It would be worth it,' said Geoffrey. The ice in his voice made Maurice regard him in alarm.

'I did my best to protect you, Geoffrey,' he said. 'I gave you letters, so people would think you were *my* messenger, not Henry's, and I tried hard to persuade him to send someone else. I am not such a terrible man, and our friendship means something to me.'

'Does it?' asked Geoffrey, thinking *he* had just lost a friend. Two, perhaps, given that Roger seemed to be complicit in the plot to deceive him.

Maurice leaned back in his chair. 'Yes, it does. But if you are going to be unpleasant about this, let me remind you that I have evidence that shows *you* carried orders for two men to commit murder. *Ergo*, we know dubious facts about each other. And you will not want your family associated with this business.'

'They have nothing to do with it.'

'You are implicated in the death of a much-loved Welsh prince. I doubt Goodrich's Welsh neighbours will be impressed by that. Joan and Hilde will never lie easy in their beds again.'

'You bastard,' snarled Geoffrey.

'Oh, come now, Geoffrey. I am sure we can end this amiably. How about I release you from your vow, so you can travel to the Holy Land and make your peace with Tancred? Would that ease the animosity between us?'

'No,' said Geoffrey coldly. 'Because *your* blessing means nothing. I will be bound by my promise until I can find a *decent* priest. If there is any such man in your Church, which I doubt. Go and take your medicine, My Lord Bishop. You are looking quite pale.'

Historical Note

There is a reference to a castle near Kermerdyn (Carmarthen) in 1093, when it seems the Sheriff of Devon, one William fitz Baldwin, raised what was probably a simple motte topped with a wooden fortified tower. He probably did so on the orders of King William Rufus. It was called Rhydygors (*rhyd* meaning ford, and *cors* meaning marsh or bog), suggesting it protected a crossing of the River Tywi just south of the present-day town, which remains salt-marsh to this day. Its location is uncertain, although an Ordnance Survey map of 1830 shows some earthworks, all of which were flattened for the railway line a few years later.

Three years later, William was dead, and the garrison seems to have withdrawn. King William Rufus was killed in the New Forest during a hunting accident in 1100, and his younger brother, Henry, seized the throne. There is no evidence that Henry was complicit in his brother's death, but he was certainly quick to capitalize on the situation and turn it to his advantage. He was to become one of the strongest and most efficient of English kings.

Henry immediately faced serious trouble all along the Welsh borders, mostly led by his own barons, especially the notorious tyrant Robert de Bellême, but the tide was turned in his favour when a number of Welsh princes fought on his side. One of these was Hywel ap Gronw, a Welsh noble who was described as a 'king' in contemporary records. He came to real power in 1102, when Henry rewarded him for his help against Bellême with a gift of Rhydygors Castle and the area known as Ystrad Tywi. At the same time, an unknown knight named Sear was granted Pembroc (Pembroke), although he did not keep it for long – it was soon passed to the better-known and more powerful Gerald of Windsor, who began rebuilding it in stone.

In 1105, William fitz Baldwin's younger brother, Richard, arrived at Rhydygors and stocked it with soldiers. Just a year later, Hywel was enjoying a pleasant evening at the house of his close friend and counsellor, Gwgan ap Meurig, when he was murdered. The story goes that Gwgan stole Hywel's sword and armour as he slept, then mentioned the fact to Richard's garrison. The castle was abandoned shortly after the murder, and a new fortress built nearer the town. Parts of the later buildings survive today, although the bulk of the site is under County Hall.

The earliest records of St Peter's Church come from documents dating to Henry's reign, in which the monarch conferred it on the abbey at La Batailge (Battle Abbey). Later, Bernard, Bishop of St David's, made repeated requests for the church to be returned to his own See. This happened in 1125, at which point Bernard gave the church with its tithes and benefits to his newly founded priory of St John and St Teulyddog. There is some suggestion that there was a Celtic monastic foundation on this site, and that Bernard replaced it with Cistercians and a Norman prior. It later passed to the Benedictines.

Other characters in the story are also real. Alberic de Felgoriis was a knight based in Kermerdyn in the early twelfth century, Cornald was a merchant, and Robert was a steward. The custodian of Kadweli (Kidwelly) was named Edward, and the Bishop of St David's from 1085 until 1115 was Wilfred. Maurice (Bishop of London, 1086–1107) built an early St Paul's Cathedral in London, and his contemporaries did accuse him of sleeping with women to improve his health. Baderon was the Lord of Monmouth in the early 1100s, and the Bishop of Durham was known to have sired several illegitimate children.

Prince Tancred was a Norman from Sicily, who went to the Holy Land to make his fortune on the Crusade. He succeeded and carved a kingdom in the east.

Some kind of castle was raised at Goodrich by Godric Mappestone shortly after the Conquest, although records indicate it did not remain with him and his family for long.